The Suppliant

Greece, 1107 BC

Fiction by Kathryn Berck

<u>The Peryton Series</u>

Part One, The Hostage

Part Two, The Hunter

Part Three, The Suppliant

Part Four, The Good Kinsman

The Suppliant

Kathryn Berck

Peryton, Part Three

For Mel Gilden, Michael Davis and Monique High, each for a very different reason. For my editor emeritus and known accomplice, Michael Carr. And for Cecelia Holland, who led the way.

... I'm glad I can't explain
Just in what jaws you were to suppurate:
You may have thought things would come right again
If you could only keep quite still and wait. [i]
— Philip Larkin

I trace my family history so I will know who to blame.
— Anonymous

It started as a simple family quarrel. But because it involved a throne, a great city, and the High Kingship, it grew far beyond its origins.

Perseus, who would be used as a rare example of honorable manhood for millennia to come, killed the Gorgon and rescued and married Andromeda. Then, at his new bride's insistence, he retired from adventuring, built Mycenae, and ruled as its first king. Because of its favorable location, invulnerability, and great wealth, and because of the strength, fairness, and wide-ranging interests of its builder, Mycenae became the preeminent city of the area, and its king became High King over the Peloponnesos and central Greece.

Perseus's son Electryon was High King when the trouble began.

Because Electryon had no sons, when he marched off to avenge a theft of his cattle, he left his nephew Amphitryon in charge, promising him his daughter, Alcmene, in marriage should he rule well in Electryon's absence. The marriage to the High King's daughter would have guaranteed inheritance of the throne, and Amphitryon believed he had kept his part of this pact. He even learned who the cattle thieves were, and negotiated the stolen animals' return for a modest ransom. But Electryon disliked Amphitryon's method: paying for the cattle instead of fighting for them. In the quarrel that followed,

Amphitryon threw a club to emphasize a point. The club glanced off a cow's horns and killed Electryon.

Thus, Amphitryon was outlawed in the first—the severest—degree. Stripped of home, family, name, and heritage and forbidden to touch any man or woman, he fled to Thebes, accompanied willingly and chastely by Alcmene. Then, raging with frustration, Amphitryon watched from afar while Electryon's brothers argued, plotted, and simply fought over who should be High King.

Purification for the killing of an elder male kinsman was astoundingly expensive. Even the wealthiest of outlaws was not allowed to pay his own fee, and even the most powerful of offenders was subject to all the rules of outlawry. By the time Amphitryon managed to convince the king of Thebes to pay for his absolution, it was too late. His uncle Sthenelus, canniest of Electryon's brothers, sat securely on Perseus's high seat.

To promote familial peace, Sthenelus agreed that he would name as his heir the next son born to any of his kinsmen. Amphitryon's hopes soared. As soon the law allowed, he had married Alcmene, and she got pregnant immediately, before all the other wives of the family. If the child should be a boy, he would rule this world. Everyone counted down the days.

Then Sthenelus's wife gave birth two months early—a single night before Alcmene. Sthenelus's premature son survived and was named Eurystheus, and he inherited the High Kingship after his father.

Amphitryon submitted at last to the will of fate. But, of course, the dispute did not end there. Amphitryon's son, Herakles, tried all his life to win back his father's rights and, thereby, his own. Eurystheus promised again and again to name Herakles his heir, as long as he could prove himself by doing— and here followed impossible task after impossible task, all designed to defeat or, preferably, kill Herakles. But Herakles returned, successful and alive.

In the end, if this could be seen as an end, Herakles died before Eurystheus. Worried that Herakles' many sons might still challenge him, Eurystheus marched against them—and died with all his own sons in the ensuing battle, leaving the high seat vacant once again.

One might have thought that Hyllus—the most prominent of Herakles' sons, and one of the few conceived in marriage rather than through casual seduction or rape—should now take his father's prize. Hyllus certainly thought he should. But instead, the high seat was stolen, as deftly as a drink at a dinner party, by Atreus and Thyestes, the younger brothers of Sthenelus's wife, and sons of Pelops, the greatest of the great Bronze Age land pirates.

Generations before, Pelops's family had migrated to the Black Sea to build their fortunes. Fleeing home to Greece after a brutal setback, Pelops found himself a refugee in his ancestral lands, welcomed only tepidly by distant kinsmen and unable to exert a claim to any place of his own. Nevertheless, he quickly won a kingdom by cheating at a chariot race and then murdering Myrtilus, the man who had helped him win. As Myrtilus lay dying, he cursed Pelops and all his descendants. But at least for now, Pelops's sons appeared to be rising unhindered. The exalted marriage of their older sister, and her timely production of Eurystheus, had strengthened their status immeasurably. Their appropriation of the high seat followed naturally.

The theft of the high seat by what they considered foreign usurpers—actually, sixth cousins, though they would never admit that—left Hyllus Herakleides and his many half brothers even more indignant. They invaded the Peloponnesos, intending to take Mycenae by force. But Atreus and Thyestes had not won the high seat by luck, but by guile and impeccable timing. They proposed that rather than spill needless blood in battle, the rivals decide possession of the high seat by single combat, at the wall of Megara.

Hyllus was a bull of a man, no smarter than his father but famous for his sword arm, and filled with resentment. Fresh from killing Eurystheus by his own hand, he came backed by a hundred kinsmen as tough and aggrieved as he. He agreed at once to the Pelopeids' proposal and stepped forward as his own champion.

Hyllus assumed that he would face one of the Pelopeids. Instead, they chose as their champion a distant kinsman, Echemus Aeropuseides, king of Tegea and grand-nephew of Auge, one of the women who had suffered most from Herakles' sexual attentions.

Echemus was forty—not old but not quite young. A thoughtful man with the blue eyes and light hair of the Pelopeids, he also had fair skill with a bow. He remembered Auge fondly and always wore a scarf of hers tied around his bow arm. Hyllus never got a chance to try his sword against the High King's champion. He died that day with an arrow in his throat, shot from fifty paces.

The Herakleids retreated to live wherever they could, nursing their grudge and breeding ever more kinsmen, until the oracle of Delphi proclaimed the time ripe for Hyllus's descendant, Temenus Herakleides, to build a new town, Nafpaktos, on the Gulf of Corinth. There he should gather his kinsmen and allies to prepare for a new invasion, from which he need never retreat.

* * *

Many years after the famous combat at the wall of Megara, and ten years before the birth of Temenus Herakleides, Echemus of Tegea found it prudent to retreat. His sons were grown men, the eldest already a grandfather and chafing to rule. Echemus's simple principles had long fallen out of fashion, and his unswerving loyalty to Mycenae and the High King was considered an anachronistic embarrassment.

The current High King was Orestes Pelopeides, who had acquired his throne in true Pelopeid fashion. His father, Agamemnon, had sacrificed his daughter, Iphigenia, in exchange for favorable winds to carry his fleet to Troy. Immediately upon Agamemnon's departure, his wife, Clytemnestra, enraged at her daughter's death, had taken into her bed a man born to her husband's uncle Thyestes and Thyestes' own daughter. When Agamemnon returned triumphant from Troy with the beautiful seeress Cassandra as his slave and bedmate, Clytemnestra murdered both husband and mistress. Orestes avenged his father by murdering his mother and her lover. Then, once the crisis of outlawry for that appalling matricide was cleared up in his favor, he took over the High Kingship and ruled as securely as any Pelopeid might expect to.

As High King, Orestes preferred the comforts of Mycenae and Athens to the hardship of travel, and so spent little time among his vassals. Offended by their overlord's neglect, those underlings eventually began to look elsewhere, even to the long-deposed Herakleids, for more attentive leadership. Thus it was that Echemus's son, impatient to rule Tegea, made no secret of his dissatisfaction with his father's political loyalties.

So Echemus put the symbols of kingship in his son's hands and retired to his own chamber, bath, and small megaron, where he and his equally aged cronies told the old stories and complained about the new ones. But that retreat was not enough. Even now his voice, still strong while turning querulous, was heard too often in his son's allcalls. Rather than bar the old hero from gatherings or find another way to silence him, the king suggested a change of air. Perhaps his father would like to leave the smoky, smelly city and make his home in more agreeable surroundings.

Echemus was old but not a fool. He would live longer if he went away, so away he went. His son the king arranged it.

Echemus would retire to the distant manor of Ladon, where his granddaughter Laothoe had been married for fifteen years to the chief, Hyades Afidameas, a stolid, loyal, though lately neglectful vassal of Tegea. Echemus's presence in Ladon might remind Hyades of his duty to his lord, as well as dispose of the old man himself in a manner both respectful and permanent.

Echemus, remembering this granddaughter all too well, did not want to go to Ladon. But no other choice was suggested, so he went.

When he arrived with all his possessions on a single donkey, he found what he had expected to find. Laothoe, thirty-five years old and the mother of three big sons, greeted him with the barest courtesy. Hyades' greeting was no more amiable, and the sons followed their father's lead, as Echemus would see them do unwaveringly from that day on. Still, there was room enough in this rambling half-stone manor for a well-behaved old man to live out his last years. They set a place for him at table, hauled in a crooked stool from an outbuilding, and pointed out a corner near the fire, where he could stow his chest of possessions and sleep. And that was all.

This was fair enough. Echemus had never expected Laothoe to forgive him, nor Hyades to like him. Although the marriage had given Laothoe vital respectability after a reckless indiscretion and had given Hyades a higher-born wife than he could otherwise have hoped for, the couple shared no bond of amity. Laothoe's face was marred around the eyes, and she bore deep scars on her hands and forearms—defensive wounds, Echemus recognized. Hyades showed the stiff, unnatural enmity of a man long baffled by his woman's loathing. So there was no love in this household except between Hyades and his sons. There were also no luxuries of any kind, but Echemus's needs were modest. A stool, a corner, a place at table—that was enough.

It was some time—days, in fact—before he noticed the other

child. When he first saw it from of the corner of his eye, it alarmed him. So small and furtive and filthy, he thought it must be a weasel or a spirit or a crippled old cat—certainly not human. It came and went with the goats, and it hung around the edges of the dooryard at dusk, with a little staff in its hands. Hyades and his sons ignored it so deliberately that he knew they were sharply aware of it. If it came into the house, he never saw it there. What it ate and when, where it slept—even what, exactly, it was—he could not learn. It offered him no hint of itself, and the first syllables of his first question to Laothoe died half-spoken in her swift warning glance.

Grape season came around. Hyades, his sons, and the servants kept busy gathering fruit, crushing it, and treating and storing the wine. Echemus's offer of help was brushed aside. So the old man sat in the yard on his stool, his back against the warmth of the house's stone wall, and waited for the child—if a child it was—to appear.

It had sensed his interest; that was clear. When it took out the goats, it crept along on the far side of them, barely visible through the maze of busy legs. It was past milking season, but two or three of the animals were still wet. If Laothoe called from the doorway for one to be brought for milking, the child would separate a doe from the herd deftly enough but then leave it to the dogs to hold it, and to Laothoe to come out and catch it herself, rather than come too near either the house or Echemus.

In this way, the first months passed.

* * *

Echemus knew stories. In fact, he knew all the tales of all the powers, immortals, and heroes since humans first came to these lands. Echemus spoke the old Arcadian language with cosmopolitan style and grace. None of these arts was welcome here. A few of the servants appeared to be of the old Perioikoi blood, but they knew nothing of their own history—they barely knew their own parents, they tended to die so young—and they spoke only a pidgin Arcadian. In the short hours between sunset and sleep, when some households gathered by the fireside for songs and stories and fine handiwork, Laothoe sat stolidly working her great, clattering loom while Hyades and his sons rolled their eyes in boredom and escaped as quickly as possible from the old man's attempts to entertain and educate.

One such night, Echemus, after giving up and leaving his story half told, had gone out for his final visit to the outhouse. He was recrossing the yard in bright, cold moonlight, his feet crunching on the frosted dirt, when he saw the child unexpectedly. It was crouched against the house's outer wall, its back pressed into a small chink between the stones, arms around its drawn-up knees, head down—a shadow amid shadows. Asleep? He couldn't tell. He stood, uncertain. If he spoke, it would not answer. If he approached, it would flee. If he tried to touch it, it would cringe—or would it bite?

As he stood there, it lifted its head and regarded him with eerily pale eyes. Not a cringer—a biter, for certain. It would flee if it could, but cornered, it would fight viciously.

When it was satisfied that Echemus would come no closer, the child rose and sidled off, never looking away until it reached a corner of the house and could duck into the darkness there. It would go to sleep with the dogs and goats. But what had brought it out here in the cold in the first place?

He went to the niche where it had crouched. It was a small space—just a careless joint in the rocks, too wide to be plastered over. Echemus bent and laid his open hand against the surface. It was warm; a thread of air from inside the house leaked through here. So the child came here to warm itself. Then he heard Hyades speak. It was only two or three words, but the voice came through the wall perfectly clear and undistorted. One of the sons answered, and they all laughed briefly, the sounds as clear as if Echemus stood among them. Then they rose and went off to sleep.

Echemus straightened. He measured with his eye the distance to the door, to the nearest window. Yes, the house's fire pit was right there, and the flaw in the wall carried every fireside word to the small soul that crouched here. Echemus wondered if such a soul could even imagine sitting with the people inside, in heat and light if not in friendly company.

Stringy grass grew all along the wall, but not in this niche. Perhaps the child came here every night. Not for the heat—to sleep with the animals was surely warmer. It must be the secret companionship of even these taciturn, hostile people that the little creature sought. Or perhaps . . .

Or perhaps the child listened to the tales that he, Echemus, told while the big boys yawned and fidgeted and Hyades sulked. Not an arm's length from here, Echemus slept every night, rolled in his blanket on the floor.

So Echemus did the only thing he could: every night thereafter, he told a story all the way through, all the way to the end, even when the men of the household had made their thin excuses to leave and no one but the silent presence beyond the wall was left to hear.

* * *

Every full moon, the king of Tegea sent a messenger to inquire into his father's health. It was always one of the older servants, himself with a servant. They rode into Ladon on caparisoned donkeys, stayed the night, and rode away the next day. Just that brief, regular attention, however, galvanized Hyades and his sons. They worked with an energy unfamiliar to them, and for a while the estate showed their attention. They even added a new layer of thatch to the roof. After every visit, Hyades would eye the chest of Echemus's personal goods, clearly wondering whether any treasure therein had been added or subtracted by the Tegean visitor.

* * *

Wine season was over, and the men spent every day with knives and hooks, pruning. Echemus spent every day by the smoldering fire, half mesmerized by the endless angry rattle of Laothoe's loom. Whenever the sun gave any heat at all, he dragged his stool outside and sat in the light. The goats and their attendant came and went, avoiding him. The dogs lazed around the yard, scratching, squabbling, and snoring in the sun.

One day, the sun was so warm that Echemus carried the hard heel of his breakfast bread outside, where he dozed off. A dog's startled yelp and a sudden sharp whack on his wrist woke him. He stared around, perplexed, and saw the feral child, still leaning after the throw, and a dog darting away, shaking its head. For a moment, Echemus didn't understand. Then he did. The dog had tried to steal the bread, and the child had thrown a stone to drive it off. That the stone had also hit Echemus apparently worried the child, and it crouched, poised to flee.

Instead, Echemus just called out quietly, "Thank you."

The strange eyes, lighter even than Echemus's, flickered as if wondering what the trick was—how the old man, from way over there, would avenge himself for the accidental blow.

Echemus opened his mouth to speak some reassurance, but at that moment, one of the sons came around the corner of the house and saw them.

The young man did not hesitate. He bent, grabbed up a loose rock, and flung it hard at the child, snapping, "Get away!" The child dodged the rock with practiced ease and vanished among the pollarded vines.

The son turned to Echemus. "My mother's trash." He glanced

at the bread crust, still in Echemus's hand. "Don't feed it," he added, and went on his way.

When the young man was well gone, Echemus rose, loosened his arm, and lobbed the bread carefully over the first rows of vines. The dogs, suspecting a trick, cocked their ears but did not go after it. The silence lasted so long that Echemus thought the child might be gone. Then he heard the faintest rustling and sat down, feeling wickedly satisfied. With such small rebellions, he mused, were the lives of old men and children brightened. What tale said that? He would have to remember, and tell it tonight.

* * *

Laothoe's trash. What did that mean? Some regretted adoption? An indiscretion of Hyades' that he would rather not be reminded of, which she had kept to punish him? Could it be her own child by some other man? Hardly possible—unlike men, women rarely survived such a scandal.

Echemus himself had arranged for Laothoe's quick marriage to Hyades after discovering her early misdeeds, but he had never told Hyades why the family ever offered him such a bride. Unless Laothoe herself had told him, there was no explaining Hyades' apparent abuse that way. And those misdeeds had obviously not produced a living child. If they had, the child would be older, not younger, than Hyades' sons. Echemus tried again to question his granddaughter but met a wall of silence he dare not probe. If she put him out, he had nowhere to go.

He studied the child. It did not seem to resemble Hyades, as the sons did. In fact, it seemed—at least in the lightness of its eyes—to resemble Echemus himself. But it was too dirty, too unkempt, and too furtive to examine more closely.

He was already familiar with its quickness and dexterity, but without some idea of its age, he could draw no conclusions from that. One thing was certain: no man in Ladon could have imparted such eyes. Only Laothoe herself could have done so. But she never behaved as if it were hers. She ignored it completely. The rare times she stepped out of doors when it was present, she never looked at it, and it retreated from her exactly as it retreated from the men. Even when she called for a goat, she did not address the child by name or even look at it directly.

When the men threw stones at it, she never interfered. Once the sons, all together, had tried to sic the dogs on it, but the dogs just looked at them as if they had lost their minds, and retreated out of sight as soon as possible. So the sons had settled for chasing it down themselves but had returned, panting and dusty and sullen, having been easily outmaneuvered in their own vineyard.

Laothoe's trash. That night, while the men snored and the loom rattled, Echemus told, all the way through, the story of the eagle and the crow, which of them won the fish dinner, and how.

* * *

The New Year came; the goats bore their babies. Laothoe half-milked each doe before allowing it out in the morning. One afternoon, standing in the welcome heat of the sun by the door, Echemus heard a new sound: a steady, muffled *thunk, thunk, thunk.* Curious, he followed the noise and found it behind the goat shed.

There was the child, its back to Echemus, so absorbed in what it was doing that it didn't sense the old man's presence. It was bent over a broken barrel, dropping small rocks into it, retrieving them, dropping them again. From the barrel came a thin, thready mewling. Kittens, it could only be. The child was dropping rocks on newborn kittens.

Without thinking, Echemus said sharply, "Don't!"

The child snapped around, wild-eyed. But for the first time, it did not flee. It straightened and stood there facing him, a rock still in one hand.

Echemus could finally see it clearly. It was a boy, maybe six years old. Its bright, pale eyes glowed through a snarled hedge of hair that might be any color. The face was well made, the nose caked with dirt and snot but shapely, the grubby fingers long and fine. This was a normal child, Echemus realized for the first time, and perhaps even comely under the filth and furtiveness.

Before the boy could retreat and the opportunity be lost forever, Echemus said more quietly, "Don't do that."

The boy's eyes never wavered. He lifted his chin, almost a challenge, and spoke the first words Echemus had ever heard from him—perhaps his first words ever. Tilting his head away, he regarded the contents of the bucket, said, "Bah. Finish." He dropped the last rock into it.

And that was the beginning.

* * *

His name, he said, was Ephialtes. Echemus must have looked shocked and doubtful upon hearing the Arcadian word for "nightmare," but the boy assured him that he had it right. That was what "the woman"—Laothoe, he must mean—had always called him, back when she still spoke to him at all.

Who fed him? The boy made a scornful face. How could anyone starve if they knew anything at all? The countryside grew edible stuff with abandon: leaves, roots, and fruit; fungus and mushrooms; insects and small animals. The woman sometimes set bread and beans outside the door after everyone—even Echemus, now—was asleep. And the villagers left things for him sometimes. Echemus ruefully understood why these unlearned Perioikoi would do such a thing: they thought the boy was mad.

But he was not mad. He had lived all his life, as best he could remember, with the goats and dogs. His vocabulary was rudimentary, his grammar incoherent. Echemus had to work hard to understand him, and it was clear that Ephialtes understood only parts of what Echemus said. With no better idea how to teach a child to speak, Echemus told stories, and from the stories Ephialtes learned new words and thoughts that made him ask questions. And he asked questions exhaustingly.

"Echemus, what is 'crow'?"

"That black bird there."

"Black?"

"Its color."

"Color?"

Again and again Echemus had to reconsider what he knew, and work out how to explain it as simply as possible. "See that goat? It's brown. That one is white. That one is white and brown. That one is black."

After a moment's worried frown, Ephialtes' face lit with understanding. Then he was not satisfied until he knew the names of all the colors he could see.

"Echemus, what is 'eagle'?"

After quickly surveying the empty sky, Echemus sketched an eagle in the dust. When Ephialtes just cocked his head, Echemus realized he had never seen a picture. Once he grasped the concept, however, there was nothing Ephialtes couldn't draw. His sketches of Hyades' sons were particularly pointed.

"Echemus, what is 'river'?"

Again Echemus struggled. "A river is running water, bigger than a stream."

Ephialtes knew "stream." He had learned it yesterday, and what he learned, he never forgot. The boy asked, "You . . . um . . . walk there over?"

"No. You can't wade across a river."

"Jump?"

"You can't jump over a river, either."

"That other thing you say?"

"Swim? Yes. You can swim across a river, if you know how."

"Huh. What is 'sea'?"

"Water wider than you can look across."

Ephialtes cast him a skeptical glance.

"Really."

"Swim?"

"No. You can't swim across a sea. Too far."

"What you say," the boy answered politely, never having seen water he couldn't step across.

Other questions were harder. "Echemus, what is 'justice,' 'kindness,' 'generosity'? What is 'immortal'?" The old man struggled to define such abstractions in words the boy knew.

Echemus had questions of his own. Why did everyone—he moved charily around this—mistreat Ephialtes? "'Mistreat'?" Echemus cited examples: throwing rocks at him, chasing him, siccing dogs on him, making him stay outside in the cold and rain. Ephialtes quirked his mouth, perhaps in scorn. That was how they lived. Knowing nothing else, he knew nothing of resentment. And besides, he preferred to live outside and sleep in the goat shed rather than in that "stink hole." It took Echemus a moment to understand that he meant the house.

What did Ephialtes think of these people? Contempt flickered in the bright, pale eyes. These people were noisy and careless. They went out hunting, but any animal could hear them coming. They were stupid. There was no pattern or logic to them. They were haphazard: they would ignore him for days, then catch and beat him for no particular reason.

Beat him? Echemus felt a surge of anger. Yes, if they caught him, they held him and hit him with sticks. But not so often recently, because he was getting faster—and even less often since Echemus had come. But still they tried to kick and hit him when Echemus was not there to see. Why did they do that? Ephialtes had little interest in their doings, and still less in their reasons for doing them. He did not know. He did not care. They were stupid.

And Laothoe? What was she to him? Ephialtes glanced sidelong at Echemus, wary now. He understood that she was a woman, Hyades was her mate, and the brothers were their offspring. If she was anything to Ephialtes, he did not know it. Why was she so scarred? Ephialtes knew what Echemus meant, but he never heard from this house what he heard from some of the village houses: the sound of blows and a woman wailing. So he didn't know.

The marks on Laothoe were long healed. Perhaps she had acquired them before Ephialtes was born. Echemus felt a pang at that, as if he could not imagine a world in which Ephialtes did not exist.

One day, when even Laothoe was out and the house safely empty, Echemus showed Ephialtes the mosaic inlaid in the top of the chest that held his things. The boy was delighted that random shapes could make a picture. After that, he would sometimes divide his sketches that way. Then, to amuse them both, he would make the small pieces of a picture into pictures themselves.

As the year moved toward summer and Ephialtes roamed farther and longer with the goats, Echemus found himself seeking the boy's company. The secret minutes they stole in the early mornings and evenings left him longing for more. Ephialtes, on the other hand, was still autonomous. Even in the midst of an absorbing conversation, he would suddenly rise and leave. He might return in minutes, hours, days.

The household owned a number of outbuildings: barns, storage sheds, the servants' hutments, even an ancient bathhouse. Echemus made use of the bath regularly, ignoring the cynical murmured comments of Hyades and his sons. Echemus devised the idea of taking Ephialtes there, to clean and delouse him and to assure himself that no inevident diseases were lurking under all that grime. The boy was highly skeptical of this plan. And anyway, how would Echemus convince the household to allow it?

Although Echemus had not exchanged a hundred words with Laothoe in the half year he had lived there, he approached her one morning when the men would be gone all day on some errand.

She was stirring rennet into milk in the room where she made cheese. Even in high summer, this was a cool, dark place that smelled strongly of milk and mold—Ephialtes' depiction of the house as little more than a cave was not so far off the mark. Older cheeses already lay in niches in the walls all around, glowing richly.

Laothoe looked up in surprise when Echemus came in. Men usually stayed well away from women's workplaces. Then her eyes narrowed with suspicion.

Echemus could think of no better beginning than to say, "The boy, Ephialtes—he needs a bath."

The bare, strong arms, streaked pale with scars, kept moving.

"I want to use the bathhouse."

She said without intonation, "Not for him."

Him. Well, that was interesting, and an encouraging start. At least she hadn't called Ephialtes "it," as the men did.

"He needs cleaning."

"He looks fine."

Echemus's legendary temper had mellowed over the years, but now it flared. "He does not look fine. He's filthy. He stinks."

Her arms still moved. "And what's that to you? When did you ever care about anything of mine?"

Ah! "He's yours?"

Her eyes flickered. "Just something I took in. Out of pity. Some Perioikoi."

Echemus said, "He's no Perioikoi. He looks like me. Like our family."

Her head snapped up, her face momentarily unguarded. She

looked terrified, and suddenly much younger.

Then, just as quickly, her face clamped shut. "He looks like a wolf cub. He looks like a viper. He looks like the world's own grief. Stay away from him."

Echemus asked softly, "Who is he?"

Her knuckles were white on the stirring paddle.

He reached out and put his hand over hers. She stopped stirring. He asked again, "Who is he?"

Her hand under his was hard as a stone.

He said, "Laothoe, I'm sorry."

She raised her head then. "Sorry?" she asked softly. "*You're* sorry? What are you sorry for, Grandfather? Are you sorry that my father was a fop and my mother a fool and I had to raise my brothers and sisters from my own infancy and you never even sent a decent servant to help? Are you sorry that you called me a drudge to my face because of the work I had to do? Are you sorry that I embarrassed you by spreading my legs for the first man who treated me like a woman instead of a slave? Are you sorry that you didn't teach me that a man like that would take someone like me seriously enough to screw but never seriously enough to marry? Are you sorry that you gave me to this goat farmer because you didn't know what else to do when that city man spat me out?"

She paused, then continued in the same calm, even tone: "Are you sorry that my husband didn't have the sense to fear an unequal marriage, but took me as he would have taken any wife, and made these brutes on me? Are you sorry that I've spent all my years in this fleapit? Are you sorry that I can say the word "screw" without a tremor, because you believed I was raised in a more refined atmosphere than that, but couldn't be bothered to find out if that was true?"

In all this, she never raised her voice. She never looked away from him. "And now are you sorry for the son I bore who finally, clearly carries my noble blood, who looks like a divinity instead of one of these beasts, and who has survived only because I let them treat him worse than a slave?

"I am glad," she whispered last, "that you are finally sorry."

Echemus stood frozen.

"Did you know that even up here on the roof of nowhere, city men still pass through? Still visit? Still claim hospitality? Did you know that when my baby began to look like my family—like you!—instead of like him, my husband suddenly began to think that maybe I'd slept with one of those fancy city visitors? As if, by then, a man's touch wouldn't be far more likely to make me vomit than sneak out in the bushes and spread my legs. Did you know how he beat me and threatened to murder his own baby son just because it didn't look enough like him? Did you know that the only way to save my one treasure was to throw him away?"

Laothoe had not moved at all, but her scarred throat worked for a moment. "Let me tell you how I weaned my baby. I put him outside in the dark and cold and latched the door. He cried. He banged on the door and begged to come in. His crying was an aphrodisiac to Hyades—he screwed me and screwed me while my baby cried.

"In the morning, Hyades found him sleeping with the goats. He thought it was a great joke—so great a joke that he let the baby live. As an animal."

Laothoe still did not look away. "My husband no longer beats me, since I threw my treasure on the trash heap. Is the relief worth the cost? Don't even ask."

She laid her other hand on top of Echemus's and said, "Certainly, Grandfather, give that child a bath. And see what happens then."

* * *

Echemus built the fire himself. When the stones were hot, he used the old wooden tongs to toss them into the rock-cut water basin in the bathhouse's sloping wall. As steam rolled over them, he peeled the layers of rags from Ephialtes' body. At the end, he had to use his dagger to trim the boy free, even then leaving some pieces that were stuck so firmly the skin would have come away with the cloth.

He let the boy ease himself into the water. When Ephialtes was fully immersed, with only his smeared, worried face and gummy hair above the surface, Echemus tucked his sleeves up to his shoulders and set to work.

The child had no memory of ever having been touched kindly. Knowing this, Echemus took great care in handling him. He carefully stroked and then rubbed the last of the glued-on rags away. He soaked the hair in oil and untangled it, painfully slowly, from the ends to the scalp. He combed out the lice. He used the softest of the rags to wash the boy's face, unmat his eyelashes, empty his perpetually running nose, and soak the wax out of his ears. He scrubbed and then trimmed the boy's ragged fingernails and toenails. He turned back the foreskin and cleared away the mire. He changed the water again and again, the boy shivering and dancing in the chill. And he marveled at the body that came forth. It was slim and strong, beautifully boned, unmarred except for the ordinary scratches and bruises. The skin was pale and pure, the hair a rich bronze, the face already stunningly handsome, the pale blue eyes dazzling, the hands and feet long and narrow and fine. Were he so inclined and not so old, Echemus realized, he could easily fall in love with this boy.

Laothoe had relented enough to give him clothes: worn leg wraps, a patched-over kilt, and a few threadbare shirts that she would ordinarily give to the servants or remake for other uses. Echemus dressed Ephialtes with his own hands, hiding him again in refuse. He cut the bright hair short to deflect attention from it. The face, the eyes, he could do nothing about. He would have to trust the men's sloth and inattention to keep them from noticing.

And at first, they didn't notice. Ephialtes was so skilled at being inconspicuous, and the men so habituated to not actually seeing him, that days passed before they noticed any change. And even then it was not the boy's appearance, but his demeanor, that caught their attention.

One night, as the men yawned and Echemus talked, the loom abruptly stopped clacking. They all looked around. There sat Laothoe, one hand on the shuttle, the other on her mouth. They followed her gaze, and there in the doorway—open for air since it was midsummer—stood Ephialtes.

His wolf eyes glowed in the lamplight. He stood straight and bold for a moment, like a lord surveying his property. One by one, the brothers rose. One held a digging stick; another put his hand on the dagger at his hip. But Ephialtes just lifted his chin and faced them.

Of course, he could be halfway up the nearest mountain before the first of them reached the door. Still, what nerve the brat had! Echemus's heart twisted painfully. If he had to rise, if he was compelled to defend this wildly courageous creature, what would happen to him?

Ephialtes himself answered that. He looked from face to face around the room, pausing equally at each one, even Laothoe's. Then he said, "Bears in cave. Stinks in here." He turned unhurriedly and walked away.

Hyades glared first at Laothoe, then at Echemus, with the malignant stare of a baffled predator. He said, "I should have sent that to Delphi years ago. If you give it any more ideas, I will. Keep it away from me."

He slapped the dust from his knees, stepped over the bench, and walked toward the niche where he slept. He lifted the curtain. Then, without turning, he said, "Wife."

Laothoe rose instantly. The sons went to the room where

they slept. There was nothing for Echemus to do but blow out the lamp, roll himself in his blanket, and sleep as best he could that night.

Come away, O human child! To the waters and the wild . . . For the world's more full of weeping than you can understand.[ii]

— *William Butler Yeats*

"That place. That house. Stinky, yes, but too cold inside."

This was what Echemus had dreaded for months. He sat with Ephialtes on a jagged rock outcropping while the goats nibbled bushes below. One huge doe set a foot against an apricot tree to reach the fruit, and Ephialtes scaled a rock at her. A solid thump to her side, and she bolted away a few strides to crop a less contested shrub.

"So?" Ephialtes added. "Why?"

Echemus asked, "What do you mean, 'cold'?"

"Mean no one like no one. No one talk but you, and they don't like. But husband, wife, you know?"

"You mean Hyades and Laothoe?"

"Them," Ephialtes agreed. "You tell me that wifes—wives—supposed to be . . . val . . . value. But I think he don't like. She don't like. He . . . um . . . hurted her before, no? Why?"

"Hurt her. He used to be angry with her, yes."

Ephialtes considered that. "But she what did—did what—to make angry? I don't see."

Where even to begin with this? Echemus answered carefully, "People remember old anger for a long time, even if they were wrong to be angry in the first place."

"I don't like that. I think—like—animals, you know? One makes one—another—angry. He bite or kick. Bah, finish. Eat together again."

Bah, finish. If only. "People are different."

"Some animals," Ephialtes conceded, "they don't ever like. They stay—um—avoid. Some female, she never like one male. People, they stay with they don't like. *Hunh.*"

Echemus was used to sorting out Ephialtes' grammar. He answered, "If they marry, they must stay together. Divorce is possible sometimes—"

"Like Herakles in your stories?"

"Like Herakles and his . . . wives." Even Echemus had come to enjoy his own sanitized, sometimes wholly invented, tales of the hero's adventures, and Ephialtes loved hearing them. "But for ordinary people, divorce is very rare."

Ephialtes was tapping his staff on his instep. He wore no shoes, probably had never worn shoes. But now he washed his elegant, high-arched feet every night. He said thoughtfully, "That story you know. What story—about the birds, and the father bird give the mother bird his own . . . own . . ."

"Blood. He gives her his own blood to drink, to keep her strong while she hatches his children."

"And that good."

"That is very good."

"Tell why."

"Because females are weaker than males. Their work makes them even more vulnerable. We must protect them."

"Male animals protect," Ephialtes agreed. "But animals weaker than people. We kill them and eat."

Echemus laughed. Puzzled but game, Ephialtes laughed, too. Then Echemus asked, "When you kill a goat, how do you do it?"

"Hyades, sons kill. I don't like that. My goats." He ducked his head a little. "Not mine, but I feel mine."

"How do they kill them?"

The boy raised his head again. "How?"

"Fast or slow?"

Ephialtes grunted understanding. "Very fast."

"Which is better: fast or slow?"

The boy was silent for so long that Echemus looked at him. He was bent over a little, the staff rhythmically tapping. Sunlight picked out the sheen of his hair, and the clean young profile. Echemus's heart moved with pride and love.

Finally, Ephialtes said, "Faster better."

"Why?"

More silence. The boy answered quietly, "I see animals eat animals. Sometimes kill. Sometimes eat anyway, still . . . um . . . still live." He paused. "Faces," he said. "Faces very . . . I don't know . . . empty. Maybe hurt, maybe not hurt. Maybe hurt so much, hurt stop, but maybe not. Don't know."

Echemus persisted softly, "So why is faster death kinder?"

"Because . . ." Ephialtes lifted his head. "Because maybe have to kill. But maybe wrong to hurt. Wrong to . . . um . . . fight?"

"Frighten."

"That. Wrong to frighten. Live okay. Eat okay. Eat while alive, no. Kill slow, no." Ephialtes gazed away thoughtfully, and Echemus waited.

"Cats wrong."

Echemus scrambled, then understood. "Yes. To kill the kittens was wrong."

Very slowly, balancing each word, "Nobody want them."

Echemus waited.

"But still kill wrong." Ephialtes cocked an eyebrow at him. "Nobody want I – me."

Echemus' heart jumped.

But Ephialtes had already turned to something else. "Okay to hit with rock when . . . when eat tree. Wrong to . . . wrong to beat and beat." Ephialtes thought longer. "Wrong," he said, "to hurt when not eating tree, not do wrong. Wrong to hurt for . . . for old things, finished things. Wrong to hurt for make feel good, bigger man. Bigger man must be . . . carefuller man." He turned to Echemus, guileless, smiling, as proud of his syntax as of his reasoning.

Then, before Echemus could answer, Ephialtes' face went serious again. "Laothoe is woman. If man protect woman . . . women . . . why do not you?"

Echemus winced a little. "Hyades doesn't hurt her now. And it isn't our custom to interfere between a man and his wife."

"But you know, I know, bad ones stay bad. Maybe not hurt now, but if hurted before, will hurt later again."

"I don't have any power here, Ephialtes."

Ephialtes' head came up like a spirited pony's. "Bah, power. You say always right, right, never mind what then. And Laothoe is you . . . your . . ." He struggled with the words. ". . . something of yours. Family?" The pale eyes were steady. "Why you come this place? Came."

There was danger here, but Echemus could avoid it. Ephialtes did not know that these people—even Echemus himself—were his own kin, and Echemus had no intention of telling him. "I came here to be your friend."

The eyes narrowed. "Not only."

"Yes, only."

Ephialtes breathed out patiently. "You tell stories, family this, family that. So important, family."

Echemus braced himself. If the boy asked directly, he would have to lie. He could not tell Ephialtes that this household of surly, ignorant souls was all the family either of them had. He could barely believe it himself.

"Even so," Ephialtes said firmly, "even no family you say, hurt still wrong."

"That's true."

"But Echemus, you is—are—a man. Would protect Laothoe?"

Echemus swallowed. "I'm a very old man, Ephialtes."

"And I," Ephialtes said, suddenly perfectly grammatical, "I

am a very *young* man." He did not look proud now, or guileless. He looked austere and much older.

Echemus's heart thrummed painfully.

Then Ephialtes' eyes lost their intense focus. He looked softly perplexed. He asked, "Who was that man?"

"What man?" Echemus asked him, but he already knew.

"That man. Long time ago. That thing on his head. He lift . . . lifted me up. He . . . What is that with the mouth, he did?"

"Kissed you. It was I," Echemus told him.

Ephialtes looked at him sharply. "No. Not you. Eyes same, face different. Like you, not you. Who?"

Echemus swallowed. "I was here. I did that."

Ephialtes was too polite to contradict Echemus so directly again, but he said again, quietly, "Not you." Then he glanced away.

Echemus looked away, too, distressed at his own lie.

That night, in his blanket by the hearth, Echemus did not sleep.

He had lied to Ephialtes, but what choice did he have? Ephialtes was so fierce, so vulnerable; so strong, so fragile. There was no safety for such as he.

Was Echemus doing Ephialtes a service by drawing him into life, language, and thought? Or was he condemning him? Echemus's own fourth son had been Laothoe's father, growing up hopeless, landless, and ineffectual in the shadow of his elders. What place might Ephialtes achieve in the wake of older brothers so favored by their father? A lifetime serving those not half as worthy as himself.

What Echemus most feared was creating a man who could never live as he should live, and could no longer live as he must. And among all the things that Echemus knew, he also knew that he himself would not live forever.

* * *

He lived six years more. The servant came from Tegea every month, and Hyades gathered and paid his dues in full, on schedule. He did not beat his wife or murder Echemus or Ephialtes. Having warned Echemus once, Laothoe ignored the old man and the boy as she always had. The brothers either ignored Ephialtes or abused him so routinely and indifferently that Echemus barely noticed.

Ephialtes did nothing more to call attention to himself. He slept with the goats. He spent as much time as he wished with Echemus, but never where the family would see. He never expressed any interest in his own origin.

His autonomy was unequivocal. Sometimes, he would give Echemus a bare, apologetic glance and disappear for days. The old man knew that human company, even his, grated on the boy. He had been alone too long. Yet even the most isolated shepherd had family, friends; had ties to others, to safety, to mutual defense. Only outlaws had no ties, and they were wholly vulnerable to maltreatment, neglect, and casual, retribution-free murder.

In the final year of his life, Echemus lay in his corner and stirred only as far as the outhouse. Ephialtes had made him a pallet of sticks and vines, deftly woven together. He stole one of the brothers' blankets, dyed it black with alumen and pomegranate, and added it to Echemus's bedclothes. The larceny was so deft that the brother beat a servant for it. If Laothoe suspected, she said nothing.

Echemus's final fading was the only thing that compelled Ephialtes to enter the house. Hyades, his sons, the servants, Laothoe—none of them cared if Echemus starved and stank. So Ephialtes came warily into the foul, smoky cave to care for his friend. When Echemus could not eat, Ephialtes fed him. When Echemus was too weak to walk, Ephialtes was his crutch and his cane. When Echemus wet and soiled himself, Ephialtes cleaned him and sat with him. Neglecting his goats, neglecting even his own need for clean air and solitude, he told him stories: sometimes simple recountings of his day with the animals, sometimes Echemus's own stories that the boy knew by heart in Mycenaean and Arcadian, both of which he now spoke with elegant fluency that would not be out of place in Tegea or even Mycenae.

The thinness of Hyades' patience was obvious. The old man's smell, Ephialtes' presence, the constant whispering in the corner—it all caused him to stamp and curse and rattle around inside his own house like a wasp in wine jug. His sons, as always, followed his lead, complaining to one another about the inconvenience of Echemus's protracted dying.

A month passed without a visit from Tegea. Another passed, and another. The king of Tegea himself was an old man. Had he gone to his dead? Did no one remember Echemus? The air of expectant waiting thickened.

Then Ephialtes came into the house one morning to find the old man stiff and staring on his pallet. Hyades and his sons had gone out. Laothoe gave Ephialtes a single swift glance.

"Get rid of it," she said. "Or they will."

Echemus had told him stories of deaths and funerals, burials, and mourning: wives and daughters and sisters singing polyphonic dirges and laments; processions of priests and mourners with the dead borne aloft on flower-drenched biers. Yet here lay Echemus, eyes glazed and mouth gaping, hair disarranged, only half covered by his blanket and nothing more.

A man was not allowed to touch the dead. But Ephialtes still wore a boy's kilt. He could not be polluted. He knelt, hesitant not because he feared the dead, but because there might be some part of the rite that didn't allow this. Then, with his own hands, he closed the old man's eyes and mouth. Laothoe did not stop him or correct him. She didn't even watch.

Still, thinking there might be more to funerals than Echemus had told him, Ephialtes asked, "Will they come for him from Tegea?"

She was busy doing something at the table, and her arms kept moving. "They don't want him, or he would never have come here. And I don't want him, either."

Ephialtes rose. "How can you not want him? He's your family, isn't he?"

"He was just some old man we felt sorry for."

He lifted a skeptical eyebrow.

"He was no kin of mine," she added. "And little good he did me."

He asked softly, "Are men only worth the good they can do you?"

"What do you think? Did he do *you* good?"

He thought about that. "Yes. He taught me . . . he taught me . . ." But he had to stop, baffled by the immensity of all that Echemus had taught him.

"Fine. Yes, fine. And now," she said, still not looking at him, "see what his teaching will get you. If you and I live through the next month, I'll be astonished."

He stood still. "What does that mean?"

She did not answer.

"What does that mean, Mother?"

She froze, her face still averted.

"Mother?"

She whispered, "How do you know to call me that?"

"What else could you be? What else could *all* of you be, but my family: mother, father, brothers? Echemus was your father—"

"Grandfather," she whispered.

"Nothing else makes sense."

"He shouldn't have . . ."

"He didn't. I never asked, because he was so afraid to tell. But why else would he have been here? Why else would I? So answer the question, Mother."

"Long ago," she said, "you knew to call me that. But then you forgot."

She turned at last. "And what will Hyades do now, with the old man dead, no more spies from Tegea, no one to know or care what he does?"

Ephialtes came and took her hand. She resisted, but he held on until she stopped struggling. Then he turned her hand over in his—it was nearly as large as hers already, and just as clean—and studied the scars on her wrist and down her forearm, pale with age but still distinct. He raised his other hand and touched his fingers to her face, tracing the scars beside her eyes.

He asked quietly, "Why?"

She stared at him helplessly.

"Tell me why," he said gently. "You, me, them, everything. Tell me how all this came to be. Tell me who I am."

She sucked in her breath and spat it out at once. "You're my son and that monster's son, but you look like the Apheidaids—the downland Arcadians." She was in such haste, the words tumbled over each other. "You look like my father and my grandfather and all the men in my family—all Apheidaids. But Hyades didn't believe, because you looked so different from our other sons and because he thought you're some other man's bastard, but you're not."

Ephialtes listened calmly. "So everything about you and him and me and . . . and my brothers—all this is wrong. All of it's not true. All my fault."

She twitched with surprise. "You never did anything wrong."

"But it's my . . ." He raised his eyes to hers ". . . my responsibility."

And just like that, Laothoe started to cry.

She had not cried in his memory, perhaps longer. But she had not forgotten how. She stood still, her son's hand on hers, and let her face knot and her eyes overflow and her nose run and her body convulse and make horrible, hopeless sounds.

Then Ephialtes did something he had never done with anyone. He drew her to him and put his arms carefully around her and said, "Don't worry, Mother. I'll make everything right."

Sobbing almost too hard to speak, she said, "No one can do that!"

She was bloated, greasy-haired, and pockmarked, scarred from years of violence before he had known her. He looked at his mother, and for the first time, a human moved him to pity.

She said, "I let them mistreat you. If they had killed you, I wouldn't have stopped them. I put you outside to live with the animals."

"That doesn't matter," he told her simply. "You're my mother. I'll take care of you."

* * *

First, he took care of Echemus.

Echemus had told him what was done with the corpses of those who died far from home. Since Ladon was not Echemus's home, since even his own blood denied him, this rite seemed suitable. Echemus had said that it was usually performed with mourning, with lamenting, with attention and ceremony and dignity, but Echemus had no one but Ephialtes, who did the best he could.

From the old man's chest of possessions, Ephialtes chose the only thing that Echemus had seemed to value: a bow with a threadbare scarf tied to one end. He spooned a coal from the firepit into a pith stem and tucked it into his pouch. Then he lifted Echemus's dry old husk onto his own narrow shoulders and carried it up into the hills they knew so well. He piled brush and desiccated flowers—it was late summer and everything was dry and yellow and fragrant, not yet softened by rain—and laid the body on the pyre and lit it.

While it burned, he called out again and again, "Echemus Aeropuseides!" so the old man's dead would come to fetch his spirit. And sure enough, as he stood there, Ephialtes felt the spirit slither free of the charring bones. He felt it circle worriedly around him. Then he felt its flare of triumph and recognition, and its swift, darting flight away, and knew that his calls had been heard and answered: kinsmen's spirits had come to fetch Echemus home.

He sat down on a rock and wondered how he felt. He knew all the words in two languages: loss, respect, sorrow. Which did he feel?

The old man had been such a long time dying that Ephialtes was mostly aware of relief that the process was finally over. But that relief was entangled with what his mother had told him, and the responsibility that this knowledge put on him. It was his own fault that this family was as it was: so empty of the sometimes arduous but always powerful camaraderie of Echemus's stories. Even Atreus and Thyestes had had better relations than these. They had fought in ugly ways but had stood together when they needed to. Ephialtes, on the other hand, barely knew his brothers' names. And Echemus must have known Ephialtes' fault in this, yet had not told him.

Of everything he might do now, the strongest impulse was to find Echemus, tell him what he had learned, and ask him what to do. That impulse opened a sharp-edged cavity in his chest. Loneliness, perhaps: another word whose meaning he knew but whose sensation he did not know how to feel. To mourn might relieve it, but it was women who sang and wept over the dead, while men stood stoically by. Their only part was to call a man's name so that his dead might fetch his spirit, and Ephialtes had already done that.

A boy had no role in mourning. Even if he had wished to sing a dirge for Echemus, he knew not a single one of the man's deeds that he might recite. So there were only crows and crickets to sing the old king's song. Ephialtes wiped water from his face with both hands and blew his nose neatly through his fingertips, as Echemus had taught him, while he watched the fire burn down.

When it was done, he gathered the ashes into a pouch and laid it on a quartz outcropping like a shelf, in a little cave he knew of—a jagged niche in stone. He wedged the bow upright among the crags on the floor and left it there.

When he returned to the house, Hyades and his sons were tearing the old man's corner apart. The chest lay upended, its contents strewn everywhere.

Ephialtes made a mistake: he let a spurt of anger drive him in among them.

He demanded, "What are you doing?"

Hyades turned on him instantly. "Where is it?"

"Where is what?"

"His purse. His pouch. His treasure. Where did you hide it?"

"What treasure, Father?"

Hyades' response was instantaneous. He roared, "Don't ever call me that!" and hit Ephialtes in the center of the chest with a closed fist and all his strength. Ephialtes staggered backward. A brother caught him and pinned his arms.

For as long as Ephialtes could remember they would slap and kick and throw things at him, and beat him casually with sticks. But now the brother held him and Hyades hit him until he sank down between them, gasping and gagging.

And that was another beginning.

| | | |

It was written I should be loyal to the nightmare of my choice.[iii]

— *Joseph Conrad*

How long was three years? In the life of a goat, time enough to be born, to play, to bear, in puzzled wonder, a child of its own. Time enough for a tree slip to root, to straighten, to put forth the first tentative branches and one or two undersize flowers. Time enough for a man to stop setting aside the king's share of his goods and forget he had ever served a master beyond his own will. Time enough for three young men to learn that they might never marry, since no father would feed even an unloved daughter to the bleak hostility of Ladon. And time enough for a man to begin again casually, almost offhandedly, to beat his wife for every error, real or imagined.

And three years was time enough for a boy to grow taller than his mother, then his father, and for his narrow shoulders and slender limbs to take on the lean, sinewy strength of early manhood. And time for the men who had abused him only casually before to turn their frustration and rage against him; time for him to understand that this was now personal, was now methodical, and finally had a goal.

They didn't kill him, didn't intend to kill him. For doing so would remove the single object they could safely vent their stunted fury on: the one victim they all could agree on; the one wall they all could piss against; the one creature they could abuse—when they could catch him—since they would never abuse a valuable animal.

On the other hand, he did have some value. None of them wanted to take out the goats every day of the year. It was all they could do to milk them and carry the buckets back and forth. It was all they could do to prune the vines, gather the grapes, and press them. It was all they could do to strip the fruit from the trees and dry it. It was all they could do to sit in the smoky cavern of a house and complain about the servants and villagers who left work undone as they slipped away, family by family, to kinder overlords. It was all they could do to follow their father out into the night and rob the few travelers still brave enough or ignorant enough to cross Arcadia by this road.

It was all they could do to fight over the one woman, a girl younger than Ephialtes, whom they managed to steal—Ephialtes never learned from where—until they had used her so hard that she died. At least, they *thought* she had crawled away and died. They never learned that Ephialtes, when he finally understood that not even Laothoe would protect the pathetic creature, had carried her over the mountain to leave her in a distant neighbor's dooryard, where her chances for survival might be slightly better. Perhaps, those people might at least feed her and keep her warm as they killed her.

This nameless girl, dragged wailing into Ladon, had been nicely clothed, with clean, shining hair, as if someone was as fond of her as Echemus had been fond of Ephialtes. She had had adults who cared for her, who . . . What was the word? Who loved her, whatever that meant. The brothers had swept all that away with the first rip of her dress.

Women were men's responsibility, to be guarded, bred, and punished if necessary. Echemus had said this. Yet there was Laothoe, whose scars the old man had ignored and whose new injuries no one cared about. And now there was this girl—not the brothers' property, but stolen and then treated badly. This was not mating; it was not breeding. Animals did not hurt their own kind that way. When the female was unwilling, the male respected that unwillingness. But these males, Ephialtes' brothers, had not.

Although she had been in the brothers' possession only a few days, the girl had already grown so accustomed to them that she insisted on spreading her legs for Ephialtes, once they were alone in the night. When he hesitated, she wept—silently, since the brothers had driven out of her any hope of rescue, along with the power of speech—until he relented.

He had seen how his brothers handled her, but clawing and biting could not be right, so he performed a simple replication of the mating act, and gently, since she was already bruised and torn. He was in no way prepared for the mighty sweep of ecstasy that left him stunned and sweating. He held her in his shaking arms, with her matted head against his chest, and pondered what he had just learned.

Once, while Echemus was alive, the four of them, Ephialtes' father and brothers, had gone to a distant town to trade. They had returned with the goods they wanted, and also with a new air of swaggering intensity.

"Prostitutes there," Echemus had sniffed privately to Ephialtes. "Very dangerous. Once the likes of them get accustomed to regular sex . . ." He had moved his old head portentously. But he would not explain that word "prostitute." Now Ephialtes knew. It had to mean a woman who was somehow available for sex with men who had no women of their own. But no prostitute could be treated the way Ephialtes' brothers treated this girl. The world would run out of women.

After leaving her in the new, perhaps less horrible refuge, he returned to find the brothers sitting in the yard in the sun, splicing rope and complaining about losing her, arguing about the places they had looked for her as if discussing a loaf of bread that the dogs might have stolen.

As Ephialtes passed them by, he heard from inside the house his father's grunt and his mother's gasp. This time, the sounds went through him like a spear. The brothers heard, too. Then they saw Ephialtes hesitate, and their eyes sharpened the way all predators' do when considering new prey. Even the dogs raised their heads off their paws to stare at him.

Ephialtes continued across the yard, not hurrying, showing no visible fear. When he got to the goats' shed, he stepped inside, pushed the door shut, and sank down in the straw, trembling.

If they, who took their right to ejaculation to be absolute, ever learned what he had done, they would . . . He could not form a coherent picture of the danger he was in, but knew that it was as real as the hemp in one brother's hand, the awl in another's.

He lowered his head to his hands. It continued to come to him in small increments, the breadth and depth of the wrong here. These overgrown unmarried men, the servants' flight, the neighbors' hasty marriages of their daughters, the scars on his mother's arms and her new whimpers of pain, Ephialtes' stunning ignorance before Echemus came, his mother's rejection, his father's hatred, the raped girl—though he had no word for this and so had to struggle with the thought.

The small coal of anger that had lit in his own chest while the girl wept now flared hotter. His own fault in being born was but one thread in the heavy, hairy rope that bound this place. Some king should come and pull the house down, fill the well with stones, burn it all. None here should survive. Not one.

He stayed in the shed, frozen in a terrified knot, until the door banged open and a brother snatched him out into the dimming evening. "Go get the goats, you lazy trash!" The powerful hands tossed him in the general direction of the nearest hillside.

Ephialtes rolled and then rose swiftly, but the brother was already striding away. Ephialtes stood there, stunned again by a new realization: they were as ignorant of themselves as he had been.

All the more dangerous, Echemus might have said. Ephialtes saw, beyond the brother's back, Hyades duck out the house door, straighten, showily adjust his loincloth, and stride off on some errand. Behind him came Laothoe, one forearm mottled with bruises, her lower lip crusted from a slap that split it only yesterday. She glanced around at her sons, then beyond them, at Ephialtes. She caught his gaze and held it, but finally had to look away.

* * *

Evil. It was a word that, according to Echemus, people should use with circumspection, and even then rarely because, as with other monsters, to say its name might summon it.

It meant a wrong so deep that it stood free of ordinary faults, of reason. It even stood free of Ate, whose compulsive, anarchic chaos was never so single-mindedly destructive. It was not a child of fate or even of chance, whose fickleness fell into patterns that one might not like but could at least understand. Evil was not a power, not an immortal. It did not even have a spirit, yet it could be anywhere at any time, and nothing could destroy it. It could only be driven back, like a great vulture that returns obsessively to feed. Like a great vulture, it hovered on a spread of heavy, shapeless dark wings—a peryton of the human spirit.

Ephialtes knew about vengeance, from Echemus's stories. If he could, someday he would avenge this. He had no such obligation, but someone had to do it, and no one else cared. If no great king would cleanse Ladon, he would have to be the one to drive evil off to hunt elsewhere.

* * *

Three years was long enough for a boy to shoulder a man's burden, finding a hundred ways to hide his mother, to distract his father, to place himself between them and take the blows meant for the woman who had borne him and denied him and never taken his punishment on herself. Yet he took it daily. Three years was long enough to learn that doing the unexpected, showing a face so reckless as to be mistaken for madness, was a way to keep his brothers uncertain and, thus, at bay.

Three years was long enough for a once-comfortable manor to complete its downward slide to a land of piracy and ruin. Three years was long enough for a woman to finally steal across the dooryard, enter the shed where he slept, and lie down beside him.

She wept sometimes. It seemed to be an indescribable luxury to her, as she lay in the fragrant straw, in the shed full of goats and safety.

She talked sometimes, telling him stories that Echemus had not. She told him Echemus's own story: of the single combat at Megara, the Herakleids, the Atreids, the real significance of the bow the old man had treasured and that Ephialtes had—he was doubly glad now—preserved. She told him the stories of their distant kinsmen the Pelopeids and Perseids—not fables and legends like Echemus's, but the true chronicle of their own times, still so far removed from Ladon that they nevertheless seemed mythic. When she spoke to him of these things, she used the language of her youth: High Mycenaean, even finer than Echemus's provincial inflections. It became a secret language that only the two of them knew.

Her husband, perhaps feeling her distraction while not knowing its source, treated her even more roughly. He would take her, not even in the transparent privacy of the bed behind the curtain, but in the open light of day. It was the one punishment that Ephialtes hesitated to challenge, and Hyades took full advantage. He would yank her to him, throw her skirt over her back and, watched by all their sons, drive into her.

"This time . . . I'll know . . . who the . . . father is," he would grunt, sweating and thrusting. She would hang from his hands, eyes squeezed shut, hair whisking the floor. She wouldn't protest, and he would grasp her hip bones and double the strength of his pounding to finally wring a groan from her. When he finished, throwing his head back and howling, she would simply pull away, drop her skirt, and limp back to her work.

His sons stared after him, filmy-eyed with lust. The stench of their male frustration gagged Ephialtes. Their sliding, calculating eyes, so dangerous, made his stomach churn. They would slink away to masturbate—yet another business Echemus had not taught him about—while Ephialtes wondered helplessly how soon trouble would start that he must finish.

Even pregnant, she continued to come to him in secret. Even then, her husband took her as he wished, clutching at her swollen belly as if to rip it away, and his sons would rush off to relieve themselves on goats, on leaves, on their own hands.

Ephialtes, however, fell in love with the magic of the new life growing in his mother's belly. He would stroke it through the striated skin that confined it, and feel it move under his hand. If she smiled, or frowned, or just waited for him to stop, he never knew. At night, the goat shed was utterly dark in every way.

The baby was born in the shed, with no one but her son to help. The birth was not hard, and she endured it in silence. When he placed the infant in her arms, she studied it intently. He watched her, not knowing what she sought in the damp, curling hair and the tiny snub-nosed face. Whatever it was, she did not find it. She laid the baby down on the straw, rose, and walked away to the house without a backward glance. Ephialtes wiped the baby and wrapped it and gave it an obliging old ewe to suck. It fell asleep, unworried, between the bony legs.

When Hyades asked for his new child, she thrust her chin at

the shed and turned her back. He hit her—a single blow that made her stagger—then stamped across the yard and found Ephialtes with the infant in his arms, and such an expression on his face that Hyades backed away.

Ephialtes called the baby Elawon for the smooth beauty and rarity of the olives that did not grow here but that he knew from his earlier years, before trade had stopped between Ladon and the lower lands. But the black hair shed away all at once, and new hair grew in, light and flat, over the delicate skull. The face lost the puffiness of birth and seemed longer, with the suggestion of a fine nose. After only a month, the baby already looked like Echemus.

Ephialtes trusted none of them. He knew exactly what would happen to this child in that house. So he carried it with him always, slung across his back in a length of cloth. He slept with it tucked in the bend of his arm. He snarled like one of the dogs even when its own mother approached.

All that fierceness earned time—time for the baby to snuggle and snuffle into Ephialtes' shirt and cling to it with tiny hands; time for Ephialtes' heart to encompass that separate life completely. But Hyades and his sons caught Ephialtes one evening, bound him hand and foot as a precaution, dragged him away past the orchard, and beat him, all of them together. As with the Herakleids later, their own eagerness made them inefficient. They could easily have killed him, could even more easily have broken bones and knocked out all his teeth, but they got in one another's way, impeding one another's reach and balance. Even their kicks were balked by tight proximity and having to wait one's turn.

Still, they hurt him. When he was limp and beaten and defiant no more, Hyades unwrapped the baby from the sling, stared at it, stared at Ephialtes, and kicked him again. Then he spat on him, pulled aside his loincloth and pissed on him, and carried the baby away over his shoulder like a sack of meal.

When their father was gone, his brothers tortured him further until they were bored and out of ideas. Then they thought of what he had always known would come next. It was a year since he had taken the girl away. Masturbation and even sex with animals were never as satisfying as another human body. They spat on themselves for lubrication and took turns raping him.

A year of frustration was not relieved at once. They took him several times each, until they were all, at last, depleted. The last one to leave said, "Clean up. We'll be back."

He had to gnaw the bonds loose and then crawl home. A ten-minute walk took hours. He meant to hide with the goats—he needed their warmth against the bone-piercing cold, which would kill him faster than his injuries. But his mother met him at the edge of the dooryard. He paused there, just to rest. She lay down in the damp grass and wrapped her cloak around them both, to warm his body with hers.

And that is how Hyades found them. Wild-eyed and bellowing, he kicked them apart. One brother held down Ephialtes, who had no strength to resist. He lay helpless, shaking and groaning, while his mother screamed anger, screamed fear, and finally just screamed and screamed. After a while, that brother released him and another dug a hand into his hair and pulled his face around toward them all. Ephialtes hid his eyes behind his wrists. The brother dropped him, kicked him, kicked him again, then kicked him unconscious.

When he woke, it was just dawn. They were alone on torn, bloody ground, and she was staring at him. Her eyes burned red in blackened sockets.

"The baby," Ephialtes whispered with ragged lips.

She hawked, spat blood, then dragged an edge of cloth across her naked chest. "Good riddance. It's not what I wanted. Let it go to Delphi with all other unwanted bastards. Food for the Serpent. Filth for filth."

Something inside him moved—some inhalation of a still more terrible wrong. And she had spoken in Arcadian, whose grammar offered a thousand ways to hide meaning.

"Not what you wanted," he said in Mycenaean. "But it's a baby. How can you want or not want it? What did you want instead?"

She looked away.

He tried to sit up, but dizziness and nausea drove him down again. When he looked, she was watching him, sharp and wary. Something in what she had said was so wrong, so big and so important, that he had never noticed it even though it was always there. As if a black blot had hung in the sky for so long that no one even saw it anymore.

He said, "Tell me."

She only blinked. Her eyes closed and opened again, like— why had he never seen this?—a turtle's.

He knew nothing, less than nothing, of how men and women dealt honestly with each other. He felt suddenly and completely lost, as if in perfect darkness or underwater, as if he still had not learned the language she spoke.

He had to poke at it as if with a stick down a dark burrow, not knowing what he might rouse. He said carefully, "There is some lie. What is it?"

"You're still a child. You don't understand enough."

"Enough of what?"

"Look at yourself—ignorant as a slave. What do you know? Nothing."

What *did* he know? Only what Echemus had taught him and what he had seen. What he had known that his brothers knew, before they themselves knew it. What she had told him: formless, nameless secrets and lies; solace, relief, words he had learned while he felt the brush of evil's formless wings against his face and thought it was only spiders' webs or her fingertips.

He said to her, as carefully as if feeling his way in the dark,

"I've defended you for a long time. Tell me what I was really defending."

She only looked away.

He reached for her. Too far. He twisted up on one hip and dragged himself closer. Then he caught her wrist, which she raised to protect herself, and he held it.

He whispered, "Tell me."

Her mouth shut so tightly that her lips were gray. He wrapped his other hand, all five fingers, one at a time, around her throat. His hands had grown, he noticed. It fit perfectly.

She whispered, "You won't hurt me." The words buzzed against his palm.

His hand tightened. She made a sound, a whine, and he felt its vibration. It was that one sound, so human, so animal, that released his anger.

He got his feet under him and rose, lifting her with him by the arm and throat. She had lost most of the fat on her body even before the birth and was light as a kid goat, her suddenly white face level with his own. He shook her, but with both thumbs locked around her larynx, the tips of his fingers fitted into the bones of her spine, all her breath in his hands.

Her mouth lolled open, and noises came out of her. He clamped tight, tighter. Her teeth gaped; her tongue protruded; her eyes ballooned; she pawed at his fingers, his wrists, then clung to his forearms with no strength at all.

He had taught himself to use Echemus's bow, had even made arrows. He had learned to count before he released, and he counted now—*one, two, three*—and let her go. She fell satisfyingly, almost as if boneless, and he kicked her. Perfect aim: the diaphragm. The last of the air in her body heaved out.

Now her noises turned truly ugly. He kicked her again, the breast dense under his foot. She writhed away, fleeing as best she could with no air, no control. He knew how *that* felt. He could kill her this way, barefoot though he was. That realization came, as unexpected and as powerful as the first orgasm had been.

What stopped him was his own pain, coming back enough for him to recognize that this much effort might provoke bleeding that would not stop. So he caught his balance and just stood over her. Her mouth was shapeless, and her nose. Blood and snot smeared her face and matted her hair. Her clothes, already torn, covered none of her: not the throat he could have crushed, not the milk-hard breasts she refused to give Elawon, not the pleated belly, not—he knew this word from Hyades—the cunt that still leaked sperm and blood, all of which now bore his own dusty footprints.

He must be exactly what she had called him. He must be the most ignorant human on earth. And with that simple thought, his rage died away.

He waited while she drew her body together into a wretched knot. He waited while she covered herself and looked up. Then he went down on one heel—feeling a spasm inside his body and the blood that soaked the back of his kilt—and reached out his hand. She snatched it and kissed the palm. The kiss stung as if she had bitten him.

* * *

Because he was bruised and beaten, his bowels cramped and bleeding, his brothers thought he couldn't hurt them. Because he was so young still and they were grown men and three to his one, they thought he couldn't hurt them. Because he had avoided or fended off or defied their violence but had never inflicted his own, they thought he couldn't hurt them. They thought he couldn't hurt them, because they didn't want to believe he could.

So he killed them all—not by stealth, but by approaching them openly, with only a kitchen knife tucked in the back of his bloody kilt, and by never quitting until he was done. Unweighted now by anger or outrage or injustice, all he wanted to do was to make it all stop, by the simplest means. Retaliation or revenge or anything else so deliberate might have been impossible to achieve, since his very resolve would have warned them. But that straightforward, uncomplicated ambition to kill them—that was easy.

They were shirtless and sweating in the noon-bright air, jabbing sticks into the soil around the vines to let the plants breathe. Ephialtes eased his goats near enough to make it seem accidental that they should all be in the same rocky swale together. Then he left the goats and walked toward his brothers.

For a moment, he wondered at the thick musculature of their arms and shoulders, their brawny hands, the dense black hair on their chests and backs. But on he came, not missing a step.

The nearest brother leaned on his stick and gave a slow grin. He said, "He liked it; he wants more," and cupped the other hand over his groin.

Ephialtes did not stop walking until he was so close he could see the man's eyes widen, see the flicker of doubt in their depths. Then he gutted him as they so often gutted lambs: in a single upward slash. *Faster better.*

The brother grunted in shock and bent over, holding himself. Another, not understanding, not seeing the knife, came to help him. Again the rapid slash. *So easy.* The third started backing away. Ephialtes walked after him, the knife showing now. The brother turned to run, hindered by the stick, by sheer disbelief that this could actually be happening, and by a bulky body inexperienced with flight. Ephialtes climbed his back, combed a hand into his hair and gripped tight, and cut his throat.

All so simple. What a fool, not to have thought of this before.

Their spirits, suddenly ripped free, fled screaming into the cracks in the rocks. He could hear their thin, furious wailing as he wiped his hands and the knife on leaves. The family's tomb was far away. He would not carry them there. The spirits would be difficult for the elder dead to find, and he would not call out their names to make it any easier. If they weren't found, the spirits would be taken by perytons, those stag-headed hunting birds that cast the shadows of the humans they once were. They were always hunting other careless men, to steal their spirits' places, and were always tied, like grotesque kites on strings, to the ground where their own bodies lay. Echemus had told him about perytons. Ephialtes had liked that story.

Then the voices faded, and the bodies lay slack and empty. Flies walked on their faces, and the sun seared his shoulders as he dragged them into the cleft that only he knew, under the shelf that held Echemus's ashes, under the shining black stare of the crows. The spirits, no longer angry, crept between his feet, whining like puppies. He laid a palm on the bag of Echemus's ashes, but could think of nothing to say to him. Echemus, wherever he was, would either understand or he would not. He left the knife there to screen the cleft from searchers, but took the bow and his own arrows.

He led the goats down and penned them. His mother had combed her hair and washed her face and changed her clothing. But her eyes were just as when he had left her, and her arms were folded tightly over her breasts as if she were very cold. The baby lay on the ground behind her, awake but silent.

Echemus had said that a man who sent another to his dead had to declare the death and the reason for it to other men. But he was not a man, and no other men were here. He stood for a moment, uncertain.

She could not speak, but she mimed Hyades: his size, his beard.

"I don't know where he is. Where is he?" Then, like the mosaics he had once loved, the pattern came together in his mind. "Oh. I don't want him."

She pressed her palms together.

"No."

She dropped to her knees and touched her forehead to his bare feet.

"No. I won't kill him. I told you I would make everything right."

She rose and backed into the house, gesturing. He followed warily. From the table, she lifted an object he had never seen before.

It was flat, like a starched cloth or a leaf, and roughly ovoid, folded across. Someone had drawn a design on the side she showed him. Four signs that meant nothing to him: a chip-cornered square, two different forks, a thing like a bush. Ugly. He himself could draw far better.

She held it out to him, making insistent noises. He didn't want it, but took it anyway just to silence her. Inside it were more marks—chains of them. Writing, this must be, but it meant nothing to him. He folded it again and slid it into his pouch. Seeing this, she closed her eyes, as if deeply satisfied.

Then she gave him her husband's sword, a bag of bread, and Echemus's cloak, which one of the sons had stolen. Sword, food, cloak, bow, arrows, and a leaf of writing—more than he had ever owned in his life before. She added a pair of sandals she had just made for Hyades, but those he would not take. He would never walk one step on that man's path.

He folded the cloak into a sling to hold both the bread and the baby. Then he settled Elawon behind his shoulder and walked away. He walked in one direction while evil, with a single heavy stroke of its wings, soared off in another.

There is a devilish mercy in the judge, if you'll implore it, that will free your life, but fetter you till death. [iv]

— *William Shakespeare*

The king of Tegea was a distaff cousin, but that had meant nothing to Laothoe and so meant nothing to him. And many years had passed since the messenger from Tegea last made the trek. If Ephialtes had other kin outside Ladon, he did not know it.

He thought about the stories Echemus and his mother had told him, and the little he knew about the world from overhearing Hyades and his sons. Then he walked down from the mountains, skirting the towns, to where he had to go.

After a lifetime of stealth and secrecy, avoiding others was both natural and easy. Although for some days he could not run or climb, could only walk slowly because of the pain in his belly and bowels, still only crows saw him leave Arcadia. It was a good time of year to travel: early spring, not yet the new year, still wet and cold enough that people were indoors or close to home. Elawon nestled against his back, sleeping or prattling softly.

When he came to the Megara wall that had stopped Hyllus Herakleides and his army, Ephialtes made a nest in a thicket of brambles and waited there a while. He shared bread with Elawon, first chewing it to a paste that a baby could swallow. Then, night after night, he crept down to reconnoiter.

The wall was stone in some places, only man-high wooden stakes in others, but watched all along its length from a string of mud-brick villages occupied by serious-looking warriors. Trying to go over or through it undetected appeared impossible. He walked to the far north end of the wall and considered the Gulf of Corinth and the mist-shrouded mountains beyond.

Although Echemus had described the sea to him, even this quiet slough looked endless to someone who had never encountered water that he couldn't step across. He hung the sword and bow loosely from his shoulders so they would not interfere with his movements. Then he folded the cloak tightly so that even if it got wet, it would not drag on him and Elawon and make them—he had forgotten the word for this—suffocate under the water. Then he paddled silently, all through the night, around the Megarans' barricade. The only casualty was the leaf his mother had given him. Wet, the writing smeared so badly that he threw it away.

Only the wolves and the fishes, the marmots and lizards and crows, knew that he traveled in the dark and hid through the day in the scrub hills and swamps along the edge of the gulf. He heard goats above him sometimes, the calls of shepherds, the howling and barking of dogs, but never saw a single human soul that he could not easily avoid.

He missed his goats. He should not have penned them. What if no one thought to let them out again? No one but he had ever cared for them, and now he had left them. They would suffer for that, and they were not to blame.

He had named them all, years ago, in secret, when Echemus told him about Akhilleas and his miraculous chariot horses, Xanthos, Balios, and Pedasos. Some of the goats' names were Mycenaean, some Arcadian: Black, Red, Spot, Sandy, Sassy, Beauty. To name animals was foolish, perhaps, maybe even wrong. It had made him miss them all the more when Hyades killed or traded them. Maybe he would never name an animal again.

Now, though, he recited the names softly aloud, like a magical song. And Elawon kicked and bobbed with the rhythm of it.

He was murmuring that song when he arrived in Delphi one midmorning. The people of the village gazed calculatingly after him as he passed among them. He still wore no shoes, so, having found at last the withy hut in the trees, he brushed off his feet with his usual courtesy, then rang the bell.

When a priest asked him, "Who are you?" he answered as the stories told him to do: "I am Ephialtes Hyadeides. Hear me, Grandfather."

He handed over the bronze clasp from Echemus's cloak, but the priest didn't let him explain why he had come. In the presence of no human, no animal, only hundreds of small clay figures that stood like a worshipful hand-high army, the priest made him kneel. Then he cut Ephialtes' wrist, filled a little cup with the blood, and poured it over the hulking sacrifice stone. The stone sucked it down eagerly. Then he finally turned to speak.

"You are outlawed," the priest said, not unkindly. "You are unclean. You have no father and no mother, no sons and no daughters. You have no kin. You have no name and no home and no king. You have no debts and no duty and no protection. Anyone can kill you without penalty.

"You may not speak in an assembly of men. You may not speak first to any man. Any man may touch you, but you may not, by volition or chance, touch a clean man. Your touch will pollute him. You may not sit with clean men. You may not touch anything a clean man might touch after you. His touching the thing you polluted will pollute him, too. Only priests, kings, shamans, slaves, outlanders, children, and animals are safe from your pollution. You may not eat or drink with clean men. You may not eat from a common vessel. Your dishes and tools and clothing are unclean. You may touch running water, but only after every clean man, woman, and animal has already touched it, and even then the spirits of water are not obliged to hear you.

"You are not a man. You may not wear a man's loincloth. You may not stand to urinate. You may not have a clean woman unless she is first prepared by a shaman or priest. You may not have a man except a slave or a king. You may not speak to a clean man's wife, nor may you remain in the same room with her. You may fight to defend your life, but you may not strike first, and every blow requires compensation. You may use no weapon against yourself. That also is forbidden."

Ephialtes still knelt on the stone-paved floor, his arms still upraised as the priest had ordered, the clay figures grumbling and giggling around him. He asked, "How long? How long am I outlawed?"

"All your life, which will not be long."

"I never asked for help, not ever before. Not from anyone."

"Then don't ask it here and don't ask it now. The Serpent doesn't want you. Delphi won't protect you. Go to the Erinyes. Go sit by the roadside and be killed. Go away."

The priest was young, perhaps twenty-five or thereabouts, with thick black hair, narrow face, and hard, judgmental eyes.

Ephialtes asked, "Are you Menetor?"

"No. I'm an ordinary priest, although I hope for that title someday."

"Am I a monster?"

"Yes, you are."

"Why?"

"There are three thousand springs and three thousand rivers in all the world, and every one of them has a name. Every crumb of soil, every stone, is accounted for. We know who you are. We know what you did. You shouldn't have come here."

The priest made a small explosive noise. "Delphi is a place of great crime and justice, not a hole for the likes of you to crawl into."

"But there *was* great crime. And I need justice for this baby."

"What would you two do with justice? Sit under a bush and gnaw its bones?" The priest made a scornful puffing noise. "Justice is for men who matter. Delphi is for . . ." He looked toward the door, where another priest had stepped inside and was waiting. The two of them talked together without words while Ephialtes waited.

Finally, the priest looked down at him again. "Your father is coming."

He started to rise, to flee.

The priest lifted a hand. "We won't give you to him. That's not what we do."

He sank down again warily.

"You believe he wants revenge. So does he." The priest looked at him narrowly, as if not believing he would understand. "What he needs is purging from his anger. To kill you would only increase it and give him no help."

"Why?"

"Because he could kill you only once."

Ephialtes sat quietly, trying to hold on to this idea. "It wouldn't be enough?"

"His lands would still be ruined, and all his sons still lost. But instead, after this, he will be satisfied. And he'll be able to repair the harm."

"How?"

"It's that way. The Serpent knows, although this is Kastalia's authority." The priest spoke the name as if the terrible nymph were a living, ordinary person, but Ephialtes knew better. Echemus had told him.

"Will she eat me?"

"Kastalia?" The priest made that sharp, soft puff again. "No. Well, probably not."

"And you won't give me to him? My father?"

"No, but we have to give him something. You understand."

He did not, but he waited obediently.

"How old are you?"

He quirked his mouth. He did not know.

"Fifteen, we'll say. A year or two either way."

The priest changed the subject again. "It doesn't matter what you really did or did not do. It doesn't matter why. Understand this most of all: it doesn't matter why. It doesn't matter if Hyades and your brothers were right or wrong, whatever that means. Those words are for women and old men.

"What matters is that you wiped out your father's future in front of his feet, and all the futures to come after. No, a baby doesn't count." The priest considered, then went ahead. "He's a man, a chief, the end of a lineage, with duties and responsibilities he has neglected too long. The world cannot afford to let him stay furious, unreasoning, and mad. If he runs wild, what then? And what of his land and his people, so many already fled away? The chaos must end. We must restore balance to him and put his world back into his hands, even if his future is gone. Do you understand?"

"I . . . yes."

"You have no place and no power. If you ran wild still, who would care?"

He already understood that.

"When we're finished, all will be resolved: shame, expiation, satisfaction, truth, Ladon's future, your mother's, and yours."

"I have a future?"

"Touch the floor."

"What?"

"Put your hand on the floor."

He did so, and the gritty stone seemed to flex under his palm. He snatched it away.

"We know who you are," the priest said again. He turned away, then back. "Stay in this chamber. That corner there. Don't try to leave. Whatever you see, whatever we do, whatever happens, do nothing except what we tell you." He started away again, then added, "And keep the baby quiet." He went out.

Ephialtes was alone except for Elawon, the stone, the sifted light, and the sharply watching votives. There was something else here, as well: a soft, chilly humming that did not reach the level of hearing, but which he felt deep in his bones. He touched the floor again, experimentally, and felt the same flexion, like the skin of a vast, hairless animal. He crept into a corner, wrapped his arms around his drawn-up knees and the baby—safe here, though he could not say why—and fell asleep.

* * *

They brought in a tall, dark-haired boy of about Ephialtes' age, who smelled of something bitter and rich. He moved like a sleepwalker and never objected when they lifted him and tied him, face up, to the top of the stone and cut away his shirt and kilt.

Then they brought in Hyades.

Naked, dripping with water, he walked heavily into the chamber. An escort of priests parted and moved to stand against the walls as silent witnesses. Only one priest followed him: an old man, short and thin and white-haired—the current Menetor, it must be. Ephialtes' priest stood in front of Ephialtes but with his back to him.

Strange. Ephialtes had never seen his father as just some man among other men. Hyades was not tall, after all. He stooped a little, and his face seemed to sag more than a man's his age should, as if he had been ill for a long time. There were pouches under his eyes, creases on his forehead, lines binding his short, wide nose to his white-sprinkled mustache. Lines crossed between his sagging nipples and his gray-haired paunch. His sex and scrotum hung shapeless and harmless, still dripping water. His wet, white-streaked hair clung to his skull and neck. There was nothing remarkable about this heavy, aging, tired-looking, ordinary man. Every one of the priests was more interesting than he, most of all Menetor, with his high crown of silver hair and his intelligent eyes.

Hyades saw the stone and the crowds of votives first. Because of the way the light sieved through the wicker walls, he did not at first see the figure bound to the top of the stone, but he saw Ephialtes crouched in the corner, behind the priest. He hesitated, his face rigid and unreadable, then turned to Menetor.

Mentor said, "That one. That one is for you."

Hyades looked again at the stone. The boy tied to it breathed out, uncomfortable even in a drugged dream. Hyades glanced at the priest with sudden surmise.

"Yes," Menetor told him, and handed him a dagger.

Hyades took it carefully, as if it might vanish if taken too eagerly. He asked, "What's that?"

"A gift to your anger."

"And what . . . what must I do?"

"Anything you want."

"But . . ."

"Anything."

Hyades closed his hand around the dagger's hilt. He stared at the stone.

Menetor said, "You are Hyades Makhaonaides. You married Laothoe of the Afeideides."

Hyades bobbed his head. "Do you know? I treasured that woman. I couldn't believe they'd give something so precious to me."

"And look what happened."

The fist that held the dagger—how many times had Ephialtes fended it off?—trembled now.

Menetor prompted, "Some monster cursed her."

"She despised me. She hatched a nest of slime in my bed."

"She was hypnotized."

"She never saw me when she looked at me. She never saw my sons, even though she bore them. She couldn't wait to get them out of her body and off her breast and toss them to me."

"And then there was the other son."

Hyades looked at Menetor earnestly, just as a sane person might. "That thing she bore, that wolf-eyed snake. It blinded her. It was all she looked at."

"You let it live," Menetor prompted.

"I let it live. And it set on us like a pack of dragons."

Ephialtes started to rise, to protest. His priest made a sharp sound, and he sank down again.

Hyades seemed to be reciting, his voice was so flat. "It cursed my house. It drove away the servants and stripped the fields and murdered the animals."

"And Echemus."

"It killed the good old king Echemus and hid his body away."

Hyades approached the stone hesitantly. The boy stirred only a little.

Menetor said, "There was once a solid, honest man named Hyades Makhaonaides. Perhaps he will be such a man again, once he has rid himself of the poison in his house. His wife is his property, so she, just like all the rest of his demesne, will be cleansed when he is."

Hyades asked quietly, "Anything?"

"Anything."

Hyades cut the boy precisely, experimentally: a slice of skin here, the end of a finger there. The boy gasped, and his eyes came open. His mouth was not blocked, and he woke as Hyades worked, and made a soft whining sound.

Hyades glanced quickly at Menetor, who murmured reassurance. The priests all around the wall never moved. Only the votives stirred and rattled.

The boy moaned, then called out, then screamed while Hyades took finger joint after finger joint, then sliver after sliver of meat, paring them neatly away and tossing them among the votives, which leaped to devour them. The boy screamed while Hyades took his ears. With every stroke, the boy screamed. With every scream, Hyades' sex rose and hardened until he suddenly groaned aloud, stood the dagger upright in the meat of the boy's arm, gripped the boy's thighs, and raped him until the anus squirted blood. The boy screamed while Hyades retrieved the dagger and cut away meat from his hands, feet, arms, legs, separating each part as carefully as if dismantling something that he wished to reassemble later. The boy screamed while Hyades—more rushed now, and careless—took one eye and the other. He screamed while Hyades began to make his own sounds: a rhythmic groaning at first, then growling and rumbling, then crying aloud every foul or perilous word the Arcadian language held. Ephialtes understood them, and the priest seemed to, as well, his mouth moving soundlessly, perhaps with the same words.

The boy screamed while Hyades opened the chest—hacking the ribs loose from the breastbone—and pried it wide and thrust his arms inside and tore at the neatly layered organs. The boy still screamed, amazingly, until Hyades buried his face and then reared up suddenly, shaking his head like a feeding dog, the writhing heart in his teeth.

The boy stopped screaming then, but Hyades was not done. No longer careful, he thrust and hacked and tore and sawed, grunting and moaning with the effort, stabbing and slashing until he could no longer lift his arms and so crawled atop the stone to continue ripping with trembling fingers and then with his teeth again when his hands failed, until he finally lay exhausted in the bloody nest he had made for himself, as if in a lover's embrace.

At last, he slid down, clinging to raw bones like a prisoner clinging to cell bars, down the stone and to his knees, as if only the force of gravity had defeated him. Then he turned and sat flat on the floor, his back against the stone, and bent forward and covered his face with his hands and howled. The walls heaved and creaked with voluptuous pleasure.

The priest reached down to Ephialtes' shoulder. "Let the child be born."

He looked up, ready to argue.

"Finish this!"

He rose and carried the soft bundle past his priest, past Menetor, through the votives, which had turned on each other now, snapping and snarling. He kissed Elawon's forehead and placed him inside the bloody cradle.

The priest said, "Take the only blood you share with anyone. Say, 'Forgive me, you are now my brother.'"

Ephialtes obediently dipped blood from beside Elawon's head and licked it up. He said to the faceless corpse, "Forgive me. You are now my brother."

"You are the twin of this boy. I hope you understand. He is the right, you the wrong. Because he is precious, you are a nameless, worthless thing. All rightness will remain here, for this good boy's spirit and for this son of Hyades. Go out and sit by the road and be killed."

Ephialtes stepped gingerly over Hyades' legs. The man could not have noticed him. The votives snapped at his ankles but let him pass. The priests who stood ranged against the walls still neither moved nor made a sound.

At the door, he looked back one more time. A huge insect was crouched on the corpse, wings lifted, antennae quivering, great shining spheres of eyes, the machinery of mandibles nibbling delicately up and down raw-edged bone. It faded away, then back again.

"What is that?" he asked.

Both priests started, stared at him, then touched closed fists to their foreheads. Menetor said, "The great nymph Kastalia, it must be."

"I greet you, Kastalia," Ephialtes said, mindful of courtesy, and the nymph paused momentarily in its feeding, then resumed.

Ephialtes' priest said quietly, "Tell us where your brothers lie."

With all his new power, Ephialtes answered, "No."

"You can't leave them as perytons."

"Yes," he said. "I can."

As he said that, Ephialtes felt the floor arch and slide under him and heard the hiss of skin against the walls of a great unseen burrow.

His priest said, "There are only three thousand rivers and three thousand springs in the world." More portentous talk. "You cannot hide."

"I didn't call evil there. I made it fly away."

"And where was it going?"

At that same moment, Kastalia rose higher on its legs, turned its great plated face to consider Ephialtes, then crouched to feed and fade away again.

Ephialtes turned and left that place.

The door was standing open. On the threshold stood a child, a black-haired boy perhaps three years old. His small, soft mouth absently open, the child stared past Ephialtes at the mess on the stone, the sobbing man, the snarling votives.

As Ephialtes approached, the child did not step aside but just stared up at him with huge dark, canted eyes.

Ephialtes ran quickly through the rules of outlawry. Yes, he could speak first to a child. He could even touch one. He asked, "Who are you?"

The little chin twitched. "Te—Temenus. Temenus Aristomacheides Herakleides, my lord."

Here was someone important, to use three names. A person, even so young, already owning the regard of men. Herakleid.

Child or grandchild of one of those whom Echemus had driven out. But right now also a little boy, confused and worried.

Ephialtes answered, "Don't call me 'my lord.' I'm . . ." He tried the word for the first time. "I'm outlaw."

The boy looked past him. "Is that Depas? Is that my friend Depas?"

"It's nothing. Don't think about it."

The depthless, tilted eyes stared into the sacrifice chamber. "My father the king is coming to fetch me. I want Depas to come, too. I can have my own att—attendants." The soft mouth quivered. "There was a party today. They didn't let me go. They ate won—wonderful things and wouldn't give me any. Depas got a bath and new clothes. Then he wouldn't play with me and just came here. I was so angry!"

"Don't think about him again."

The child's voice, raised for a moment in resentment, fell to a whisper. "Is it my fault? Did I do that?"

"Don't be stupid," Ephialtes snapped, finally impatient. "Get out of my way."

The child did not close his mouth. But he raised one hand as some children could, confident that an adult would take it and lead him safely away.

Ephialtes lowered his hand. Temenus's was so small that two of Ephialtes' fingers filled it. The little grip was strong and warm. He turned the boy away and led him out among the cypress trees, then leaned down and painted his face with blood from his other hand: two lines across the forehead, and a dot on each cheek—a ceremonial marking, although he did not remember how he knew it. Then he twisted his fingers free and went on his way.

That was the first and only time that he spoke harshly to a child.

All you need in this life is ignorance and confidence; then success is sure.[v]

— *Mark Twain*

When he paused in the town to collect his cloak, sword, bow, and arrows, he already could recognize almost nothing in the new tale, breathlessly told, of the savage slaughter of peerless young men by a changeling demon, a gryphon, a monster of some new and terrible kind. For fear of the monster's retribution, they called it "the Good Kinsman." Already, the ignorant speculated and debated which were more terrible: the Erinyes—the Serene Sisters—or the Kinsman. Already, Hyades was a hero, saving his infant son, his wife, and his province from waste, all while the actual Hyades still wept and wailed under a dribbling corpse

So, good. Hyades would let out the goats.

The priest had said Ephialtes should sit by the road and wait for someone to kill him. So he stole a pair of sandals from an unguarded door and left. He walked over mountains and rivers, past rangy fortresses and wolf-haunted hills, and then on and still on until he was amazed at the sheer vastness of the world. At first, the landscapes were familiar. Then the mountains grew higher, the trees taller and wider in spread, the undergrowth wetter and denser, the plants increasingly foreign and strange. He passed valleys flecked with sheep, and steaming villages where men farmed and women cooked, and no one, not even Echemus, had ever told him the world was so large.

He was usually hungry, but he found enough to stay alive. Even in alien forests, he could find edibles both familiar and new: nuts and seeds, tubers and shoots, sere winter berries, squirrels' caches, and many small creatures to dig, shoot, or snare. He found mice and voles in abundance and already knew a hundred ways to catch birds.

For variety, when near human establishments, he robbed traps and stole seed from field granaries. He had no use for larger animals and dare not approach goats to steal their milk: fierce guard dogs were everywhere. He saw his first cattle and kept a respectful distance from the huge horned beasts. He saw his first horses and kept away from them as well—they were too watchful and wary, and their keepers would no doubt be interested in whatever was making them snort and whicker.

The local people hunted sometimes for deer and bison, and although they left nothing behind from their kills but bloody smears on the ground, their hunting camps were large enough that they could be careless with the meat once they had taken it. They dried racks of it over smoky fires that were guarded by children who were alert enough to keep dogs and weasels away, but not fast or clever enough to deter a human thief.

Clothing was more difficult to acquire. The sandals were awkward in the soggy, vine-knotted forest, and although the cloak was of good, heavy wool and tight against rain, his shirt could not keep out the seeping cold. His kilt left his legs bare below the knees. After many chill days and sleepless nights, he managed to steal a shirt and leggings of bear leather with the fur turned inside. The legs and sleeves were too short, but they were warm. Then he used his sandals' soles as a frame for knee-high boots stitched together from slices he cut from the tail of the cloak, using the tough skins of vines as thread. They were clumsy but warm, and they protected his legs from thorns, nettles, and biting flies.

He walked steadily, never stopping for longer than a single day and night no matter how good or plentiful the food, or how warm and dry the shelter. Some days, he traveled very far, others not, but his motion was steadily forward, north and east toward the sun's solstitial bed.

It never occurred to him that he might beg food from people, let alone step forth and live among them. Instead, he kept to the rough, unproductive edges and fringes—a shy, wild creature traveling unseen through the quiet interstices between worlds, watching with interest as the world changed slowly but continuously as he passed over it.

And as the landscape changed, so did its inhabitants. Each settlement, studied warily from a distance, was distinct from the last. Each population dressed differently. Their cooking smelled different, and when he crept close enough to hear them, their languages were different—again and again, everything new in small but undeniable ways.

Even with so much variation, the inventive fancy that had made all this never seemed to tire. Whenever he began to sense a drift toward repetition, he would suddenly come across a dell or a cliff, a strange flowering plant, or a distant human face of such originality that he could only stare in respectful amazement.

Three thousand rivers and three thousand springs. *Huh.*

* * *

Guided only by the shape of the land, he turned more and more eastward and watched the forest thin, lighten, and finally stop in a trickle of stunted saplings. And then there was nothing ahead but grass. It flowed like never-ending water, like the sea that Echemus had tried to describe but that he hadn't credited until he saw the gulf below Delphi, and this was infinitely wider even than that.

Just as the wind ruffled water, here it lifted and turned the downy pale heads of grass, making wide, soft waves of changing hue—silver-white to silver-green—that streamed gently up and over the low hills and on beyond the reach of sight.

He stood watching. He had walked the winter and the spring and the summer away. He had walked incalculable distances, and still there was no end. It was inescapable: the world must be enormously bigger than anyone had told him, or perhaps bigger than any one person could know. Here, at what had to be the absolute end of it, it still went on with no sign of weakening or weariness. He could feel it in the solidity of the ground under his feet, and the gleaming resilience of the stalks that leaned and turned and leaned again in a vast and regal dance, to the horizon and beyond.

This, then, was the true meaning and the power of Chaos. It made itself unknowable not through emptiness or madness or illogic, but through a perfection too immense and too complex for the mind to grasp without coming apart. Echemus had once told him, "There is Chaos, so there must be order. There is order, so there must be Chaos." He had never said these might be the two sides of the same hand. But what else could this be?

There was no answer. Driven by some impenetrable need, he found exactly one hundred small stones. These he stacked in a tidy four-sided cairn at this juncture between two of so many worlds: trees and duff and clay behind him, grass and loam ahead.

He slept for many nights beside this, the only thing he had ever built in his life, before he finally gathered the courage to move away from it and forward, into whatever would be.

* * *

Even now he could not let go. The slightest peculiarity, the subtlest variation on sameness, still drew his need for order. He could not just walk, but must walk along folds in the ground— must find something, anything, that would make a fixed, certain place in the emptiness, so that he could sleep beside it. A rock, a flower of deviant shape, a spot of dead grass he could encompass with his arms—these things he clung to as he had clung to his cairn of a hundred pebbles, as if to save himself from disappearing.

When mountains showed themselves as a shy gray smear on the horizon, he couldn't make himself go elsewhere.

He walked a quarter moon to reach them. Every day, they rose a little higher, until the ground itself began to ascend and he was wading uphill through a running sea of flowers, which broke and foamed at the feet of sheer cliffs. The wind called like women, Sirens, perytons, spirits of the dead.

He tied the bow and sword to his back and climbed.

Sometimes, it was easy: a swooping trackless path along quiet saddles ankle-deep in loose dust and gravel, or over leaning shoulders sprinkled with tiny tufts of sedge, the air singing softly through the stones. Other times, it was straight up, risking death with each finger- and toehold; pressing so tightly against indifferent stone that he could hear only his own prudent breathing and the mountain's deep, slow heartbeat; finally sprawling, freezing and sweating and shaking, on narrow ledges with the sun glaring red above, and nothing below but the backs of wheeling eagles and the bright abyss.

He slept in heaps of soft stone dust, or wedged in a hollowed dihedral—wherever he was when night caught him. If there were storms, he crept into fissures and covered his ears while lightning hissed and shattered and glazed the walls outside.

Always he was cold, and sometimes he was hungry. But cold had been his companion for so long that it did not concern him, and hunger, even in these strange places, he could find ways to relieve. He was never actually afraid.

He climbed not over, but up, always up the highest surface he could see, until finally he thrust his head and shoulders out of a narrow black chimney, and the screaming wind ripped him bodily from his hole. His fingers scrabbled along pitched rock, and he stopped himself halfway over, legs flailing in bottomless air, hands clutching a blackened, enormous human foot.

He looked up. The mummy, three times his own height, leaned over him, arms outstretched against the rock. The hawk-nosed, eyeless face looked westward over one shoulder, bare teeth shining against black skin and veined gray stone, black hair blowing in great, rippling waves out into empty sky.

He hauled himself onto the stone shelf. The bronze staples that pinned the ankles to the mountain gleamed as if new, from endless scouring by the wind. He crept into the sloping shelter between the spread legs. From there, he could see that the outstretched arms were also stapled, at the wrists. The shriek of the wind was so huge, he had to open his mouth to relieve its pressure inside his skull, and then the driven air filled his cheeks like a wine bladder.

Echemus had told him the story of Prometheus, the man who dared to learn too much. Bound to the farthest mountain and ripped every day by a great eagle, healing overnight to be torn again the next day. Who else could this be?

Clinging to the hard black thighs with the full strength of his arms, pressing his back against the stone, he stole upright and looked along the giant's line of sight.

He saw the tracts of grass he had crossed, his precious cairn and his tiny footprints almost invisible and utterly inconsequential. Beyond that, he saw glittering islands in rich seas, tall citadels gleaming with bronze and gold, Delphi, his own dear mountains, and, past all this, the vast upright shadow of the warlord Atlas, carrying the sky on his shoulders.

He looked straight outward, to the south. He saw warm riffling lakes, thorny hills, plains white as salt, and beyond them, towering wet jungles rich with monsters. To the east, the direction he still traveled, lay not emptiness but more wide steppes of flowing grass, then black forest, milk-white rivers, bottomless lakes, spidery cities swarming with ghosts. The farthest limits lost themselves in mists that glowed of secrets.

He looked straight up. The huge laddered chest protruded, taut as a drum. Above that, the blowing black hair wrapped and unwrapped the sun as it slid along the sky in an endless caress.

* * *

Only the deer knows where the buds first grow.
Only the wild ass knows where the greenest grass is.
Only the wolf knows all the different trails.
Only the fox knows the scents of the seven streams.
Only the nightjar knows if caravans pass in the darkness.
Only the camel knows how heavy his load is.
Only the horse knows how well his master rides.
Only the mother knows the father of her son.

* * *

It was autumn again when he met fate on an ordinary riverbank, nowhere he could have named, while fishing.

He had known all this life that fish were food for dogs, not people, but he had more recently discovered that they were easy to catch and edible, so he taught himself to catch and eat them.

He devised two methods for catching them. One was simply to shoot them with arrows as they drifted near the edges of calm water. The other way worked best in running water. It was to wade upstream, fingers laced together between his knees. When he came to a fish resting quietly while facing away from him, he would ease the mesh of his fingers around its body, then flip it out and onto the shore before it could react.

He was using this method in a quick, noisy little stream that shot through a cleft in a bank of grassed-over stones. The fish twisted wild silver and blue in the air and fell—between a horse's hooves.

He straightened. Three, four, five men on horseback, with bows arching over their shoulders, watched him. The water's racket had masked any sound they might have made: the swish of their horses' legs in grass, even their words if they had spoken. He was acutely aware of his own bow and sword, resting with his boots and cloak in the grass downstream.

The horses were immense, half again as tall as the few donkeys he had seen in his lifetime, and taller than the horses he had seen only from a distance. But the men sat on them easily, with perfect balance. The nearest man was leaning forward, arms crossed as comfortably on his horse's withers as if he were leaning on a fence. Ephialtes turned to face him more squarely.

The man was beardless, and his round, high-boned face was colored deep brown, with black slits for eyes. A single white braid hung over one shoulder and down to his horse's withers. The men behind him were also beardless, but their hair was black and their cheeks fuller. They must be younger, though he could not judge the age of such alien faces.

The older man spoke. His voice was soft and the words guttural, rising and falling like song.

"I don't understand," Ephialtes told them in his best High Mycenaean. The man spoke again, longer this time. Ephialtes spread his dripping open hands. "I don't understand."

The old man turned to his companions. They talked together briefly. Then one of the others slid off his horse. Ephialtes tensed. The man walked a few steps on short, bowed legs, then leaned forward. His waist-length braid, woven with red feathers, swung over his shoulder, and the bow on his back flexed slightly, like a heron's wings before flight. He picked up something. The fish. He half turned and held it up, still struggling, for the others to see. They laughed.

Suddenly, Ephialtes was angry. "Laugh," he said. Then,

louder, "That's mine." They all turned toward him again, alert. "My fish. Give it back."

The old man murmured something. Red Feathers bent again, pressed a clump of grass down, and laid the fish carefully across it. He stepped back and crossed his arms over his chest, daring Ephialtes to come close enough to retrieve it. The slit-eyed faces were unreadable, but another mounted man strung his bow and rested it across his horse's neck. An open leather sleeve hung near his knee: an arrow case, bristling with bi-colored fletching.

Ephialtes weighed things. There were other fish in this river, and other rivers. He doubted that he could outrun horses, and these tall animals could certainly cross the shallow water in pursuit. And yet, the men could have killed him and had not.

And something else. What had that priest said, so far away? Ephialtes had touched the fish; that must have polluted it. Then Red Feathers touched it after him. He had imagined that polluting someone would harm them immediately. Yet there the man stood, whole and sound, arms crossed, as if nothing had happened to him. Did these beings not count as men? So what did his outlaw status really mean here? Perhaps nothing.

Never looking away from the mounted man's bow, he waded slowly ashore. The old man tilted his head to the side, encouraging him. He came dripping up the grassy bank, hands open at his sides.

Nearer, the men were larger than they had seemed. They were not nearly as tall as he, but the shortness of their legs and the slightness of their bodies had made them seem even smaller—that and the surprising height of the horses. Their eyes, long and canted, hidden by flat, thick lids, were no more readable this close than at a distance.

Alien as they were, though, their eyes were still strangely familiar. *Like the boy's.* Like the child in the sacrifice chamber with the long, dark, canted eyes. Temenus, little friend of Depas.

The men smelled of leather, horses, sour milk, smoke, and acidic alien sweat. Ephialtes stopped an arm's length from Red Feathers, at an angle that put the man between him and the mounted man's bow. Then he stooped boldly for his fish. It still pulsed and gasped, drowning in air. He laced one finger through the gill and stood—and the tip of a nocked arrow touched his chest.

He was too stunned to react. Red Feathers had strung the bow, nocked the arrow, and drawn it back while Ephialtes picked up the fish—two blinks, three at most. Red Feathers sighted casually along the shaft, correcting his aim for the heart. The arrow's head was bronze, with three lobes, like the pod of a flower. Driven by that bow, it would pass straight through Ephialtes, hardly slowing at all. The limbs of the bow never wavered. Ephialtes stood perfectly still.

The old man said something quietly. Ephialtes told him, "Tell him I'm not afraid. If you were going to kill me, you'd have done that already." He swallowed and gripped the fish hard.

The old man turned on his horse's back and talked briefly with the others. They all twitched their heads to one side, apparently agreeing.

"And if I live until tomorrow," Ephialtes said directly to the man before him, "I want you to show me how you did that so fast."

Red Feathers grinned: black teeth filed to points, and bright blue gums. The old man leaned again on his horse's withers. They were waiting for him to do something. What?

Something symbolic. He thought for a moment, then reached out his empty hand and touched the arrow. Red Feathers did nothing. Ephialtes closed his fingers around the shaft just in front of the chock, then snapped the head off. He turned swiftly and tossed it to the old man, who caught it automatically in both cupped hands.

There was a moment's silence. Then all the men threw back

their heads and roared laughter. Ephialtes took a long breath, relaxing. Red Feathers tossed the broken arrow shaft into the air, juggled it quickly with the end of his bow as it came down, then flipped it into his arrow sleeve. He unstrung the bow and slung it behind his shoulder, turned, and went back to his horse. He mounted, swinging up from the ground in a single leap onto the horse's back. The others put their bows away.

The old man spoke to Ephialtes again, then looked carefully along the whole arc of the horizon, one palm open under his chin as if directing his own eyes. He moved the open hand toward Ephialtes, then lifted just the thumb. *You are alone. There is no one else.* He turned the hand, curling the fingers over the thumb, and indicated the mounted men on either side. *Join us.*

Echemus had taught him never to refuse a gift. He had even taken his mother's written leaf, and still regretted having thrown it away. He looked one more time around the horizon, then decided. He repeated the old man's gesture: the lifted thumb, the closing hand.

"Thank you," he said. "I'll come with you."

The old man tilted his head gravely.

He went down the stream to collect his few belongings: the boots, cloak, a neat shoulder basket of seeds, roots, and sun-dried fish. The bow and sword. When he carried them back, the men were watching him keenly.

He lifted the bow. They glanced at it politely, clearly not impressed. He gripped the sword. The men lifted their chins sharply, indicating something negative. He demonstrated briefly, roughly, because he himself had never used it. The men blinked and glanced at one another, then twitched their heads up again. Did not know.

Ephialtes reversed the sword and gave it to the old man, pommel first. The old man turned it over and over, murmuring. He held it as Ephialtes had done, but even more awkwardly with his smaller hands. He weighed it on his palms and stroked the metal as if it were gold. Finally, he leaned to give the sword back, speaking in a respectful tone as he did so.

"Keep it." Ephialtes made a pushing motion.

The old man tilted his head, querying.

"Keep it. My gift to you." He gestured broadly.

The old man straightened, his face lighting. He turned and talked excitedly with the other men. Then he turned back to Ephialtes and touched his palm to his heart. Without waiting for a reply, he slipped the sword under his thigh, against his horse's side, and lifted the reins. The horse raised its forelegs, turned like a dancer, and cantered away. Most of the other men followed, but Red Feathers leaned down, reaching toward Ephialtes. Ephialtes backed away.

"I never rode a horse. I don't want to."

Red Feathers said something, still reaching. The horse was sidestepping, yearning after the others. The man said something, jerking his head toward the darkening sky. Ephialtes swallowed, got a grip on his fish, and raised his other arm. A powerful hand closed around his elbow. He jumped, up and up, and the hand tossed him free. He landed on the horse's rump and slid wildly, snatching for anything, finally wrapping an arm around the rider's waist. Seated, the man was as tall as he. The braided hair was solid as a club and smelled of rancid fat. The feathers got into Ephialtes' mouth.

Then the horse seemed to lift into the air. Ephialtes held on with all his strength, the fish trailing against his leg, and the horse flew.

* * *

Later, a woman in the old man's household fed the fish to the dogs, and marmots boiled in milk to the people. It was the first cooked food, and the first fire, Ephialtes had seen this season, and the first time ever he saw women eat with men.

Later, the old man, as head of the family, traded the sword for hundreds of arrowheads and gave Ephialtes a proper bow—layered wood and hide with recurved limbs—to replace the child's toy he had carried when he came to them. Later still, Ephialtes learned to hold arrows, one between each two fingers, and shoot them less than a second apart. Even later, he was as fast and accurate with the new bow as UlaänUsu Red Feather was with his own. And like every adult, male or female, he had his own fletching so anyone would recognize his arrows: gray and white with the lightest touch of red at the tips of the feathers. He never had to ask UlaänUsu how he could string a bow so quickly: it was obvious.

* * *

They called themselves Bajgani. They called him G'atag'atu-olos, the Foreigner, and they taught him the things all young men knew: how to pluck his beard and tend his mustache; how to urinate neatly while squatting or riding—in this country, only women and old men stood to pee. They threw away his fetid rags and gave him proper leggings and shirt of silk-soft leather patterned with stain and beads. They considered weaving to be both quaint and a waste of time. Like farming, it was indulged in by the lower orders of man, who were too stupid, cowardly, or incompetent to herd and hunt. His rules of outlawry meshed with their common rules of living; these people could only be the outlanders that Delphi had exempted from his pollution.

It took time for his near-starved body to adjust to their diet: cattle, camels, elk, birds, rabbits—more meat than Ephialtes had seen in his life—served at every meal. They didn't raise grain, roots, or fruit, but traded milk and meat for such things. They ate the grain as porridge, never bread. They consumed the milk of their cattle and camels, never making cheese or yogurt, but simply drinking it directly. They milked the horses, too, stirring the milk in hard leather vats until it was sharp and sour enough to bring tears to the eyes, and fermented enough to addle the mind. Although its consumption was reserved for adults, no child would play at hunting without a little leather bottle of fresh milk slung over one shoulder, to sip from importantly in imitation of adult hunters who would sooner leave camp without their horses than without koumiss.

They could count, and did so with relish. Everyone knew how many horses, cows, and camels each neighbor owned, and precisely who owed how many to whom. They had no fear of counting the living or even the dead. They knew how many children had died from what causes and how many lovers everyone else had had. On the other hand, they never measured anything. Sizes were demonstrated by hand gestures and hyperbole, distances by days to walk or ride, the time of day by the proximity of night. Years were identified by memorable events, but every clan had a different opinion of what merited remembering. And so, from camp to camp, fixing a past event in time was risky at best and usually impossible, resulting in more laughter than accuracy. Only the months of the year had reliable names and attributes. The seasons, too obvious to require identification, went nameless.

They were garrulous, these people—always chattering, laughing, singing, interrupting each other. They gossiped, lied, and told stories about themselves, each other, their friends, relatives, ancestors, and eponymous animals. G'atag'atu-olos's story, however, they never asked for, and he never offered.

He learned their songs and rhymes, which they had in seemingly endless number: for riding, for racing, for counting the months, for naming new babies and sending older ones to sleep, for pitching tents in summer, for digging their winter lodges, for hunting the elk, for calming the cattle, for attracting a lover, for repelling the Wolf when storms howled over the smoke holes.

He learned to speak as if for the first time, using words as they did, to tease and pun, and then to persuade. There was a power in words that he had never sensed before, and he set out to master them and their potency.

Marriage was promised very early here. Children were sometimes matched and mated in babyhood. But this was not the onerous and abusive infant marriage Echemus had told him of. Promised couples, as they grew, avoided each other as much as they could, partly to maintain mystery, partly to resist the temptation to breed before the right time. As they grew, they flirted with each other but never spoke directly. When they neared marrying age, they sent each other gifts: flowers, shiny stones, puppies. When at last they married, they jumped on each other like starving animals.

But sex was not a marriage gift. Any child born before or between marriages was welcomed as a full member of the mother's family and of the clan. The only loser might be the man who was—or fancied himself to be—the father, who might mooch around the outskirts of the girl's family compound, longing to claim a child whose grandparents, aunts, uncles, and cousins airily ignored him. "Good enough to plant a seed, not good enough to marry," was the sometimes devastating dismissal— doubly insulting for its reference to farming, which the Bajgani despised. There was, predictably, a whole body of songs purportedly written by fathers longing for children they had fathered and for the mothers who would not marry them. Any such already-born child brought into a marriage came as a gift, not a dishonor. Sex was not a dark threat or curse. It was not a treasure to be fiercely guarded and viciously punished. It was an agreeable diversion.

G'atag'atu-olos avoided touch, avoided familiarity, but in the end could not avoid the bold gangs of girls who teased and tempted all the boys, even him. Intrigued by his odd looks and strange manners, egged on by one another's dares, the girls taught him the inverse of the only sex he knew. Bemused by their forthright innocence, soothed by their audacity, finally seduced by their skills, he pretended to know nothing, and let them teach him as if for the first time—kindly, comfortably, and with laughter.

Their language had no word for privacy. For all the open space around them, they preferred to huddle together, to ride in tight packs, to sit crammed together, to trip over each other's feet and breathe in each other's faces, to cram inside tents or underground like colonies of marmots. The girls taught him, and the children taught him, and the men and old women taught him that other people were not always peril. He even learned to find a certain precarious pleasure in their company, in good-humored jostling around a warm fire, in singing and laughing together, in sleeping shoulder to shoulder in smoky darkness while the horses stamped and snorted outside in the cold.

Only the dead were left alone, laid gently by trail sides or raised into the arms of trees for the sun—their single, overwhelming deity—to claim and bring back again. Death was a temporary condition, a failure of the body but only a misplacement of the spirit, which would return in a new frame. Their language spoke of a person "being" dead, as if death were a state of health rather than a final exit to unreachable lands where all the dead dwelled together.

He learned an astonishing way of rearing children. Here, childhood did not mean solitary labor, cold, hunger, and fear. Fathers loved their children, took interest in their rearing, and bragged about them to other men. Mothers hugged and cuddled and fed them, then sent them forth among their siblings, knowing they would not be hurt. Older brothers joked with younger brothers, teased them, indulged them, taught them gently and kindly what they needed to know, and never harmed them. Sisters babied and scolded younger siblings and followed their older siblings worshipfully.

Sometimes, the unremitting noise and sociality and affection and strangeness would drive him up and out, aching for solitude and silence. He walked alone in frosted grass, his head throbbing and nerves jangling from the perpetual guard that he could never fully relax and that they unknowingly violated a thousand times a day.

* * *

By the time he had learned the language and performed all the rituals for his adoption by the old chief, it was spring and he was, by his own estimate, about seventeen years old. So, with much teasing, he went through the quadrennial initiation with much younger boys of the chief's lineage.

After the fasting and praying and dancing and eating, the chief gave each boy a horse. Which of the chief's horses would go to which boy had been the subject of intense speculation among them for months—including the night in the hothouse at the third quarter of the Riding Moon, when their conversation was expected to turn to pious thoughts of herds and hunting.

The boys had ridden their fathers' horses all their lives, but these would be the first horses of their own, so the individual selections were vitally important to them. An improper match would embarrass a boy at this critical point in life.

Unknown to the boys, the matches were also discussed at length by all the adults in the family and were made with great care and understanding of each boy and each animal.

G'atag'atu-olos alone was less than thrilled with the idea of owning a horse. Ownership would require that he finally learn to ride—a skill he had managed to avoid for all the months he had been among them, since in winter they went into the ground like lemmings and rode nowhere. The horse chosen for him was a lank spotted stallion with a tail reaching the ground, and a soul of vast tranquility. Now he could skip to his own age step and be married.

* * *

All the girls in the chief's family were married, promised, or hoarded for a better match. But an elderly second cousin, a cripple-legged widower with very few horses, had an unpromised daughter who might be willing to marry a stranger. UlaänUsu Redfeather acted as intermediary. His mission was favorably received. So he arranged a formal meeting between G'atag'atu-olos and Solong Rainbow.

Taller than any other Bajgani, man or woman, Solong had no chin, no visible eyes, and deplorable posture. She also had a deep, contagious laugh and a wit so dry and sharp that her few tentative suitors had quickly sought matches elsewhere. Nevertheless, when Redfeather and the Foreigner called on her and her father, she fed the spotted stallion honey with her own long hands, and half a month later she and G'atag'atu-olos were married.

It was most common for men to live with their wives' families, but this was not required. Since his wife's father was so poor, everyone expected G'atag'atu-olos to bring his wife to the rug-hung, meat-fed warmth of the chief's winter den. Instead, to everyone's surprise, he chose to move his few possessions into his wife's father's dank hole in the ground.

The old man, H'oolee the Horn, had lived for years in his winter dugout, flatly refusing to leave it for summer or any other reason, smoking hemp and feeding himself and his daughter on offhand scraps sent by his sons, who had married into luckier families.

But G'atag'atu-olos had heard what the Horn himself barely remembered: that before the fall that shattered his knees, the old man had been the best rider of his generation. He asked H'oolee to teach him to ride, but the old man refused—amiably since he liked this strange young man, but firmly all the same.

Although H'oolee refused to come out of his hole and refused to talk about riding with the Foreigner, he saw that his daughter was happy. His stony old heart softened to see how the young man looked at her with—as near as could be told from so alien a face—interest and respect. He saw how she looked at him with amused affection. He found no fault in the Foreigner's courtesy to either of them, and he liked to listen to his daughter and her husband talking, like friends and equals. He liked to listen to them making love; the Foreigner seemed unskilled but kind, Solong fearless and indulgent. That was the most he had ever wished for this daughter: kindness and companionship. H'oolee the Horn was pleased with his son-in-law.

Now that H'oolee had refused to teach him to ride, G'atag'atu-olos might have practiced anywhere. But he rode directly behind his father-in-law's den, out of the old man's line of sight but maddeningly within his hearing. It did not take long for the sound of regular hoofbeats, irregular hoofbeats, and his daughter's wild laughter to drive the old Horn outside, leaning heavily on the lodge frame and blinking like a turtle in the light.

The Foreigner did not notice him. He was too busy clinging to the spotted horse's mane while Solong, from the back of her own mare, tossed the end of a knotted rope into her husband's other hand. The spotted horse whirled to run beside the mare: it knew this game. As the horses reached full gallop, Solong smiled sweetly at her husband, jammed the mare into a sliding halt, and yanked him bodily off his horse.

H'oolee straightened his back, sucked air into his lungs, and bellowed in the voice that got him his name, "Daughter, bring that pair of buffoons to me!"

* * *

The next day, Solong gave her father two heavy sticks with

carved forks and grips, so that he could stand alone and stump after his pupil, roaring orders. And G'atag'atu-olos finally learned to ride.

He joined UlaänUsu Redfeather on a few hunts, as he was entitled to do through his adoption tie. He had no reason to be careful, so his riding improved rapidly. And because he had no reason to be careful, when their party's attempt to trade at a settlement was rudely rebuffed, it was he who suggested they take what they wanted.

Thievery was not unheard of. Desperation had sometimes driven the people to steal from their neighbors. But the novelty of thievery for its own sake was revelatory. The men loved it. They took to it as if they had stolen all their lives. Raids on horseback became, first, the habitual celebratory end to successful hunting excursions, then the whole purpose of going out at all.

G'atag'atu-olos was a bold, audacious thief. He brought with him strategies learned from years of hiding, foraging, and stealing—strategies that were new to the steppe, based in a culture unknown to them, and thus both illogical and devastatingly effective. He altered them only enough to adapt to vast distances on horseback.

When he could, he avoided repetition. He had no interest in stealing what he had stolen before, in raiding the same people twice, in riding a road he had already ridden. Although he had no right to lead any hunting party, he did what he could to draw the parties he was a part of into new places—always a different direction, farther each time. Always, while the other men skinned and quartered their kills or squabbled happily over plunder, he would walk to the edge of the camp and stare at the horizon, wondering what lay there, beyond his sight. Wondering if Prometheus on the mountain had been right, wrong, or even there at all. The other men would glance at his straight, still back and fall somewhat quieter, and set aside his share plus a little more.

It was not long before all the chiefs wanted G'atag'atu-olos in their hunting parties, and hunting yielded more and more often to the ever more interesting raiding. His portion of the booty increased with every outing, and after every outing he laid his share of game and goods at his father-in-law's feet.

The more he traveled, the more he understood that Bajgani horses were far from perfect. He asked, and was told that of course the men knew the differences between the horses they owned and those they fancied owning. As much as they wanted better horses—taller, stronger, sounder, more resilient, more intelligent—they couldn't afford better.

Stealing, however, was free.

Within a few seasons, young men of the Horn's lineage began to drift back to this part of the steppe, attracted by the Foreigner's amusing ways and the apparent change of luck in their old kinsman's household.

* * *

The first child was a boy, who died immediately. That was the source of their first important disagreement. Solong insisted that the corpse be left beside the road so that it might come into a passing woman and be born again, while G'atag'atu-olos insisted that it be buried under the dirt, to travel to the land of the dead. Each was certain that the other's way would doom the tiny spirit to be lost forever. Solong never quite forgave her husband's ignorance and willfulness, although she eventually managed to set her resentment aside and still be what she had to be—and also wanted to be—for him: friend, companion, and partner.

She would willingly have served as his confidante as well, but he seemed to have no need to speak about himself beyond the affairs of the world: grazing, trading, H'oolee's health, preparations for winter, and, later, the children. Nor, she knew, did he speak of himself with her father or any other man. He was too strange for them to know even how to begin a conversation that might tell them anything of his history, and he did nothing to encourage such talk.

Their second child was a girl, who lived. Solong washed her in milk and laid her in her husband's hands. Though he remained as unreadable as ever, still Solong could see something terrible in G'atag'atu-olos's face as he took the tiny body and gazed at it. For an instant, she thought he might bite it in some alien rite he had not warned her of. But he only kissed the forehead with such tenderness that Solong's careful heart moved with compassion and envy.

It had never occurred to her that G'atag'atu-olos might love anything—that foreigners were even capable of that. But here was a clear sign. He held this baby as if it were a precious jewel, and returned it to her only reluctantly. Then he rose abruptly, strode outside, and caught a horse and fled. It was summer, with lingering twilights and early dawns, and he did not return until well into the long evening, coming so quietly into the tent that she barely woke.

He stood over her and the baby, not threatening, not speaking, not moving, for so long that she nearly slid back into sleep. Then he wiped his palms on his leggings, streaking them with mud, and knelt beside her.

She had seen him, from time to time, crouch down and press his hands to the earth as if to get its attention, to speak with it, maybe to ask of it some favor or gift. One more of his inexplicable habits. What had he asked the earth this time, out there alone in the rising dark? What could be so frightening about this tiny new life that he might ask an alien power to do . . . what, exactly? Kill it now to relieve some hideous suspense?

While she watched through nearly closed eyes, he laid both open hands on the baby's swaddled body—it made a squeaking noise and a cranky face at the disturbance—then bent his head, curled his hands into fists, and pressed them to his forehead. It was too dark to see whether he was speaking soundlessly, or weeping, or just waiting.

* * *

It was customary to close a birth with the promise of the next. They knew that practice, and performed it the next night with punctilious care. Women were normally too tired and raw to take much pleasure in this rite. Certainly, the first time, separated by the quarrel over the dead infant, their act had been only cursory and distant. But this time was different. This time, he was so gentle, solicitous, silent—and, yes, passionate—that he lifted her up and swept her with him to some unknown country where disagreement had no place. Her orgasm was unlike any before or after: not only completely unexpected on this night, but so overwhelming as to leave her blind, breathless, and utterly in love. And for that one timeless span, he seemed to love her, too.

Then it was gone—banked, buried, hidden behind those unfathomable wolf's eyes.

* * *

With the survival of that child, Solong was now counted a grown woman and the Foreigner was counted a man. He did not even try to hide his strangeness: his height, the length of his arms and legs, the skin that even this harsh sun could not darken enough to match his neighbors', the straight, thin nose, the long narrow hands, the heavy, sun-bleached hair and long mustache, and, most of all, the pale, unreadable eyes. He knew that visitors feared his looks. Even old women were cautious around him. He, in turn, could hardly decipher Bajgani faces, and their thoughts often eluded him. He took as his own their habits and gestures, their speech and its long, punning idioms. He wished on the

Blood Star as they did, and was never surprised when his wishes came true. But their most fundamental beliefs—those so visceral they were not even thought of as beliefs—those he could not touch.

I came here too late, he once thought with deep sadness. *I was already too old.* Then he remembered Echemus, Hyades and his sons, Elawon, and did not know what to think. Had he been born here in a tent or underground, raised on horseback with a pack of loving, squabbling siblings, with an amiable father and a happy mother, believing without question in a vast, high, single, benign, all-seeing deity . . . No. He could not imagine any of that. Then he would remember that he was outlawed in his own country—despised, inhuman, to be killed by any fool who came along—and he realized that he understood nothing at all.

The clan's children grew used to him much faster than their parents did. The smallest of them had already known him all their lives. What mattered to them was not how strange he looked, but that he was kind and patient, easy to tease, never offended, and always amused by their antics no matter how outrageous.

When he was at home—not hunting, raiding, or trading—he kept his own children with him. Even to walk over the hill to see a horse, he would take at least one along, gladly carrying it when it grew tired. Solong was often irritable with the larger ones, reserving her leniency for the current baby. But G'atag'atu-olos had a bottomless well of patience for all his children. It was he who taught them to clean themselves, to eat tidily, to do up the frogs and buckles of their clothes, and to groom the horses, though H'oolee taught them to ride. It was G'atag'atu-olos who sat up with them if they fell ill. It was he who feared for them so much that at times, he could not breathe.

But after the first, none of them died. In fact, they thrived. With their mother's coloring and a combination of their parents' features, they were Bajgani enough to look familiar to those around them, foreign enough to be arrestingly exotic. They came, girl after girl, and here girls were treasured here as readily as boys.

Girls were not burdens, not property. They did not depend on men to keep them alive. They could own horses, herd and hunt, inherit. They were petted, admired, and depended on to bring useful, hardworking men into the family. They were their parents' guardians in old age, as Solong had been H'oolee's. The best—the most sensible, most beautiful, bravest, and funniest— were in much more demand for marriage than any such boy would be. In cases of early marriage agreements, it was the boys who struggled and worried and fretted about how to keep their future brides' interest. Either side could break off a marriage promise, but it was most often the girls.

The fathers of girls were not subtly pitied; they were admired. G'atag'atu-olos, with his succession of lovely, intelligent girls, was indirectly courted by any number of men whose sons would need wives. Even he, the outsider, the stranger, the unknown and enigmatic, found himself often flattered and favored for the sake of his daughters.

And then came Juchii, his son.

* * *

It was not unheard-of for a man to have several wives. Successful men—and there was no comparing G'atag'atu-olos's success with any ordinary man's—might keep two, three, or even more, visiting them one by one. Or, in some families, one might break the convention of matrilocality and gather the women together. The king, it was said, had eight wives. Even the old chief who adopted G'atag'atu-olos had had three. Sometimes, men and women came to him with offers. Would G'atag'atu-olos care to have one more wife? Younger? More beautiful? Owning herds and tents of her own, and with brothers who would be happy to ride with him? Although he was skilled at slow negotiation, his refusals were so abrupt, they bordered on rudeness.

It was not unusual for an adult to negotiate his or her own marriage, sometimes quite informally, by finding a way to be alone with the target of their interest and then offering sex. If they slept together and the other person stayed, the marriage was considered concluded. If the target refused—left the assignation too quickly for sex to have occurred—those who had helped arrange the encounter would often spread the word that one or the other had fled due to a lack of either womanliness or virility.

The few times that hopeful women found ways to approach G'atag'atu-olos so directly, he simply walked away from them. He seemed not to hear or care about the good-humored mocking that followed. When Solong, who could use the help, asked him why he refused, he did as he always did when wearied and balked: he went out, caught a horse, and galloped over the grass as if pursued by fanged eagles, until fatigue soothed him.

She thought his resistance might come from fear of marrying a woman who wanted only his wealth and would secretly despise his looks and ways. Yet he seemed completely accepting of his own differences and the staring and uneasiness of those not used to him. She would never suspect the truth, until it was much too late for the truth to matter.

* * *

They returned from the north just before the solstice, wrapped in furs and driving new horses. Everyone ran out to meet them, shouting greetings and shaking bells and rattles to chase off any spiteful spirits that might have followed them home. G'atag'atu-olos rode a little ahead of the others, holding his horse to a prancing walk while he searched for his family.

There was H'oolee the Horn, waiting in front of his beautiful bear-skin tent, leaning on his sticks and laughing, and behind him Solong Rainbow, carrying one child on each hip while the older girls stood together, smiling radiantly. Clutching his grandfather's hand, three-year-old Juchii stood his ground when the huffing, sweating horse stamped beside his toes, and his father's weird eyes glared down at him from the shroud of gleaming black furs.

The red mare—stolen the year before from armed guards who had fought to the death to keep her—snuffled the Horn's face. The old man rubbed her jaw. Then little Juchii, never flinching, raised both arms over his head. G'atag'atu-olos leaned down, grasped both small hands in one of his, and swung the boy up in front of him. Juchii dug his fingers into the horse's mane and looked up at his father, laughing.

For a moment, the child's slick, flat, narrow-eyed face was as alien as a dog's: not his own child, not even anything human, but some strange animal in his arms. G'atag'atu-olos felt himself tense to throw it down, and he hunched his shoulders and closed his eyes against that compulsion.

Something touched his leg. He covered the hand on his thigh with his own. He didn't need to look. Solong, his wife—Solong the tall, the intelligent, the ugly, the contrary, who laughed but never smiled, fated to live her life in her father's hovel until one even stranger than she appeared. Solong knew. He gripped her hand until the bones grated, and she did not protest.

Then H'oolee lifted Juchii down, and G'atag'atu-olos slid off the horse's back. While the other raiders streamed by with the horses, he stripped off the furs, heaping them over the old man's twisted feet, until he knelt, naked except for the single tattoo on his back, and the long plait of his sun-faded hair. All the people were quiet, bemused to silence by the wealth he had brought them yet again.

G'atag'atu-olos stared into the sheen of ermine and sable,

eyes wide open, mind deliberately blank. He heard the hooves passing behind him, the old man's labored breathing, his son's joyful chatter, his daughters' solemn replies, and the comprehending silence of the woman who was his wife.

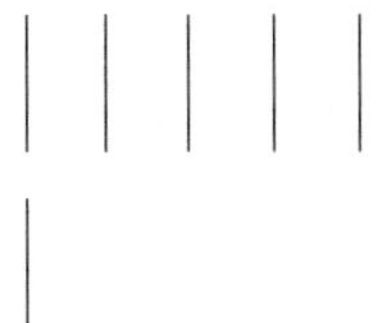

One, you'll find sunshine,
Two, you'll feel rain,
Three, you'll learn laughter,
Four, you'll learn pain.
Five, receive sorrow,
Six, receive joy,
Seven's a woman who'll give you a boy.
Eight brings a kinsman whose promise is true.
Nine means your children will remember you.

When H'oolee Horn died, he left five grandchildren, seventeen kinsmen with their families, twenty-two tents, one hundred six horses, four hundred cows, fifty camels, a pair of gold-sheathed walking-sticks, and a ruby ring for every finger. He was reckoned the richest man for eight days' ride in any direction. He had not slept a single night underground in many years, but had indulged his son-in-law's preference for tent dwelling year-round, and had learned, as all had learned, how to make a tent impervious to snow and wind.

Like her sister, Solong Rainbow inherited two horses, twenty cows, three camels, a four-pole tent, a bow, and a gold thumb ring. The other goods and animals were divided among her brothers, who had already moved nearer in anticipation of the death haul. H'oolee Horn's followers, however, chose not to go with the newly rich heirs, but to pitch their tents with the Foreigner.

Before the full of the Elk Moon, G'atag'atu-olos and his

raiders had stolen back every one of the Horn's one hundred six horses. When the brothers-in-law went to the king to complain, they found the twenty best of those horses in the king's personal herd, and their baby niece promised in marriage to the king's favorite grandson. And they found everyone in the royal camp still talking about their recent visitor, the Foreigner: a strange-looking creature, an appalling rider, and the most inventive thief in living memory or legend.

* * *

The king had said, "I have heard of you, Foreigner, but you have never come to see me."

"It seemed insolent for such as I to trouble you, my king." The title of king was long and nearly unpronounceable, but G'atag'atu-olos had spoken it easily after practicing it with Solong for hours.

"Come and drink koumiss. I'm glad you've chosen to trouble me now."

They had sat together on a thick patterned rug laid under fruit trees. The king's house was part dugout, too, but walled in fragrant wood and carpeted everywhere. Half the carpets, G'atag'atu-olos had already seen, having stolen most of them personally. It had been H'oolee, as family head, who circumspectly sent so many gifts to the king over recent years, anticipating a future need for favor, for H'oolee had mightily disliked and distrusted his own sons. Beyond the low wall of the garden, Juchii sat in the shade of a tree, holding horses: the red mare, his own first horse, and a dozing pack animal.

The king's wives brought cups of silver and bone—also familiar—and poured the drinks and departed. The king drank straightaway, but G'atag'atu-olos raised his cup in six directions, then spilled a drop on the ground before he drank.

The king watched, bright-eyed.

"It's a dirty habit," G'atag'atu-olos admitted, "but one I can't help but maintain."

"And what powers of what places drink through the ground? Really, that is a strange notion." The king smiled. His teeth were long and narrow and very white. "But the ants will certainly be grateful." Then he raised his own cup directly to Utsir, the single power in the sky, whose eye, the sun, saw everything.

So, clearly invited to speak of himself, G'atag'atu-olos instead told a story he remembered from Echemus: the tale of how the ant outsmarted the wasp. The king smiled again, repeating the story's lesson aloud, as if fixing it in his mind.

They drank and talked: the weather, the last year's breeding, a recent illness among the old men of a distant family. The king was a high-level clan leader really, chosen by the lower family heads to keep order in his far-flung extended family and to arbitrate disputes. But his decisions were binding.

It was perhaps with his role in mind that the king said, "You are a puzzle, as I'm sure you know. We share no blood between us, but I cannot disregard you as I might some out-of-clan stranger who marries into one of our families. You are too . . ." He paused and arched a thin eyebrow provocatively.

"Too *busy,* my king?"

The king laughed. "Not exactly what I was thinking, but it will do."

Having reached toward the purpose of G'atag'atu-olos's visit, they backed away from it again and talked of the grazing this summer. There had been no rain between the rivers, but the grass by the lakes was still rich. Most of the herds were there already, and the king's would follow shortly. They touched on the sizes of herds, and how families and households defined themselves by the numbers of animals they could claim.

They withdrew again and talked of their children. The king was not an old man, but already he had three grandchildren. The one he favored especially was a boy, he admitted—a boy as dazzling as a star.

They talked then of travel, and the stories G'atag'atu-olos had collected of lands beyond those either of them knew. Monsters, chasms, mountains that belched fire, birds of prey as the size of camels. He told the king about elephants and why he believed they really existed, and how dearly he wished to see one.

They talked of children again and of how worrying it could be to provide for them. Of how sons were favored over daughters in inheritance by some laws they barely remembered. Of G'atag'atu-olos's daughters and their legendary beauty.

Then they talked of horses. The world envied G'atag'atu-olos's red mare and her children. To what stallions did he breed, that she threw such perfect foals? G'atag'atu-olos led the king into a discussion of breeding, and how his own people did not recognize the difference that careful selection of an animal's mate could make in its offspring. That line of talk, although he himself had chosen it, briefly choked him—his own people knew little about breeding, but he knew all too well the consequences of children who did not resemble their parents. The king arched a brow again, noticing his pause but not asking about it. G'atag'atu-olos smiled self-deprecatingly and agreed with the next three things the king said, whatever they were.

Finally, the king said, "I was born in the spring of the Lost Moon year. I am old and have few ambitions now. When the Blood Star comes, I wish only to see my grandson's marriage, to see my herds enriched in quality, to feel a soft carpet under my elbows—these are the simple matters that concern me now."

G'atag'atu-olos lifted his head. From his post under the tree beyond the garden, Juchii saw, and took down a certain rug from the packhorse. When the boy came before the king, he knelt, then stretched himself on the ground as custom required and as he had already seen his father do when they came to this place.

"Your son?" the king asked.

"Juchii, my son," G'atag'atu-olos agreed.

"He has been horsed?"

"This year."

"I see that his first horse is of a quality even old men would aspire to."

G'atag'atu-olos murmured modestly.

"He has his own bow now? And his own arrows?"

"Blue, striped with black."

"He must sit and drink with us. Come, boy."

Juchii glanced cautiously at his father, but a woman had already handed him a cup and was filling it. Juchii sat up, crossed his legs, and sipped politely. G'atag'atu-olos could no more readily know what the boy was thinking than the boy could read his father. They did not look at each other again.

The king feigned casualness. "So what is this bundle you've carried here?"

"Nothing, my king. Some scrap I found, I don't remember where. A cover for an unfavored horse, perhaps. A rag to wipe your nose and your beautiful grandson's bottom—no more than that."

Juchii opened the knot that bound the rug. Even the women gasped.

The pattern was as dark and complex as the night sky. It was thicker than felt, supple as a scarf. Even in sunlight, it gleamed.

The king set his cup aside and caressed this treasure of treasures.

Then he composed himself, found his cup again, and drank. He did not take his eyes from the rug as he said, "I would so like to see my grandson married."

* * *

Always a stranger, Juchii, brave as a bear with other boys, bold with men while still a child, but from an early age tense and clumsy and speechless before his father. Wanting, always wanting, and terrified of asking, although G'atag'atu-olos had never spoken harshly to him, never slighted him, never turned him aside.

Not for Juchii the fearless mirth of his sisters, teasing their father, leading him by the hands, climbing his legs, cuddling, bribing kisses. Not for him even the easy camaraderie of the other boys, whom G'atag'atu-olos treated as equals even before they were horsed. G'atag'atu-olos saw Juchii's skills only obliquely as the boy took a modest place at the rear of the hunting troop, as far as possible from his father's eye although he could freely have ridden at G'atag'atu-olos's side.

And G'atag'atu-olos heard of Juchii's wit and kindness from his sisters and from other men, as if hearing of someone he had never met, while the boy himself stood humbly before him, head down and eyes averted, silenced by the depth of some need he dare not voice.

* * *

Unable to provoke the king's indignation with the injustices done to them, H'oolee's three sons waited a year, two years, then rode with twenty followers to G'atag'atu-olos's camp on a day when they knew that all the other men were away with their own herds. They rode into the circle of tents and called their sister.

Solong came out with a baby on her hip, then set the infant carefully aside in a young daughter's arms. She wiped her hands on her shirt and went forward to meet her brothers.

She stood among them. They did not dismount as they should to greet her, but sat high above her.

The eldest said, "That thing you sleep with—it stole from us."

Her temper flared. "My husband steals from those who

haven't the wits to keep a hold on their own goods. Why should you be different?"

There was a stunned silence. Finally, another brother said, "Where is he? I want my horses back."

Solong turned calmly toward him. "He's clearing the spring of weeds. His work is too important to be troubled by something like you."

"He stole from us!"

"So steal back, and see what it gets you."

Juchii and his oldest sister came out of the tent laughing, then stopped, stared, and fell silent. They glanced at each other; then Juchii spun and raced away. The daughter came quietly to stand behind Solong.

The eldest brother glanced at her, then looked again. He said, "I have an unmarried nephew I might take this girl for—if she can even cook."

"She's already promised."

"Your mate doesn't mind breaking promises."

"He never does that."

"He stole our inheritance. A patrimony is a promise."

"Like your promise, when I was born, to care for my interests. So why did I live alone with my father, ragged, hungry, with almost no horses, and too old to marry? That"—she made a rude gesture—"for your promises."

Women and children had come from the other tents, and they stood scattered and still, watching, uncertain.

The eldest brother leaned over his horse's shoulder. "You've lost your manners, sister. Sleeping with animals can do that to you. So I'll rescue this girl from that kind of future. Who knows what might happen to her otherwise?" Kicking his horse forward between Solong and her daughter, he leaned and snatched the girl up before she could even back away.

All the women murmured. Stealing the bride was a normal marriage practice, but it was ceremonial only, and a great deal of fun. This, on the other hand, was as rare as it was ugly. Solong stared up at her daughter, hanging from her brother's arm, unable even to give words to her outrage. The other brothers rode in her way. In a moment, they would turn and gallop off, and when would she see her daughter again?

Then one brother raised his head and said, "Well, now, what's here?"

Solong turned, relief flooding her. G'atag'atu-olos came around the tent, a long, sharp-ended digging stick still in his hands, and the front of his shirt muddy. Behind him came Juchii, looking solemn and scared. G'atag'atu-olos stopped there, his colorless eyes as unreadable as ever.

There was nothing they could really do, one man and one boy against twenty mounted men. But at least, G'atag'atu-olos was here to see this, to voice his objections. Then he could go to the king at once to complain. Solong was already planning what clothes he should wear, what gifts he should take. He would ride the red mare, the one the king so envied. He would . . .

Then Solong realized that G'atag'atu-olos was standing still, saying nothing. He did not protest. He did not complain. He did not seem surprised, or disapproving, or even distressed. He just stood there flat-footed, not even looking directly at her brothers, as if simply waiting for this to finish happening.

For all his oddness, she had never thought that he lacked courage. But what was this, then, that let him stand by and watch these men steal his daughter? Did he care so little that he wouldn't even object? Was he afraid?

She drew a hard breath, ready to turn her anger on him. But even as she opened her mouth to begin, Juchii took a rapid step away from his father. An instant later, G'atag'atu-olos raised his head and looked at the men on horseback. Solong saw then that although he stood perfectly still, holding the stick, his jaw was taut. His face was perfectly still, but the eyes glittered.

He said to Solong's brother, very softly, "Put her down."

Solong felt the hair on her neck and arms rise.

The man stared a moment, then recovered and laughed. He had laid the girl across his horse's withers, like some lifeless booty. Afraid of falling, she didn't struggle.

The man said, "So, dirt digger, come to my camp when you've cleaned yourself, and we'll talk. Returning our horses might get this girl back. Or maybe not."

G'atag'atu-olos's eyes were fixed on him. He looked nowhere else, did not move, did not even seem to breathe. He said in the same soft voice, "Put my daughter down and leave, or I will kill you."

The man laughed again and raised his bridle hand to turn his horse and ride away.

He never finished the motion. The digging stick hissed like an arrow with the speed of the throw. It struck the center of the man's chest with such force, it propelled him backward, almost unhorsing him. Solong snatched the reins before the horse could bolt, and the man slid the rest of the way off. The other brothers started to yell, started to turn, to flee, but too late.

G'atag'atu-olos ran for the nearest and yanked him bodily down. The man hit the ground hard as the third lashed out with his riding whip. The copper-tipped tails slapped G'atag'atu-olos's face, but he was not distracted. He dropped on both knees on the downed man's chest, locked his hands around the throat, and crushed it, just like that.

As he sprang from that crouch directly onto the back of the third brother's horse, Juchii reached Solong and took the reins from her frozen hand. He backed quickly away, leading the horse out of the melee. Then he helped his sister slide down.

The riding whip had lashed G'atag'atu-olos's face three times, but a fourth blow never came. With the horse staggering under the double weight, he combed one hand into the man's hair, dragged his head back, and—Solong would never believe this, even years later—bent over him and bit his throat, in the way that a lion or a wolf might. Her brother howled and struggled, the horse spinning in place, until G'atag'atu-olos grabbed the man's forehead with his other hand and, still holding the hair, twisted it under his teeth. Solong heard the neck snap even over the frantic drumming of hooves.

As quickly as the body slid off, G'atag'atu-olos did, too. He went to retrieve his digging stick, setting his foot against the dead man's chest and pulling it free. Then, without a moment's pause, he raised the stick vertically to the full reach of his arms and stabbed the corpse again. Then again. At each thrust, the body jumped. Each time, he had to hold it with his foot to free the stick, which sucked a spray of blood out after it. The third or fourth time, the end of the stick was brown again. He had plunged it all the way through, into the ground.

Solong looked at Juchii. His face, usually so like hers, was now as cryptic as his father's. The daughter had covered her eyes with her hands.

Before Solong could think what to do, how to stop her husband's rage, Juchii tossed the reins to her, then ran to G'atag'atu-olos. Solong herself would not have dared go so close, but Juchii laid his hand on his father's shoulder.

The reaction was instantaneous. G'atag'atu-olos spun around, the stick already whipping toward Juchii's head. Juchii ducked, suddenly as graceful as his father, and in the same motion threw his arms around him. G'atag'atu-olos froze. Solong could see his face. It was unrecognizable as his, as any human's. The leopard, the wolf, the bear, the vulture—he had told her of the peryton and the gryphon; they would surely have been closer. Had she been of his people, she would have pressed both fists to her forehead for self-protection.

Instead, she looked frantically around, to send away any of her smaller children who might see this. None were here—only the neighbor women, who had already pressed their own children's faces into their coats and trousers to shield them.

Solong's daughter stood with her eyes still hidden by her own shaking hands.

And there stood her husband, that mild, courteous stranger, looming over her brothers' corpses with a blood-caked stick and the face of a monster. Juchii held him tightly, his arms wrapped around him, his face next to his father's—when had he grown so tall?—murmuring something she couldn't hear.

The air did not move. Even the sun stood fixed in the sky. Then finally, the stick began to sag, and the fists eased open. His shoulders sank, and he closed his eyes.

Juchii finally, very slowly and cautiously, let his father go. He took the stick from him, stepped around the corpse, and went part of the way to the brothers' friends, who had taken no part yet and were clustered together on their horses, just staring.

Juchii bent down and laid the stick on the ground: a barrier none should cross. He straightened and stood there until G'atag'atu-olos turned, slow and halting, as if he had forgotten how to walk, and went to join him. G'atag'atu-olos looked at each rider, one by one. He asked them calmly, "How far does this quarrel go with you?"

"Nowhere, Foreigner," one of them volunteered. "It's over."

"I'll keep all the horses. Those that I took before, and these three as well."

"They are yours."

G'atag'atu-olos turned back to his family. His face was finally familiar again, although his eyes were still strangely bright. His cheekbones and the bridge of his nose were torn in crisscrossing stripes from the whip. He stood there, blood threading down his face and neck and spattered up his leggings from below; his hands, still muddy, open at his sides. For the rest of her life, Solong would remember the day a demon transformed back into the man she had thought she knew; the way he waited, not knowing, perhaps not caring, whether he still had a place here;

and the particular way the sun had lit his long straw-colored plait and the silvery hairs of his bare forearms as he murdered, over and over again, a corpse.

It was the daughter who finally crossed that space, passed among her dead kinsmen, took her father's hands in hers, and held them to her breast.

He asked her quietly, "When is your marriage? Remind me."

"In summer. The first of the Grazing Moon."

He looked up past her, at Solong. He said, "I've been stupid."

There was absolutely no answer to that. Of all the words Solong might use to describe what she had just witnessed, "stupid" was not among them.

Juchii brought a basin of water. The daughter dipped her father's hands and cleaned them, then dried them on the hem of her shirt. She also used the hem to blot the slashes on his face until they stopped bleeding.

Her cheeks were scuffed with mud. He wiped them away with his clean fingertips. She closed her eyes, still so trusting of his touch even after what she had seen.

He drew her face to him and kissed her forehead. Solong wondered whether he remembered some other young girl, freed by him from another set of brothers, in his alien past. But from the way he kissed his daughter, Solong understood that he would never again kiss any of his children.

The dead men lay as he had left them. Their followers still sat their horses uncertainly, a safe distance away. G'atag'atu-olos turned back to them.

He asked, "How will you all ride now?"

They looked at one another. A few murmured, "With you, Foreigner."

"Wherever I ride? Whenever I say?"

"Yes." More voices, and stronger.

"Then go home. And come when I call you."

They understood themselves dismissed. A few of them

dismounted, stepped deferentially into the space Juchii had marked, and gathered up the corpses. Then they all rode quietly away.

Juchii had collected the other two horses. G'atag'atu-olos took the three sets of reins and led them to his daughter.

"These are yours," he told her. "They're good horses. I know their mothers and fathers. Marry that boy as soon as you can, and bring him to ride with me."

* * *

That night, in their nest of furs and blankets, he lay with his wife—with her, but separated by a powerful silence.

He told her, "If you wish to leave, you may."

"Where would I go?"

"To the king. Or to live alone with your children. You're rich now, and I will give you all that you need. All that you want." He smoothed her hair back from the face so straight and dark, smelling of smoke and babies. "Something like that will not happen again."

"I will not go."

"You could marry again. You could forget this. Forget me." He was silent for a moment. Then he said, "All the good things, all these years, have been markers that I myself laid down, to teach evil the way to find me."

He used the foreign word because nothing like it existed in her language. Yet she surely caught its meaning from the way he used it—he could feel it in the sudden tension in her back against his warm chest.

He said, "I don't know why I am so important to it. I don't know why it hunts me. But I will destroy everything myself before I see it lay its shadow over anything of mine again."

She did not answer.

"Will you at least send the children away?"

"You need them."

She pressed her hips back against him. The Bajgani preferred to make love this way, front to back. Face to face was considered selfish and demeaning; front to back purified the pleasure by avoiding the distraction of faces and leaving the man's hands free to caress.

G'atag'atu-olos caressed his wife. Her skin was as smooth as on the day he married her. How long had that been? He had no idea. And it did not matter. They were no longer a man and a woman, a husband and a wife, making love in their comfortable, accustomed way. They were a warrior and his comrade, a monster and its mate, a killer and his accomplice, a pair of mummies scraping dried bones and leathery skin together. His climax was the ugly last spasm of death.

* * *

The king sent a messenger to inquire about the incident. G'atag'atu-olos sent no answer in words, but a double handful of seed gold and the red mare's two-year-old son. That was the end of it.

* * *

It was just a miscalculation, the Bajgani later told one another. The widow only wanted what all women wanted: a lucky husband, a rich camp, a successful leader for her growing sons. Her father had sent a marriage offer to the Foreigner, who had refused it so quickly, the woman thought that perhaps he had not fully understood. She thought to present the proposal herself. She thought her beauty and her well-known sexual skills could tempt any man to change his mind.

Her timing could not have been worse. She believed that G'atag'atu-olos would be feeling bold and triumphant after defeating his enemies. So when he walked into an acquaintance's tent ten days after he sent his gifts to the king, twenty days after he murdered Solong's brothers, he found not the man he expected to find, but a beautiful, perfumed, completely naked woman, who rose from a fur-upholstered couch to come toward him.

He realized at once how neatly he was caught. If he stayed long enough to be courteous, everyone would think he had acquired another wife. If he left now, everyone would tease him as unmanly. Twenty days ago, he would not have minded the teasing.

When he moved forward to meet her, he saw her smile and open her hands on both sides of her silky mound—the clearest of invitations. He saw her eyes and mouth soften in anticipation of kisses, of orgasms, of wealth.

Then he saw her eyes freeze and widen as he closed his hands on her shoulders and bore her, not gently backward to the couch, but straight down to the floor, where the harsh camel-hair carpets would scrape her back raw. He was on her, in her, and done with her while she was still gasping in surprise, then afraid to struggle, then—she could see his face clearly— afraid to breathe.

He rose, closed his leggings, and said, "If you want me, bring a better offer." He walked out.

The joking applause that was waiting to greet him died uncertainly as he caught the red mare and rode away without a glance to either side. Many minutes passed before anyone dared enter the tent.

He never spoke about the incident except to tell Solong, "If you had anything to do with that, never admit it."

That was one of the rare times that Solong Rainbow did exactly as she was told. And it was the last time that any Bajgani presumed to know what G'atag'atu-olos might want—or might tolerate.

Solong's brothers' followers brought their tents and their families to his camp. The brothers' widows brought their tents and their unmarried sons, their married daughters, and the daughters' husbands. When he rode out to raid that year, sixty men rode with him.

* * *

His daughter was married on the first day of the Grazing Moon, in the Year of Many Elk Twins. The young man, almost unrecognizable in his ornament-laden shirt and densely embroidered trousers, rode a black horse at full gallop into the camp. Behind him thundered all his male relatives, whooping and bellowing.

Solong and a score of other women of the clan clung to the girl, screaming curses and terrible threats, defending her with flowers. The groom swung down from his horse, fought his way through to her, and tore her from her mother's arms. Lifting her, he raced back under a ruthless pelting of blossoms. He set her astride his horse, whose hooves had been gilded at considerable expense and who showed considerable desire to bolt and so was being held firmly, against all logic, by the kidnap victim's own brother, Juchii.

The groom turned to the women, and a heavy bouquet caught him square in the mouth. The bride stifled her laughter, pulling her face into a semblance of horror and sorrow.

The groom spat petals and shouted, "Mourn, mother and sisters! Your daughter is taken from you! Now she's mine!"

Great wads of blossoms battered him. He ducked, swung onto the crazily rearing horse, and rode as if for his life. The bride held fast to the back of his belt while stretching her other hand to her kinswomen, wailing for help and showing off her matchless horsemanship by the daringly casual way she leaned out over the jeweled crupper. The black horse dived into the crowd of milling riders, and they charged away, whistling over their shoulders at the screaming women.

Atop a nearby rise, the groom's father turned to G'atag'atu-olos.

"Nicely done, if I may boast a little."

G'atag'atu-olos refilled the man's bowl from a golden jar shaped like a koumiss skin. "If your son can plunder as well as he rides, you'll see a rich old age."

"Ah, now. There's flattery, coming from the father of the best riders on earth." The man laughed uneasily. "And the best plunderers."

Over the rims of their bowls, their eyes met. G'atag'atu-olos felt acutely the other man's acquisitive gamble. He knew that the murders had caused the man to reconsider this marriage, but in the end he had allowed it to go on. So be it, then. If yet another family had chosen to ride into the path of the coming tempest, it was nothing to G'atag'atu-olos.

They drank together. At the last moment, as he raised the bowl to his mouth, G'atag'atu-olos looked into it. His own skull looked back at him.

* * *

With each year, G'atag'atu-olos stretched the boundaries further: hit a harder target, increased the complexity of the strategy, and—most important to him—went farther north or south or east. Not by a day's or two days' ride as he had before, but by a full month's. And men eagerly rode with him. They rode straight south across the Takla Makan—the desert waste that everyone knew could not be crossed, but G'atag'atu-olos didn't care what everyone knew. They took silver and brocade and carpets from between the very feet of the World's Roof Mountains, the true sky-holders that put Atlas's to shame. They rode for days into black, icy forests to bring back furs and gold:

not a few skins and trinkets this time, but loads of treasure that staggered the packhorses and attracted all the steppes' traders like choughs and magpies to a wounded camel.

Every man thought himself a skilled trader. G'atag'atu-olos had been good before. Now he became a master. The traders would talk for hours to gain a single concession more, and G'atag'atu-olos would wait, wait, wait, then strike at the offer so quickly that the trader wouldn't think to regret it until days later.

To attract even more followers, he used the men's inability to decipher his face. He used his formidable reputation. He used his own unleashed ambition. He used the tenacity that had kept Ephialtes alive in the years before and after Echemus. He used Ephialtes' feral caution and headlong recklessness. He used the looming dark wings above him. He used the clan's blood and bone, but they didn't know that and so they were happy.

* * *

While G'atag'atu-olos had willingly promised his third daughter to the king's grandson when both were small, he had resisted making other promises since he had not known how his or others's fortunes would change over time. But even as his successes grew and matches that might have seemed flattering a few years before appeared less so, he hurried to complete them and see his children wed. One daughter after another married and brought a new young man to ride with her father.

Juchii, fourteen, fifteen, sixteen years old, with his mother's face and his father's nerve, was the prize of all prizes in the sport of marriage. The girl who won him would bring to her family all the prowess of her husband's father, and his help in any dispute. But Juchii resisted marriage and G'atag'atu-olos did not insist. When men and women came to make offers for the boy, they always went away fed and flattered but promised nothing.

Juchii refused to marry, and that was that.

For himself, however, G'atag'atu-olos took no such caution. Offers began to come for him again, presented very cautiously at first, formally, publicly. The best of those, he surprised everyone by accepting. He married a second wife, a third, and more—all widows with herds of their own, near-grown sons eager to ride with him, daughters who could be married soon, to bring him still more followers. If the women winced to look at him, he did not care. If they tried to avoid sex, he simply took them as firmly as he had to, so that they would understand the bargain they had made. If that left them dismayed, so much the better—they would remember longer. If they fought with Solong or tried to displace her, he divorced them without a thought. If their families complained, he bribed them into silence. And more offers came.

He still rode poorly by steppe standards. His bowmanship, on the other hand, was faultless. He sometimes still used the old wooden bow with the faded scarf tied to it, which he had brought with him—the bow that had killed the claimant to some small throne in a land far behind him, long ago. He had forgotten the names and all the stories, but the bow he had kept. For serious work, he used the same kind of recurved wood-and-sinew weapon that all men carried here. He could hold three arrows between the fingers of his bow hand, two in his mouth, one at the nock. With six arrows, he could take five rising herons from the back of a galloping horse. Even UlaänUsu Redfeather could not do that.

He no longer offered food and drink to six directions. He knew where the absolute power, Utsir, lay: in the clouds and the rainbows, in thunder and lightning, in metallic bright sunlight and the distant, trembling stars of the night. He knew the names of all the pictures the stars made, and he knew their stories. When he wished on the Blood Star, he used the name the Bajgani had given him, but then wished for things they could not have imagined. When he spoke to Utsir, he looked up as all the Bajgani looked up, directly into his eyes. To speak to kings, men would prostrate themselves as a sign of respect on earth. For Utsir, though, they stood upright, to show that they were worthy of benefaction.

He never bothered to remember a dank withy shack, a black and bloody stone, a monstrous feeding insect and the creaking undulations of a terrible serpent under his open hand. They were there always, in the dark, cold center of his spirit. But no one knew, sometimes not even himself.

As he and his followers ranged farther, they found still better horses to steal, even surpassing the first red mare. But he kept her daughters, crossing them with the finest stallions he could find. His favorite mount of these years was the red mare's last granddaughter, the child of one mating with a stallion stolen for a single night from the stable of the sabak, the potentate of Mohanj, whose friendship G'atag'atu-olos would have preferred to retain but who was, in G'atag'atu-olos's opinion, regrettably stingy with his horses.

If his own warriors, those who pitched their tents by his year after year, should fall short of horses, they could borrow from G'atag'atu-olos's personal herd of four hundred. Should they need still more, it was a simple matter to ride out to new lands and take them.

G'atag'atu-olos's deeds were etched on his body as Utsir loved to see, not only in the scars from arrows and knives and horse bites and the lines across his cheekbones from his brother-in-law's riding whip, but in the black and red tattoos that splayed across his back—a new picture for each successful year. As the greatest honor of all, his name was changed, by the king himself, from G'atag'atu-olos Foreigner to H'olgaichi Thief.

* * *

She alone, his eldest daughter, could still reach him. She alone still dared to go to him when he sat alone in the night. She alone would fill his pipe for him and sit quietly while he smoked and stared at nothing. She alone dared to take his hands and lift his arm around her shoulders, and lean on him. She alone would wait and wait until finally, tentatively and awkwardly, he would do what had once been so easy for him, and rest his face in her hair.

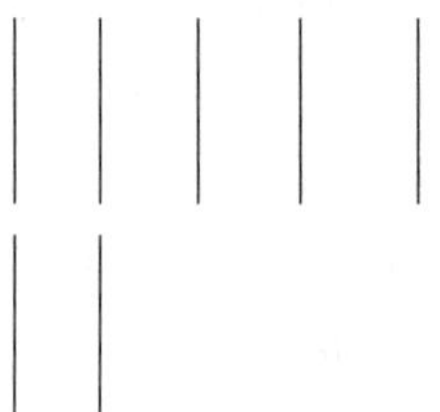

Let them think what they liked, but I didn't mean to drown myself. I meant to swim till I sank—but that's not the same thing.[vi]

—*Joseph Conrad*

H'olgaichi told his men to pack for a long journey. They kissed their wives and children, mounted, and trotted east under the Riding Moon. They passed the fallen ruins of their own winter dugouts, unused for years, and their own ancient hunting grounds where they hunted no longer. They passed all the familiar hamlets and visiting places, crossed the big river, and looped carelessly through the territories they had raided in years past. They rode on through bare, dry highlands that they knew only from stories, then into plains and plateaus that none had even heard of.

It was a land poor in everything but vastness: too high to hold water, so the grass was short and hard and blue-stemmed and the saiga were scarce and undersize. There were no buffalo, no bears, no elk, not even snakes, and even the few fish in the brackish water were tough and full of bones.

The people they met were hole dwellers, as they themselves had been, and too poor to rob. They knew little beyond their own horizons. They had only heard rumors of other lands beyond their own, and in their ignorance, they peopled them with giants, dwarves, and monsters. But they welcomed the diversion of visitors and were happy to accept the Thief's gifts, share their millet and rank mutton, and trade stories with the strangers.

The Bajgani rode on. The farther they went, the more H'olgaichi removed himself from his men, riding and even sleeping apart. This was his normal behavior on raids, and long considered a lucky sign. They rode away a full moon, then another. Then a third.

They came out of steep passes, abruptly into a land so green it hurt their eyes. From under their horses' hooves, tilled fields stepped elegantly downward to a wide, slow river. All along the river's edge, little shining towns were surrounded by squares of boggy water obviously designed to stop galloping horsemen. The men grinned at one another over their horses' ears. In towns so carefully protected, they might find something really worth stealing.

Although the treachery of the land dictated caution, they raided three towns in six nights without losing a man or a horse. The people fled, shrieking and wailing as if they all expected to be murdered, and the tiny forces of men who stood against them were ridiculously easy to kill.

Yes, they killed the guardians. They had not done that before. But H'olgaichi drew his bow against these men so straightforwardly that his followers never thought twice about doing the same. So they left dead men behind them for the first time.

Among the novelties they found were lean domestic birds that could be tied by the legs and strung together over a horse's withers, like so many fruits on a string. There were many terrifically ugly animals like nothing the raiders had ever seen before: short legged, heavy headed, black and nearly hairless, and possessed of voices to terrify the dead. These were as wayward in behavior as the fowls were cooperative: they could be neither led nor driven, and the raiders were skeptical of H'olgaichi's explanation of swine. But when he could convince them to overcome their revulsion enough to pitch a few into the flames of a house that had caught fire in the occupants' haste to escape, the meat was the most delicious they had ever tasted.

The cattle were nothing like the sober, hairy, courteous stock they knew. The fat, heavy-horned beasts simply refused to be driven, either lying down neck-deep in silt and lowing mournfully, or fleeing at the mere sight of the horses. So except for the fowls and pigs slaughtered and smoked for the road home, the raiders departed with no booty animals.

There were only a few horses, in a single compound near a well-traveled road: small, sheep-necked, bony creatures that reminded the elders among them of the horses they themselves had once valued. The animals' hips and shoulders had been marked with signs burned into their skins, and they seemed never to have been ridden. The men stared uncomprehendingly at the one broken-wheeled chariot while H'olgaichi explained. They listened to him, polite but unconvinced.

Even stranger: the horses had been born to be stallions, yet they had no testicles. The men knew of injuries that might do this to another man, but it appeared to have been deliberately done to these animals *by* men. Perhaps that was what made the horses so docile.

The idea prodded at H'olgaichi's memory. Some story Echemus or his mother had told him, perhaps, about a quarrel between powers, which ended in one of them doing this—he couldn't remember the word for it—to the other. So this act was known in this part of the world as well. Interesting.

They found, among the round-headed, yellow-skinned people of this country, a few slaves who did not resemble their masters, each other, or any other people the raiders had ever seen. At H'olgaichi's insistence, they brought these people out of the towns so he could question them. Gently and persistently, sometimes through whole chains of trembling captive interpreters, he learned their stories.

They could describe their own countries, and did so eagerly

when they got over the worst of their terror and saw his genuine interest. But they had been sold and traded so many times, they had only the vaguest notion of what direction those countries lay in, and how far away. When H'olgaichi finished with them, he felt more troubled than informed. For their part, they were relieved when he gave them safely into the hands of traders who, even here, ventured to his camps to do business.

The traders would barter the slaves to new homes nearby, or perhaps even sell them back to their old owners. H'olgaichi knew the slaves' fear: that with his interest in their origins, he might want to release them to find their way home. That would have been a cruel and hopeless favor. But he well understood how lost they were. He traded most of them, to their great relief, keeping only five. Those, he packed onto horses and carried along.

Despite the distraction of the slaves, and the difficulties with animals, the raiders rode home with silk and gold enough to make their women the envy of the entire steppe. A hundred fowl were soon pecking as contentedly around the tents as if they had never left the eastern villages. Solong and the other wives got the household help they needed: two young women and an older man from a land so remote, not even they could say with any certainty where it lay. But they were skilled cooks and tailors. H'olgaichi sent the other two slaves—sisters who wept at the thought of being separated—as a gift to the king.

Amid the booty were bags and bags of wheat and millet. They had also brought enough of the bog grain to feed everyone they knew for an entire winter, except that no one really liked the tasteless paste it made when ground.

So they boiled it and gave it to the camels, who ate it happily until a trader from the far southeast offered to exchange the entire supply for double its weight in rye. While H'olgaichi's youngest wife served tea, he squatted with the trader. The negotiations went normally, and the strange stuff was gone at a profit.

H'olgaichi also took information in his usual way from the traders, in return for slightly more favorable bargains. Ye, they knew about cutting away horses' testicles. Yes, it was done to make stallions more docile. 'Yangguh' was the Shang word for this custom, and for the animals themselves. There was no word for it in any local language, since only the Shang did it.

** * **

The slaves spoke little of any known language, so the smaller children set about teaching them. It was only a few months before the older man, the tailor, could speak well enough to tell stories from his own country—tales that touched at the edges of H'olgaichi's memory. He told how the world was made from a turtle shell, how the snake lost his rabbit dinner, how the ferret and the magpie became kings. H'olgaichi, who until then had liked the man well enough, considered trading him, giving him to the king—anything to get rid of him. But Solong insisted on keeping him, so in the end H'olgaichi kept him, though he was not happy about it.

** * **

His first grandchild was Chinowa Wolf. Named for him, he was born to the laughing, black-eyed daughter, who rode to meet him the day he returned from the east, and placed the infant in his hands.

She said, "He's for you as much as for my husband, because you love babies so, my strange and wonderful father."

He smiled because she expected him to, and because he had some memory of loving her. He held the baby because she expected him to. Then he gave it back to her and forgot it. He had business to attend to.

* * *

This second year, they traveled by a more northern route, raided ten different towns, chased screaming people through the streets to amuse themselves, and slaughtered the militia that finally came out to resist them. At the height of one place's confusion, H'olgaichi swung off his mare, wrapped around his hand the long plait of a man who was annoying him, and cut the man's throat. Then he continued the circular motion around the front line of his hair.

It was amazingly easy: there was a harsh sucking sound, and the scalp and all the hair came free in H'olgaichi's hand. He stood there a moment, flat-footed with surprise. Then he thrust the bundle into his belt, mounted again, and rode across the newly bald corpse in search of further plunder. Later, a new slave cleaned and smoked the scalp for him and tied it to the horse's bridle. Many more would join it.

A trader with a chain of camels found them at the edge of the highlands. He eyed the plunder respectfully, then hunkered down to bargain with these savages. By the time he rose again, he had gained enormous respect for the savages and their twice-alien leader. He had won some respectable goods. And he had told all he knew of the lands hereabouts.

There were, he had reported, maneuverings of power in the extreme east. "Farther east even than this?" the leader asked quickly. The strange wolf-eyed man was clearly intelligent but hopelessly ignorant. People called Chous, the trader patiently explained, were extending their rule in all directions and upsetting the order that the Shangs had maintained since time out of mind.

These Chous, the trader said, were not high political men, but their will was strong and so were their powers of enforcement. They could field the fiercest warriors the world had ever known.

Remembering the yellow-skinned, flat-faced round-heads who always ran shrieking from their horses' hooves, the raiders laughed politely, but the trader insisted it was true. The Chous' fighting men came from the uttermost east, he said, from the edge of the world—at this, the Thief carefully set his koumiss cup down, listening—and no one had ever seen men fight as these fought.

They drove two- and four-horse chariots like a terrible wind, and when they went to war, they killed not only warriors but anything that wandered into their sight: babies, dogs, cattle. Towns that resisted were destroyed to the last life, then burned to charcoal and trampled to dust. Rape was considered a kind of loot, and women were captured and shared out accordingly. They never practiced it on the bodies of dead enemies, though, as some others did. The Chous reckoned that an abomination.

The Chous placed their dead kings in high barrows in their own land, but their enemies, they buried facedown under the ground. Sometimes, the trader said, they sacrificed their own children for luck in war.

He added that the Chous were even now negotiating with the Tsaidam kings to trade far south of here, in the wild white mountains, and no one seriously considered opposing their desire. But they had no interest in the outlands except for the herd animals they might provide. It was the Shang countries they wanted, whose farthest western boundaries H'olgaichi had violated. It was the trader's advice that the steppe people call no further attention to themselves until everyone was more certain of the Chous' intentions.

H'olgaichi thanked the trader cordially. He put him to sleep in stolen silk and returned to the fire, to squat and smoke and think, alone except for Juchii, who also squatted and smoked, and watched him.

After hours, H'olgaichi raised his head and looked at his son.

He said to him, "Get married," and Juchii answered, "No."

* * *

Only a few years later, H'olgaichi met the Chou Warlord.

The raid to the east had become an annual event, which other clans envied but lacked the courage to imitate, and to which all young men of the most tenuous kinship begged invitations. H'olgaichi's raiding luck was legendary. He was fearless but still clever and careful as a crow, never losing more than a few men even when the round-heads sent fleets of chariots after them. Those few who died were most often killed by their own kinsmen, because they were too injured to ride— better than leaving them to the enemy. It was an ancient rule of theirs, which H'olgaichi endorsed.

H'olgaichi now wore a hundred gold beads in his long plaited hair, and twenty black scalps on his red mare's bridle. The tails of his extravagant mustache hung below his collarbones. He dressed as others dressed, but finer: the leather softer, the beadwork more intricate. He wore a belt of silver links and bosses, hung with hardened leather pockets to hold incidental treasure, buckled not with metal but with bright jade ovals carved in high relief with facing tiger lizards, taken from a Chou who had defended it as if it were itself a treasure. Besides his old and new bows, he carried a slim bronze axe, pried from the hand of a dead and desiccated unknown warrior on an ice-swept mountain pass. The tattooed tales of the Thief's adventures and triumphs covered his entire back and chest and trailed down his arms and thighs like points of lace.

Solong Rainbow, the mother of six living children, the most senior of seven wives, mistress of twenty slaves, was still lean and supple, still rode better than her husband, and still served every meal to him with her own hands, in rock-crystal bowls so pure they burned the fingers. Every one of her slaves wore brocade and silk. Her own camels and cattle numbered in the hundreds, even after all debts were figured.

While Juchii remained immovable on the subject of marriage, H'olgaichi's younger children were greedily bargained for. But what goods could anyone offer him? What promises would tempt the richest man anyone had ever known? He, for his part, barely knew these children, and they were wary around him. He was away so much, they had lost their ease with him. He left the business of their marriages to Solong and spent his time building the force for his next ride east.

H'olgaichi's men—the ones who did not gamble—were unimaginably wealthy by the standards of only a few years before. Those who did gamble spread wealth still farther across the steppe. The king's personal horses numbered over a thousand, nearly all of them gifts from this single clan. And the trader's advice was long forgotten.

The clan drifted eastward, or rather, the warriors returned less far to the west every year as their camps rambled casually after them, deeper into the regions H'olgaichi's men knew from their yearly passages. All their more distant kin and familiars followed, too, in an unplanned migration toward the sources of their wealth. They shouldered aside other nomads, pushing them into the territories of yet others, who also pressed outward. They barely noticed the hole dwellers they passed through or over.

In this way, they met the Chou Warlord.

In the Year of the Wall, the Thief led a troop of three hundred men and six hundred horses by a route paralleling the trade road but ten full days below it. Passing far to the south of the places they had raided before, they crossed a new chain of forested mountains and came down in sight of a jewel-like city shielded by a tall stone wall stitched with towers.

H'olgaichi directed some younger men on three nights of reconnaissance Then he led the raiders to an unwalled, boulder-choked defile that the flatlanders apparently considered impassable. They trotted quietly onto the plain—no grain bogs here—and took from that city wealth enough to buy every king they knew of, six times over.

To the city militia, they lost twelve men and thirty horses—three of those men killed by their own kinsmen to save them from capture. But experience had shown that the round-heads, wedded to their chariots, would not follow them into the high, dry lands. They crossed back over the river valley and camped atop the first plateau to admire their prizes.

It was at sunset that Juchii, sitting sentry, hooted a warning: horsemen coming fast. The troop scrambled, loaded, and moved as only they could move. They did not travel but flew, leaving behind a neat mound of horse droppings on a flat rock in the middle of a smoldering firepit.

Whether oblivious to, or infuriated by, the insult, the mounted troop followed them for seven days, until they were out of arrows, most of their horses had been shot from under them, and they were too parched to go on. When H'olgaichi saw that they were finally at a standstill, he sent the booty on ahead and rode back to take a look at these strangely dogged flatlanders.

The few surviving men and horses were in a sorry state: many wounded, all plainly thirsty and exhausted. Only their leader still sat his horse like a whole man. And he did not move as H'olgaichi and his warriors, on their leather-tough horses, dropped straight down an impossibly steep slope to meet them.

The leader, old for a warrior, was enormous for a flatlander. He had broad, drooping shoulders and, under an elaborate hat, a round yellow head as featureless as an egg: no hair or brows or lashes, no ears, and eyes tinier than a baby's. He sat perfectly still as the steppe men ranged around his troop, and did not move his eyes from H'olgaichi.

When all the horses were still, the leader asked calmly in the trade language, "Who are you?" His voice sounded like the distant rattle of thunder.

The warriors tittered, and H'olgaichi said, "Who asks?"

"I am a warlord of the Duke of Chou. I am responsible for the peace of this borderline. We're tired of the trouble you're making. But we've never seen a creature like you, so of course, I must know who you are: a man or a demon."

"I am a man. These warriors"—H'olgaichi gestured—"are the demons." His men murmured appreciatively and nudged each other.

"Why are you so ugly? What kind of man are you?"

H'olgaichi said, "Greek." For lack of a ready word, he had to recall and use the High Mycenaean name. "What kind of sorry master is this Chou, to produce no better riders than these?"

"We fight in chariots in our own land. This is only my personal troop, and I am only one of an army of warlords. The Duke of Chou holds this land in the name of the king, for distances you couldn't imagine. From here to the edge of the world."

Against his will, the Thief's heart jumped. He said carefully, "Then the world must be much larger than this Chou imagines."

The Warlord paused, then said, "If that's true, then you should go back to the part you came from. Because I swear, if you trouble us again, I'll lead you to my duke yangguh, blinded, and in chains."

The steppe men murmured. Juchii raised his bow and shot the Warlord's horse between the eyes. It dropped straight down, and the Warlord hit the ground hard. The steppe men wheeled as one and vanished up the rocks.

Later, they laughed long and well at the Warlord: the bold way he spoke, and then the ungraceful roll in the sand. Juchii parodied brilliantly both the deep, scratchy voice and the tumble. He kept one cautious eye on his father as he did so, but H'olgaichi made no sign that might discourage him. Still, H'olgaichi and a few others were quiet that night, thoughtful about nothing in particular.

Deep in the dark, alone at the last coals of the fire, H'olgaichi looked again at his son and said, "Please get married."

"I won't leave you," Juchii answered. He passed the hemp pipe to his father, and that was all.

The Warlord was wrong, of course, as well as right. He and H'olgaichi met many times again before the final time.

* * *

The old king died in midsummer. His body, stuffed and draped, was carried to all the camps of his people on a camel cart, and at each camp, all who could be spared mounted and followed. They had to ride a full month west, to the wind-scoured, treeless sacred plateau that had once been the heart of the lands they knew. The ground was spotted with old mounds and was taboo for hours in every direction. Even scavenger birds, normally bold as roaches, never came here.

After the funeral and the sacrifices, the shamans sang while the living horsemen threaded through the impaled ones in a slow rotation around the immense gift pile with the platform rising above it. The hanging legs of the dead horses swung at an idle walking pace. The living horses moved slowly, too, from time to time breaking into a trot so their riders could catch up to friends. The patterns of hundreds of riders, men and women, broke apart, reformed, then broke again like strings of foam on turning water. The sun was brilliant and cold, Utsir watching everything.

When H'olgaichi pulled out of the procession to let the red mare rest, Solong and UlaänUsu came up beside him. They leaned on their horses' withers and watched the circle turn, the living and the dead, around the king's burial tree. The smell of sweat and blood and excrement, and of the sweet grass that stuffed the body, rolled over them like smoke.

UlaänUsu looked strange without the long club of his hair—mourning required all men and women to crop their hair for the king, just as it required all men to pierce their left hand with an arrow. Old men might carry the history of many kings between the bones and tendons of their hands. This was UlaänUsu's third and H'olgaichi's first. H'olgaichi's hand burned despite the ointment the shamans had plastered over the wounds, but he had been honored, with only a few other chiefs, by being allowed to leave his own pale plait under the king's dead hands.

"Someday," UlaänUsu said suddenly.

"What?"

UlaänUsu turned to him, his face twisted with emotion. "You gave us life and made us rich. You're greater than any king. Someday, we'll do this for you."

Solong looked swiftly at H'olgaichi, alarm shifting her face. But H'olgaichi only moved his head calmly affirmative as, inside his skull and high overhead, he heard the deep, steady pulse of invisible wings.

* * *

The traders knew of his interest in unusual things. That was why one of them brought him opium. It came, the man explained, from flowers grown beyond the mountains, harvested by insects as large as horses. When H'olgaichi gave a start of unpleasant surprise, the trader elaborated. These insects—he shaped their actions with his hands as he spoke—ate the pollen of the flowers, then defecated this pure, precious flesh-like paste that could form itself into the most fabulous of dreams. With a flourish, he presented a hand-size casket of filigreed gold.

H'olgaichi opened it and saw a plain, pale clod inside. It looked as unremarkable as mud or animal scat. The smell was distantly familiar, although he couldn't place it right away. Then, like the memory of the giant insect: Delphi. Hyades. And then the boy Depas.

His mind stopped for a moment. When he recovered, the trader was talking again.

One consumed it, the man explained. Ate it, drank it—how didn't matter. Another flourish. Paradise!

And the price? The trader's first price seemed huge for a treasure of unknown worth. They bargained all afternoon, torpid and cagey in the midsummer heat, unable to agree.

Finally, the trader called one of the slaves and gave him instructions. They rested again, talking idly of camels and colored stones, until the slave brought out a heavy silver and bone drinking cup half-filled with warm koumiss. With a jeweled spoon, the trader stirred a small knob of the paste into the drink, then presented it to H'olgaichi.

Paradise, indeed. He sipped the koumiss slowly, shocked by, then savoring, the flood of sensation. It was exquisitely sensual: richer than hemp, deeper than sex, stunning in its usurpation of mind and senses. No wonder, then, that Depas had survived for so long.

When he recovered, he gave the trader the last price the man had asked, plus an additional gift of seven matched amber beads and a bronze Shang vessel in the shape of a celestial dragon.

He was never without the filigreed casket, filled again and again whatever the price.

* * *

Every year, H'olgaichi threw himself and his warriors into the teeth of fate, tempting, provoking, daring it to take them. And every year, they escaped again. The Warlord seemed a sorry representative of the powers that could have risen against them, but he was all H'olgaichi had. So every year, he led his raiders ever deeper into Chou lands. And every year, the Warlord dutifully hunted them. Twice, he followed after them, each time faster and farther, before he had to turn back. Another time, he circled around through the hills to cut them off. The steppe men waited politely for him; then H'olgaichi sent the plunder home and led the flatlanders forty days in exactly the wrong direction, finally leaving them in the forest behind the Great Hook Lake, at the full of the Fat Horse Moon.

Once, the Warlord crossed to the north with an enormous troop of chariots, along the lake line, apparently searching for cities to burn. But the steppe people had no cities, only the long-abandoned winter dugouts, in this season empty of even the poorest squatters—sorry kindling for the Warlord's fires. The people drifted, unharmed and amused, around the great clanking army, picking the men off at their leisure and taking the horses that they fancied.

Twice, the Warlord traveled up from the Takla Makan trade road and spoiled the end of the hunting season by tramping around the steppes until all the elk left for quieter districts and the women complained that they hadn't the time, amid all the packing and riding, to do up their hair properly.

Each year, the Warlord lost men and horses, and each year, at the point that he would have to turn back, H'olgaichi made sure he saw him at the head of the men who had beaten him yet again. Each year, the Chou sat his horse, his face expressionless under the wide hat, the reins buried in one great fist, staring silently at H'olgaichi across a broad swale of grass, unable to touch him or harm him in any way. But each year, after the eastern raid, the Warlord came back.

Although H'olgaichi's men didn't understand it, they respected his need to drive toward the goal he never spoke of: the world's ultimate end, which the trader and the Warlord and even Prometheus had promised him. It was his one remaining ambition, to know the truth about the shape of the world before evil finally took him.

To his men, this craving was a sign of luck: the stronger it pushed him, the better the loot. As long as he took time to rob with ingenuity and skill, they would follow him eagerly. The other things—his vagueness and distraction, his incessant questioning of slaves and traders, his thoughtful smoking when everyone else was long asleep, his occasional days of reclusive opium dreams—were other well-known portents of luck.

He dismounted at last on a spume-blown beach where no horse's hoof had ever stepped. The air was full of icy spray, and the water beyond the roaring breakers was darker than blood and netted with yellow foam.

This could be it, could be the end at last. But this sea was alien and wild. No part of it knew more orderly lands. It had never lain quietly between warm islands or touched the face of Charybdis. It had no memory, however distant, of drinking the waters of three thousand rivers and three thousand springs, all of them with names. No half-grown boy had folded a cloak around a sword, a bow, and a baby and paddled quietly through it.

While his men gazed, indifferent and uncomprehending, over the heaving, endless water, H'olgaichi Thief lifted with both hands a twisted knot of driftwood and held it to his face. It smelled of new places: lands complete unto themselves and utterly foreign. Then he knew what he had feared for so long: that he was beaten and had always been. It was not over and never would be. He stood on frozen sand and stared at infinity.

That was the year the Chou Warlord found his camp at last.

* * *

That afternoon, the sky was yellow, with crows circling. They rode swiftly up the valley, all but H'olgaichi too filled with dread to be cautious. The smell was heavy as smoke. Dead children sprawled like wads of rag.

His tent was the only one standing. He rode to it at a gallop, only because all his men were galloping. He dismounted calmly and stepped through the flap. Flies rose up in a cloud. He held his sleeve across his mouth and nose and considered what he saw.

He knew that it was Solong Rainbow. The fan of hair was the right color, where it wasn't caked with dried blood to the texture of wood. One leg was still drawn up, the foot tangled in stiff, filthy clothes. There were two ragged black eyes on the narrow chest, and no other face at all. Black-crusted fingers were hooked like the feet of dead birds. White larvae squirmed everywhere, disturbed by the light.

No living man from his prior life would approach such death, but H'olgaichi didn't mind. He knelt by her side and moved his hands over her, finding at last what he sought: a clot of blood, still slightly liquid under a thickened shell. He scraped up a lump of it, sucked it from his fingertip, and told her, "Forgive me. You are my sister."

Then he rose and walked out and stood and waited. By his feet lay Chinowa Wolf—five years old or a little more, or less, and the grass already growing up around him. Fingers still clutching a fine small bow. Reaching but never touching him, the hand of H'olgaichi's daughter was nearly severed at the wrist, her arm wrapped in the cord of the baby hacked from her womb and stamped to paste.

Then Juchii was shaking him, shaking him.

"What do we do? Tell us what to do!"

He raised his head and looked at his son. Juchii's face was finally open to him. Shock, horror, panic, pain—H'olgaichi marked them one by one, like an inventory of trade goods. Then he answered calmly, "There's nothing to do."

"Everyone's dead! Everything—"

"So are we. Don't you know? I called this, and it came."

Juchii stared at him for a moment, then twisted away. He snatched his bow from his back and ran for his horse. He threw his head up and howled.

He ran straight into a sheet of arrows. Every one of them hit him, and he went down without a sound, first to his knees, then twisting to one side, still holding the bow, reaching out toward nothing. The arrows stopped instantly, but the other men, scattered through the smoking camp, snatched their weapons and charged, mindless, hopeless, screaming, up the hill toward the line of Chou archers.

The archers waited. H'olgaichi waited. The archers selected, nocked, waited. Then they all drew at once and fired. His warriors threw themselves into the murderous cloud. They screamed while they ran, then died in perfect silence.

As for H'olgaichi, even now the Chous feared him. Unwilling to touch him, they only took his two bows, and his dagger from its sheath—mistaking the axe for some finery, they left that— and prodded him forward with arrow points, until the Warlord's voice stopped them.

H'olgaichi's head came up blindly, dragged by the hair. The Warlord sat his huge yellow horse, the reins in a fist like a rock. H'olgaichi had never been so close to him. The spherical head turned slowly toward him. H'olgaichi was on his knees, arms held outstretched, a Chou fist in his hair.

The Warlord's lips were narrow and rigid as a frog's, and his mouth was white inside. "Now, my children," he said. "Now, here is a puzzle."

H'olgaichi knelt, waiting.

"You have been a lot of trouble to me, for much too long a time. Perhaps you thought you would teach me war?" The Warlord lengthened his back, looking over all their heads at the smoldering camp, at the dead. "But perhaps not."

H'olgaichi waited.

The flat black eyes turned back to him, interest flickering in their depths. "Still not afraid? What does it take, I wonder, to turn the likes of you . . ." The Warlord sought a word in the simple trade language. ". . . to turn the likes of you abject? To make you grovel and whine. If this doesn't do it, it will be interesting indeed to learn just what will."

He breathed out loudly—his way of laughing, perhaps. "I made you a promise once. Do you remember? To bring you to my duke blinded, yangguh, and in chains. And I will make you another promise as well: before long, you will be happy to grovel and whine for me."

They dragged him backward, fixed him to the ground. Yellow faces leaned over him in a circle. They pinned his head in place.

The knife was an old one, with a rune-carved wooden haft. It was not sharp, but the man was strong. The tip of the blade touched his eyebrow, paused, then plunged in. The pain was invasive rather than acute; more intrusion than laceration. The blade did not stop until it jammed in the cheekbone. There it paused and drew out. The other eye saw it rise, dripping yellow fluid laced with blood. It hesitated in the air; then the hand tensed and the knife came down. It cut the other way this time and grated again on bone. It rose and moved to the other eye.

"No," the Warlord said. The Chou paused and looked at his master. "Do the other thing first. So he can watch."

The Chou turned back—a young man, half H'olgaichi's age, with a high-boned face, and skin fine as paper. He bent to open the belt, pausing at the interlocking jade cats that served as its buckle. The ends of his hair brushed H'olgaichi's mouth. None of the Warlord's men spoke, but the hands that pinned him all tightened at once. Sweat dripped onto H'olgaichi's forehead.

The belt loosened with a soft click. Then the laces of his leggings opened, and a cold hand clutched his genitals. The young Chou laid the blade against his skin, paused for a moment, raised his face, and smiled.

Then his head nodded hard one time, and his front teeth spattered outward, replaced by a trefoil arrowhead. The eyes bulged as if they might burst out, too; then blood fountained from the nostrils. The blade slid along H'olgaichi's groin, cutting deep but turning outward, lodging under the tendon and stopping as the Chou curled forward onto H'olgaichi's chest, as if he had suddenly fallen asleep. A feathered shaft projected like a waxed braid from the back of his skull. Blue fletching striped with black.

All the weight came off H'olgaichi's arms as the men leaped up. He moved instantly, rolling with the dead man, dragging the belt along. Then he was free of the corpse, snatching his bows from someone's hand and running, holding the belt and leggings up with one hand.

The Warlord's voice thundered behind him. He couldn't tell distance, couldn't gauge where things were. He stepped into a hole, and his good leg folded, but he rolled twice and was running again. He thrust fingers into his mouth and whistled.

An arrow sizzled past his ear. The red mare was trotting, then galloping to meet him. She veered nearer, matching his speed as he had taught her and her mother and grandmother, but he couldn't tell where she was. He reached, missed, and nearly fell again, then wrapped his hand in the flying mane, bounced once, and swung onto her back. Jolting pain shot down his leg. The knife still projected from his thigh. He jerked it free and stuffed it hilt-first into his shirt. The mare jumped a corpse.

Juchii knelt before him, quilled with arrows, his bow still in his hand. He spread his arms in the gesture they all knew. H'olgaichi snatched his axe, leaned sideways, and swung the length of his arm. The blade hissed over Juchii's shoulder. The distance was wrong, and he was already past. He twisted to look. Juchii swayed, still alive. The Chous were running. He must go back—the inviolable rule, to kill one's own rather than let them be taken.

Arrows slapped the ground all around him, and a blanket of crows rose and scattered, shrieking. Then he was up and over the rim, with open steppe before him.

* * *

I am the Aleph, the snake, the sphere. I remember everything.

* * *

The red mare carried him for days and immeasurable distances. When he felt the first hitch in her stride, he began counting down the time she had left.

It was hot. Heat, no sound, flat reddish light, the mare. Too far in the wrong direction to believe that even Utsir might see. There was no grass here, only gray hardpan figured evenly with deep octagonal cracks. No graze for a hungry animal, no water for a thirsty one, no shade for a dying one.

Standing upright, H'olgaichi cast no shadow but a tight black smear between his feet. The horse didn't lift her head, not even when winged shadows skated over her. But H'olgaichi looked up, shading his eyes with the flat of his hand. Ragged black against the burning red sky—the shapes of great birds passed and wheeled and passed again. Vultures, choughs, kites. No. He looked down again.

He had already cut the scalps from the bridle and stuffed them, carelessly wadded, into a pouch on his belt. He had slid the bridle itself from the mare's head, only to ease her discomfort. He would not take it. Now she lay still, so diminished that it seemed impossible she could have carried him at all.

She nickered wearily as he knelt. He cut her throat with the Chou's stone dagger, then licked blood from the blade.

"Forgive me," he whispered. "You are now my sister."

* * *

The Thieves' Moon child is white as snow,

the Coming Home child has far to go.
The Calving child is born to play,
the Elk Moon child would hunt all day.
The Fat Horse child is bold as thunder,
the Day-too-Long child makes his mother wonder.
The Grazing child is thoughtful and sweet,
the Berry child will always eat.
The Turning child is silly and dear,
the Trading child will persevere,
the Eagle Moon child will have no fear.
The Riding Moon child means certain danger,
the Night Moon child's forever a stranger.

* * *

Arrows sleekly fletched in his own gray, white, and red; tri-bladed heads in bronze as bright as gold. A tall, foreign bow much older than he, and a much better bow of heartwood and sinew. He could hold three arrows between the fingers of his bow hand, two in his mouth, one at the nock. With six arrows, from a galloping horse, he could take five rising herons. Even UlaänUsu could not do that.

* * *

The rivers lay milk-soft in beds of white sand. In highest summer their water was tepid, and in winter they froze in swirled patterns of white and clear. Marble was never so sleek and flat. They rang like gongs underfoot, and the horses would shy and slither while the riders' laughter echoed to the vacant black forests and beyond.

* * *

There was a valley that everyone knew of but few visited. Cupped smooth as a bowl, it was, and grass filled it from rim to rim— short at the edges but, in the center, as high as a mounted warrior's head, so that it seemed not hollow at all but flat and ordinary as the rest of the land for days around. At the level of the ground, the stems were thick as a baby's wrist. The scent of the grass was spicy and rich, but neither camels nor cattle would graze it. No one knew why.

* * *

Once, he rode all day alone under a sky filled with rainbows. Never in Arcadia had he seen the whole vault of a rainbow—only stingy disjointed segments, as if the sky begrudged even that small extravagance. But here rose full arc after full arc, to one side and then the other, and between them a sky deep blue and black, and the grass gleaming like a billion separate threads of bronze.

* * *

Golden eyes between black branches; the chitter and hiss of sables; lizard moons; a flawless trembling foal just born, trailing placenta like silken wings; golden cups steaming with new milk; a sea of purple flowers no taller than his thumbnail; hoofprints full of rain.

* * *

He rose and stood and looked down. He laid the fine recurved bow across the horse's corpse, shouldered the ancient foreign one, and slid the young Chou's dagger into the empty sheath at one hip. The axe hung at the other.

If he could remember where he had buried his firstborn

child, he could bring it to lie with its mother and brother and sisters and nephews so that it, like them, might come back again with no memory of him. But he did not remember where the child lay, and could only hope that they would.

He owned exactly what he now wore on his body, which would have seemed a vast treasure only a few years before: scores of rings and bracelets; gold beads in the plait that had grown long again since the old king's death; jade-buckled, silver-bossed belt, its pockets crammed with casual treasure; twenty or more Chou scalps; axe, knife, bow and arrow case, beaded shirt, painted leggings, fringed boots; the deep paths of healed and open wounds; the tattooed stories of so many years.

There would be no moon tonight. He knew this already. There would be only the Blood Star to watch whatever he might do; to hear, as was the custom here, him speak aloud his name and then his desires.

But he owned no name, and "desire" meant nothing. The future would be only what would happen, and what would not.

He never thought of doing this; he simply started walking.

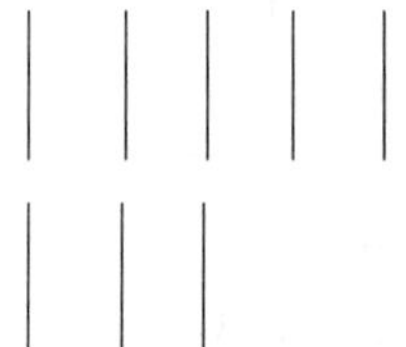

There are no stars
there is no grief
I will never arrive
I stumble when I remember how it was
with one foot
one foot still in a name [vii]

— *W. S. Merwin*

A walk down a corridor, Elawon had said, with pictures along the wall. Each picture a point in the walker's life, each lit in turn by a lamp in his hand. The rest of the corridor dark.

Goatherd. Apprentice. Defender. Protector. Murderer. Beggar. Outlaw. Wanderer. Alien. Husband. Father. Thief. Murderer. Refugee. Beggar. Protector. Lover. Murderer.

Was repetition allowed? Akhaïdes hadn't thought to ask.

If Elawon was right, there was no sense in asking fate for anything. It had already painted what it would paint. Nor could any other power change what would happen. He had felt this when he walked away from a horse's cooling body. How could he have forgotten?

Be what you've always been to me, whatever that is. The first time that Ephialtes lifted the baby into his arms, fate already held a knife to its throat. Yet it was his own hand that had wielded the knife.

One, two, a thousand times, he saw himself, as if from above and at a distance, step away from Aristodemus's door, choose a direction, and go. By the time the other door opened, he was too far away to hear it, and Temenus would not have raised his voice to call him back.

Pausing so long, turning to the opening door, speaking, walking forward, stepping inside, trying to sit but so shaken he could only trust the floor—every separate instant had felt like a choice freely made. But what had fate painted before either of them was born?

The baby blinked and rooted, the days of its life already counting down.

If you can't tolerate something for a year, you can tolerate it for a month. If not for a month, for a day. If not for a day, for a breath. If not for a breath, for a horse's stride. If not for a horse's stride, for a heartbeat. You can. See? Yes, you can.

* * *

Pictures lit in turn. The road heaving up a ridge so steep that a misstep could plunge the horse all the way down into the gulf. The soil had crumbled away, baring lime and quartz like bone in old wounds.

Pictures in turn. A fertile valley dotted with rank, disordered fields and roofless villages. Through open doors, as certain as dreams, neat pyramids of skulls on the hearths.

Pictures. Against a mottled sky, geese and swans raveling southward.

Thin mist between quartz pebbles, and in the same line of sight, the blunt head of Parnassos, far away, maned in cloud. He lay curled tight on bare ground, the coat draping all but his face, the blanket pillowing his head, with no idea when he had fallen or how he had so carefully covered himself.

Eyes patiently watching, following, never showing themselves, never going away.

Parnassos's veins and shadows different with every sunset,

its clouds raw, unworked silver. Not bothering to expect him. Or warn him away.

* * *

"Here, let me."

He jerked awake and turned his head. Arms slid under his knees and shoulders and lifted him up from stony, dry ground.

"*Fah!* You're all wet."

Groggy and bewildered, he closed his eye. Someone carried him easily and then laid him down. There was heat on his face, and the smell of smoke. He opened his eye to see fire and a small, fleshy mouth smiling from a broad bearded face.

"Karnus, my mother called me," the man said. "And folks still do, for lack of something better. I assume these are yours?" He shook out the wolf skin and spread it over a bush, then did the same with Makhawis's blanket. "This is the wrong season for bathing, and that little pond's not near deep enough for fish—if you eat such things. What were your plans, exactly?"

He turned to rearrange the fire, humming, with one eye still cocked toward Akhaïdes. His shirt was Delphic red.

Akhaïdes stared at the coat and blanket. He'd been wearing them. How . . . ?

"You wanted water, maybe, and fell in. Try this."

Karnus offered a water bag. Akhaïdes reached for it, then stopped. Karnus smiled again. The face behind its short silky beard was plain, but the tiny eyes glittered with intelligence.

He said, "I really am a priest of Delphi. Even outlaws have to use poison to poison me. And this is plain spring water. Drink in safety."

Akhaïdes tried to hold the bag, but his right hand would not close and the bag slithered free, slogging over his legs.

"*Tchh.* Never mind."

Karnus opened the skin and raised Akhaïdes' head on his

arm to feed him, then corked the bag with a smack of his palm and helped him off with his shirt and boots. He glanced at the pictures on Akhaïdes' chest, then looked again.

He did not stare but did not look away, either, as all amusement cleared from his face. He turned to spread the clothing to dry and busied himself at the fire. When he turned back again, he held, like a magician, a roasted rabbit on a stick. He tore off a limb, ate it to the bones, then offered one to Akhaïdes.

A picture: Elawon, curbing exasperation, teaching him to feed himself again. With no warning at all, his throat closed and his eye flooded.

"This is the time," Karnus said, looking only at the meat in his fingers, "when you tell me who you are. But then, you probably won't do that."

Beyond the ring of light, the horse yawned, shook itself, then lay down to sleep. Karnus fed Akhaïdes as one might feed a child or a puppy: bite after tiny bite, with long pauses in between for remembering how to chew and swallow. At last, he laid the bones aside and sat wrapped in a red cloak while Akhaïdes grew sleepy in the glow of the fire and the priest's small, reckoning eyes.

* * *

In the morning, Karnus shouldered his pack and walked ahead. The horse followed him, and Akhaïdes had only to stay on. Parnassos stood out clearer still, with the cliffs and tables of Delphi like a great curled paw against its breast.

Karnus glanced back. "Don't look," he said. "Don't look if you don't want to." And so he did not look.

* * *

Time reeled backward. They passed the place where Akhaïdes had awaited the Herakleids. They climbed Krissa's terrace, walked through Delphi town, passed the ruined house where he and Elawon had sheltered, the shelf where the Mycenaeans had camped. People stared as they went by. The roadside corpses still had nothing to say. Akhaïdes bent to press his forehead against his hands as the horse strode past each silent skull.

In the space before the sanctuary, a score of priests and slaves in Kastalia's red stood as if ready to defend it. Karnus left the horse on the road and scaled the steps, Akhaïdes leaning heavily on his arm. They climbed between the cypress trees.

"Menetor, look what I brought you."

Akhaïdes dare not look up. He knelt and opened his left hand in the dirt by the priest's bare toes. He held the right hand protected against his chest.

A familiar voice asked, "Who are you?"

"I am Akhaïdes Outlaw."

Beside him, Karnus drew a quick, soft breath.

"We told you not to come back here."

"There is nowhere else."

They led him to an ordinary room in an ordinary building, stripped off his shirt, and laid him facedown on the cold dirt floor. Male slaves stood on his arms and legs. A bull-shouldered priest spat on his own palms and spun a stiff leather goad between them, a forced grin showing his teeth.

With the first stroke, Akhaïdes' breath caught like cloth ripping. The second made an explosion of light. The pain was like the fire's, but this torch he could not throw away. The men's weight held him immobile.

The priest paused, crouched, and laid a cold hand on Akhaïdes' back. The skin shuddered like a horse's. When the priest rose again, the next stroke carried all the certainty of fate behind it.

Akhaïdes moved in one moment from defiance to assent,

from assent to need. He stretched out, giving all of himself to the lash. It did not stop until it stopped.

* * *

Later, Menetor found him sitting stiffly upright by the moss-laced white stone stele among the cypress trees, staring at the wall of Kirfis across the vale. Menetor stopped in front of him, his fists on his hips.

"You. You have a lot of names. What are they?"

He licked his lips. "Ephialtes Hyadeides. G'atag'atu-olos. H'olgaichi. Akhaïdes. Hunter. The Good Kinsman."

"I'll use the one you gave yourself, the one that everyone knows has no meaning. 'Akhaïdes.' Gibberish. Do you know what this is?"

Akhaïdes turned to look. Menetor's open hand lay atop the stele. There was carving all down one side: writing, he remembered.

"This is a name, too." Menetor slid his slender finger along an incised line of four symbols. "This is the name of the High King Orestes, who came here to beg absolution after he murdered his mother and her husband to avenge his father. Here it says, 'Orestes, son of Clytemnestra, planted these trees.'"

Akhaïdes studied the carving warily. It told him no more than it had either time he came here before.

"The Serpent does not like its food whole. Anyone who would come to it must come in pieces. There are three ways to break any man. One need only find them and then choose between them."

Akhaïdes raised his chin. "Break me," he said. "I don't care how."

Menetor started to go on, but then some confusion moved into his eyes. He blanked his face, but it was clumsily done, like the defense of a man who has no idea what to say next.

Finally, he managed, "I won't change my mind about you," and walked away.

* * *

Faceless, Solong Rainbow lifted her hands—black-fleshed, with gray bone exposed at the tips. White, fat worms writhed in each palm.

"H'olgaichi." The voice not her own sizzled from the black chasm of her chest. "H'olgaichi, my husband." Shreds of cloth and sinew pulsated softly.

Behind the naked plate of her shoulder, Elawon stood. Some light glossed the curls of his hair, and when his hands parted, entrails tumbled forth in a spill of precious stones: jade liver, rose crystal stomach, ropes of pearls, heart of deepest ruby.

"For a time, you seemed to sit content at fires." This time, Solong's lips moved, whole and pliant below dark sockets and the jutting raw bone of her brow, but the voice had the same atonal, uninflected sibilance. "But even then you must go out, go away, go and see. Every time you stepped out of sight, even for a moment, I knew we might never see you again. I didn't believe you would die, but that you would find a road that led on until you simply forgot about returning."

Elawon said, "At least, he gave you wealth. To me, he gave only lies."

Solong turned her head to him. Her spine creaked like an old chair. Her black hair was dense at the sides of her face, but the back of the skull was bare, with a mossy tracery where it had lain so long against the ground.

She hissed, "I don't know you. Who were you?"

Elawon stood with the soft heap of jewels around his feet. He lifted his head to Solong's eyeless stare. "I knew exactly who I was, until he came back."

"More fool you." The cutaway breasts with their backing of

splayed ribs blinked with idiot wisdom. "You wanted him; you got him. So did I. He knew what was coming. He told me, and I chose to stay. And so did you."

She turned back to Akhaïdes and said again, "I chose to stay. So did he."

Behind her, Elawon glanced down, scowling his customary disapproval, and bent to gather his guts in his arms. The stones clattered.

Elawon's stoop revealed behind him a third corpse lingering. This one wore clots of rusty-brown hair stuck to white-bone scalp. She had eyes still—black and comprehending above a mouth withered into a permanent rictus, a frozen scream. She said, calmly and in her own voice, "He is my perfect, beautiful son. I will not hear a word against him."

Behind her, a hundred more shadows pressed, robed and masked in blood, murmuring, waiting to speak.

Akhaïdes ripped awake. He was in Delphi's slaves' house, where they had sent him to sleep. He was clutching Menetor's wrist as Menetor gripped his head. A crowd of slaves stared wide-eyed around Menetor's shoulders.

Menetor said harshly, "Stop this. Don't bring your dreams here."

Menetor's eyes were crumbed with sleep, but his voice and his grip were strong. Akhaïdes hung dazed and speechless between his hands. Menetor shook him. "Delphi doesn't want your dreams. Send them away."

"I don't dream. I don't know what this is."

Below them, under the floor, something shifted and slid: stones, sand, dry skin against earth. The sound was almost below hearing, but the lift and shiver of the floor could not be mistaken. The slaves all looked at one another. Menetor released his grip and sat back on his heels.

Akhaïdes pressed his left hand and, carefully, his right to the ground. The noise faded; the floor stopped shuddering.

Menetor glanced behind himself. All the slaves shuffled their feet but didn't actually move away. He turned back to Akhaïdes.

"Do you think I haven't watched an outlaw decompose before?" He tucked his hands between his narrow thighs. "I was born at Pheneus. I'm Arcadian, too. Maybe you know, in the old language—our *real* language, before this Mycenaean gabble came along—there's no word for 'accident' and no word for 'once.'"

Akhaïdes whispered, "I know that. I remember."

"But there is a word for 'alone.'"

"It's a curse."

"This name you gave yourself, that everyone knows means nothing. You turned the old language back on itself, in a way that no one would understand now—certainly no Mycenaean speaker."

The low lamps cast Menetor's face in shadow, but each line of his scalp was deep as the cut of a knife. "'Akhaïdes.' It means solitude, and it means he who must be mad, because he is alone. It also means the grief that picks a man out and makes him alone and mad—the sick grief he calls to himself through his own actions."

Menetor turned and took a lamp from a slave's hand. Facing Akhaïdes again, he said in pure Arcadian, "Everything that happens, happens for a reason. Everything that happens has happened before. Everything that happens will happen again."

Akhaïdes whispered in the same language, "Everything that happens is someone's fault."

Menetor switched back to Mycenaean. "Your great-great-grandfather Tydeus ate the brains of his enemies."

Akhaïdes sat silent.

"But at least, he knew what he was doing." Menetor circled Akhaïdes' head with the lamp. Then he puffed out the flame and poured a few drops of the oil onto Akhaïdes' hair. Akhaïdes shivered.

Menetor said, "Your life lies inside this circle. Nothing enters; nothing leaves. There are no dreams. Someone, give him back his blanket. And all of you, go to sleep. This is not your business."

* * *

It was only the Culling Moon, but the weather stayed cold. Every morning, Akhaïdes collected the priests' and guests' chamber pots and firepots, emptied them, and scoured them with sand. Then he scrubbed the floors with sand and stones. Since he had to perform it one-handed, this work took him most of the day. The right hand, still unhealed, the bone shards always threatening to shift, was useful only to steady things, never to grip or lift. The chill damp of the paving seeped into his knees until they ground painfully, all the time.

He ate after the slaves, after even the sick and the polluted, and said nothing when only greasy rinds were left in the pot. At midnight, he washed himself in the stone slaughter basin behind the barns before going to the slaves' room, where he lay down in his corner beside the door, drew Makhawis's blanket over his head, and fell instantly asleep. No dream even approached him.

Everything he did was on Menetor's orders: "Sit there. Do that. Eat this." When Menetor wasn't actually there, he still heard the old man's voice and did what it told him. He worked and watched himself working. He watched his own hands as if they were someone else's. He never thought, never spoke. They beat him for every infraction, real or imagined, on any whim. He never resisted.

Menetor watched him, his mouth pulled tight. There was nothing he could make Akhaïdes do that Akhaïdes would refuse, nothing he could refuse Akhaïdes that would elicit a word of protest. No force he could use that Akhaïdes would resist. Even when Akhaïdes was punished—for some error, for effect, to impress a visitor, for nothing at all—the sight of the lean, frivolously decorated body stretched across the gritty floor, devouring every stroke with a shiver and a groan, filled Menetor with profound dissatisfaction.

He turned caustic and short-tempered. He wasn't sleeping well. That was the reason.

* * *

The priest with the goad was a master of his work. Nevertheless, an imperfect stroke split the skin across Akhaïdes' spine. Untreated, the wound festered and putrefied. As if eager for this opportunity, all his recent injuries started up again. Infection spread to every scrape and scratch on his hand and arms, to the nearly healed bruises from Hippotes, the olive grove, the beating in the street. His teeth loosened; his neck and armpits and broken hand bloated. His lungs filled with yellow fluid laced with soot from the Nafpaktos fire. His eye dribbled pus. His throat and knees swelled until he could barely swallow or walk.

He crouched in the corner of the slaves' room, seared with fever. Afraid to come within reach, they pushed food toward him with sticks, but he would not eat; he only drank water. At the fever's worst, he could not think, could not see, could not understand anything said to him. And the Serpent rumbled restlessly under the house, cracking the floor and spilling dust from the rafters until the slaves moved out to sleep elsewhere.

Menetor came to look and went away shaking his head. And just when they were certain the patient would die, he started to recover.

* * *

Still stooped and trembling, he crept to the shack that held the Serpent's stone. No one stopped him. A few morbidly curious slaves and small boys followed.

He sat on the threshold and fumbled his boots off. The one-armed guardian scuttled away. Akhaïdes stood, leaning on the wicker door frame. He did not touch the bell, but simply stepped through. An explosion of pure energy, like lightning, blasted him back out again.

He lay sprawled on the ground, blinded, ears ringing. The slaves and children had scattered. Priests crept inside to set back upright the little forest of clay votives—also knocked flat by the stone's vehemence. The one-armed slave returned warily and used his well-worn whisk to brush the ants from Akhaïdes' face until he woke enough to crawl away a safe distance and lie facedown beside Orestes' stele, his fist full of loam and cedar crumbs.

A few boys came to sit around him, discuss him, and, finally, bring him drinks of water in folded leaves. Eventually, he could sit up, arms around his knees, face in the crook of his elbow. He would not talk to them, but they followed as he dragged himself—alternately walking and crawling—to the slaves' house, where he sank back into his corner.

Then the boys wandered off to catch beetles and race them, while Akhaïdes waited for Menetor to find and punish him.

That night, he crept out again. It took a very long time to crawl and stagger all the way down to the Serpent's pool at the river.

He had never come here before and had no idea what he would find. But there it lay in bright moonlight: a rough-edged well of black water where the earth's four folds met. Someone long ago had paved the sides, but the stones were neglected now, split and lifted and separated by mats of dried grass. He remembered a fortress and his dreams of it: a confusion of paving stones and weeds, and a presence he could not see. To crawl to the edge of the pool and look over, he first had to gather all his failing courage.

The sides were smooth and vertical and coated with slime. Once in, there would be no coming out. The water's surface was too low to touch, even lying flat and reaching down with the whole length of his arm. Below the night air, unmoved by any inward or outward flow, the water nevertheless reflected nothing: not the moon or any star, not the Serpent, not an Erinye or peryton or gryphon, not his own face. It lay black and silent with a chill rising off it, not inviting, not beckoning, not tempting, not repelling—simply waiting for him either to slide in or to go away.

He never remembered how this ended. At one moment, he lay reaching down to the silent surface; the next, he crouched once again in his corner of the slaves' house. If he could have wept at all, he would have wept then.

* * *

But inside him, something was beginning to open. Not like the door between him and Elawon, not like the wound that had torn open for Temenus, this unfolded outward from its own center like a pod, like a hatching insect, like a fist or a flower, but a flower made of stone or metal that would break if forced, and so must be allowed to open on its own. It strained in a harsh, cramped unfurling, every tremor plucking the net of his nerves and setting them screeching. He huddled in the corner, his left hand hiding his face; besieged by light, by breath, by the faintest scrape of sounds, by the clatter of dust falling through shafts of sunlight; empty even of dreams while this thing tore itself abloom within him.

When he finally could bring himself to rise, to move, to shuffle outside, it was raining. He lifted his face to the fall of blistering sparks without flinching or shielding himself. Instead, he pulled off his shirt and opened his arms to take more of it. In an instant, the flow doubled. It battered his face, coursed down his arms, sizzled through his hair, filled the well of his eye, and washed clean the wrappings of his hand and head. He lifted his arms to the posture that men took when they addressed the greatest powers—the pose of the votives he had disturbed—freely submitting.

Then the slowly unfurling thing inside him banged open. The substance of his body liquefied, and the rain poured through unimpeded. He did not exist, and that transcendent nonbeing lifted him to a surrender so pure that nepenthe was only a sorry hint of it and he would never have to breathe again.

The priests, watching from an open window, exchanged worried glances. Then they looked warily at Menetor, who stood and stared, as expressionless and immobile, as unapproachable and cold, as pitiless and unyielding, as the Good Kinsman and H'olgaichi Thief had ever been.

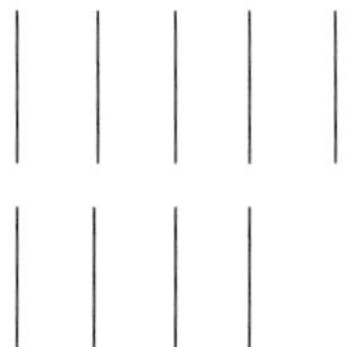

You might be looking for reasons but there are no reasons.[viii]
— *Nina La Cour*

For some, to carry one's crimes to Delphi was worth bragging about. Even now, with winter begun, sailing riskier, and Phocian banditry bolder, the guesthouses and camping places were populated with parties small and large, bringing offenders for absolution.

Most of those absolutions could be performed anywhere, by an ordinary shaman. To walk or ride or sail so far and give the gifts that Delphi demanded seemed excessive even to the priests themselves, but there were plenty who happily did so. For more complex errors, a bath in the spring called "Kastalia's" sufficed, even though the suppliants complained that the water clung and burned.

One or two men whose crimes required drinking the water fared less well. Taken into the stone's sanctuary for the rite, one of them lost his nerve and fled. The other strangled in the water's grip.

A high-ranking Attican, whose crime required that he face the Serpent itself, never returned from the high cave. *Eaten,* the slaves whispered. Dragged down into the lair, meat and bone for the cave's terrible guardians.

Still others, urgently seeking news and information, brought gifts for the oracles. Sometimes, the priestesses—never seen in the town or the sanctuary, but existent nonetheless—provided advice and foretellings that only they, in their intimate contact with the underworld, the dead, the nymph, and the Serpent, might know. Other times, the seeker entered one of the underworld portals—a cave, a well, others less known—to meet directly with a power or an Erinye. It was the priests' responsibility to choose.

The slaves did not know how absolutions were performed. They knew only what they saw: crouching and whining and ringing the bell; nervous bragging; locked rooms in the guesthouse, with food slid in through slots in the doors; priest-escorted processions to the spring; to the cave, to the stone; a door firmly closed and terrible noises within.

The young boys at Delphi numbered fewer than a score these days, even including the smallest of them and those on the brink of manhood. Unwanted boys did not come to Delphi in the numbers they once had. In earlier generations, they themselves said, all fatherless infant boys came here. But now their numbers were fewer—a good thing, perhaps, since so few were used for sacrifice and there were already enough slaves. Male slaves were still rare outside Delphi—unwanted because of their supposed fractiousness when they grew up. That was fair and sensible enough, but people now seemed to ignore the rules that governed the disposal of unwanted male infants. Instead of sending them to Delphi where they belonged, most simply left them to die of neglect or accident, or helped them along with plain old infanticide.

During this season—and, said the boys, many seasons before—no one required the kind of sacrificial extravagance that would use one of them whole. Many boys in recent years had lived from infancy to adulthood awaiting the call. Once they reached the age when their voices changed and their facial and pubic hair grew—the age after which they would never be chosen—they could leave their fellows to take up other work, become priests, or even marry if they could find unwanted, willing women.

Most of the priests and many of the ordinary workers of Delphi were of this kind: safely grown. Even as adults, they still yearned for the glory of feeding the forces of order: fate, chance, the Serpent, Kastalia. Sometimes, in the shed where the young ones slept, restlessness would keep them awake at night, and their talk would turn to how courageously they would walk to the stone and accept the embrace of immortality. They would finally fall silent and sleep, unaware of how closely this talk resembled that of other boys in the world, also obsessed with ideals of courage and fame, and without a single thought— except offhand scorn—for longevity.

* * *

Menetor found Akhaïdes in a barn, wrapped in a tattered shawl against the cold, a small goat upended in his lap, doing something with a knife to one of its hooves. Watching from the low doorway, Menetor saw the taut line of Akhaïdes' back, the authority with which he held the calmly blinking animal, the slow, deliberate grace of his hands.

Despite the abuse the long fingers had taken here, they worked smoothly, almost hypnotically. *Thieves' hands,* Menetor thought. The right, crippled for so long and still wrapped across the palm, now looked clumsy only by comparison with the left.

Akhaïdes paused in his work and said something quietly. Menetor saw a black-haired, ragged boy, one of Kastalia's children, squatting on the other side of the goat, skinny arms around his knees. The boy asked a question. Akhaïdes answered, showing something on one palm. The boy studied it, then twitched his head, showing that he understood.

Menetor held himself in check until Akhaïdes finished and set the goat on its feet. The animal jerked awake in one enormous leap and dodged out past Menetor's knees, bleating furiously. Akhaïdes looked after it and saw Menetor. He quickly lowered his eye. The black-haired boy looked up sharply.

"What are you doing?"

"Trimming goats' hooves, Master."

"I didn't tell you to do that."

"I'm sorry."

Menetor shifted his stare to the boy. The boy returned it stalwartly. Menetor twitched his head toward the door. The boy sank down rebelliously on his narrow shanks. Menetor sharpened his stare. The boy glanced at Akhaïdes, but Akhaïdes did not look at him. The boy got up and stalked out, giving Menetor a mutinous glare as he passed.

Menetor squatted with some effort, tucking his skirts between his knees, and took Akhaïdes' right hand. The swelling was gone, the skin pale with cold and dirty but otherwise healthy, the bones disfigured but firmly knitted. He reached to untie the tattered fillet, then touched the outer rim of the socket.

"It healed," he said.

He cupped his hand over the deep, chaste, tangled scar—not touching it, only hiding it. "It healed," he said again. "There's no canker, no fever. It healed clean. Why did it heal? The rain?"

"It wasn't rain."

Menetor twitched his head up. Something else. He had to say something; he could not let his own wonder stand so exposed. He took his hands away.

"What was it that drove you back here?"

"Hubris." His voice trembled. "Ignorance. Arrogance."

"What is it that you won't say?"

Akhaïdes moved his head negative.

"Tell me."

"I can't say it. I can't say that word."

He closed his eye and shivered. For that moment, he looked so forbidding and at the same time so fragile that Menetor felt his spirit yearning against his own harshness.

Menetor got up and left the barn. In the bright yard, he pressed the heels of his hands to his eyes until he saw bursts of light. Then he slid his hands down his face. The dark-haired boy stood under a tree, waiting coolly for him to go away.

Menetor said to the boy, "I know what the word is that he won't say."

The boy glared, not understanding.

He flung his hands down. "Remember this, child: there are three ways to break any outlaw."

The boy stood straighter, listening.

"This way worked for Tydeus and Orestes, so how was I to know?"

The boy tilted his head, now fully attentive.

Menetor made his habitual puff at the irony of it all, and again at the boy's alarm. After a lifetime of outmaneuvering Pelopeids, he was trapped at last by the least likely Pelopeid of all.

* * *

Just after the first snow, the army of the Tribes passed through Delphi. They stayed two nights while their leaders visited the sanctuary, added a score of figures to the votive population, gave plain but plentiful gifts to the priests, and built an extravagant stone altar down by the river to offer gifts to War. They marched away toward Arne on a bleak, windy morning that made more snow before noon.

Akhaïdes spent those two days up the mountain, weaving straw hives under the critical eye of the master beekeeper. The beekeeper had burned his hands when a disorderly dream made him mistake his own firepot for a bowl of mead. So Akhaïdes' help was plausible if not essential.

When he returned to Delphi, the children were still

chattering excitedly about the army. *Hundreds* they said. Dorians, Aetolians, Akarnanians, Dyropians, Thessalians, and more. Spears and shields and swords. Greaves and gauntlets. No chariots to be banged to pieces on these roads, and the Herakleid who managed the chariot troop, they said, had flatly refused to waste his drivers on ordinary combat. Even the Herakleid king walked.

Yes, Temenus Herakleides had walked quietly into Delphi. For the first time anyone could remember, he did not visit the prostitutes, trying to charm them out of their services at a price he could afford. Instead, he stayed with his younger brother, slept in his own tent as chastely as any virgin girl, and spoke only with Menetor. His brother bargained hard for the votives the king wanted, watched the king with atypical warmth and worry, and never left his side.

Besides the Herakleids came also the one-handed Dorian king and the Dorian lawagetas with the patchwork scalp, who secretly asked the boys about Akhaïdes but did not press when they refused to answer.

They were traveling to meet the mass of the Dorian army and to take Arne. None of the boys had seen Boeotia, but the slaves' descriptions of it thrilled them: a vast double plain walled by cliffs and hills; Thebes's ruins, transfixed in time like a sculpture in carbon and stone; Copais's complex waterworks; Arne's black vertical walls with gates like jaws; Orchomenos with its crumbled gatehouses and its mad king tended by Amazons. Oh, it would be a war worth witnessing.

Akhaïdes listened patiently, and volunteered nothing.

* * *

The priest was not old, and no one suspected that he might be ill. But he didn't come to breakfast one morning, and they found him in a twisted knot on his bed, lightning-struck, clutching his blanket with claws that could not be pried open, one eye staring and the other locked shut. His pillow was soaked with saliva, and his sheets with urine.

The slaves had other work to do, as did the dwarf cook who also served as Delphi's physician. He declared the priest incurable. They all fretted about the time his care would take from other duties. All were happy to leave him to Akhaïdes.

As in Nafpaktos, not even a slave could touch feces without undergoing purification afterward. But an outlaw could, and the priest's body produced an impressive volume of diarrhea—semisolid at first, then sandy black water—before it was finally empty. Washing his arms in the ice-rimmed slaughter basin, Akhaïdes found himself thinking of Elawon, dead on the beach, covered with sand, and stinking of all the waste a body could hold.

Elawon had hated to be dirty, hated to smell, hated anything untidy. His eternal anxiety— to fit, to fix, to belong—had been both a shield and a burden he could never cast off. His acquisition of the goods and daughters of the unfortunate had carried that air. Even his seeming carelessness with his clothes and shoes had been the same: he had never been careless with them until Deione was there to pick them up and put them away—a test, perhaps, of whether his worries were valid and could be acknowledged.

Akhaïdes wondered whether his brother had been purified before he was burned. The Shaman had secured the house and furniture, and Deione had been careful. Both he and Elawon had compulsively minded the rules, but they were together so much at the end, he could not believe that Elawon had died unpolluted.

Then Akhaïdes stood blank, up to his wrists in cold dirty water, trying to grasp what had just happened. It was not possible, but it was so: he had thought of Elawon without the grinding shame he was accustomed to, so potent it was physical agony.

He lifted his hands. Water trickled down his forearms—thin icy rills inside his sleeves. He saw, clearly and coolly, Elawon's corpse and how many others: a sack of heads, a dead pony, Xanos frightened, Temenus fearless, and then, in a rush, Solong, Juchii, his daughters, his brothers-in-law, the children, the Shangs and Chous whose scalps had swung from his bridle, his Arcadian brothers, the butchered boy Depas. All of them he saw, and yet, he stood here, still whole and was not blinded or crippled or consumed.

What was this terrible gift? He did not deserve it, had done nothing to win it, dreaded welcoming it, did not want it. Perhaps he was finally losing his mind.

* * *

The priest's funeral was quiet but festive, attended by all the priests and village men. They got a haunch of pig and a string of onions out of storage and roasted them, then drank two jars of Attican mead while the men told every story they could remember about the departed priest. Since he had come to Delphi as one of Kastalia's children fifty years ago, there were a lot of stories to tell, and the party lasted until after dawn, by which time the slaves had dug the weeds and rocks out of the dromos of the common tomb, and the body—washed, tied in a folded position, and wrapped in a linen shroud—could be put away.

Priests carried the corpse on an eight-armed wicker bier, moving slowly over the ground, partly because of the thin rime of snow, partly because of the night's drinking. Akhaïdes knew how light the body was by now, like a bundle of dry branches. He had handled it before the priest died and was purified. Now, of course, he could never touch it again.

At the entrance to the dromos, the priests stopped and set

the bier on the ground. The passage was too steep and narrow for the parade to enter, and Menetor waved at two of the stronger and soberer slaves to carry the body down. Then he lifted his palm to Akhaïdes, allowing him to follow.

Akhaïdes and the slaves knelt to pull off their boots. Menetor was already barefoot. Then the slaves lifted the corpse in their arms, sharing it between them. The circle of priests opened to let them pass. Akhaïdes followed Menetor and the slaves down the ancient passage. After a few steps, the dromos turned slimy underfoot, and he clung to the worked stones with the soles of his bare feet, curling his toes over the edges.

As they moved downward, the light reflected more sharply from the rough, damp walls, but nothing was truly visible. To see the way more clearly, Akhaïdes closed his eye. He felt over the raised sill with his foot, then stepped into the chamber.

The floor was sandy and cold. There was no smell of death here, only the honest odors of damp stone, roots, verdigris and rust, and one faint, pure scent he could not name. He stepped to one side to avoid blocking the light, and looked around. Everywhere lay other parceled bones, brittle cloth, and powdery wooden coffins so old that a fingertip might pierce them.

Menetor and the slaves went to the center of the space, where an earthenware burial box stood on four stumpy feet. On each corner of the lid, a little Erinye perched, head bowed and bladelike wings raised. The slaves lifted the lid off and set it aside. As they did this, Akhaïdes could have sworn that he saw the wings quiver for a moment, and heard them buzz in warning.

Then Menetor reached into the box and lifted out a skull. It was white and clean, with only a soft mat of brown hair clinging to the back, and even that gave way under a single stroke of Menetor's hand.

"A good departure," Menetor said aloud. The circular stone walls softened his voice, but those waiting outside must have heard, for their contented murmurs drifted down the passage.

Menetor carried the skull to one side, where Akhaïdes saw wooden shelves holding row after row of skulls. Menetor placed this one carefully among its fellows, then returned to the box to gather the rest of the bones.

While he did that, Akhaïdes crossed to the shelves and stood and looked. The skulls all looked back quietly. They had nothing to say, no complaints to make. They were not even waiting, really, but simply being there. Here, the clean smell was stronger, and he realized that it was indeed the smell of death, but a different kind of death from the one he knew. There was no violence. No mutilation, humiliation, terror. No sinking through the earth to live in dark and tedious squalor, more bound in death than even in life; no being dragged up into the sky to soar and shriek and hunt living prey, desperate to murder and steal the victim's resting place.

This was the quiet death that flowers knew, and sliced fruits, fallen trees, eggs when broken, and tools and clothing honorably depleted. It was the death of animals when they kicked clear of their bodies and ran free. It must also be the death of men when they stepped out of life peacefully, without fear. He had so rarely seen this kind of death, he was surprised to recognize it at all. H'oolee Horn had died contented in his daughter's arms. Akhaïdes could think of no one else.

160

Traffic to Delphi continued. Here, peace held, even as the Tribes swept through Boeotia, burned Orchomenos, besieged Arne.

The camping grounds were still sprinkled with tents, and visiting oxen grazed the meadows above and below. Gift animals arrived and were marked and put among the herds. For all the cook's grumbling and predictions of a hard, hungry winter, people came steadily, bringing ever more gifts. Sufferers came seeking relief from pernicious ailments: lung rot, infection, gangrene, leprosy, atrophy. A young woman was carried in, her body locked in an unopenable knot from fear of her marriage bed; and an ancient man, borne on a curtained litter and tenderly guarded by elderly sons, his only problems extreme old age and heirs not yet named. A short, stout man came, pouting and puffing and glaring, unable to father a child; and men in pairs, to swear bonds; and oracle seekers, barefoot and furtive and clattering with gold. And sometimes, the sanctuary bell would sound, and the slaves would run to see an outlaw beg for purification.

The one-armed slave who had minded the sanctuary door for so long now had other duties. So it was Akhaïdes who guarded visitors' shoes, sheltering them from rain and brushing ants away with a leafy branch while the owners made their pleas and presented their proofs and gifts.

Akhaïdes' presence served as a lesson for any who thought to bargain. Nearly everyone knew who he was. For the few who did not, the priests would explain. Akhaïdes heard again and again that he had no place, no family, no friend, no patron, no wealth, and no hope of absolution. The priests could do as they pleased with him, the Serpent would not talk to him, the nymph would only eat him, and he had nowhere in all the world to go except to join his kind by the roadside or else step, on his own, into the Serpent's pool.

One by one, the suppliants came.

"Hear me, Grandfather."

"Did you leave all lies, all guile, all deceit, on the threshold stone?"

"I did."

"What is your plea?"

"I ask for relief from my faults."

"What is your fault?"

Now would follow a recitation of errors and complaints and excuses.

"Truth is here, and Oath. But so are Untruth and False Swearing. What have you brought for them?" A rustling and rattling as gifts were turned out for inspection: gold for Truth and Oath, stones and dry sticks for the deceptors, and last, a gift for the priestesses, to feed Revenge and Retribution.

"These are your own things. No kinsmen have provided any help to you."

Denials, more excuses, lists of supporters. The discussion and criticism sometimes went on for painful hours while the priests dissected the suppliant's story. If, in the end, it was believed and the support was adequate, a priest would say the magical formula: "You are fortunate to have such friends. We will consult together and tell you the day and time, and what to do."

Then the final statement: "You will stay in the guesthouse. A place has always been ready for you."

It was true. Rooms were always ready with fresh bedding, water, new bread every morning. The suppliants moved in and disappeared until whatever rite was over. Relatives and patrons waited patiently to receive men restored to manhood. Akhaïdes watched them come from even the farthest islands: from Asopus, even the Propontus. And he cleaned their chamber pots and floors.

The Tribes took Arne and Orchomenos in a bloody storm. No dainty Athenian dike-strolling for them, no civilized ransom-holding or tiptoeing through planted fields. They wanted murder, and they made it, and marched home still smeared with it. Passing by Delphi, Temenus Herakleides gave six hides of gold and the blood of twenty men to War. When he visited the sanctuary, though, another slave guarded his shoes. Akhaïdes was sent to spend those days with the larder keeper, replastering the floor of his storage cave while the keeper, himself fat as a cheese, told bad jokes, farted, and licked butter from a spoon.

The Herakleids still numbered in the scores, the children reported. And with them came a hundred, maybe two hundred, non-Dorian allies who had fought for Temenus, all parading back to Nafpaktos in triumph. They brought slaves too, of course—all Cadmean or Perioikoi women and girls, no Boeotians. The Boeotians had gone over almost before Arne closed its gates against the Tribes. Temenus donated a crowd of salvaged boy children to the priests. The bigger boys of Delphi curled their lips. *Babies,* they said. Just babies, and who would watch them? It would have been easier to kill them, too. Besides, everyone knew that even the smallest baby boys taken this way would later grow up to avenge their fathers. Keeping them alive was like breeding asps and adders under one's doorstep. Akhaïdes heard them voice these complaints without a trace of irony, as if totally unaware of their own origins.

The Tribes had protected the mad king of Orchomenos in spite of himself—he had wanted to die fighting—and left him here as well. The priests would care for him.

The vast Boeotian cattle herds stayed where they were born, with Dorians now to worry over the pastures and the waterworks. The Boeotian horses, however, had crossed to Euboia Island long before the Tribes arrived, and their caretakers had burned the bridge behind them. And so the Herakleid king still walked. Some slaves, some treasure, no horses, fewer fighting men. So many Herakleids gone to their dead, and little to show for it but unadorned victory.

Temenus met in private with the priests. What he asked of them and what they answered, none said. Even the children noticed how haunted he looked despite his triumph, his flawless dignity and his elegant new clothes. He seemed as sick and distraught as one who has received news of unavengeable murder. His brother walked in his shadow, stood at his elbow, followed him everywhere, his forehead creased with worry.

* * *

Akhaïdes spent these days with the larder keeper. At night, safe in darkness, he returned to the slaves' house to sleep in his customary place.

And he was sleeping the night before the Tribes would leave, when the door quietly opened. He woke to see the overseer rise in protest, expecting, perhaps, some lost Dorian seeking a prostitute. Then the man retreated silently, his hands lifted in alarm.

It was Temenus Herakleides, the conqueror of Arne, beautifully groomed and dressed. He stood erect, calm, and contained as if triumphant kings routinely visited slaves and outlaws in the middle of the night. He stepped inside the low room as if he owned it. The overseer retreated farther, then returned to his own bed. No one else dared to stir.

By the faint shadow-light from the open door, Temenus found where Akhaïdes lay. He came silently to sit on the edge of the low, narrow pallet, arms on his raised knees, face in the crook of his elbow.

He whispered, "You were right. Arne was . . ." He shuddered, and for a moment, Akhaïdes thought he might vomit, or weep. But he breathed deeply, calming himself. "I did nothing. It was all Xanos, Dymas, Kresphontes. I hid in a tent while they did the work. But when it was over, I had to walk through it. Across the fields, through the . . ." He swallowed. "Through the citadel itself. All the Tribes—the Dorians, so many traitorous Boeotians—they lined up and I walked through them and they cheered for me.

"They had piled bodies here and there—stripped them and just piled them up like hay or firewood. It's the Dorian way."

Akhaïdes could not see his face, but the small sound told him that Temenus had tightened his lips and touched them with his tongue. "Some places, I was *ankle deep* in blood. Clear over my shoes. Kresphontes had to lead me along, blood slopping in his shoes, too, and everyone shouting, and the piles of naked bodies. I never knew there were so many Cadmeans."

"Maybe they weren't all Cadmean."

"The Boeotians killed so many for us, you're probably right. They probably used me to settle old quarrels."

"With the quarrels settled, maybe they'll be more docile."

"I hope so. But it's the Dorians' problem, anyway, not mine. All of that—so many of my cousins gone to their dead, so much blood—and not my problem." His voice trembled at the end, and he cleared his throat.

"The Regent?"

"Fled. He knew his life was worthless, even if he won. He left his friends and family to die and ran for Mycenae. I wonder what I would have done."

"You would have stayed."

"I don't—"

"You would have stayed."

"Thank you for that."

Then Temenus sat silent, not moving.

Finally Akhaïdes prompted gently, "And now?"

"I'll never be clean."

"It was war. And as you said, you yourself didn't take part."

Temenus moved his head negative, his hair as dark and dull as soot in the dim lamplight. "Not from that. From something else, long ago. A dream I have sometimes, but this time I saw it even in the daylight, even awake. While I looked—I had to look—while I looked on the murder of Arne. There was the blood, the bodies, as real as anything, but what I saw over it all was . . ."

Akhaïdes waited.

Temenus drew a deep breath. "It's a dream. It's not the blood that makes it so terrible; it's the *mood* of it. I can't describe it, not even to you." He swallowed. "It's that, that always kept me from striking out in anger. Remember how hard you had to work to make me hit you with the whip? It's that dream, that vision, that makes me sick over blood. And there it was, like a picture over a picture. It had such power, I couldn't even see the faces of the men and boys dead in Arne. And I thought, what sort of monster am I, that in the middle of all this horror I have wreaked on others, all I can see is something about myself?"

He breathed quietly for a moment. "I come here often and beg for absolution. They always say that I'm not unclean, but I am. I must be."

"Tell me."

Temenus still looked away. "I see a cage of bloody ribs pointing upward. I see my own hands—a child's, but I know they're mine—cupped full of blood. Sometimes, they hold a human heart, still beating." He paused, and again Akhaïdes knew that he tightened his lips and touched them with his tongue. "I see eyes like yours—without color. And the feeling is heavy, like drowning. A feeling that there's nothing I can do, nothing anyone can do. It's too late and has always been too late. It's so final, so absolute, I can't breathe."

"It's my fault."

Temenus turned to gaze at him.

"His name was Depas. He was your friend. They sacrificed him for my father's sake. Because of what I had done. You were three, maybe four years old. You saw it. The sacrifice."

"I don't remember."

"Yes, you do."

They were silent together.

Without sitting up, Akhaïdes laid a hand on Temenus's head. The texture of his hair was so familiar.

For a moment, Temenus did not move. Then he turned and lay down under Akhaïdes' arm. Akhaïdes lifted the blankets to cover both of them. Temenus's hands, always warm before, felt cold as death.

Akhaïdes could smell the blood and smoke of Arne, and Temenus's shaken horror. He held Temenus's head against his heart, just as Temenus had sometimes held his, until Temenus's breathing slowed and his hands grew warm again.

Then he helped Temenus shed his clothing: the brocade shirt, leg wraps lined with fur, gold on every finger—all of it. They made love in a silence as pure and clear as the stillness after a bell's chiming. The slaves in the room never moved or murmured. Akhaïdes thought Temenus might weep at the climax, but he just breathed out in such cleansing relief that Akhaïdes' heart stirred with pity.

Temenus did not withdraw, but fell asleep as he was, still embraced and coupled, as if he could not bear any separation, as if he had not slept for many, many nights.

They had never slept together. That was the luxury of respectable lovers, not the likes of them, and their bond had never included ordinary comforts. But Temenus fell asleep as cleanly and simply as if the body, arms, and heartbeat of the lowest creature in Delphi could be the only sure haven for a puissant and victorious king.

Akhaïdes did not sleep, but all through the night, strange visions rolled past, one after another, after another. The theme was always consolation—vast, formless, absolute.

In the morning, long before dawn, he helped Temenus dress, as Temenus had so often helped him. He kissed Temenus's forehead. Temenus kissed Akhaïdes' mouth and both his hands and left him there, without another word between them.

By sunrise, the Tribes were gone.

* * *

Almost at once, Nafpaktos began to produce trouble. The stories marched like a covert army up the road. A storehouse burned, and again famine loomed—midwinter famine, the deadliest of all. Plague came, out of season and all the more lethal for it. The Herakleids' priest died of it, as did all Akhaïdes' onetime neighbors in the hovels along the beach. Desperate enough to eat vetch, Nafpaktos watched the stiff-leg disease take its children. There was endless fighting among too many warriors, already blooded and hungry for more, but who had won only paltry booty and could not turn their battle skills against the troubles that beset them now. For all their triumphs, they could not stop the march of their women and children and parents to join their dead. An Akarnanian, two Akarnanians, then three, who had not acquired slaves at Arne, were caught in adultery with other men's wives. Delphi saw friend-murders and cousin-murders. It saw a young Aetolian, sullen and glaring, who had raped and then strangled his own sister.

Even for him, there was no first-degree outlawry, for she was only a girl and younger than he. He had sisters enough that his father was no doubt furtively glad to be relieved of the burden of her dowry. The murderer's grandfather brought him to Delphi, with huge absolution gifts. The priests contented themselves with twenty whiplashes, which reduced the boy to a wailing, quivering shadow. They poured Kastalia's water over him while he writhed and wept.

Then they released him to a year's warm exile in his grandfather's house, while Akhaïdes sat among the shoes, stared at and murmured over. Menetor had said it: the old language had no word for "accident" and no word for "once," and solitude was the greatest offense of all.

As the boy staggered off, leaning dramatically on his grandfather's arm, Akhaïdes herded an ant gently off a worn ribboned slipper, then let the whisk dangle. Only when Menetor touched him did he come back to himself and raise his head reluctantly to meet the old man's eyes.

Menetor did not remove his hand. "What are you thinking about?"

He looked away, unwilling to speak.

Menetor pondered him a moment longer, then patted his shoulder and went on his way.

It was hours later, while Akhaïdes was chipping ice from the goats' water basin, that he realized Menetor had come to him on his blind side and touched him without warning—worse, had touched him kindly. But he had responded peacefully to something that, only two months before, would have provoked either flight or instant, unthinking violence. There was no accounting for this. He could not imagine what sort of creature he was becoming.

A goat nudged his elbow. He smiled at it, cracked an edge of ice, lifted the bucket, and spilled water into the trough.

* * *

A few days later, Menetor found Akhaïdes, again in a barn, digging a drain channel around the inside of the walls while three boys made impudent remarks and carried away the dirt in little baskets. Akhaïdes straightened as Menetor came in, and the boys mumbled excuses and scattered. Menetor took the mattock from Akhaïdes' hands and leaned it against the wall.

"I'm walking my rounds now," he said. "Come with me."

Akhaïdes followed him out. Once in the open, Menetor made him walk beside him, and they strolled around the village together in the thin, cold sunlight. They stopped at a storehouse, which Menetor opened to return Akhaïdes' wolfskin coat to him. It was wrinkled and musty. Akhaïdes asked no question, just shook it out and threw it over his shoulders. Menetor wore, over his usual red robe, a long, sleeveless vest of sheepskin with the fur turned inward.

A few boys, suspicious of Menetor's sudden and unlikely kindness toward their friend, trailed behind them while Akhaïdes followed Menetor up a thready path he had never noticed before. At the top, balanced on the rim of the high meadow and overlooking the shining windy vastness of crags beyond Delphi's vale, stood a stone hut and a huge heap of cut wood. As they approached, the hut banged and shuddered, and a stout man came panting out. After bending double through the low door, he straightened, eyeing them with hostility but not surprise.

"Menetor," he said severely. "Where's my kindling?"

"Coming." Menetor was composed. "I told you, Kepheus: new kindling once each month, no more."

Kepheus slammed the door, and the little building shook. "Hah. If it were up to you, I'd have two rocks to clap together when the time comes. All this trouble, and the thanks I get . . . Who's this?"

"Akhaïdes Outlaw."

Kepheus was mostly bald, with a flying gray fringe of hair

over his ears, ten or more long shirts tied one over another, and bent, hairy legs thrusting firmly out of the pile. He glared at Akhaïdes for a moment, then snorted and turned to the heap of wood.

He grumbled, "Not that it'll make any difference, any of it, if that fool on Crathis Mountain is asleep when the time comes. I wouldn't trust him to set fire to his own mother's barn."

Menetor drew Akhaïdes a few steps away.

"The problem is . . ." Kepheus strode to the pyre. He lifted one end of a long, crooked branch, studied it, then fitted it carefully between two heavier logs thick with dry moss. "The problem is always with the draft. In winter, if it's raining, the wind comes up from below, and I'll need the big wood over here."

He got his shoulder under a thick trunk and heaved it up. Akhaïdes started forward to help, but stopped when Menetor touched his arm. Kepheus ignored them both, chewed his lip for a moment, and said, "But when the weather's fine, the wind comes straight down off the mountain. And in midafternoon, it stops completely." He paused, deep in thought, the damp trunk still against his neck.

Akhaïdes glanced at Menetor. The priest was smiling, and he suddenly understood. "The beacon," he said. "The beacon chain. For when the High King goes to his dead."

Menetor touched his finger to his lips and led Akhaïdes away. When they had gone far enough to speak aloud, Akhaïdes said, "I remember, in Arcadia. There was a sanctuary on the mountain—I forget its name—with keepers and a watcher, and always a fire ready to light."

"Yes. They're everywhere, on all the peaks that can be seen the farthest. When the High King leaves us, everyone will know."

Akhaïdes looked back toward Kepheus's rattling and grumbling. "He takes his responsibility seriously, doesn't he?"

"Exceedingly."

As they descended the path, they could still hear the

watcher's impatient rearranging.

"Will he ever organize the pile to suit him?"

"He's been organizing it since he came up here. That's been—let me see—forty-two years."

Akhaïdes stopped and stared. *"Years?"*

Menetor turned, smiling. "Forty-two. And he's still not satisfied. He was here when you came the first time. And consider this, too: it's the same wood."

"The wood is forty-two years old?"

"He won't take any newer. He's always after fresh kindling, but he says modern logs aren't trustworthy. Here, watch your step. Put your foot—yes. Does your back hurt? When were you last beaten? I don't remember, but I suppose you do. We won't be doing it again, by the way."

"I don't mind."

"That's why. Come. Let's see what's for dinner. Tonight, you eat with the priests and guests."

"I don't—"

"Sitting meekly beside the door."

"As you say, Grandfather."

* * *

In Mycenae, Tisamenus stared straight into the eye of the sun. It was low now, dimmed by stringy clouds, apparently unconcerned with him although he had addressed it correctly. The diffuse light spread like his own scattered attention: wide and thin, with no real focus. He lowered his hands to his sides and sat down where he had been standing, on the wide parapet of his chamber's balcony. He hugged his knees.

People were moving behind him, talking quietly, deferring to his disregard of them though still not willing to go away. Their small noises intruded more and more until he finally gave in and turned his head. Instantly, they were all around him, crowding, jostling, murmuring for his attention.

All this sudden regard happened when Orestes was weakest. On the High King's good days, Tisamenus was just an unwelcome outsider, with even the slaves showing him only scant respect. On bad days, they all clung to him, grudging but dutiful, demanding his permission to do what, both he and they knew, they would do anyway, only more furtively, if he refused.

He picked out Baron Hawmai and listened to him, agreeing to whatever he said, and Hawmai went away satisfied. Tisamenus glanced over the rest of them. His friend Philaios was the only welcome face. Philaios smiled and raised a hand, signaling both his greeting and his willingness to wait until Tisamenus wanted him. The rest he could easily dismiss, and did. They backed away reluctantly, and some actually left, though most just lingered a little farther off. He turned away from them again, back to the low white sun crawling over Argos and the High King's demesne: the wide, deep plain where his father's aged chariot ponies grazed, untouched by anyone from year to year.

Something brushed his shoulder lightly. Aranare, the slave who had raised him, murmured, "Do you have a headache? Can I help?"

"Yes, thank you."

She stood behind him and pressed his temples. He closed his eyes. Feeling her cool breath on his ear, he said softly, "What news?"

"Limnea's labor stopped again, and the baby is still alive. If she keeps it, it may be born at half-solstice." Her fingers worked lightly in the hollows behind his eyes.

Tisamenus thought of Limnea, Penthilus's daughter, and her unborn child. More of them. Oh, always more. And this one could be the most difficult of all, because its father was his own blood brother, the baron Philaios, waiting patiently right now for Tisamenus to talk to him.

Philaios was his dear friend, his loyal friend, his *only* friend. The friend he could relax with, talk with, laugh with, dice with, drink with, sleep with, who meant him no harm, no hardness, no deceit, no ill will, and who held, he claimed, no ambition beyond serving Tisamenus all his life. But Orestes had refused Philaios's father an exchange for his useless land, which had never been fertile and was now depopulated by famine. So when his father died, Philaios had married Penthilus's daughter. Philaios had never told Tisamenus the details of the marriage bargain. And Philaios had never told Tisamenus his wife was pregnant. Philaios had never told him, and would not tell him now, the trouble his wife was having to keep this child. Only Aranare would tell him these things.

If Philaios's child was born at half-solstice, Tisamenus would be glad. He would give the baby wonderful gifts. He would serve with pride as its luck parent. He would laugh someday that this birth had once been one of the many things that haunted him sleepless.

In Mycenae, many things haunted him sleepless. The loss of Orchomenos and Arne was one of them.

The Regent had gone to his dead just this morning after reeling south with a mere score of other survivors. All the man's swagger had left him. He had sprawled at Orestes' bedside while the High King drooled and stared and Hawmai fired questions whose answers anyone could have given him.

The Megarans, the guardians of the wall, had let the Regent pass for amusement's sake since he had nothing to give them. What he did have was an arrow through both jaws, which made his speech devilish hard to understand. It could not be withdrawn, the Egyptian doctor had said, except to kill him faster. But the Regent got out the gist of his story before his tongue swelled enough to stifle him to death.

The tale was simple enough and had been told a thousand times before this time: siege and treachery. A sally port eased open in the darkest hour of the night. The soft rattle of armor on stairs. Tisamenus could have told it as well himself, though he had never been to war in his life.

The only worthwhile news was that the horses had not been taken. Those superb animals, bred there since before the Cadmeans and even before the Boeotians, guarded like gold for all these generations, had moved to Euboia Island while the Tribes' army was still only a shadow on the horizon. Although Temenus and the Dorians had taken cattle by the hundreds, the richest prize eluded them. The Regent had ordered this, and the Perioikoi herders had been pleased to comply. They had hurried their families and the horses over, burned the bridge behind them, and now sat smiling, free at last of all domination, protected, probably forever, by the ripping treachery of a current narrow enough to throw a spear across, but impossible to traverse.

Why had the Regent thought to move them to the island instead of taking them, as usual, inside Arne's walls? A dream, the Regent's slave said. A dream came to him and told him to do that. A dream of anyone they knew? Yes, someone the Regent had once held, and lost. Who? The slave looked away. Then the Regent died, and Hawmai turned from his questioning to stare at Tisamenus with curt speculation, as if all the treachery of this generation lay in the quiet heart of the High King's son.

Aranare worked unhurriedly, and Tisamenus felt his nagging headache flow out through her fingers.

"Not many lice," she murmured. "The cold weather."

"Who's still here?"

"Only Philaios."

"Then tell me what else I need to know."

Her fingers paused, then dug deeper. "Your great-uncle in Lacedaemon is ill again. They won't tell you."

"Is he dying?"

"No."

"I want to see him."

"You will call him here?"

"I'd rather go there, but I suppose I shouldn't leave Mycenae."

"That's why they won't tell you. If you go to Lacedaemon, they can't watch you so closely."

"They're right," he said. "I want to go home."

Eyes still shut, he let his head pull back with each circuit of her hands, enjoying the luxury of this unguarded pleasure.

"What more, Aranare?"

She made her voice still softer. "There is one who sat like a slave at your feet but was no slave. Then he lived in Nafpaktos but was no slave of the Herakleids, either."

Tisamenus's eyes opened themselves. He made himself wait two long breaths before he said, "So?"

"You might want to know this. He left the Herakleids."

"When?"

"At the equinox."

"Where is he now? Is he alive still?"

"No one knows."

"I know."

Aranare laid cool fingers on his shoulder, and he realized he had spoken too loudly. He lowered his head, acknowledging the warning. But at the same time, he inhaled hard, sucking damp, cold air down into his chest, feeling his heart swell. He knew this sensation, although he knew it only rarely. It was hope, the frail and terrible child of fear and chance.

He had maltreated Akhaïdes and allowed Oxylus to assault him. He had sent him away when he had nowhere to go, and had forced him to the Herakleids, who had tormented him even more callously. Akhaïdes must hate him. He would never come back.

There was a light rustle of movement behind him. Aranare's hand lifted away, and another replaced it. He recognized it at once.

"You worry too much, little brother," Philaios murmured. Now his warm fingers kneaded Tisamenus's shoulders, working the tightness out.

"I don't know what to do," Tisamenus replied.

"It's hard for you. I wish there were more I could do to help. I could be your lawagetas. I would love to serve you so well."

Philaios as lawagetas, in place of Hawmai. Just the idea made Tisamenus's heart jump. What a comfort that would be, to have at his side a man he could trust utterly, instead of one whose every move was thrice calculated.

"If I can do that later, when I am High King, I will."

Philaios moved his hands down Tisamenus's arms and drew him gently back until he leaned against his chest. Safe in his friend's embrace, Tisamenus let himself relax completely.

* * *

Akhaïdes found that Tisamenus, of all people, was much in his mind—more so as winter deepened and there was less work to do. He saw him at Arne, the only light in a cold, dank cell; slouched like a boy in an armed chair and wearing a wrinkled shirt; at Delphi, standing steadfast at Akhaïdes' shoulder while Menetor spoke of blood; leaning over a grim circle of Mycenaean faces and saying, "I know you"; watching, clear-eyed, unblinking, compassionate, as Akhaïdes wept; standing tall and still in torchlight, telling Akhaïdes to go away.

He felt Tisamenus's presence powerfully, as if, by turning quickly enough, he might see him. He felt that near. It was like the instinctive awareness that could link two people who wanted each other—so potent, there could be no question that the other person felt it, too. It was like the bond he knew with Makhawis, with Temenus, who had also told him, "I know you." But there was nothing dark in this tie with Tisamenus. It was as clear as water. It was a connection that, entirely of itself, wove a web between them that did not need their consent or even their awareness in order to grow.

Where it came from, he did not know: something he could not fathom, meant only for the two of them. The decision he had made to sit with the dog by Tisamenus's feet may have been the beginning. The end must be a rapprochement he could not yet imagine. With everything else now, he felt it, looked at it, and let it be.

* * *

He took over the daily task of carrying Kepheus's food up the mountain. Sometimes, the black-haired boy went with him partway, though he always stopped well out of sight of the watcher's domain. Kepheus still glowered, intent and grim, over his heap of timber, his little hut creaking in the wind, his coal box nestled between stones. The skin of his bald head, with its busy gray wings, was as thick and scaly as a turtle's. If he noticed the cold, he never said. He just slapped the snow off his arms, added a few more shirts to the layers already there, and yanked his rope belt tighter.

Akhaïdes' depthless sight made the steep path more treacherous. His knees rasped and groaned with the stress and ached all night afterward. But he enjoyed sitting wrapped in his wolfskin coat on a rock worn smooth by Kepheus's own backside, while the old man rearranged the ancient pyre and made dark pronouncements of the consequences should it fail to light.

Once, Akhaïdes said, "You might find someone else to watch for a while. I'll do it for you. Why not go down for a hot meal? Sleep in a warm room?"

The Watcher turned, exaggerated horror on his face. "Please," he said severely. "Please. I have my duty." He lifted another log into place. "And if that stubborn hulk thinks he's going sneak off to his dead without my knowing it after I sat up here through forty-two winters, he's as wrongheaded as he was in Clytemnestra's Year."

Akhaïdes bowed to him and turned to face the vast spread of bright air and mountains that was the watcher's hearth and garden. Then he carried the basket down the mountain.

If that is not enough, what is enough? [x]
—Vincent van Gogh

Nafpaktos smelled worse than ever. The stink was not only the usual sewage, sea, and rot, but also stale smoke and death. Even in Temenus's hall, the stench was so strong that many of the Herakleids wore the ends of their cloaks wound over their mouths.

They had returned from Arne in triumph, but troubles had reared up around them like wolves around a sleeper in the woods. Temenus had seemed puzzled at first, then hesitant, and then stunned into immobility. Now no one could talk to him; no one could get a decision from him. He ignored his brothers, his wife, his cousins. He even seemed to ignore the ruin of his city, which could neither feed nor clean itself with his distant victory and so had sickened and starved. With Aristodemus ill, it was left to Kresphontes and his cousins to keep what order they could. Indeed, it was Kresphontes, not Temenus, who had sent to Delphi for a new priest.

And tonight that priest, Karnus, stood in the center of the room, with all the Herakleids in attendance. A thin thread of smoke curled, low and surly, around his ankles from the only fire that burned there, on the hearth. It wasn't a real fire, just dried seaweed and grass. A few lamps smoked and stank as well, the oil so rancid it hardly burned.

From his high seat, Temenus said, "You are most sincerely welcome, Grandfather. As you can see, things aren't good for us here. I hope that your coming will mark the beginning of better times."

Karnus pursed his small mouth and brushed his dimpled hands together. He said, "That's a hope for you to hold on to."

He turned, surveying the room slowly: all Herakleids, every one of them with black hair and canted eyes, and, far enough outside a doorway that he couldn't send her away, a woman with a wine jar in her arms, who looked like them. The three tallest chairs held Temenus himself, a younger man, and an older one who was pale and drawn and gray. The only non-Herakleids were Dymas, the Dorian king, and Xanos, the lawagetas.

Karnus said, "I was thinking I should talk to all of you. I thought there was something important to tell you."

Temenus's elbows were on the lion's paws, his hands clasped together between them. He said, "Please go ahead."

Karnus still brushed his hands together, dismissively now. "I was mistaken, grandson. There is no point in talking here."

"Why not?" In the light of the dim lamp, Temenus's face was shadowed.

"You see the road before you, but it does not lead where you want to go."

"Then I'll travel another."

"You may travel any road you like. You may carry with you any tools you fancy. They will not help you."

Temenus sat still.

Finally, Kresphontes had to ask, "What tools do you mean?"

"He discarded the only tool he had that could get him what he wants."

Only Temenus's mouth moved. "All I want in the world is to be High King."

"Time flows only forward, grandson."

"I haven't made any errors so big as to close the door to my own future." Temenus unclasped his hands and interlaced his fingers with the lion's claws. "I will be High King."

"You will be many things, for sure. But High King you might not be."

Temenus half-closed his eyes. "What can I do?"

"Use the tools that come to hand, and hope for luck."

"What tool is left to me?"

"Only Orestes' son."

The megaron fell into baffled silence.

"Tisamenus?" Temenus blinked. "How would he help me?"

Dymas answered, "By being himself: young, scared, indecisive, still a child."

Kresphontes added, "Maybe he'll go to his dead before he goes to Rhion. Hasn't that other Oresteid promised? What's his name?"

"Penthilus," Aristodemus reminded them, in his forceless voice.

"Penthilus was never acknowledged," Temenus murmured. "He can't be called a son of Orestes."

"But . . ." Aristodemus coughed softly. "But everyone says it's true." He sat back, pressing the heel of one hand to his chest.

Karnus looked from one to the other of them. "You have the wheels, the wheat lands, the lion's skin. And women are easy enough to skin, as well. What are you missing?"

Hippotes was rising from his stool. He was gaunt, almost thin, and a terrible sick color. And yet, from habit, the men around him stepped away.

"Priest," he said.

Karnus turned and saw him.

"We rid this place of vermin already. We don't need some fat man talking riddles."

Karnus glanced past them all, as if listening to a different voice.

Temenus said softly, "Hippotes, don't."

Hippotes stopped but did not sit again.

Kresphontes reminded them, "Penthilus?"

"We have less likely allies," said Temenus. "I once said that to the baron Hawmai Aquileides."

"Hawmai is the High King's lawagetas, though," Hippotes growled. "Penthilus is a spider."

"Spiders have long legs," Meydon said.

"And teeth," Satnios added loyally.

Aristodemus whispered, "But he's Orestes' son for sure, even if Orestes never admitted it." He paused to catch his breath. "And the three-eyed man? Who knows? We never understood that. How many eyes does a spider have?"

Satnios said, "Two. Four. Hundreds."

Aristodemus sat back, laughing softly, then again pressed the heel of his hand to his chest and closed his eyes.

Temenus sat still, considering. Finally, he said, "Well, it must mean him: Penthilus. I get messages from him all the time. He offers to be my spy, my steward, my blood brother. He offers to wash my underwear."

The Herakleids all laughed this time. Satnios said, "I'm sure he'd be happy to grow an extra eye for you," and they laughed again.

"That's what it means, then: I must find someone who would try that hard to please me. That would certainly be Penthilus. And he knows everyone and everything. That's a part of being a spider sitting in the middle of a web. It's part of being three-eyed as well: he sees everything in Mycenae and all around it. Perhaps he can be more useful than I thought."

They all considered Penthilus while Karnus stood patiently before them.

Temenus finally said, more quietly, "I need something that's more than useful. I need magic."

A hard crash startled everyone. They looked. At the inner door, Makhawis stood, the shards of a wine jug around her feet, horror in her face.

Temenus stood up. "Makhawis? What is it?"

She stared at them, stared at Karnus, then snatched up her skirt and fled.

* * *

Temenus found her in her workroom, surrounded by slaves, all weaving furiously. Keeping his distance from women's work, he asked, "What was that?"

She didn't look at him. "What do you mean?" Her hands moved as if independent from her, the different shuttles clicking.

"Tell me what happened. What did the priest say that frightened you?"

She swallowed. "You were there. You heard him as well as I did."

"It was something about Penthilus, something in all that talk that made no sense. You figured it out. Tell me."

She finally looked up at him. "I'm not allowed to talk to priests. How could I ever understand what they say?"

Temenus turned his face away a little but didn't take his eyes off her. Under his beard, his jaw muscles worked steadily.

"Are you mocking me, Makhawis? I may have to put up with that from a priest, but I don't have to take it from you."

All her women had stopped working.

He said, "The High Kingship is too important for women's games. If you know anything that I should know, anything that matters, tell me now."

He had never looked at her this way: as if she were an enemy, a tormentor trying to thwart him—someone he would hurt if she didn't do his will. A sacrifice to the temperament of Nafpaktos, as Akhaïdes always had been. She suddenly remembered Akhaïdes in the olive grove, and her throat cramped shut. Would they beat a *woman* so? A pack without prey was no pack. And this pack, which had fed badly at Arne, was starving again. What would it eat? What would it not? Would Temenus do that to her? A woman's skin—what had the priest said about that? This new Temenus might do anything.

He turned his face to her fully again, his eyes hooded. In a cool, soft voice cool, he said, "I've indulged you in almost everything. But if that's served to make you ungovernable, I can correct it."

The room was utterly silent.

"Makhawis?"

She rose, went to him, then knelt and bowed her head. Temenus stared down at her. Finally, he said, "My city is dying. My brother is dying. I went to war and won nothing by it." He twitched his head. "Now you—you, of all people—defy me. I have no time to play games with you or with anyone. Think about your life and how it could change on you. Then come and see me very soon." He walked out.

Makhawis sat back on her heel, then sank all the way to the floor. She ran her hands over her face, then up her arms. When she turned back to the room, her women were all watching with anxious faces.

She rose and shook out her skirt. She went to the entrance and looked out. Temenus was not there. She stepped into the hall. He did not appear.

Behind her, one of the slaves said, "Lady?"

She turned and looked at the warm, lighted, well-ordered room full of women and their work. This passage where she stood was cold and dark. She had walked its length for years, but tonight she had no idea where it might lead her.

She pressed her skirt against her legs and started down the corridor alone.

* * *

"Grandfather."

Karnus turned. Makhawis watched his face go through the changes of puzzlement, surprise, then dismay. He was younger than he had seemed in the megaron, surrounded with such dignity. He might be no older than Meydon.

She said, "Grandfather, please. I have to talk to you."

"You know that priests don't talk to women."

She raised her hands, palms up. "Please. Please. It's so important . . ."

"And I certainly don't talk to women alone."

"What you said. I . . ." She glanced back the way she had come. "Please let me in, Grandfather. If anyone sees me, I don't know what will happen."

"And if anyone finds you in my room, what will happen?" He lifted his eyebrows. "Where are your women? Why are you alone?"

"If my brother catches me, he'll punish me. But he'd kill any slave I brought with me."

"He could kill you for this, too."

"He won't." She wished she were as sure of this as she would have been yesterday.

Finally, Karnus stepped back into the cell. She came in, turned, and latched the door to its peg. Then she went down onto her knees before him.

"What do you want that's so urgent?"

She put her open hands on the hard dirt floor. Its coolness steadied her.

"What you said in the megaron . . . about the three-eyed man, about tools, about Penthilus . . . I understand it."

"So?"

She looked up. "My brother didn't understand. No one else did." Her throat ached with panic, with anguish. "He doesn't know, either, does he?"

"Your brother?"

"You know who I mean! You have to go back to Delphi, send a message, do something. You have to warn him."

"Delphi is a long way."

"My brother has a long reach."

Karnus sat down on his stool. "Granddaughter, the world needs to know."

"But not this way." She put her hands on Karnus's knees. "Temenus never wanted to let him go. If he knew this . . . Warn him. Give him a chance to survive."

Karnus started to answer. Then the barrier behind her slammed open. The peg flew wildly across the room. Makhawis turned, her arms already raised to fend off blows.

Not Temenus. Hippotes.

Hippotes, pallid but still massive, stood spread-legged in the entrance, filling it. The door rebounded from the wall, hit him, and bounced back again. He did not seem to notice.

He said, "What's this?" He said it not to Makhawis, but to Karnus, who was rising, far too late.

"Priest, what do you want with this woman?"

Karnus backed the two steps to the wall and had to stop.

Makhawis dragged her skirt out from under her knees and stumbled upright. By then, Hippotes was inside. For a man in so much danger, Karnus looked perfectly calm.

Makhawis grabbed Hippotes' arm with both hands.

Hippotes turned on her. All the dog-soft weakness that came over his face whenever he looked at her was gone. He looked at her now as if she, too, were an enemy. He lifted his upper lip in a sneer, then turned back to Karnus.

"This woman doesn't talk to men. She doesn't send them messages. And neither do her go-betweens."

As simple as that, without even bothering to shake Makhawis off his arm, Hippotes hit the priest. Once in the midsection. As Karnus pitched forward, Hippotes held him up with the other hand. Once in the chest, then again in the chest, right over the heart. Without a sound, Karnus sank to his knees. Hippotes doubled his hands, his fists interlocked, and clubbed downward.

"Stop!"

Makhawis spun around. She had feared seeing Temenus. Now she crouched at his feet.

He ignored her, staring only at Hippotes, who turned and faced him and stood still. Behind Hippotes, on the floor, Karnus did not move.

For a moment, nothing. Then Temenus asked quietly, "What did she do?"

Hippotes uncoupled his hands. Only then could anyone see, still in one fist, a bronze dagger with a gold deer running down the blade, looking out. "She wanted this priest to carry a message."

"What message?"

Hippotes grunted, not concerned with that.

Temenus looked down at her. "What message?"

Makhawis stared at her brother's shoes. *Dusty,* she thought absurdly. His shoes were dusty. Perhaps she could lick them clean.

As if hearing her thought, he moved his foot away from her. Then he bent, combed his fingers into her hair, and pulled her head up. "What message?"

Her eyes watered with pain, but she had never been further from crying.

He shook her hard. He dragged her face closer to his. "What message, woman? Hippotes killed a priest for this. Tell me why!"

She squeezed her mouth shut. He threw her away in disgust. She hit the wall hard and slumped into a protective crouch. Kicking her, he missed her face and hit her chest instead. He kicked her again. Then he stood over her.

He was quiet for so long that she risked a glance at him.

He looked bemused. He was not even breathing hard. His self-possession, his silence, was more frightening than any rage. He asked calmly, "What message, Makhawis?"

Hippotes said, "She said the priest had to warn somebody. She said, if you knew something . . ." He stopped, not caring.

Temenus knelt and took Makhawis's face in his hand, his fingers gripping her jawbones. "I told you before to tell me." His voice was soft, reasonable. "Tell me now, or I will kill you."

Unbelievable. This was Temenus, her own sweet brother, whose violence was never, ever physical, who got sick at the sight or smell of blood, who had come home from Arne too shaken to eat meat. Yet she believed him absolutely.

So this was how she would die: keeping a secret for a man who didn't know he had one. She never would have suspected it. Temenus closed his fist and hit her.

For a moment, she thought she was blind. But then her head hit the wall and her eyes came open. He was still looking at her with that mild, detached expression, as if he had never seen her before in his life and didn't care who she was.

Hippotes had dropped the knife. It was right beside her. She kicked it away so Temenus would not think she might touch it, use it, have anything to do with it. It clattered and slid, caught on the uneven floor, and spun, the gold deer flashing in the dust.

Temenus reached for her again, then turned to stare at the knife. Makhawis followed his gaze. With dust obscuring its antlers, the deer did not look like a deer anymore. It looked like a horse.

A horse, gazing out of the blade with both eyes.

Temenus's hands sank away from her. He stood up, turned, and stared at Hippotes, at the dead priest, at the knife, at the wall, at nothing.

"I know what it is," he said. He ran one hand down his face, then stared blindly down at her while she winced and cowered.

Frantic running footsteps. Kresphontes skidded into the room, took in everything instantly, grabbed Temenus's arm. "What is this?"

Temenus turned on him. "What is it? It's me, Temenus Herakleides, king of the Herakleids, High King, finally bringing this family to order." He snarled in Kresphontes' face. "And you're just as bad as she is. Spoiled, selfish, willful, looking out for everyone but me. Ruining everything."

Kresphontes stared at him. "What? I never—"

"No?" Temenus ripped his arm from Kresphontes' hand and hit him without warning, with a closed fist and the full swing of his arm.

Kresphontes staggered against the wall. Then Temenus turned and walked out of the room, Hippotes following.

The door hung open, but they were alone: Makhawis, Kresphontes, Karnus, and the knife on the floor, saying all that it said. She crept away from the wall to the priest's body. Karnus stared over her shoulder, at irrelevance.

Kresphontes sat on the floor, legs outstretched, hair down over his shoulder, the wooden pin dangling. He looked stunned. He whispered, "What happened? What did I do wrong?"

The side of his face was already discolored and swelling. He whispered again, "What did I do?"

Makhawis turned and sat and held her aching head in her hands.

Think. Think. He would go as soon as possible: ten days, three days, tomorrow. How could she convince him to take her along?

Even as she thought, she heard voices—new voices, calling from a distance. She and then Kresphontes lifted their heads to hear them. To hear them calling, then crying, then wailing, "Aristodemus Herakleides!" as if it were a spell, a song, or a magical chant meant to bring the dead to life again.

190

The best is the deep quiet in which I live and grow against the world, and harvest what they cannot take from me by fire and sword. [xi]
— *Johann Wolfgang von Goethe*

When Akhaïdes came down from the watcher's aerie in the morning, the black-haired boy was waiting. White with cold and huddled inside his own many layers of rags, the boy bore a striking resemblance to the old man on the mountain, though Akhaïdes would never have told him that. The young priests' awe of Kepheus was palpable, and the children feared him most of all. Kepheus was fey, and everyone could feel it.

He and the boy finished the climb down together. Not trusting his knees to hold him, Akhaïdes often used a stick on the steepest parts. He sometimes wondered whether the boy came to meet him for his company, to help him if he needed it, or simply to assure himself that Akhaïdes had come down safely once again. Any one of those reasons was enough to touch Akhaïdes' heart.

Today, Menetor met him just outside the kitchen door.

"How now, grandson," the priest said. "Staying busy?"

"Useful, I hope." He rested the basket against his knee. "Kepheus takes his duty very personally, doesn't he?"

"He does indeed." Menetor cocked his head and waited.

"He thinks the High King is holding out on him deliberately."

"Ah, yes. When Orestes was hit by lightning and didn't die,

he was furious." Menetor waited again.

Menetor's anticipation made it easier for Akhaïdes to say what he wanted to say. He understood that this was intentional, but still the words were difficult to gather. "Is it arrogant to ask to replace him if he should go before the High King does?"

Menetor's head wrinkled from brow to nape. "There's always a High King. If not this one, then the next. And I can't release a watcher until there is another to replace him. It's like Atlas or the Spinners; the crows, Megarans, corpse tenders, Erinyes. The job must be done."

If not this one, then the next. Was that the link between Tisamenus and himself? To light his funeral beacon?

"It's no work to waste a priest on. Or a perfectly good slave."

"It's lonely."

"I don't mind that."

"You want to pass your life perched on a rock, with a fire to light, someday, perhaps?"

Alone forever in a palace of stone and sky. No need ever to speak again. Menetor raised his hand and touched Akhaïdes' face gently, just at the corner of his eye.

Akhaïdes said with quiet passion, "I would see it. Believe me."

"I believe you." Menetor smiled abruptly, forcing a change of mood. "It's a job that needs doing. But I hate to waste you, either, on that kind of work."

Akhaïdes did not yield. "Why? I have no skills more useful, beyond what I've been doing. I wasn't exactly trained to priesthood. Nor to slavery."

"Well, no. You're right, as far as that goes." Menetor blew into his bony hands to warm them. "And as outlaw you have fairly limited utility, even for slaves' work, although you certainly have managed to keep busy."

Menetor wrinkled his head again, but Akhaïdes would not lighten. "Come in to the fire. Come in. I want to talk to you."

Akhaïdes stamped snow off his boots, then followed Menetor under the low lintel. He turned to check, but the boy had gone away. Children were not welcome in the kitchen; the fierce little cook said the sight of too much food aroused base passions.

After the bright, dry cold of the mountainside, the kitchen was steamy hot and, to Akhaïdes, black as a cave. He stood waiting courteously until a slave came to take the basket. This gave him time to orient himself by the sounds around him, and then move through shadows across the room without stumbling, toward the bright smear of the stone hearth, set like a legless firepot directly in the ground, which the cook used when the ovens were not working.

Closer to the light, he could see a little. That reddish blur was Menetor, rubbing his hands together over the coals. Akhaïdes threw back the wolfskin coat, moved one calf to touch a bench, and sat down. His knees grated.

Menetor was not smiling now. "There's something I have to tell you. You won't like to hear it."

Akhaïdes' hands were extended to the fire. The right hand did not respond to Menetor's warning, but the left tensed. He waited.

"Karnus is gone to his dead."

Akhaïdes' heart went suddenly silent. "How?"

"I sent him to Nafpaktos. They killed him."

He kept perfectly still, listening.

Menetor said, "He knew it might happen when he agreed to go. I knew it when I sent him. And still he went."

"Who? Who did it?"

"If I said I don't know, it would be a lie. But I won't tell you." Menetor leaned forward. "Your life doesn't lie with Karnus. You are not responsible. He is, and I am. Not you."

Akhaïdes felt the old transfixion, the forcible stillness he had lived under so long, pinioned and gagged by responsibility and shame. He let it hold him now.

"I didn't want you to hear from anyone else, at any other time." Menetor leaned closer yet. "Men will go before you: men you know, men you love. They are not all your personal fault.

"And if you believe I would trade you for Karnus, you haven't been paying attention. Even Karnus himself would have refused."

Akhaïdes looked up at him. "What does that mean?"

"I will tell you when I know you're actually listening to me."

The dwarf cook was rummaging through the basket, muttering about what Kepheus had and hadn't eaten. They both glanced at him, and their tandem motion eased the strain between them. Menetor turned to Akhaïdes again.

"You never thought, when you left Nafpaktos, what it would mean to them. There are three thousand springs in the world, and three thousand rivers. They all can be counted, and accounted for. Yet it never occurred to you to wonder why you were in Nafpaktos? Or how they would manage without you?"

Akhaïdes laughed, short and harsh. "It was managing *with* me that baffled them. I assume they're only relieved that I'm gone."

"Your assumption is incorrect. Of course, some of that is my own error. I've always done right by you, it seems, but for the wrong reasons. You have no idea what I'm talking about, do you?"

"No, Master."

"'No, Master.'" Menetor puffed out his usual small explosion of pique. "Your eye healed. It healed right in front of me, and I almost didn't realize. Your eye, your hand. But everything that happens . . ." He stopped and raised a thin brow.

"Happens for a reason. What reason? Do you know?"

"I believe I do."

Akhaïdes sat silent, his hands lifted to the fire. The right crept closed, as it always did when he did not purposely hold it open.

Menetor said, "The Herakleids are our own people. Amphitryon really was Herakles' father, despite all later efforts to make his birth mysterious and magical and place it here instead. Herakles' first wife, Deianeira, the mother of Hyllus, from whom everyone who calls himself Herakleid today claims to descend—Deianeira was your own ancestor by blood, before your people carried their line into Arcadia. You know all this."

"My mother talked about it."

"And I'm sure your brother used that distant kinship to the Herakleids to help him win a place in Nafpaktos."

"Yes."

"All the Herakleid rulers were born in Athens. They respect the High King's law and the powers familiar to us."

"Tell Elawon."

Menetor gazed at him serenely. "Their friends the Dorians— it's them I fear. Unless the Herakleids can rule them like Perioikoi, when this Herakleid generation and the next one pass on they all will be Dorian, however carefully they believe they are guarding their own blood and dominion. And when they are Dorian, so will we be."

"Do you fear for Delphi?"

"Delphi will remain. We survived the Mycenaean coming and the one before, and will survive this coming and the next. But each time, we are changed. Each time, the Serpent threatens to leave; each time, it changes but remains. But it, like me, is too old to anticipate change with pleasure."

Menetor rubbed his hands together over the fire. "We're in the fourth age of the world—the one that was foretold to us. Promises are broken; prophecies are not fulfilled; lives are thrown away; deaths have no meaning. Wars are fought as the Tribes fought for Arne: slaughter and butchery so far beyond the necessary. Men are . . ." His smile was brittle now. "Men are like you: blood and fire and brilliance, all wasted. And before it's over, things will happen to make our hardships now seem like the powers' great feast for the sacred."

Akhaïdes glanced up. The shadows of their four hands over the fire moved across the ceiling like a dream of spiders.

Menetor mused, "How much of a king is Temenus? I knew him as a small child and have met him from time to time as a man. He is deeply intelligent and nearly fearless. And yet, what man lives who can ride demons? I mean, except you."

Akhaïdes watched his own hands closing. "He doesn't—he hasn't grasped his power. He looks too much to others."

"But not to you."

"I couldn't convince him to hear me."

Menetor thought for a moment. "It might have required that he change beyond his ability. But if anyone can change another person, it is you."

"Not to change *him*. Only what he does. That should be simple."

"*He* must change what he does," Menetor said. "Also, who he trusts, why he blinks or does not blink, and what he sees when he looks into the dark and still dares to walk forward."

Menetor made his puffing noise. "And by the way, there is not, never was, and never will be anything simple about you and Temenus Herakleides."

Akhaïdes dismissed that. "Can he change now?"

"He has already begun." Menetor glanced away. "By allowing the murder of Karnus. You might feel that the change won't serve him well, but that's you. That's you and Temenus. fate has a longer view."

Akhaïdes closed his eye, fearful.

"Temenus also has his own story to live."

"Separate from mine."

"No. With yours always, as much as . . ." He stopped himself. "But both of them, perhaps, lived in ways you would not ask for, were we to offer you choices. Still, choices are a luxury we are not granted."

Menetor reached out and took Akhaïdes' right hand. He cupped the callused fingers in his and stroked the crooked bones until Akhaïdes finally yielded, cautiously, to kindness. He even closed his own hand slightly, and they sat for a moment in a small mutual embrace.

Menetor said, "You were not made to light beacons."

"I was not made for anything useful."

"I have a useful job for you. There's a message to be carried."

"An augury? I can't—"

"You can. You may not touch it, of course, but you won't need to. The priestesses will tell it to me. I will tell it to you, and you will remember it exactly. I will also write it on pithleaf, which you will carry in a sheath like an arrow case."

Menetor paused. "My priests and priestesses never travel anymore. If you want Delphi, you must come to Delphi. But this is different. For the first time in generations, a message must be carried. And not just carried quickly because the recipient's feet are already on the road to his dead, but carried because he is important, the message is important, and it must travel by land. It must go through Boeotia, because I won't entrust it to a boat even though the other shore is in sight. The Herakleids kept order while they were there, but the Dorians don't. No priest, no slave, even in Delphic red, would be safe there now. So I thought of you and your horse. At the very least, you could travel faster than word of your coming. Will you carry it?"

"Why are you asking? I'll do whatever you say."

Menetor slid his fingers up Akhaïdes' arms and drew him down until Akhaïdes' forehead rested on his shoulder. Menetor held all of Akhaïdes, finally stilled, finally submissive, in his arms, his mouth against the parched hair.

"You don't even ask where I'm sending you, but I'll tell you. Mycenae."

* * *

The gray horse's plushy coat was pure white, its legs mud-packed, and its mane and tail woolly as a pony's. No one would recognize the sleek, dark-dappled animal of Arne. It greeted the first sight of Akhaïdes with an explosive snort, then crossed the sheep meadow to meet him.

The Waiting Moon, called the Night Moon on the steppe, was fat and full. The solstice, celebrated even here with bonfires and drinking, was only a few days past. Soon would come the Dark Moon—Akhaïdes' own Thieves' Moon—then the most dreaded moon of all: the Hungry Moon. This was not the time when humans stood in the greatest danger of starvation—that came later, in the spring, just before the wheat harvest, when Nafpaktos's hunger had taken root—but it was the time when the soil sucked the nourishment back from the grasses, and animals wasted away no matter how much grazing they found.

On the steppe, where the extra horses and cattle were sent ten days' ride to the south to graze and no enemy could reach the camps through the snow, the Hungry Moon was called the Coming-Home Moon or, better, the Storytelling Moon. For Akhaïdes, it evoked memories of warm tents glowing with light and thrumming with life, and the people all at home together— and himself standing deaf and heedless in the cold, thinking of going away.

Menetor said, "This is the message case. It's like an arrow case—see? A lid keeps the pithleaf dry and clean. You may touch the case, but never the message itself."

Menetor said, "You know the message now and must recite it word by word. It is written here, too, but only so that the recipient can confirm what you say. I won't have my oracles misheard. We're already blamed too often for others' confusion."

Menetor said, "This is the Serpent's ring. It will prove that you are under Delphi's hand."

Menetor said, "This is the envoy's cloak—red—and the hood

is black to honor the Serpent and its dead. The hood can fold like this, to hide your face if you need to. All hosting courtesies are owed to you, but you will owe nothing in return except safe delivery of the message to the man who requested it. Anyone should feed you and give you a bed, to their honor. But you still are outlaw, and the law is not suspended for this. And with Boeotia as it is . . ."

Menetor said, "If anyone can get through Boeotia now, it is you. And your story is not Karnus's. No one in Mycenae should want to harm you."

Menetor said, "Go with confidence, Ephialtes Hyadeides. And don't neglect to come home."

* * *

Akhaïdes went: horse, cloak, ring, message case, and a bag of food that the cook insisted he carry. Menetor watched until long after he was out of sight, after the idlest of the slaves wandered back to work, after the children who had run whooping behind him trailed back, after the black-haired boy stalked pointedly past Menetor with a malignant glare.

Then Menetor went down to the sanctuary, pegged the door, and opened his own wrist over the sacrifice stone.

——— │ │ │

*"We are all humiliated by the sudden discovery of a fact
which has existed very comfortably and perhaps been staring at
us in private while we have been making up our world entirely
without it."*[xii]

— George Eliot

The first time, he had paddled around the Megara wall in the dark of night, carrying a bow and a baby. This time, he rode straight to it in full daylight and waited while they let him in.

The wall, one end rising from the gulf, the other from the sea, was now built of stone along its entire length and stood almost as high as the walls of Arne. Its two gates framed a stone palace where, on a terrace under a sleeting gray sky, Akhaïdes met the king of Megara, flanked by weapon-laden guards.

The man was as tall as Akhaïdes, skeleton thin, and of a clean white color that made him half invisible against the frosty balustrade and a heavy coat of black ermine. His hair, also ice-white, hung unbound, down to the back of his knees. He turned on Akhaïdes a pair of eyes as pale as Akhaïdes' own, but rimmed with pink.

He said, "You are bold to pass through these countries alone—even as Delphi's envoy, even as swiftly as you can travel on horseback. Surely, the men of Phocis and Boeotia were less impressed than I by the nature of your mission. Still, you came, and you are welcome."

Even making the swift adjustment for the sound of the king's voice, which surprised him with its resonant depth, it still took Akhaïdes a moment to understand what he had said. Then he realized, with a jolt, that the king spoke his own Arcadian. He answered with pleasure, in the same language. "No creature exists but risks fate daily. I am only one of these, willing to wake each morning hoping only for the luxury of sleep that night."

The king smiled at the familiar adage. His gums were also pink. "As I thought, you remember the tongue of your fathers. You are doubly welcome, then, for your envoy's cloak and for the sake of Echemus, our comrade." He glanced at his guards. "Has our guest been warmed and fed? No? You will see to it, then."

One of them hurried away.

The king said, "We rarely eat our guests anymore, since we took our oath to Echemus and the High King. We may seem whimsical in our choice of who passes and who is turned away. And even with passage granted, our fees can be painful. What are you prepared to give us for admission to the lands of the High King?"

Menetor had told him about this. He said, "I can offer only the Serpent's friendship, my lord, whose runway from sea to sea your walls adorn and respect. And the regard of Echemus, who always remembered this place."

The king glanced at him, suddenly guarded. "Any man who saw the living face of Echemus is sacred here. But do not tell me all you remember. Instead, just walk with me, will you? Come see the wall you did not see when you passed before by night."

Akhaïdes followed him to the edge of the terrace. "How can you know who I am?"

"Better ask, how can I *not* know who you are. Your face is the face I would expect. This is the time I would expect your return. And remember that Megara is one of the many heads of the High King. What he knows, I know. What I know, he knows.

I am thus bound both by oath and by affinity. I never travel. No Megaran leaves the shadow of our wall. But words have legs of their own."

"And wings."

"And wings," the king agreed. He stood at the edge and raised a thin white arm, sleeved in ermine, toward the distant bastions of the Peloponnesos. "Look there, and tell me what might happen yet remain secret from me."

Akhaïdes had not been this close to Arcadia—not in Nafpaktos, not in Delphi. The shapes and colors of the peaks, their vaulting heights and noble bones, made his heart clench. The word for "home" in Arcadian was a complex construction. He spoke it aloud now, savoring the way it crimped his tongue.

"Yes," the king said. A toss of the head set his frosty mane shimmering. "But perhaps not the home you expect. Or even the home you deserve."

They stood side by side for a moment, the High King's lands flowing from below their feet. Then the king turned the other way, facing the wall that rose above the flat roof of his palace. Armed men walked and stood along its crown. It blocked any view of other lands, but straight through the palace's rooms, open windows framed segments of the world beyond. More world than anyone here would care to know existed. The road to Boeotia, Athens, the steppes. To Korea and the most distant sea.

The king said, "I would give much to know what is in your mind at this moment, Envoy. Even more, I would like to know what is not there but should be. And that, you cannot tell me. Come. Eat, rest. There is warm food in a warm room, and a warm bed. All will be purified after you leave, so use them with an untroubled mind. There is a warm stall below, and water, and fodder aplenty for your horse. There will also be a warm welcome here when you return this way." The king gave him a dazzling smile. "Whoever you might be by then."

* * *

The sleet had turned to even colder rain when Akhaïdes passed Corinth. The gray horse hated rain, and the novelty of walking a paved road did nothing to improve its disposition. It clopped along, head and tail down, sullen and sluggish. The red felt cloak did not shed water as well as his wolfskin. By the time he reached the Mycenae crossroads, Akhaïdes was soaked, and stiff with cold.

He rode into the city in midafternoon. The deserted streets were ankle deep in running water. The horse waded upstream, turning its head constantly side to side. Arne and Nafpaktos long forgotten, it was used to the high meadow of Delphi now, and these narrow, unnatural defiles unnerved it.

Mycenae was a labyrinth of walls, stout, ranging roofs, and heavy foundations splayed over older, even heavier substructures. The moss thick as loaves in the roof gutters, the profusion of lichens and vines over every wall, the dense bristling of grass from every breach in the paving, declared age and permanence. Here were stone walkways cupped and polished by generations of anonymous feet. Through half-open doors and shutters, he glimpsed floors of pounded earth that shone like glazed tiles.

He tried to follow pavement, thinking that would lead to the citadel. But the streets branched and branched again, and what seemed the likeliest passage ended in a blind courtyard. He went back and chose again, with the same result. Finally, he simply followed whatever route led uphill. The horse walked sideways, trying to watch all around at once.

They turned and climbed, turned and climbed, until, without warning, the houses backed away at either side and he faced the tomb of Perseus and the High Kings.

It was a monumental vault fronted by a long, slanting passage that ended in a towering portal and closed double doors.

Three men were at work there, hammering the doorposts under a scaffold's shelter. With their arms fully extended above them, they could not have reached one third the height of the doors. He touched his forehead and looked away.

The horse walked on, and a new passage closed around them, leading upward again in a long blind curve. Then Akhaïdes faced another wonder: the stronghold of the High Kings.

Nothing he had heard or seen before could have prepared him for this. A wall stood like a cliff before him, but no natural cliff could rise and curve so smoothly. The walls of Arne, although blacker and straighter and three times as high, never had the authority and perfection of this straw-gold stone. A narrow passage led up between two sculpted standing lionesses, whose beautiful, intelligent eyes studied him with neither interest nor passion. Below their feet, a great double-leaved gate stood open, showing edges of structures and bits of sky beyond. The sky was slick and gray above, but still his eye was filled with gold.

He slid stiffly down, feeling the shock and then the familiar grating in his knees, and led the horse forward. It went only a few steps and balked. Pressing its ears into its mane and planting its hooves, it raised its back and stopped as decisively as if determined never to move again.

He had seen no one on the wall, but two men in leather armor came from under the lionesses' feet to meet him. Their wet cloaks slapped their legs. The horse snorted in half-feigned alarm to register its irritation with everything about this place.

Both men looked vaguely familiar—from Arne, perhaps. Akhaïdes pulled the red hood farther forward to hide his face, then held his right hand up, palm inward, so they could see the ring. They raised respectful fingertips to their foreheads. A smaller man, wearing only leg wraps, a plain shirt, and an outsize coat, dodged between them and around the horse's menacing rump. Recognizing him as a groom, Akhaïdes yielded the reins.

"I'll care for it well," the groom said. "May I also keep your bag for you while you're the High King's guest?"

Akhaïdes handed him the shoulder bag but kept the arrow case. The groom slung the bag over his arm and turned to the horse.

The horse eyed him critically. He spoke to it, trying to draw it away from the gate, but it stood undecided. Then the rain intensified, and it strode past him with such sudden energy that he had to trot to keep up. The knights fell in at Akhaïdes' sides, directing him to the gate without seeming to, looking anywhere but into the hood. One of them said, "We knew it was you, of course, Envoy. We saw you from far off. We already sent for the king."

The other said, "Not the High King—he's ill, but he would meet you here if he could. Only the king of Lacedaemon."

They were already under the lionesses' feet. There was nothing to do but step onto the great cracked threshold stone, into the High King's dominion.

The entry court was a narrow curve wrapped around a slab-sided tomb and a wide ramp that rose under a patched and faded cloth canopy. The sentries led Akhaïdes to a sheltered bench, then stood erect and formal, one at each end. Under another portal's wooden eaves, men and slaves had already gathered, talking softly and glancing at him. Akhaïdes stretched his legs, working his knees straight. His right hand ached.

Footsteps approached from above, and all turned. A familiar voice said, "My lord Envoy, forgive our poor hospitality. Please come up."

Tisamenus looked older, with fine wrinkles gathered at the corners of his eyes. He was still clean-shaven. His hair was lighter, a sun-faded olive gray, and he wore it loose still, down to his belt. He moved with quick, familiar grace, descending the last few strides down the ramp and touching his forehead with both hands. Akhaïdes copied the gesture. As he lowered his hands, he saw the flicker of a question in Tisamenus's eyes, then saw it quickly dismissed. Akhaïdes slipped his hands into cover under the cloak as Tisamenus smiled blandly, graciously, and turned to lead the way upward.

The ramp ended at a flat walkway under wooden roofing. The gap between cloth and wood dribbled water, and he paused to let his eye adjust to the shadows. This lane was still more outdoors than in, the center running with thin sewage.

A woman, backed by two slaves, appeared at the far curve of the lane. She was immensely fat, nearly as wide as the passage itself. She raised both hands in showy invitation. The edges of the red cloak swept each roof support that Akhaïdes passed, and that faint swish was, for a moment, the only sound. Then the fat woman sank to her knees and placed her hands on the ground, forehead on her hands.

"Envoy," she said. "We welcome you." Her voice had a rasping, sexual edge.

Akhaïdes stopped in front of her, and she raised her face again. Through the smiling, distorted facade, brown eyes examined him coolly. Akhaïdes half-turned, asking. Tisamenus said, "Limnea, daughter of Penthilus Mycenades. Wife of the baron Philaios, who is like a brother to me."

The slaves helped the woman stand. She smiled boldly at Akhaïdes and stepped aside into an open doorway, pulling her skirt showily up under her abdomen to avoid the touch of his cloak. The tail of her dress was soaked with sewage, and Akhaïdes' saw that she was not only fat but also hugely pregnant. She bobbed her head as he passed her, but to Tisamenus she whispered something Akhaïdes did not hear.

They turned into a high, cold hall packed with oil jars, then out again to another roofed passage, wider than the first. Men, women, and slaves paused in their work and dipped their heads.

Akhaïdes and Tisamenus passed through a maze of rooms and turnings, then up more steps to a roofed and pillared gallery.

No one else was in this room, and they walked side by side. Tisamenus said, "We weren't sure when you would come. My father didn't expect you so soon. He'll be grateful."

They passed a massive table, and Akhaïdes brushed it with the cloaked back of his hand automatically, locating it in his two-dimensional space.

Tisamenus stopped, and Akhaïdes turned politely toward him. Tisamenus was staring after Akhaïdes' gesture, and his face showed, only for a moment, a naked, haunted need. Then the gracious mask slipped back into place.

"Excuse me, Envoy. I was thinking—you just reminded me of someone. I suppose the comparison wouldn't please you, but it would not be meant disrespectfully." Now his smile was self-effacing.

They moved carefully forward again. A team of slaves spilled into the hall, glanced at Tisamenus, then saw Akhaïdes and scattered out of his way. They approached a heavy door. Akhaïdes was so bemused by all this that he raised his hand to push it open before remembering he must not touch it. His hand stopped in the air, fingers spread, and he felt Tisamenus's shock of recognition.

Tisamenus turned fully toward him, grasped Akhaïdes' wrist, and placed his own hand palm to palm with Akhaïdes'. Tisamenus's hand was clean and cared-for, unmarked and unornamented except by plain gold rings. Akhaïdes' was larger, swollen at the knuckles, hatched with a hundred flaws and a long scar between the tendons, but the same shape exactly. A reflection in a wicked mirror. The perfect dark twin.

They stood facing each other, absolutely still, until Akhaïdes spoke for the first time in Mycenae. He said, "Yes."

That released Tisamenus. He jerked into motion, shoved the door, and led the way through. The latch closed behind them with finality. They were alone in yet another corridor, this one plastered and frescoed and lit by narrow high windows. Tisamenus wheeled to confront him, and Akhaïdes thrust the hood back onto his shoulders.

They faced each other, Tisamenus erect and pale and so rigid that he barely breathed.

Akhaïdes thought of a hundred things to say. He said, "Wanax Tisamenus, I mean you no harm."

Tisamenus did not move. "But will you do me none?"

"I swear I do not know."

"How can . . . How do we . . . ?" He stopped, out of words.

Akhaïdes said, "We'll just do what we should do, until this is over."

"You and I."

"You and I."

Tisamenus closed his eyes for a moment. His lips repeated soundlessly, "You and I."

Akhaïdes raised the hood again. They turned and walked together, matching stride without thinking, the red cloak spreading behind them. Peeling frescoes slid by.

They strode under a portico painted in a pattern of birds and vines. Two Mycenaeans with spears and shields straightened and saluted lazily from the sides of the door. Here in the palace proper, there were carpets everywhere, even under standing water. From a shadowed corner, three men watched with fixed and insolent stares. Two richly dressed women gazed after them.

When no one was close enough to hear, Tisamenus said, "I lost Arne."

"You aren't the lawagetas. Hawmai lost Arne."

"We should have fought for it. Hawmai said no, but I was so sure he was wrong." He lifted his head. "My father doesn't know."

"He won't learn from me."

"Some blame me, though. I don't know what they thought I

could do; if the High King and his Lawagetas say one thing, how can I say another?" Still walking, Tisamenus added, "I had no idea you'd still be alive."

"Neither did I."

"How is Elawon? I always especially liked—"

"With the dead."

Tisamenus stopped in mid step. Though he didn't look at Akhaïdes, his shock was palpable. Akhaïdes paused, too, hiding Tisamenus's hesitation with a half turn and a riffle of the cloak, as if it were he who stumbled. Tisamenus recovered, and they went on.

Tisamenus said, "My own rooms are awash, but I know there's a place somewhere that's not leaking, and hot food if you know who to ask for it. I need to give you refreshments. I need to . . ." He scrubbed his hands over his face. "I liked Elawon. I missed him after he went with you."

He despised you and was relieved to be rid of you, Akhaïdes could have said.

They moved into a wide hall with a painted floor, full of people who all turned at once, like a shoal of fish wheeling. Tisamenus met eyes and smiled, met eyes and smiled. To Akhaïdes, he murmured, "Oxylus left here some days ago. His exile is over. I gave him that horse he liked to ride, and got him passage across the gulf from Patras, when he gets there. He— Oxylus—can't walk far now. In fact, he's lame forever, but doesn't seem to hold a grudge. I've heard him bragging about being . . . *marred* by you. He even tried to get Sigewas of Argos to set it to verse. But I haven't forgotten the rest of the story."

A dark-eyed, handsome young man—unbearded, richly dressed, a few years older than Tisamenus—approached boldly. He touched his forehead to Akhaïdes, then looked at Tisamenus, smiling warmly.

"Envoy, my Companion, the baron Philaios."

Philaios turned that smile on Akhaïdes. "Welcome. I hope the news you bring will relieve my lord's worries." His teeth were white and straight, his skin perfect, his hair glossy and, yes, perfumed. He laid his perfectly manicured fingers on Tisamenus's sleeve. Even the folds of the knuckles were immaculate.

Akhaïdes almost said, "Take your hand off him." That surprised him, for there was nothing obviously wrong with Philaios, except that his open affection for Tisamenus did not fit in the air around them.

Akhaïdes stepped past him and kept walking. Tisamenus followed.

Akhaïdes looked back. Beyond Philaios, who stood flat-footed and surprised, others were smiling. Akhaïdes knew these smiles. They were familiar and chilling: the lust with no name, which only blood sacrifice would satisfy, and even that for only a moment. As he spoke and smiled and touched reaching hands, Tisamenus was walking the narrowest of bridges over snake-infested waters. At the first misstep, he would be gone.

Akhaïdes drew the hood tighter across his face. He said, "I don't need refreshment. Take me to Orestes."

* * *

Fragrant, almost smokeless wax candles lit the High King's chamber. Below the warm, scented light, though, the stench of sickness lay thick and stale, and the walls were patterned with blooms of mold. A cluster of men turned to look, sullenly respectful, as Tisamenus came in. Then they saw Akhaïdes' cloak and parted to let him pass.

Beside a high, curtained bed, another cluster of people had gathered: three men and a pair of slaves. The slaves barely glanced at Tisamenus, then saw the envoy and slid into deep curtsies, at the same time scuttling backward, out of the way.

Akhaïdes stopped. Of the three men, one was bony and black

skinned, with a jowled, sagging face, lank black hair, and bagging eyes: Egyptian by appearance, and a doctor by his long, straight dress. The second was shorter and wider, with a trim gray beard and a modest paunch. Then the third man raised his head.

He was small—not naturally, but as age and disease had bent him. A generation ago, he might have been as tall as Akhaïdes. Now the bald, scaly back of his head, the highest point of his body, wouldn't quite reach Tisamenus's collarbone. One skinny hand, warped as a leper's, was cocked across his chest. His head—his entire body, swathed with stiff gold cloth— twisted down and to the right as if pivoting on that withered arm and hand. The cloth seemed to stir of its own volition, throwing light around the walls. The face . . .

Akhaïdes' heart missed a beat, then started again with a painful lurch. Tisamenus said, "Father," and dropped to both knees. And Akhaïdes, despite the cloak, the ring, and everything he knew, sank down instantly beside him. He could not have done anything else.

Familiar eyes looked out of a face he knew. It was tinged yellow now, with skin like cloth that had been wadded and never smoothed, hanging in deep folds from the two hard knobs of the cheekbones. There was no beard anymore—just thin yellowish hairs clumped here and there amid crevices and pale warts.

But it was Akhaïdes' own face, and more his own than any reflection could ever be. It was the face in his first, oldest memory: young and hale, helmeted in gilded leather, lifting him up, kissing him, turning away. Orestes. The High King. Not Echemus, despite the old man's insistence, and not himself, not a dream, not a prophecy. Orestes.

Tisamenus said, "The envoy from Delphi, Wanax."

"I will see him." The voice was high and broken, dragging at the ends like a frayed coat.

The other two men raised the High King by his elbows as

they might a piece of furniture, lifting him to sit on the curtained bed. The warped body straightened reluctantly, as if it might break before it would yield, and they were speaking to him, to the High King, to Orestes Agamemneides, about medicine and worry and getting too tired. Akhaïdes held himself immobile, feeling all that it cost him, even safe inside the hood, to show nothing of himself.

Orestes perched there, one waxy eyelid drooping, that eye uncommitted and uninterested, but the other as cold and quick as a cock's. A corner of his thin mouth twitched, drooling slightly, and when he spoke, that side of his mouth did not move. He said in a high, wavering voice, "Leave us."

The two men still leaned over him, holding his arms, talking. The doctor's glance at the shorter man was rich with enmity, but when Orestes twitched, they both together held him tighter, closer.

Tisamenus stood. "He said to leave us."

Hawmai—the broad man was Hawmai, the High King's lawagetas; Akhaïdes had not recognized him until that moment—barely glanced at Tisamenus.

Akhaïdes stood, too, pushing himself away from the refuge of earth. He felt his mouth moving. He heard his own voice say, "Go away, all of you."

Hawmai looked at him, startled. The doctor turned to Tisamenus. "He shouldn't be excited," he said, not unkindly. His accent was Egyptian. "Keep him calm. His heart."

"Yes," Tisamenus answered him.

The doctor released Orestes' arm and stepped away, then turned to wait for Hawmai.

Hawmai stood fixed. "If there is a message, we all should hear it."

Akhaïdes made himself speak again—something Menetor had taught him. "I'm here at the High King's call, not yours." His voice cracked, and he swallowed hard. His knees quivered as if they might give way again. He needed to lean on something. Tisamenus stood firm as a tree beside him. It required an effort of will not to reach for him.

"He won't understand," Hawmai said again. "The message will be wasted."

Akhaïdes breathed past the constriction in his chest. "That's not your concern. Orestes Agamemneides asked an augury, and he will receive it. I am the Delphic envoy. I say leave us now." He raised the ring toward Hawmai as if brandishing a weapon.

In moments, the three of them were alone. Even the slaves had fled. Then the High King stirred, twisted his head to the side and up, and said in that ragged whine, "Show us your face."

Tisamenus murmured, "The envoy is always anonymous."

The High King ignored him, waiting.

With shaking hands, Akhaïdes pushed the hood back.

The harsh Pelopeid eye moved over him, unhurried, assessing. The distorted mouth worked, and a thin string of spittle, fine as a spider's thread, descended slowly from his chin. "What is your name, Envoy?"

"I am Akhaïdes Outlaw." His voice came out just above a whisper, but it seemed to echo in this room. He also said, "Ephialtes."

The eye flicked over his face. "Who was your mother?"

Akhaïdes felt Tisamenus straining beside him.

"I have no claim on kin, Wanax. I am first-degree outlaw."

"Answer me."

"Her name was Laothoe, of the Afeideides. Her father was a son of Echemus." He cleared his throat, swallowed, and rubbed his mouth with the back of his hand.

"A distaff Herakleid, Echemus, but a good man for all that. And damned handy with a bow, lucky for us. You look like him. And your mother's mother?"

"Great-great-granddaughter of Oineus, lord."

The one vivid eye fixed on him. "Subtle, subtle Envoy. Oineus was father to Tydeus and had only that one child. Tydeus had only Diomedes, who had one child, who died childless."

"There was a son. A young boy when his father died, but he survived."

"You get that blood through women, so it's not your own. There are no more Tydeides. The madman is finally gone. Unless you think he lives in you."

Akhaïdes swallowed.

"Your father?"

"Hyades Makhaonaides from the line of Aphidamas. Chief of Ladon in Arcadia."

The grim, bright ancient eye searched Akhaïdes until he had to close his own eye and lower his head.

Orestes said, "You look as Arcadian as my son's dog did. Tell me, Akhaïdes Outlaw, did this Hyades acknowledge you?"

Akhaïdes tried to speak, but no sound came. He stared at the floor.

The old man's head began to bob, his whole racked body working, the scrawny strings of whiskers sliding and catching on the gold of the gown. The thread of spit widened.

"But then," Orestes said, "why wouldn't he? And what did you do with your eye—leave it on some Arcadian's pointed stick? I'm not impressed."

Half his face smiled—a gnarled grimace to himself. "I want my message."

Akhaïdes unhooked the lid of the case, fumbling. He extended the tube toward Tisamenus and watched his hand reach into the dark and withdraw the curl of pith. His own hands shook so that the hanging lid tapped softly.

Tisamenus unrolled the pithleaf and read it through silently. Then he looked at Akhaïdes.

Akhaïdes began, "To Orestes son of Agamemnon, son of Atreus, son of Pelops, son of Tantalus, Wanax of Mycenae, and High King. Greetings from the priestesses at Delphi."

Akhaïdes glanced at Tisamenus. The young man was following along with one fingertip on the pith.

"The ladies answer you: What comes at evening except the dark? No power can turn back the sun. Touch fire, and you flame like a torch against the coming night. Leave the dead to the living, and the living to the dead."

Tisamenus lifted his head to confirm, "That's all."

Orestes' spittle thread broke, droplets rolling down the stiff cloth like beads from a broken necklace.

"Yet it's better to burn than to rot," Orestes said. His eye rolled toward them, full of cool malice. "And which of you two, I wonder, is the living, and which is the dead? The answer would surprise all three of us, I suspect." The eye shifted from Tisamenus to Akhaïdes and back.

"Hyades was an idiot," Orestes said. "I'm only sorry that before you ran off, you didn't grill his balls and make him eat them. *That* would be worth being outlawed for."

Akhaïdes swallowed. "He was not available."

Orestes' brow lifted on one side, sketching amusement and perhaps approval. Then his head began a bobbing motion, up and down, mechanical as a well-cock. "I went to Delphi. I was younger than this one, still a whelp. I'd killed my bitch mother and her filthy lover. My sister, being female, got off easy. But I'd been outlawed all winter, living in that hole in the mountain you call home—that sty, Ladon. Nothing to do, crap food, piss to drink, no one worth talking to. And Hyades and your mother and that roach pack of sons. What a nightmare. They named you correctly. 'Ephialtes.'"

Orestes breathed out hoarsely, like a pot whistling. "I was exiled and outlawed, my kingdom beating itself to death. I crawled to Delphi for help. They made me carry filth, muck their chamber pots. I was like a slave—me, Orestes Agamemneides Pelopeides. Then they whipped me—in front of my friends, my supporters, the men who would do anything, give anything, to see me on my throne. They whipped me with my own chariot goad.

"Then what did they show me? A *bug.* A giant bug in a carpenter's apron. Me? I don't think so. They must have laughed themselves sick, them and their stinking snake. They made me . . ." Hard red knurls appeared at his cheeks. "They made me plant trees. *Trees.* My kingdom rotting away, and I'm planting trees." Orestes paused as if thinking, and Akhaïdes watched the beads of spit roll slowly down the gold cloth gown.

Finally, Orestes said, "Now my kingdom is rotting away again, and I can't even hold a tree slip in my hand.

"I wonder whether you had the balls to stand up to those smutty priests, or you just spread your cheeks and let them screw you. Running off, waiting on Herakleids, now carrying notes like a slave—I know the answer. You're not what I need. Not you, not this child."

Orestes' withered arm twitched. "I sleep with young girls so I won't die in the night. Sleeping is all I can do with them. But I made many sons in my life." The unresponsive mouth twisted his tone into a high flatness.

Akhaïdes' chest contracted. He stopped breathing at all.

The eye shifted again to him. "I didn't sleep with your mother for her beauty. I slept with her because she was Echemus's granddaughter. The rest of his family was nothing. They married nothings and created nobody. The blood deserved another chance. When she didn't get a baby the first time, I had to try again, even though by then she stank of goats and that pig husband. I stopped there once more on my first rounds as High King. I saw you and thought I'd succeeded. Hah!"

Akhaïdes whispered without sound, "I remember."

"I made many sons in my life. I thought you might be the best of them all."

Akhaïdes did not move, did not breathe.

"But instead, you wasted your life. You may leave me."

Akhaïdes stood still, trembling.

"Leave me," the High King said.

Akhaïdes turned and strode out.

* * *

He stopped in the hall, stooped, and held himself. His back and shoulders hunched like a cripple's, like Orestes'. He pressed his hands against his thighs, shaking uncontrollably.

Tisamenus gripped his arm, dragged him down the passage, and kicked open a door. Slamming it behind them, he said, "No one saw." He added fiercely, "I hope he enjoyed that, the hateful old crow."

Akhaïdes sank to his knees, clutching himself, shaking and rocking. "Utsir," he whispered in Bajgana. "Ah, *Utsir, Utsir, Utsir, nadad tuslaäch.*"

"What did you say?" Then, very softly, "What did *he* say?"

Akhaïdes groaned.

Tisamenus ran a hand through his own hair. "We're both idiots. What did Menetor say about blood between us? He even called us brothers. I thought he was insulting us. Maybe *he* thought he was insulting us. But he was telling the truth."

Tisamenus laid both hands on Akhaïdes' bowed head. Akhaïdes gasped and shivered. Tisamenus said, "I think it must be true. I think we have to believe it."

"I can't." Akhaïdes raised his face blindly between Tisamenus's hands. "I can't. I don't know how."

Tisamenus threw his long hair back, knelt on the floor, and took his brother in his arms.

* * *

Akhaïdes stayed in that room until after nightfall. He sat on the floor in a corner, wrapped in the red cloak, turning and turning the envoy's ring on his finger. Tisamenus did not seem to want anything, only to sit together, sharing the same space, breathing the same chill air. A tall slave woman—Akhaïdes remembered her but had forgotten her name—guarded the door, perfectly silent, motionless on a low stool, never looking at Akhaïdes but allowing only Tisamenus to enter.

Tisamenus left often but always returned. Once, he brought food with his own hands: a steaming, fragrant meat stew. The bowl was solid silver, and Akhaïdes understood the generosity, but he couldn't swallow food. He didn't touch it.

Once, he whispered, "Everything he said is true."

"He doesn't know. He doesn't know anything about you."

"I thought everything was done. But it wasn't done. It hadn't even started yet. It hadn't even begun. My mother lied me into murder. Hyades was right. My brothers were right. I killed them for being right."

"Just move from moment to moment until it's over."

Akhaïdes looked up. "This will never be over."

Tisamenus did not disagree.

* * *

What Tisamenus did do was something Akhaïdes would never have expected, would never have predicted, and would never have asked for. He went back to his father's door and stood outside it for a moment, drawing a calming breath. Then he turned the latch and walked in. And before he could lose his nerve, before he could notice who else was in the room, and consider what they might say or do, before Orestes could spit out something caustic, Tisamenus said, "I've never asked you for anything." Then he drew a still deeper breath and continued.

* * *

After moonset, the slave led the way with a raised hand lamp, through a chain of passages, a small, unguarded gate, down wooden steps outside the wall. They met no one.

The rain was finished, the night raw and dark. The lamp threw a splash of light on muddy pavement. The horse was waiting, held by a sleepy, incurious groom. The slave stopped and stood, still as statuary, the lamp high in her hand.

Akhaïdes mounted and took his bag from the groom. It was quite heavy.

Tisamenus said, "There is food to carry you safely home, and payment to Delphi for the message to our father. Go in peace, Envoy."

There was nothing more to be said between them. The horse shifted, wanting to move.

Tisamenus stepped away to stand, erect and utterly alone, in the lamplight. The horse strode past him, into the black night.

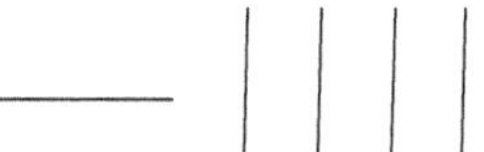

There's a darkness living deep in my soul
I still got a purpose to serve
So let your light shine, deep into my home
God, don't let me lose my nerve.[xiii]

— *Erik Francis Schrody*

The boys and the slaves were waiting for Akhaïdes, fretting impatiently while he slid off the horse's back, straightened his knees, and flexed his stiff hand. They took the ring and cloak and message case from him, took him by the sleeves and led him, without explanation, to the priests' hall.

A crowd of acolytes sat on the floor around Menetor's door. They all looked at Akhaïdes, but no one spoke. He ducked into the cell and found the dwarf cook surrounded by priests, all of them also sitting on the floor, and Menetor on the low pallet bed, sallow and still.

As if concluding a longer conversation, the cook said, "But he's much better now." He glowered as if defying Akhaïdes to contradict him.

Akhaïdes sank down on his heel and took Menetor's hand. The wrist was cinched with muslin. Menetor didn't open his eyes, but his cracked yellow lips moved. He said, "You."

Akhaïdes sat on the gritty stone floor. He wrapped both hands around the old man's cold claw and held it, watching his face, trying to understand. He finally had to ask, "Did you know?"

"Did I know what?"

Akhaïdes got up and went out.

He carried the heavy shoulder bag through the village to the pigs' shed. The villagers, though still cautious, drew away as he passed, but the little boys skipped around him, heedless as pigeons.

Akhaïdes lifted uneaten food from the bag—bread, dried spiced vegetables, sausages—offering it first to the unpollutable children, who either snatched and gobbled it or refused it with disdain. He dropped the rejected items into the pigs' feed basin while the animals watched as critically as the boys did, and then jostled each other for the best leavings.

In the bottom of the bag, among the crumbs, was a box: wooden, twice as long and wide as his hand, and a finger deep. It was carved in swooping spirals, and closed with a bronze latch as clever as a piece of jewelry.

The payment that Tisamenus had mentioned. He did not touch the box, but carried the bag back to the priests' house. The crowd at Menetor's door looked up all together. He stepped inside.

One of the priests said, "What."

"This is from Mycenae. Payment for the oracle."

The priest took the bag, set it on the floor between his shoes, and lifted the box out.

Without looking, Menetor said, "The fee for the oracle was paid before you left here to deliver it. We don't work on credit. Open that, someone."

The priest turned the bronze latch. A folded square of pithleaf opened a little as the lid lifted. The priests all leaned to see. The leaf was covered with row after row of marks and symbols: writing. Under black silk so thick it looked at first like leather, a bundle of dried twigs—thorns, herbs, and flowers— was tied together with heavy silver thread. Under this was a gold chain, folded over and over on itself. Everyone sighed together.

The chain was as long as the priest's arm, the plain, perfect links the size of a looped thumb and finger, but so thick they could barely pass through each other. The priest lifted it, and it moved as if alive in his hands, as heavy and disinterested as a snake. He curled it back inside the box.

Under a fold of silk, the priest found a ring—massive, silver, scummy with age, holding a big oval lapis stone. He held it out on his palm for all to see. The face of the stone was incised with two animals rolling over each other, perhaps fighting. The ring looked old but seemed never to have been worn.

The priest returned the ring to the box, on top of the chain, and opened the pithleaf. He studied the marks, then passed it to a neighbor, who did the same while everyone else watched. A murmur, so low that Akhaïdes did not catch the words, followed the pith around the room. When it finally returned to the first priest, he asked his fellows, "Do we agree?" They all murmured assent. The priest rose a little and whispered into Menetor's ear.

Menetor drew a sharp breath, and his eyes flew open, then closed again. He said, "Give him his message."

The priest handed the leaf up to Akhaïdes.

For a moment, all that Akhaïdes could think was that Tisamenus must have painted this himself. Whatever it said, it could not be the kind of message to be entrusted to a clerk. He tried to picture Tisamenus at a table, in lamplight, one leg extended and his back bent, holding the slip of beaten pith in place with one hand and . . . The picture failed. He had never seen anyone write and had no idea how it was done. Elawon would have known. In one corner of the leaf were two brown smudges, side by side.

He finally had to ask, "What does it say?"

"These blots are Tisamenus's blood and Orestes'. The High King claims you as his own son, and his heir concurs. The gold is for your absolution."

In the silence that followed, Menetor laughed softly, airlessly, then murmured, "Now give him his father's ring. You all have work to do.”

* * *

The sanctuary door wobbled open, and the priests filed in, vanishing instantly into the dark. Bees swooped and hovered in the doorway. The one-armed servant, back at his old post, touched his forehead to Akhaïdes. Akhaïdes returned the gesture, pulled off his boots, then grasped the bell rope. It was warm from the sun. He pulled and let it go. The bell sounded, sudden and low, echoing against the Faedriad cliffs before it died away.

Bees hummed around his head. He left his lies on the threshold stone, stepped into the sanctuary chamber, and knelt. For the third time in his life, he said, “Hear me, Grandfather.”

The sun was so bright, he could see nothing beyond the carpet of light around him—not the priests, not the stone, not the army of votive figures guarding it. But among the votives, a disapproving rattle started, like the vibration of a thousand thin clay wings. He pressed his open hands against the gritty floor, and the noise faded.

A familiar voice asked formally, “Who are you?”

“I am Ephialtes Oresteides, outlaw in the first degree.” The name came off his tongue as smoothly as a lie, but it had to be true.

No blast of rage this time. The votives chirped, then stilled.

“Have you kept to the terms of your outlawry?”

“I have.”

The voice was cool, disbelieving. “For all these years, you did so?”

“I swear it.”

“Then what is your plea?”

“I ask for purification from my faults.”

“Whose are you? What place is empty for you? Who would

pluck you from the jaws of the Serpent, carry you home, and set you by their fire? What friends would speak for you?"

The same questions since time out of mind. He licked his lips. "I belong in Mycenae, with the High King Orestes and Tisamenus Oresteides." He paused. "Xanos Lyceides Lawagetas Dorian might speak for me. The shaman and the armorer of Nafpaktos. Menetor Priest." He cleared his throat. "Elawon Hyadeides and Karnus Priest would speak for me if they were still with the living."

"Who stands behind you? Who confirms what you say?"

"The Great Eye that sees all the world. The spirits of my fathers' and mothers' places. The lioness and the crested boar. Orestes Agamemneides, High King of Mycenae. Tisamenus Oresteides, king of Lacedaemon and heir to the High Seat." He swallowed. "I will put the truth before the Serpent and let it be judged. And see what the Serpent sees when it looks at me."

"You may not like what you see."

"I'm not afraid to look at what is mine."

Still his heart was too constricted to work smoothly. He waited. If he was to be expelled again, to the roadside or the black pool, it would be now. And he would go.

"Truth is here, and Oath. But so are Untruth and False Swearing. Was that gift for them?"

His heart jumped like a bird from cover, its whir momentarily deafening. He struggled to control his voice. "Yes, Grandfather. Is it adequate?"

The voice was amused. "More than adequate, Grandson. Even for you."

His right hand shook and would not stop.

Voices mumbled together. One said to him, "You know, the defense of the High King himself turned on the value of kin blood. He paid a terrible debt for purification, and he only killed his mother. It is very, very difficult to excuse lineage murder. Only the Serpent can do this, and the Serpent eats more such outlaws than it heals."

"I was not kin to these brothers." He raised his head but did not even try to see them. "Their father was not my father. We shared only our mother's body, not his."

The bees sang. Under his hands, beneath the stone flags, something listened intently.

"It is a perilous fault to harm any elders. But if you shared no father, you were closer in blood to your mother than to those you killed."

The voice paused. "It would have been an error to leave her unprotected despite her fault in this matter, including the adultery that made you. Orestes was outlaw when you were conceived, so your very birth was defiled. You have never in your life been unpolluted. Perhaps, that might explain some things to you."

Akhaïdes looked up sharply, into the dark.

"You want to say something?"

He lowered his head again.

"Your mother gave herself not only to another man, but to an outlaw. Orestes and she could have made you only when she was already long married and he was in exile. Her husband should have strangled her and drowned you at birth, but he didn't. We wonder why."

The whole length of his life turned inside out yet again.

"You had blood in common with those you killed, with the spirits you doomed and wasted. Making a peryton is always outlawable, whatever the kinship. Because you were born polluted, you had no right to touch them, even in affection. It will be more dangerous than you can imagine, but the compensation is given, and powerful voices speak for you. You can, perhaps, be cleansed of your murders and of your birth, if the Serpent chooses.

"Writing is an art as well as a tool. There is a word in your note that we have no precise spoken word for. It means that a person will go out without saying where. The High King intends that you be released into the world, to do as you must."

Akhaïdes could barely move his lips. "And may I confess the rest?"

"How many times are you outlawed?"

"Just the one time, Grandfather. But—"

"Then one outlawry is all we are concerned with here."

"Elawon. His death was my fault. And I brought death to people who never harmed me. I murdered my own children."

"You did not, yourself, spill Elawon's blood, nor did you take any part in the plan to spill it. In addition, he is with his dead, so any problems between you are resolved. Even your role, whatever it was, in his birth and survival.

"The people who took you in are like Lokrians and Perioikoi: of no account. That, we assume, is why you chose to live among them."

He moved his head slightly, affirmative.

"They are dismissed and will not be considered further." The voice was comfortable again. "The High King's support is unequivocal. You are fortunate to have such a kinsman. We will consult together and tell you the day and time."

Feet moved away, then came back. "This is for you." A familiar hand passed the silver ring to him. "You will stay in the guesthouse. A room has always been ready for you."

The formula again. All the times he had heard it, he had known it to be, in a way, true. And it was, in a way, still true.

He raised his head again, this time to locate the stone in the darkness. He could not see it, but he heard a low rumble and hum—a warning that it, at least, had not forgotten. He slid the ring onto his right forefinger and closed his other hand over it, then pressed his interlocked thumbs against his front teeth.

So simple. All so simple. He backed out over the threshold, got stiffly to his feet, and looked down at the ring. The animals carved into the stone might be fighting but might equally be playing, or even making love. They were a lioness and a crested boar. Mycenae and Arcadia. Tydeus, Echemus, his mother. Orestes. Tisamenus.

He went to stand in the shade, beside his father's stele, under his father's trees.

* * *

In the guesthouse, the black-haired boy tended him. This was the boy's first formal work, and he performed his duty precisely and with awed caution. As the rules required, he did not speak to Akhaïdes. Akhaïdes did not speak, either. It was not permitted, and also, he did not want to.

The night before the purification, he did not sleep. He lay still in the warm little cell, staring beyond the ceiling and rambling through his own thoughts.

The terms of his outlawry were as familiar as his own skin. They gave him, however lowly, a place: all the margins and interstices that no one else wanted. He had entered them on leaving this country, as he walked unseen between alien lands. And he had never left them again. Exile could encompass the breadth of the sky or of a fingernail, or both at the same time.

All who passed through outlawry had some pattern awaiting them when exile was over: home, family, obligations; a fabric reweaving itself, with the man an irreducible part that weave; a door closing, and the man securely back on the path he must follow—a path that Akhaïdes could not imagine for himself.

As a child, he had sometimes reached out his arms and felt as if invisible threads from his own fingertips tied together himself and every plant, every animal, every particle of soil, and every person, past and future. During those moments, he had been as solidly embedded as the ancient rock that his brothers once worked for days to uproot from its matrix of loess, pulling the dirt and stones from its sides and base until it balanced, bare and dusty, on a narrow finger of soil—and *still* could not be moved.

He had known the magic that the rocks and the plants and the animals knew. It was the only magic they had, and all they needed to have, to be exactly described and bound by their fixed natures, so that they could say only "I am here," and "This is mine," and know that nothing more was necessary.

The goat said, "I am goat." The bird said, "I am bird." The bull said, "I am bull." And then they were silent, for they had no need to say more. That was their magic, and he had held it, had understood it completely. But even as he had grasped his own right to say, "I am Ephialtes," the enchantment had dissolved. There was no Ephialtes he could have described without using the word "not," and the dislocation of his actual, temporal life had closed again over his head.

And what would it mean to say now, in this place, "I am Ephialtes," or, worse, "I am Akhaïdes"? A cat's yowl had more meaning. A single live lizard at an anthill had more purpose. But tomorrow, he would look through the eyes of the Serpent and know the purpose of this pointless creature with the meaningless name.

Orestes had told them to purify Akhaïdes and release him. But if the purification succeeded, he would not even own his own outlawry. What then?

He could refuse. Tisamenus had lied to him about the gift he carried back to Delphi, knowing that he might refuse it if he knew what it was for, or might discard it along the way and pretend it had been stolen. If he refused, he still had his place with the slaves of Delphi. If he accepted, he might emerge clean, and far more useless than any slave.

He lay awake through the night, waiting and aware of his own waiting, afraid and aware of his own fear, but waiting still.

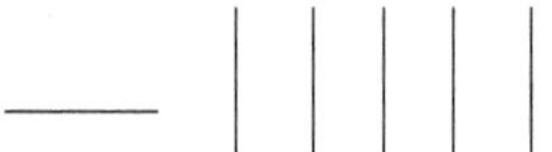

You knew damned well I was a snake before you took me in.[xiv]

— *Oscar Brown*

They dressed him in a long shirt like a child's, red in color, and led him to the Kastalia spring. There, where the water welled forth into a carved-out stone trough, the priests stood guard against the nymph while he put the shirt aside and lay down in the roil of sacred water. The trough was barely larger than a box for the dead. Eye closed, he crossed his hands over his chest, and the water shoved and plucked and eddied over him. It was cold, hot, thin as air and strong as a serpent, as penetrating and many-legged as the monster that guarded it. It handled every part of his body, leaving no secrets. It fizzed and whispered in his ears, around his throat, over Orestes' ring. If he stayed long enough, it would speak.

He stayed as long as he could without breathing. But the water held its own counsel and he came out at last, disappointed.

He had been clean before; now his skin burned with cleanliness. He pulled the shirt back on, over his head, and the priests, cloaked in red and gray, led the way up a path he knew, above the village. Some people stood to watch them pass. Up the escarpment they climbed, along the side of the Serpent's furrow, then up the precipitous trail to the cave of Korkia.

The cavern's mouth seemed unremarkable—a low, rough

doorway into nothing much. But when they stepped inside, Akhaïdes' breath caught.

The chamber was so vast, they could have held horse races inside. The walls were creased, folded limestone and natural pillars, and the ceiling was rough with great crag-edged, upturned wells of darkness. In the torchlit distance, the down-curving sandy floor rose again to a small, rounded, many-fanged opening like a second mouth, with only darkness beyond.

At one side of the entrance, a pair of rubble huts like the Watcher's were piled against the walls. A bowl was carved into the floor before each. Akhaïdes heard rattling and moaning, and from each hut crept a living creature. In shapeless, filthy clothes, with hair that sprang in wild shocks and clumps like piles of mown weeds, they squatted and grumbled before the dark doorways. It took Akhaïdes several moments to identify them as human and, eventually, as women. A collar and chain bound each to the doorpost of her kennel.

"What did you bring us, Menetor?" one mewled, and the other repeated, "What is it? What? What?"

"A suppliant, ladies, but not for you. For the Serpent."

"Outlaw," one sniffed.

"*Pah,* outlaw," said the other.

They spat together.

One sidled closer to peer up at Akhaïdes. "This is a comely one, at least," she said.

The other said, "That last few were ugly, ugly, ugly."

"What does it want?"

"What they always want."

"To make excuses."

"To be hugged and kissed."

"And made all better."

"The Serpent knows how to hug and kiss." A short two-voiced snigger.

"We get the crumbs it leaves—we and our cousin, the

nymph."

"Look, he's afraid of us."

"They're all afraid of us." They cackled again together.

One said, "We are the priestesses of Delphi."

"The Serpent knows us."

"It never eats us."

"It tells us things."

"And we tell you."

"Oracle."

"Maybe."

"Maybe."

"Sometimes, we lie, but not usually."

"But sometimes."

They shifted on their haunches. "Afraid? Afraid? Afraid?"

Suddenly, he was not. He stepped to the nearest, sank down on his heel, and offered his hand, palm down. She snatched it, smelled it, pawed it, licked it, then lifted it onto her head. He stroked her chaotic hair. She wriggled, baring black stubs of teeth.

The other sulked. "Me! Me! Me!"

Menetor came forward. "There will be a gift for each of you. And if the Serpent comes, more gifts."

The priestesses looked at each other. "Good things to eat."

"Outlaw bits."

"Maybe."

"Not this one."

"Maybe not."

Akhaïdes rose. The priests had brought out a wooden table and some baskets. Akhaïdes' eye was adjusting to the darkness. As the priests mounted the torches in brackets, the light stopped shifting and he could make more sense of this.

Up on the walls, on surfaces that seemed naturally smooth, pictures were frescoed: birds and animals, the Old Woman with her bulging eyes and protruding tongue, the Deceptors treacherously intertwined. Truth and Oath leaned precipitously from truncated stalactites. Over the distant toothed portal, a panel displayed the Great Eye. It was the same eye that had ignored and then finally acknowledged his gifts in the hills behind Nafpaktos. It had never lost patience, never cursed him. Of all the signs here, this was the one that might not mean him harm.

The purifying priest called him softly. He turned.

The young man's uncanny looks jolted Akhaïdes. Except for his smaller stature, he might be Hippotes' twin. His poise was all his own, though, as he tilted his head in query. The Herakleid eyes were guileless and patient. Akhaïdes placed his cold fingers in the priest's soft palms and bowed his head.

Four other priests staggered into the cavern, bearing between them a boar with a fiercely crested back. The animal was bound head down, legs tightly folded. Immobile on its litter; it could only snort and glare its wrath at the men who carried it. The priests strained to hoist the litter up and slide it atop a stone plinth. The priestesses murmured, pleased.

The purifying priest still held Akhaïdes' hands, so tightly that Orestes' ring pressed against the bones. "Listen to me, child." His voice was deep and throbbing. "The sun and the moon both make light, but when they are in the sky at once, the day is no brighter. And when they couple, all is dark. Explain."

Akhaïdes lowered his head and thought, but nothing came to him. He looked up again. "If there is an explanation, Grandfather, I don't know it."

"Argus the dog knew his master's scent after twenty years. Did he die then of joy, or of sorrow at seeing Odysseus a beggar in his own kingdom?"

"No one knows."

"Remember this. Some things can be known but are not, and some never can be known. That is not the same, and not different. It is two sides of the same blade. There is Chaos, so there must be order. There is order, so there must be Chaos. A man is a cairn built in a wilderness. You built such a cairn, so you know."

Akhaïdes stared at him. The mellifluous voice went on. "At your birth, the Bull, the Demon, and the Reborn Prince lay between the sun and moon. It was a mighty hour, the hour for the birth of a man who might surpass all others, from the beginning to the end of time. But power belongs to itself, not to us. It uses us for its own purposes, and we are helpless to resist or to step a single stride from the path it drives us down—as you have learned and must remember.

"You will die under the eye of the Bull alone. That also will be a potent hour, because it will relieve the world of both the benefit and the burden of hosting you. And how will you die, child?"

Akhaïdes swallowed. "How can I know?"

"You know. Tell me."

Akhaïdes gazed at the wide, implacable face so like Hippotes'. His throat was dry. He suddenly saw, bright as flame, a javelin in a leather-gloved hand. Then this faded away.

The priest said, "You more than anyone understand that birth and life, dying and death, are not separate, but simply blend one into the next, like the Proteus. As with so much else, the mystery lies not in these things themselves, but in our fear of them. In Kashi they know, and you know, too, that death is not the opposite of life; it is only the opposite of birth. You have never feared death. You have feared the dead."

The priest glanced away, then back at Akhaïdes. "If I asked for your life now, would you give it to me?"

Akhaïdes looked into the untroubled Herakleid eyes. "Freely."

"Now tell me how you will die."

"I assume I'll die as I have lived, in the midst of some ill-informed error of judgment."

The priest's eyes opened a little wider. He smiled. Off to one side, Menetor made his puff. This time, it sounded amused.

"Wrong," the priestesses gloated. "Wrong, wrong."

"I hope I will die fulfilling my responsibility, whatever it is."

"Good," a priestess whispered.

"Good," said the other.

"They always say, die by the fireside, warm and old."

"Good outlaw. Good boy."

The priest released Akhaïdes' hands, then turned and lifted a bronze dagger from a basket. The boar rolled its eyes in helpless warning. Akhaïdes closed his eye and heard the animal's swift, hard thrashing. He looked again. The boar still struggled as the purifying priest held a tall gold cup under the flow of blood. When he took it away, two other priests slid a silver basin under the plinth to catch the rest. The boar sighed and relaxed. Its spirit wriggled free, sank to the floor, and went to sit like a dog at the side of the nearer priestess. She put a companionable hand on its back.

Two more priests came in, carrying a lioness between them. It was a statue of some material or other, covered skillfully with pelt, and would have appeared amazingly lifelike to someone who had never seen an actual lion. Like the boar, it, too, was bound.

They heaved it up onto a second plinth, and the purifying priest pressed the dagger against the statue's throat. There was a growling, gurgling sound, and blood surged again into the waiting cup and then the basin. Then, unaccountably, a spirit lowered itself from the effigy, stretched, and curled up on the floor, by the second priestess. A lioness, perhaps. Or the lion of Nafpaktos still.

The priest took Akhaïdes' hand again, turning his arm to expose a vein inside the wrist—one already scarred by so many futile bloodlettings. The priest opened it yet again, pressed the lip of the cup against the skin, and caught the flow neatly. Another priest came after him, to take more blood into the silver bowl.

Then the purifying priest pressed a pad against the cut, and another wrapped Akhaïdes' wrist with a fillet. The purifying priest swirled the mixed blood in the cup, lifted it to the six parts of the earth, and offered it to Akhaïdes.

"Never forget this. You live in the boar, and the boar lives in you. You are your mother's son. You live in the lioness, and the lioness lives in you. You are your father's son. Drink."

He had tasted the lion's blood, tasted boars', and expected this blend to be spicy and fierce. But it was flat and dense, with no savor. He took a mouthful and lowered the cup. The priest took it from him.

"If you would ask the powers for your life, now is the time."

He looked past the priest, at Menetor. "Will I be sorry?"

Menetor hesitated too long. "I can't say," he answered finally. "If I knew, I would tell you."

"I know what Prometheus saw."

"I believe you."

The purifying priest held out an earthen bottle. "Share this with the ladies," he said. "It is water from Kastalia—the water of life and death, of forgetting and remembering. Birth is forgetting. At death, we remember everything. Drink with them, and you will never be the same."

Akhaïdes knelt and poured water into each priestess's bowl. They lapped it up, neat as cats. He lifted the bottle and drank. Still flavorless, still lethal. It searched through the inside of his body as it had searched outside, fingering every flaw, leaving him unharmed, perhaps more from contempt than from satisfaction.

"Ah."

"Ah."

And he, too, said, "Ah."

The frescoes, impossibly bright, tilted over them, their red mouths and tongues like those of the priestesses who watched him keen-eyed with malice and delight. The priestesses. Suddenly, he knew them.

He asked, "Where is the third? Where is your sister?"

They exchanged startled glances.

"He knows."

"They never know."

"He knows."

The boar and the lioness looked quickly away, keeping their secrets as animals did. One priestess said, "Our sister Alecto."

The other said, "She is not here."

"She is hunting."

"Hunting," confirmed the other.

"Where are your wings?"

One unfolded hers out of nothing, lifted and shook them, then folded them again and they disappeared.

"You have only two houses. Where does she live?"

"One of us comes."

"One goes."

"Two stay here."

"And sometimes, we all hunt together."

They looked up at him, suddenly ferociously intelligent.

"We hunted you, all together."

"But you were gone."

"Now you come to us."

"But not to see us. Not to hear our advice. Not to let us catch you."

"Give us a gift . . ."

"And maybe we won't eat you."

"Maybe."

"And maybe the Serpent won't eat you."

"Maybe."

"But maybe the guardian of the cave will come and eat you. She eats all her husbands."

"Like the spider does."

Akhaïdes said, "They say she's gone from here."

"They wish so, maybe."

"Down there in the dark."

"With the Serpent."

"And the bones of men."

"And of fools."

The priest took the bottle from his hands and gave him the cup of blood.

Akhaïdes poured, and the Erinyes drank. They threw back their heads and wiped their mouths with their fingers. Their eyes shone like bats'.

"Now call, outlaw."

"Call."

The cavern was filling softly with a kind of smoke. He crossed the floor, the cup in both hands, and climbed the slick, damp rise to the far portal. Among the stone fangs, a third bowl was carved into living rock. He trickled blood into it, then straightened. Under his feet, the earth stirred.

He could not call, but he said aloud, "I am Ephialtes Oresteides. Please come to me." His voice was so strained, he himself hardly recognized it.

Staring into the immutable black of the passage beyond, he was alone, blind, and oh, so cold. Shards of reflected light from the cup in his hands and from Orestes' ring shivered against the walls but found nothing beyond the stone fangs and the bowl of blood. Something like steam or smoke wreathed, twisting and furling, across his sight. He could hear a faint, coarse, rhythmic hissing: his own blood as the slivers of ice scratched past one another. On his face and hands, he could feel the rising pressure of air from some massive, silent approach.

He could not feel his own lips or fingers. His throat was paralyzed. He could not breathe—did not want to breathe, in case that sound masked other sounds. The passage exhaled softly. Somewhere inside and below, some small stones fell.

He backed down the incline to the gathered priests, never turning from the ringed black mouth. The purifying priest took the cup from him and called, "Here is a suppliant. Come forth and speak to him."

Behind them, the Erinyes chorused, "Come forth, come forth, come forth!" and cackled mocking laughter.

Larger stones rumbled. The sand under their feet shifted and hissed. The other priests retreated a little, closer to the entrance.

Up the tunnel's throat came a gust of air, icy and pure as wind off a glacier, then hot and rank as the lion's breath, finally becoming a squall of sulfurous putrefaction that set even the Erinyes coughing and gagging. Akhaïdes did not move. If something was coming to eat him, he would let it.

The Serpent came: first, through a roil of filthy mist, just the eyes, like lamps; then the glistening loll of a tongue like the finest leather riding whip. A thin-skinned black skull, trim as a lance head, then length on length of lustrous keeled scales, patterned gray and pink below, dense blood red along the spine. The head lifted, the body arching upward, higher than any man. Akhaïdes could not have encircled the neck with both arms, and the head was larger than a bull's.

He heard soft thumping as the priests all knelt.

The sleek head turned side to side, gleaming like a jewel in the smoky light, eyes like caves in bas-relief. The nose tilted downward to the bowl, and the tongue dipped and flickered. The head lifted again.

The Serpent said, "I am fate. I am chance. I choose the Chosen. Another Pelopeid comes, as deep in trouble as only a Pelopeid can get. What do you ask?"

Akhaïdes had to try three times to speak. "Purification of my faults. And knowledge of myself and my future."

"Who are you, that I should give you these?"

"I am Ephialtes Oresteides Pelopeides, son of the High King. I am Akhaïdes Outlaw. I am the Good Kinsman of Arcadia. I am the Hunter of Nafpaktos."

The head wove rhythmically for a moment; then the entire vast body flexed sideways down the slope toward him. The head swooped low, and the tongue glided over his face and hands, light as a flirting woman's scarf. It was dry and surprisingly warm. The round, lidless eye did not actually see him. It was too deep, too distant, although he could have raised either hand and touched it. The skin around it was precisely carved, gleaming black.

The head split open side to side, the mouth amazingly long in so delicate a face. Fangs swung forward as if to strike, a clear drop of venom at each tip. Akhaïdes had locked his knees to keep upright, but there was no stopping his body's quaking. The open mouth turned sideways, and he could see down the long reptilian throat as smooth and clean as marble.

Then the fangs folded neatly; the mouth closed; the head elevated away. The Serpent said, "This one corrected his errors. He killed the abomination that should not have lived. He will set everything right, whether or not he knows that he does so. I don't want him; he is clean. He already knows where his future lies. I will show him no pictures. He may use me for his sign."

The purifying priest made an inquiring noise.

"The sign of the Serpent for his shield," it said. "And his doorposts. His linens if he wishes. He is mine."

It was leaving already, curling away, gliding back toward its portal. The other priests stirred, rising.

Akhaïdes said, "Don't."

The body stopped its sidelong passage. The head swiveled in his direction.

He said, "What about Elawon? What was your role in that?"

The tongue flickered. "You accuse me. But you believe you are responsible. And Temenus Herakleides, because he loves you, which makes you responsible again, in your mind. That has nothing to do with me."

"You were there. I felt you. You let them take the thing I valued most." It was his old reliable anger, loosening the knots that held him.

"There is more in the world to value. Go find it." The Serpent's head lowered, weaving a little. A habit of thought rather than a threat, Akhaïdes recognized, and more fear sloughed away.

"He was mine. You let them kill him." He thought of something. "I wonder if you can be killed."

There was a stunned silence. The Erinyes backed into their kennels until only their noses and hair looked out, and the priests stepped closer to each other, passing the cup between them like evidence of a crime.

The Serpent said mildly, "Interesting. You threaten me. Perhaps you believe you have nothing further to lose? Yet even you know that is not so."

"Prove it."

The Serpent tilted its nose and looked down it to finally, really see him. The eyes both reflected light and absorbed it, giving no information.

"Who is this fool who thinks truth is more important than his skin? I told you once, you would not like where I could take you."

"Take me there. Take me anywhere. Don't leave me here with my hands full of snake shit and think I'll be grateful."

The purifying priest ventured, "He doesn't know what he's saying."

The tongue flickered. "Really? He seems in consummate control of his wits, to me. You haven't brought me one like this in a long time. When he calls me, you don't need all this mystical babble. I come willingly."

The tall head pivoted, regarding Akhaïdes again. "But you? If you want truth from me, try it first with yourself. Remind yourself what you already believe: that you let Elawon go deliberately. That Temenus Herakleides released you from him because he loves you, because you made him love you. Is it true that you could have saved Elawon? I don't know, and neither do you. But it is guilt, not loss, that you have mourned so lavishly. Do we understand each other now?"

"We do," Akhaïdes whispered.

The Serpent lowered its head and looped sideways, almost casually, up the inclined floor. The long nose tilted. The tongue wrapped smoothly around the inside of the bowl.

They all waited. The head lifted vertically, then leveled, in a motion so graceful it could only be female. "Yes," she said. "Pure Pelopeid blood, indeed, upholding your heritage. I would recognize the taste of one of you anywhere. Lineage-murdering son of a mother-killer and a fouled adulteress. Pretty birthright. Pretty boy." The head tilted toward him. "But blood is the token everyone gives. I think you would give me more than this."

Without realizing it, he had followed her up the slope. He was again close enough to touch her. "I'll give you whatever you say, in trade for the kind of truth that you know."

"Now, what could you give me that I might want?" The slender tongue lolled provocatively. "Body. Mind. Will. Hope. Hunger. Fear. Love."

"Willingly."

"Then walk with me," she said. "Are you afraid?"

"A little, still."

"You think I'm a danger to . . . what? To your body? Your spirit? Which you have already pledged to me? That's not it. You think I would not deal with you fairly, because evil touched and turned you. I am certainly a danger to you, but that is not the reason. In fact, I may be your only true friend in this world."

The head dipped farther, lower than the arched neck. They were nose to nose. The tongue brushed his face again. Her breath smelled of rot and ice. "You think as others do, in their cramped little ways: that evil is attracted to a man's deeds. That a man is wicked because he kills unbefittingly, or tortures the wrong people, rapes the wrong women, burns the wrong children, refuses to share with those he owes sharing to, leaves or harms his companions. But that is not the work of evil any more than it is goodness to stand firmly at a shoulder you are already obliged to defend, or to give in apparent generosity to those who would take anyway."

The tongue curled around his wrists—the softest of manacles. "I'll tell you something you already know, if you can remember. Evil is not of the hands; evil is of the spirit."

"What does that mean?"

"You know. When you saved your mother and the infant, you knew. When you killed your brothers. When you buried a baby. When you threw so many souls to Death. When you left your son alive and tormented yourself every day thereafter. When you killed horses and men to spare them torture. When you fought that man Oxylus. When you wept under Tisamenus's hand and then under Makhawis's—the only safe places in all the world to do so. When you accepted Elawon, despite what you *still* fear of him. When you knelt by his corpse, afraid to touch him. When you faced Xanos, Hippotes, Satnios, Orestes. When you opened your heart and body to the only man who truly . . . You knew. What is the most terrible pain? What is the cruelest thing to face, to submit to, to let grind away your spirit and your reason? Not fear, not death, not murder, not cowardice, nor even living with your own fear, death, murder, and cowardice."

"Love."

"How carelessly you treat it or how late you are to recognize it is less important than you can imagine. You have failed every time, though not in the way you believe. Your flaw is not that you do not love. In fact, you love very well. But you do not know how to be loved, and the harm you do is for that reason alone. What is the bait for evil? It is not you. Never you."

"That's too easy."

"Only because you would punish yourself if you were me. But you are not me, and I won't do it. Besides, with or without permission, you will always punish yourself more relentlessly than any other man, power, or Erinye could do. You parse blame so painstakingly that you can always find your share. I bite with a larger tooth."

She glided among the priests, who bowed rapidly out of her way. Unasked but knowing that she meant him to, Akhaïdes followed. At the mouth of the cave, they looked out and down. Ordinary clouds and sky, ordinary day. A few houses, goats. A cow. Plain, common sunlight on the plated head of a snake. And the sacred way—her own path to the Faedriads, Kastalia, the pool of the dead, the underworld, the sea. Where she hunted the bodies and souls of men. Where she once had propelled him to shore just to warn him.

She said, "The Herakleids are coming again. They killed my priest—a singularly stupid move even for men as arrogant and ignorant as those.

"Herakles never came to me. If he had, I might have hindered his annoying busyness, but he did not. This present Herakleid king, the one you love and who loves you—he, also, has never deigned to speak with me. And so they wander deeper and deeper into trouble.

"But who are these other people, these Dorians? They have no flavor, and I can't hear their thoughts even in my own dreams. It is their coming that I will not survive. They will turn my wealth into bookkeeping, my sanctuary into warehouses of double-dealing, my precious spring into bathwater, and its guardian into some tedious, pretty human virgin. My love into trade goods. My vengeance into little sticks to slap at each other. My wrath into fire they can carry in a pocket, to light their pipes. They will change the glory of sacrifice into whining and carping and begging unearned favors, and call it love."

Her head lifted sharply. "Ah, I am done with this. It disgusts me. Walk with me, where only you and I and my nymphs and Erinyes can go."

She turned back along her own length, the torchlight catching on her folding, rippling skin. He laid his hand on her head. It was sleek and hard and cold as an arrowhead: black skin, pale fingers, silver ring, blue stone.

They walked together.

Leaving the priests and the light behind, they crossed the cavern, climbed through the saw-toothed stalagmites and under the Great Eye, crossed another, smaller chamber into an unlit channel that curved away and down. Even without light, he could see. His feet found, unerringly and without his hands' assistance, balance through pathless boreholes of scree and gravel and precarious boulders. The Serpent moved easily beside him, the head like polished stone, her unblinking eyes reflecting the no-light and the sheen of damp rock. They descended unscalable slots and cliffs, traversed ceilingless caverns clouded with bats, skirted phosphorescent lakes through immeasurable time.

They passed the guardian nymph Delphine, clinging like a monstrous gnat to an upper wall and pulsing, as gnats did, with a rhythm they alone could hear. Her woman's head on its many-jointed neck followed his path exactly, but her wings remained folded. She only lifted one foreleg to nibble pensively at the toes as she watched him go by.

They passed racks and drifts of human bones, bent and shattered like the knot of the Serpent's stone, but also gnawed at the ends and stripped of marrow. The Erinyes were right: With such a trove below, Delphine need not hunt above.

The Erinyes themselves, unleashed somehow, trailed behind, muttering and mumbling, carrying the gold cup between them, and the spirits of the boar and the lioness followed. The Serpent ignored them but, inexplicably wary, glanced sideways at Akhaïdes once in a while. They descended without stopping for hour after hour, perhaps day after day. The rough, pathless rock did not hurt his feet, and he was not tired or hungry or discontented.

They came out of a narrow vertical cleft, into the land of the dead.

It was as he had heard: flat and gray, with low hills robed in mist and pale trees. Little villages. Tilled fields sprouting dull gray plants with dusty leaves. A few furtive dogs, languid oxen, dull, high-spined horses. As they trailed into the sourceless light, the boar and the lioness slunk off to find their own kind. Some house doors opened, and people came out.

The Serpent stopped, and Akhaïdes stopped with her. They watched the torpid approach of a man, a woman, a few others.

"Don't fret," the Serpent said. "When you finally come here indeed, all your own dead will assemble. They are much more interesting than these."

"My own dead? But most of them are from elsewhere. If the land of the dead can include all the dead, what are perytons?"

The Serpent's head lifted a little. "Not everything men say is wrong just because they say it. My perytons exist, for certain. You have made more than your share, and them you will not find here. Do you believe you will not find your wife, your daughters, your grandchildren, the warriors who followed you? By their own laws, they were not lost, and so you are correct. They have gone and will come again in new wombs. And as for the boy whose name must not be spoken . . ." Her tongue flicked. "We shall see."

To face Juchii—it was worth being a peryton to avoid.

Reading his thought, the Serpent added, "This is a land of many parts. There are those like this, with the dull, the hostile, the loveless, the grudging. But there are others as well. Some are beautiful, and worth the search to find them. Anger and ill will find each other, but so does love.

"Look. These you should know."

The group approaching was led by a man not much older than Akhaïdes. In shape, he was like the baron Hawmai. But he was Hyades, whom Ephialtes had called father, full of years now, gray-haired, and fat enough to be termed prosperous.

"You two," the Serpent said. "You should be comrades and clasp hands. You made each other."

Hyades stopped and stood, empty eyed. Behind him stood a woman who was nearly faceless, so carefully had she hidden her thoughts throughout her life. Behind her, Akhaïdes recognized Echemus, stooped and blinking. The rest were strangers: Tydeus, perhaps; Diomedes; more: his legacy of crazy, vicious men. His mother glanced at him and they both looked away, unreconciled.

The Serpent said, "That man Hyades kept you alive. Who would do that for the bastard spawn of an outlaw and his own wife? You should honor him as your true father, more than that thug in Mycenae. There are times that I regret letting him go."

"Orestes?"

"I should have bitten him. If he had given me as much trouble as you, believe me, I would have—and shared his bones with Delphine. But he was content with so little: rites, formulas, talk-talk-talk, profligate payment. Confirm whatever he said; draw a picture for him. He never realized it was Delphine herself—our little joke—and he went away bragging about how he had suffered. As if he might have survived even a heartbeat of what we *could* do."

Akhaïdes turned to take the cup from the Erinyes. The shade of Hyades waited, face blank. But when Akhaïdes raised the cup to him, the shade reached and took it.

Hyades drank a little, then reared back. "*Pah*," he said. "Pelopeid. Disgusting." His eyes shifted, intelligence rising in them. They moved aimlessly for a moment, then locked on Akhaïdes.

"You," he said. "I know you. What do you want?"

"To tell you that you were right. To thank you for your kindness."

The eyes wandered. "Well, I'm glad you finally figured it out. And I'm glad you don't dare use the word 'sorry.' Neither will I."

"I lost Elawon."

"That? An heir, nothing else. He won't come to see you. He's new here. He'll be all right after a while. But give me my real sons."

Yes, they should be here, slouching and sullen, like Hippotes' brothers, grouped behind their father. Better yet, still aboveground, living in Arcadian halls with sons and grandsons, all better men than they.

"What have you told Elawon?"

"Nothing. We don't talk much here. Give me my sons."

"What you believed, don't tell him." Akhaïdes looked past, at his mother. He repeated, "Don't tell him." Her head, still turned away, moved negative.

"And you'll give me my sons?"

"If I can."

"Then I won't tell him. And she won't. It would hurt him, which she would enjoy, but it would hurt you more." Hyades turned away.

"Wait."

Hyades turned back, impatient.

"Show me the future. You must, if I ask you."

The shade's sluggish face woke. A shadow of pleasure, transparently unpleasant, played over it. Akhaïdes remembered that look and the horrors it once brought him. Now it seemed only tiresomely, uncreatively malicious.

Hyades said nothing, but raised an arm and pointed past Akhaïdes.

Akhaïdes steadied himself and turned. Turned and sucked in air and held it, shocked out of breath, out of motion, out of thought.

Not two steps away, the pale ground ended in a crumbling edge that looked out into nothing. Not ordinary darkness and not the rich blackness of sky or cave, but a deeply neutral void, unmarked even by stars, with no further surface beyond or below, utterly real, for as long as he could look at it and beyond. Forever.

As he looked, he saw that the edge of the ground was corroding in reverse: bits and shards rising from some unfathomable depth to fasten themselves to the fragile rim, settle, then mate with the next crumb that rose, and the next. The surface crept slowly forward, constructing itself in a slow generation. And beyond it, still nothing at all. No pictures, no corridor, no light, not even an abyss. Just featureless, colorless, eternal nothing. How loosely he had used that word before, heard it spoken, and thought so little of it. *Nothing.*

He turned back to Hyades, who had crossed his arms and stood waiting.

"Well," Hyades said. "So much for the tidiness you were wanting."

Akhaïdes turned to the Serpent. Her head was cocked like a hound's.

"What . . ." He had trouble finding words. "What is that?"

"What you asked for."

"Is it true, or is it a snake's lie?"

If she could have smiled, she probably would have. "It is true. Even for the likes of you and me."

His sight clouded. He felt for the ground and sat, head between his raised knees, breathing deeply, struggling to stay conscious.

Someone—himself? The Serpent?—whispered, *"Utsir, Utsir, Utsir, nadad tuslaäch."*

The Erinyes were talking to the Serpent—words that skated past Akhaïdes without touching him. Asking, then insisting on something. The Serpent made a hushing noise. They stilled for a moment, then started up again.

He finally could lift his head. "Tell me, please."

She lowered beside him, her chin on the ground, suddenly collegial. "I won't tell you what you want to hear. You want to know how you went wrong and what to do to set it right. Trials, terror, pain, hard labor to repair history. You want to know that the future exists. That it is tied to the past in a steady flow of feats and deeds that someone—I, perhaps?—monitors, and that all you have to do is shape yourself back into it, like the bones in my stone in that hut you know of, and all the wrongs will be gone as if they never were. That your future will then be some trim little path that you can set your feet back on, and off you go."

She swiveled her head back to the Erinyes, whose voices were rising again.

"Toss him in," one said. "See if he can swim in it."

"Stop that," the Serpent told them, and they quieted. She laid her chin back down on the ground beside him. "Put your hand on my head. I like it, and it will help you understand."

He laid his palm on the cool skin. What flowed up his arm was not life, but something equally forbidding. It gave Orestes' ring a dull, sullen shine.

"Where do you think all this right-and-wrong foolishness came from? Not from me. From that ninny Pandora, with her box and her hysteria. From your friend Prometheus, who had too much idle time. Why do you think he ended up where you found him? He wouldn't stop meddling, trying to change what could not be changed because it didn't exist. He understood even less than you do, if that's possible. He wanted this thing—free will, he called it. It frightened him because he mistook it for chaos. And he did not like chaos; he liked order, as all of you do. Building little cairns of stones to anchor yourselves to nothing. But still, he thought he wanted it. So typical of your kind, to try to hold two or three contradictory ideas at the same time and then wonder why you are torn to pieces, why you go mad."

He ran his free hand over his own head. "I can't think like this."

She waited.

"But you said I had to correct what I had done. I thought that meant something would change. I could go into my real future. Fit a pattern that I lost but could find again. If there is no pattern . . ."

"Would you have understood anything else?"

"I still don't."

"Even the priests don't know this. They couldn't understand it any better than ordinary men do. Had I shown you this last year, when you thought you had reached your furthest extreme but you had not yet, what would you have done? I showed Tydeus, and you know what happened to him. Others have thrown themselves over the edge. From what you see, it seems they should come back up, but they never do. I'm not sure why." She glanced up at him. "I prefer that you stay here."

He struggled through this. "There is no fate."

"None."

"But chance still is."

"It's in front of you." She showed just the tips of her tongue. "Think of a kitten, unique in shape and color and mind, just living and learning, then dropped into a bucket and stoned by a child for no lucid reason at all. Can you really believe that it was born for that purpose?"

"How can anyone have hope, then?"

"How can you?"

"But I didn't know until now."

"And knowing now, is there still hope in you?"

He tested that. Although it had no form and no picture, hope was still there, sitting quietly in a corner of his mind.

She said, "Like my lion. When he faced you, he saw his death clearly. And still, he fought you. What did you say to Temenus about that?"

"'The lion himself ran onto the spear. But he didn't enjoy the experience.'"

"So, for the future, fate, and all that."

"Pandora was right?"

"Despite herself."

"And Prometheus?"

"For the wrong reasons."

"The Bajgani, what I did to them . . ." He stopped, overwhelmed again.

"You performed their destruction, yes. Wives, children, grandchildren, friends, followers—every soul that believed you. You alone are responsible. And you alone know that their deaths were relief and release for you."

He shivered.

"Why else would you mourn them so mercilessly? Why else have you drowned yourself in pain for them, whose pain lasted so much shorter a time? That guilt, also, is your own doing and responsibility. Utsir indeed!"

"How can I live with that?"

"How can you live without it?"

"It made me a monster."

"It made you Akhaïdes. It gave you that value."

"That makes no sense."

"It doesn't have to make sense. I don't calculate that way. There is no grand balance scale into which I dump souls like seeds or gold, intending that the cups hang even. I am not Elawon any more than you are."

Memory flooded him. "There was . . ." He stopped, ashamed.

"You were your version of happy. Ephialtes, G'atag'atu-olos, content with the life he had made for himself. There was a hard, cold kernel at the center of him, but perhaps it would never have sprouted. A man as good as any, better than most."

"What was wrong with that?"

She remained serene. "You ask me that, when you were so well prepared to change at the first hint that you could do so? You think you saw evil coming after you? I think you knew you would have to return here, and so you made that happen in the only way you could."

"I could have left them and come back here at any time."

"No. You would have just walked on."

He sat still, his hand on her head.

"And what good would you have done for me and mine and all those who need you, by living rich and happy and *blah, blah, blah* in distant lands? You had to return—whatever it took to drive you home."

"But that's fate again, isn't it?"

She waited with a predator's patience, unblinking under his hand.

He said, "There are more than three thousand rivers and three thousand springs."

"There is no end to their number."

He thought of something else. "How can you know what the coming of the Dorians will be like, if the future doesn't exist?"

"Because I'm not stupid, and some things are obvious."

"When we say that everything that happens, happens for a reason . . ."

"Ah, I do love my Arcadians."

He still struggled with this. "Temenus was troubled all his life by what you and I did. If he feels better now because of fate, yet fate doesn't exist, then what?"

She breathed out, making her patience more obvious. "He believes it does. It gives him the pattern and the limits that all of them want. Is the flea grateful when you take it out of your pocket and set it down on a mountaintop?"

"It prefers boundaries. They are easier."

"Even for you."

He looked at her. "How does the priest know when I will die?"

"Because you know *why* you should. Knowing, you'll try to make it happen. If you succeed, fate will get the credit. If you fail, it will get the blame."

He gave up.

"Of course, being still a man, even you want to know what this means to your little vision of some cramped, dark passage, only one way forward, all neatly laid out before you were born."

He was ashamed at the commonness of his desires.

She breathed out with thunderous patience. "What are you? Do you still not know? And if you decide to be somehow different, what are you then? Should the lion mend its ways and be a deer? Then who will be the lion? Should the Arcadian murderer come down to the sea and become a tamer of horses? Then what of the murders? And what of the horses?

"You are Akhaïdes. You always have been and will be. You might be the most annoying man alive, but if you were not you, who would be? You should keep that name. It suits you."

She turned her head to the clamoring Erinyes. "Shut up," she told them. "He may sometimes be stupid, but he is my perfect, beautiful son. I won't hear a word against him."

The Sisters fell quiet, sulking.

She turned back. "You are what you are. Pattern or no, it is you who belong to the world, and not some other man the world might prefer. For a sign of yourself, use mine. I did not offer it lightly, even before. What else do you need from me?"

Akhaïdes held his own head again.

"Temenus and Makhawis each know the parts of you that the other cannot comprehend."

Waiting for him. Reaching for him. Locking hands with him. Weeping while making love with him again and again, never getting enough. Killing for him.

Holding him while he wept. Singing to him. Arguing with him. Defending him to himself. Kissing him. Shouting down her own people to save him.

"Always believe Makhawis. She is the key. You can heal Temenus, and Makhawis can heal you. Remember, you were never unclean. You were Akhaïdes. Just as the clean, perfect Serpent comes forth from a bent and filthy egg, you came forth from your mother and Orestes."

He looked up. "May I tell the priests that you said this?"

"Anyone who looks at you will know."

"Take away—"

"Your burdens? I would not think of depriving you of them. I will, however, assure you of what is yours. Your dreams and visions are yours. The people you must love are yours. And if you see something that must be done and there is no one else to do it, that also is yours. However repellent, however perilous, however desolate, however necessary. You cannot do anything unsuitable to you. You are Akhaïdes."

"How can I be so . . . special?"

"Who are you? Tell me again, and this time believe it."

He said slowly, "I am Ephialtes Oresteides Pelopeides."

She extended only the tip of her tongue, to caress his hand.

"I am the High King's eldest son. Tisamenus's only living brother. Great-grandson of Echemus Protector. Akhaïdes."

"Lover of Temenus Herakleides. Husband of Makhawis, even if you never touch her, nor she you. And you are my consort. The first since Tydeus, your ancestor, who betrayed me, but you will not. Perhaps the last. You are the man who stood with Prometheus. You are the man who will never excuse himself, never forgive himself, never stop until he's done what he has to do."

He looked down again. "It is very hard to live as you say."

"And, for you, impossible to live any other way." She made a scornful puff just like Menetor's, just like the Bajganis' when they spoke of farmers. "I would never think of giving you instruction. I only give you information that you now have permission to know."

He rose, unsteadily. Behind him, the spirits were gone. The flat gray land, dull houses, ordinary animals—all gone. The surface of the ground faded into a dirty mist, as packed full of unseen detritus—the sad, shabby little treasures of men—as the future lay empty of it. Only the Erinyes stood, fog swathing their ankles, finally quiet but tapping their feet with impatience.

He turned back to her. "If you leave the world, where will you go?"

She raised her head to his height. "I will go where there is no returning. But if you want, I will give you a gift."

He stepped back warily, then glanced toward the crumbling edge.

Her head wove in the air, amused. "What did I promise to give you, when first I spoke to you?"

"Nothing, you said. Nothing at all."

"And what have I given you? And what more do you dare to want?"

"When you go, take me with you."

The head turned away, as if she feared he might detect a human emotion in her eyes. "On all the worlds ever made, of all the men ever in them, it is your company I would prefer. But from where I will go, you could never return—not even to here, to meet your dead. I would not be the cause of regret."

"Give me what I need most, then."

"Your son died before the Chous touched him."

There was still room for grief.

"And that is true, even by your own obstinate measure of truth. Twice." Her tongue flickered. "In those lands, even a buried spirit whose name must not be spoken can find a womb and come again."

His head whipped up; then he understood. "Thank you," he whispered.

"Even over very long distances, if they are drawn so far."

"What draws them?"

"Memory. And love. Once reborn, they don't remember."

"But that's enough."

"I thought it might be." She paused. "If you ever need my Erinyes' help, call them. I am strongest at Delphi, underground, at sea. That place, Nafpaktos, is at the edge of water. If they had killed you there, the world would have seen revenge such as it hasn't known in a long, long time."

The image was instantaneous: a vast pulsing shadow over jumbled roofs, a man's awestruck face turned upward, gutters swirling with blood, shoals of fleeing rats and roaches, knots of bowels like windrift.

"Why for me and not for Karnus?"

"I have many priests. I have one Akhaïdes."

"You would have avenged my death. Would you have saved my life?"

She did not answer. He knew.

"Give me one more gift."

She drew up and back.

"Give it to me."

She reared away in a powerful double curve. "Forgive me," she said. "You are now my brother."

She struck.

He had purposely exposed his throat, but still the drive of her fangs was shocking. The jaws closed steadily, stopping breath, cracking cartilage, crushing vertebrae. The venom did not numb—it stung like Lokrian poison. The pressure increased steadily, and his knees weakened. She threw one coil, then another, around his body and laid them gently down together.

The coils shifted and tightened, squeezing flesh, bending bone. The venom crept along his veins. One by one, his joints cracked and tendons snapped free, rebounding like bowstrings. The bones spalled into shards that ripped through the skin in a thousand cuts from within. The links of his spine separated in a slow, sucking chain.

He groaned as his body arched backward in the agony of the Serpent's embrace. The two of them, an irreducible helix, rolled slowly along the un-crumbling edge of time.

* * *

The purifying priest snapped awake instantly, his heart thrashing. He swung off his cot, snatched up a loincloth, and was already running as he tied it on, shouting for Menetor. But Menetor was still up the mountain by the priestesses' kennels, still stubbornly waiting long after the time by which any suppliant would ever come back.

He slammed out of the priests' house. "Here, here, here!" he roared, dodging between buildings. The sanctuary was a slightly darker shadow, inconsequential in the darkness of night and trees. His own shadow spilled before him, picked out by a sudden torch behind. The shadow strengthened, racing more sideways than forward as torches bobbed and thrashed. The dogs in the village howled, all together. The wolves on Parnassos answered.

He straight-armed the wicker door, hurling it against the inside wall. The lightless room stank of sulfur, rot, and blood. He raised an arm to breathe through his sleeve, then remembered that he wore no shirt. He stepped forward as if wading through mire. Another step, and he could move no farther—neither forward nor back. Whatever would happen had summoned him as a witness and nothing else. All the little clay statues shivered and squeaked. The sludged blood around the stone drained like quicksilver down between the flags and disappeared.

Outside, up in the night sky, something groaned. The earth answered with a shudder. His feet skidded on the gritty, damp flagstones, and he dropped through invisible density to his knees. His hands hit the floor a moment later.

Breathless voices behind him, torchlight skipping around the walls and over the sanctuary stone. The stone reflected nothing, devouring light as it flexed and bowed.

He called, "Don't come in here!"

Someone asked, "What? What is it?"

"Stay out!" The stench gagged him. He could not move, not even to creep backward to safety. Outside, all over the mountain, dogs and wolves keened in chorus. The votives chittered like bats and flapped their tiny arms.

The stone stretched and moaned, whined and snarled, shifted with the heaving of the ground beneath it. The knot of bones writhed like sea wrack in a tidal surge. Then one long rod suddenly arched and paled. Light and dark raced across it as it bent and rose, spurted blood, widened, became a man's shoulder, shoulder blade, spinal bones, the back of a neck sleek with wet hair, an arm streaked with blood and white aqueous serum.

The men's voices at the door stilled, and the dogs' howling shut off.

The pale, filth-banded body heaved forth, joint by joint, limb by limb. It rolled sideways, bonelessly flaccid, with the legs and feet finally extruded, and sprawled onto the floor.

The earth gave one final quiver. The stone sighed and subsided. From under the ground beneath his hands, the priest heard a vast exhalation and the creak and slam of a door. The mire that held him dissolved.

He crept forward cautiously, touched the slack arm. It was cold and wet, like the skin of a frog. The fluid that covered it came away like spider webs, on the ends of his fingers. Still on his knees, he shuffled closer and tugged. The corpse rolled slowly onto its back. The one-eyed face, hooded with blood, stared past him, sightless.

He sat back on his heels and pressed his shaking hands against his legs. Behind him, someone coughed, reminding him of the others.

He said, "Bring a blanket. We need to cover it. Carry it to our own tomb. It—he—is sacred now."

As he turned away, just at the corner of his vision, one long finger twitched. He whipped back, pressed his hands on the slimy body. It remained unresponsive and cold. He pulled his hair aside and set his ear against the spume-clotted chest.

Someone started to speak, and he waved him quiet. Then he heard it, quiet and slow: the deep, sepulchral throb and pause, throb and pause.

He scrambled up. "Blankets! Towels! Now!" He bent again, clutched a greasy wrist, and hauled the corpse up and over his shoulders. Even as he turned, the light shriveled—the priests and slaves racing to obey and taking their torches with them.

Only the black-haired boy stayed, clutching a cloak at his throat, a lamp quivering in his upraised hand.

Together they descended the dark path between reaching trees and clutching bushes. The weight hung, slack and stinking, across the priest's shoulders. They climbed to where the spring sluiced out of the mountain and rattled in its stone trough. The priest leaned and let the weight slide down off him, braking it against his hip. The boy reached out to help, but he made a warning noise and the boy backed away.

Feet, legs, body, lolling head, staring face, slack arms and fingers, a slimy silver ring: all went unresisting under the water. Blood and fluid boiled up and spun away in strings and wads. The priest waited, bent over, straddling the trough, his hands wrapped in hair like weeds. Waiting . . .

The water heaved and broke. A hand floundered upward, pawing at his arms. He squatted, lifted, and Akhaïdes came up gasping, clutching the hands in his hair. The priest shifted his grip to wrists, then arms, and hoisted Akhaïdes out of the water.

Torches, lamps, thundering feet. Eager hands wrapped Akhaïdes in wool and linen and rolled him onto another blanket on the ground.

Akhaïdes gagged suddenly. He turned on his side, on one elbow, retching and coughing, vomiting blood and water, wet hair across his face and looped around his throat. They all drew away in awe. It was the boy who knelt by him, wiped his mouth, and looked into his eye.

Whatever he saw there sent him up on his feet and three steps back. Then Akhaïdes lay back, arms over his face. A half-score of hands raised the blanket and carried him swiftly away, leaving the priest and the boy with their single lamp, facing each other across the defiled water.

The priest asked softly, "What did you see?" and the boy only looked away. The priest scooped up water, scrubbed the slime from his arms and shoulders and the side of his leg, then palmed water over his face. It buzzed in his hands and stung his eyes and lips and inside his nose. The stench of death and birth faded.

High between the Faedriads, air moved; a leaf whispered; a few loose pebbles slid and bounced. The priest looked up at the wedge of sky between the stones. It changed shape, the narrowest point filled by something darker and spider-legged that rose and flexed and lifted narrow, vibrating wings.

"Let's get away from here right now," the boy murmured, and the priest agreed.

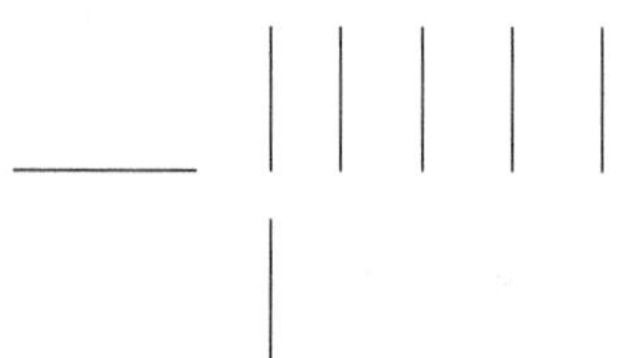

When I stand before thee at the day's end, thou shalt see my scars and know that I had my wounds and also my healing.[xv]

—*Rabindranath Tagore*

All he saw first was brilliant white light. Waking or sleeping, it lay before him, thin as veil, dense as cloud. He thought at first he must be finally blind, and was relieved to find that blindness meant unending light instead of unending darkness. But the white coalesced into shapes and images: bleached walls, curtains, his own hands, translucent as any aesthete's, resting on the soft white blanket that covered him.

He recovered slowly, but there was all the time in the world for that: to hear, to smell wood smoke and dust. To see. He studied the hands while hearing the voices of birds outside the bright barred window and while feeling, exquisitely on his naked shoulder, the soft movements of air. Dawns and evenings passed gently. Midnights found him unmoved, and noons did not concern him. The hands were his touchstones and his talismans. In their quiet repose lay the silent waiting of his own mind.

The black-haired acolyte tended him and fed him: first clear, saltless broth, then, morsel by slow morsel, lamb simmered in seawater and soft winter greens. The boy helped him sit up, first on this pallet propped with fat pillows, then in a padded chair by the window, with a view of a tiny sunny courtyard that hosted a single silvery tree and a flock of quick little crimson birds that squabbled in its branches and gorged on its seeds.

You are purified. You are clean. You have a father and a mother. You have kin. You have a name, a home, a king. Your debts and duties are returned to you. You are a man, and you may do the things that men do, be the way that men are. You may wear a man's loincloth. If you have children, you may wear a man's beard. No one may harm you without risk of revenge. You may speak in assembly. You may touch anyone and anything clean. You may sit and eat and drink with anyone. You may have any suitable woman or man who will have you. You may touch an unclean person, but an unclean person may not touch you. If the unclean touches you, you will be polluted.

He had not really heard this spoken, but he knew it. Perhaps it had been recited over him while he was deaf and blind and far removed from words, then stored for later contemplation. Even without the words themselves, he knew that it was true. The Serpent had told him, and he could feel it in the centers of his body, in the marrow of his bones, in the curve of his waiting fingers.

This was what he had craved, what Orestes had commanded, what Tisamenus had spent such courage for. Just this: to lie in perfect stillness, all time and thought suspended, and see, as if for the first time, his own hands.

They were immaculately clean, the nails trimmed and shining, all memory of dirt gone from the creases. But they were not an infant's hands. In a thousand lines and flaws, their history still was written, and they retained each tale of that history: horse bites, dropped knives, snapped bowstrings; dog bites, grass cuts, cinder burns; human bites, the Regent's horsehair shackles, Tisamenus's compassionate bonds, work that had hardened them like those of an honest man. The wrists looked wolf-gnawed, so deeply and repeatedly scarred were they. One hand was crooked because the Herakleids had shattered it, although work had retaught it almost normal motion. The base of the thumb was scarred by Tisamenus's dagger, and the forefinger wore Orestes' ring. The other palm was marked with a vertical scar of tribute to an alien king long with the dead, whose name he remembered. That also was his bowstring hand, with telltale calluses still at the fingertips. With six arrows, he could take five rising herons from the back of a galloping horse. Even UlaänUsu could not do that.

The hands lay at his sides like well-used gloves, waiting for their owner to slip back inside them. The Nafpaktos shaman had said it, in a different rite: "Do what you are made to do." Her formula now carried both meanings in full.

He was the Serpent's, and how she had marked him was extraordinary. She had devoured and created him exactly as he had come to her, unchanged in any way. It was with both pity and awe that the purifying priest took Akhaïdes' hands, felt them gently, turned them over to examine them. He touched the half-healed incision from the sacrificial knife, touched the blinded eye, traced the scars on his cheekbones and the tattoos visible above the white blanket, then pressed the heels of his hands to his forehead as if back in the presence of the Serpent herself.

When Menetor came to see Akhaïdes, the purifying priest placed himself, subtly but certainly, between them. Menetor looked haunted and anxious. He did not speak, but reached past the sheltering arm to take Akhaïdes' hands and examine them, too. Then he laid them carefully back on the coverlet and peered into his eye cautiously, as if fearful of what he might see there.

Other priests also came, to stand in the doorway and murmur greetings, not expecting responses and not getting them. The slaves, Akhaïdes' old companions, peered around the doorposts, faces hidden behind their hands, and ducked away before he could recognize them.

Menetor came again. Kneeling like a penitent beside him, he

said, "What did you see?" Not needing the purifying priest's warning glance, Akhaïdes only touched the papery old face. When he did this, Menetor looked away as if something hurt his eyes.

Bird says, I am bird. Bull says, I am bull. Akhaïdes says, I am Akhaïdes. And then they are silent. There is no need to say more.

* * *

The third time Menetor came, he found Akhaïdes standing, wearing a new white fillet and new leggings of soft leather. His hair, still clean, fell lightly around his elbows, and the pictures on his skin blazed and flowed as he and the acolyte lifted up a white shirt by the sleeves.

"We were just wondering," Akhaïdes said, "how to put this on. Do you know?"

Menetor studied the garment. It appeared to have an excess of lacings while lacking something in length. They turned it over and around, discussing it thoroughly. Finally, they got Akhaïdes' head into it, his arms through the sleeves, and the deceptive twist out of the torso. The tail fell nearly to his knees. The cuffs, soft and generous, lapped over his hands.

Menetor said, "You can wear a loincloth now. There's no reason you shouldn't."

Deione had presented the leather leggings with touching pride.

"I'll keep these," he replied.

"And you can use your real name. You're entitled to that." Menetor's eyes were darting around the room, as if searching for something mislaid. "You can even choose a new one—whatever you like."

Akhaïdes lifted his arms, watching the linen's supple flow. "Do you have suggestions?"

"I've considered a few. Zagreos. Tychenos. Perhaps

Cleobulus. What do you think?"

"Restored to life. Fortune. Honored justice. I don't know that I merit anything so grand."

"Orestes gave enough gold that you don't have to choose. You can have them all." Menetor said it lightly, but his scalp was wrinkled from brow to nape.

Akhaïdes studied the cloth, picking at a flaw in the weave. "Eurylas might be more appropriate."

"No. Your roaming is over."

"Is it?"

"You're ours, if you'll stay here."

"Stay here and do what?"

"What we need. What you please. You would always find something to do."

"No one lives here that way."

"You would have—contentedly—as less than a slave. You still could, and wouldn't even have to carry our night soil anymore. Could eat warm food. If you chose."

"If I chose?"

"You've always wanted to take care of your business in Arcadia. You can do that now."

Arcadia. The clean air, the vast sky, the peaks all around, the calls of the wind, the fox, the hunting bird. The cleft in the rocks, and the perytons anchored there, waiting for him.

He raised his head and said, "Tell me."

"Tell you what?"

"What you came to say but don't want to."

Menetor looked nonplussed.

"The sooner it's told, the sooner it's over."

Menetor relaxed a little. "Only this: the Herakleids are here."

Akhaïdes stood still, taking the time he needed to understand. *Herakleid.* The name sounded as remote as the name of the moon. Yet the Serpent herself had mentioned them. Finally, he said again, "Tell me."

"They came days ago, to give amends for Karnus's murder. That's what Temenus said, and he did it, very correctly. But that wasn't the real reason he came."

"How do you know?"

"Temenus never has just one reason for doing anything. You know that even better than I. And this time . . . this time, it's even more complex than usual." Menetor reached out to adjust Akhaïdes' cuff. "He brought a large number of cousins. He brought his younger brother." He paused. "And he brought his sister."

"Makhawis."

"And he asked for you. When he learned where you were and why, he looked . . . well. I've never seen him like that."

Akhaïdes glanced down at his own hands. He hadn't worn a ring since he traded his last amethyst for a handful of rancid venison, coming back into forest. He wore a ring now, with no memory whether he had put it on or someone else had done it to him.

"He says he'll wait as long as necessary to talk with you. That's all he wants, he says: talk."

"You know what he wants to talk about, don't you?"

Menetor stood silent.

"It's a good thing I love you, because you are damnably trying sometimes."

Menetor puffed. "And you aren't?"

Akhaïdes considered this for a moment. "Do I go barefoot from now on?"

"Your small friend has new boots for you. We copied them from the old ones. I hope they fit."

They did. They were exquisitely made of softest lambskin from knee to foot, then toed and soled with layers of ox. Much finer than the boots that Solong had made for him and that Makhawis's women had repaired for him. He would not ask where those were now. No doubt forgotten already on a midden.

He stepped back and forth in the new ones while the boy beamed and Menetor said, "You don't have to see the Herakleids now. Or ever."

"I will"

"As you wish, but don't . . ." He stopped, and Akhaïdes looked at him. The old man grinned suddenly. "Don't kill any Herakleids in my district, will you?"

"What degree outlawry would that be?"

"With your family connections, no more than third, I'm sure. Quite tolerable after what you're used to. But still . . ." His face went serious again. "Remember. From now on, anything you are, you will have chosen."

Akhaïdes walked out of the hall and along the path lined by cypresses. He passed Orestes' stele, then stopped and went back to look at the first line of symbols. A chip-cornered square, two different forks, and a thing like a bush. "Orestes," it meant, and he could appreciate that the answer to a riddle had been right here, in bright sunlight and open air, all his life. He should have recognized it the first time he walked by. He should have . . . he couldn't imagine what.

It was a fair winter afternoon: luminous air, and a thin frost on the ground. He felt clumsy from resting so long, and he had to pay attention to the placement of his feet and to his balance, as if learning all over again how to walk in a two-dimensional world.

At the bottom of the steps, he paused, recalling another time he had walked here this way—down the steps to Oxylus, to Elawon, to Nafpaktos—and everything strung between that moment and this one, less than a year later. The roadside dead, veiled in silvery grasses, ignored him.

Moving forward again was difficult. He moved.

After the austere serenity of the sanctuary, the Herakleid camp looked chaotic. On an irregular shelf, tents and pavilions stood crowded together. One of the largest was cream and scarlet—Makhawis's colors.

Then Akhaïdes saw Temenus Herakleides himself, head lifted toward him, arms folded, Kresphontes at his side.

Temenus's gaze stayed on him, appraising his every stride, until Akhaïdes came near enough that he could stop walking. The eyes were more shadowed than Akhaïdes remembered, with deeper creases at their ends, and discolored pouches beneath. The angled folds at the corners of his long mouth were sharper, the cheekbones more prominent, with no softness under the skin. Even his hair was flat and dull. He looked worn and spent and much older, and also sly in some new way. He had not looked like this when they last met, despite his anguish at that time. Then he had been as transparent as clean water. Even if Menetor had said nothing, his appearance alone would have warned Akhaïdes.

Temenus said quietly, "Exactly as you always come to me when I ask for you." His voice, at least, was the same. "You look well, as if someone has finally fed you. As if even your blood were new."

"And you look terrible. What's happened to you?"

Temenus made a soft exhalation, as if too aware of the truth to disagree. Then—so typical of him—he set aside his own fluid complexity and said, "I don't know how to talk to you now. It's too different."

"It is."

"And talking with you in front of others—that's different, too, but I want to do it. They all have to know." Temenus touched his lips with the end of his tongue, as he always did when tense. "I see that your situation was corrected."

"Only you would call lifelong first-degree outlawry a 'situation.'"

Temenus smiled. "My first undeserved insult. Now I know it's really you."

"You killed a priest of Delphi. Why? What did you think it

would get you?"

Kresphontes said suddenly, "Don't talk to him that way."

It had none of Kresphontes' usual puristic force, but Akhaïdes turned on him. "Don't talk to him what way? As if he were a murderer? I know how murderers are talked to. I'm being extremely polite to your brother."

Kresphontes started to answer, but Temenus laid a hand on his arm and he subsided.

Akhaïdes looked back and forth between them. "Temenus, just tell me. What is it you want?"

"Can we do this inside? I'd rather plead with you in more comfortable surroundings."

There were so many possible answers to that. "Inside, then."

Under a thin-walled canopy, in chilly half-light, they sat on painted stools and regarded each other across a wooden trestle table laid swiftly with food and drink by silent slaves in Makhawis's colors. Temenus sent his own bread to Akhaïdes and watched while the women served stewed meat and cheese, then set cups around and filled them.

One by one, like players in a Cretan drama, other men came in, served themselves, and stood against the walls to eat. Someone rolled up one panel and tied it, and in the stronger light Akhaïdes was able to put names to the faces: first Xanos, then Meydon, Satnios, others. So many men he had known.

No one spoke. A few shadows at the edges of the canopy stirred and rose and coalesced into dogs that yawned and stretched and went to sit under the men's feet, watching their hands rise and fall, more from habit than from hope. Slaves carried in a few firepots, and the air warmed.

Temenus reminded Akhaïdes, "We can eat together now."

"So we can," Akhaïdes answered. He looked down at his bread and the savory stew on it, scented with cardamom, and the rich, veiny cheese. Neither of them touched food.

Kresphontes, intent and uneasy, hunched over his bread,

throwing occasional glances at his brother or Akhaïdes. His hair, in its pegged knot, gleamed in the firepots' light.

Finally, Temenus cleared his throat and said, "I did not kill Karnus with my own hands, but I take the responsibility. And we were punished for it."

"Good."

"Aristodemus is with our dead."

"I'm sorry." That sounded miserably inadequate.

Temenus looked directly into Akhaïdes' eye. "I didn't come here to consult the oracle. I didn't come to pay for Karnus. I didn't come to do penance for a murder. All of that, I could have performed from a distance."

There was no sound at all, inside the tent or outside.

"Do you remember how the oracle told me to find the three-eyed man to lead my Tribes? A three-eyed lawagetas?"

"I remember. You didn't know what it meant."

"It means you."

Akhaïdes' breath went out of him. Behind him, Xanos shifted his feet with a sliding, embarrassed sound. At the corner of his vision, Satnios, juggling his cup wildly, dropped it anyway. Kresphontes watched, tense and wary.

Akhaïdes spread his hands, palms down, on both sides of his bread. The right hand quivered. "Now, how . . ." He cleared his throat. "Now, how do you reckon that?"

"No man in the world has three eyes. But you have one eye and your horse has two. That makes three. It can't be anyone else."

Silence.

"Do you remember," Temenus asked, "when you told me you didn't know why you were in Nafpaktos?"

Akhaïdes remembered.

"I think you were there for me. And now I've come for you." Temenus looked nowhere else. "I want you back, and I'll do anything to get you."

Akhaïdes waited still.

"With you beside me, I know I'll win all that I'm entitled to." He leaned forward. "And so will you."

Akhaïdes said, "You killed four men to save me. And now you killed a priest for this?"

"You learned who you are, they say, in Mycenae. But you came back here. That means you still need a place. And I believe it means that you still can be tempted, which is what I intend to do."

Everyone watched in silence.

"You were right when you tried to advise me and I pushed it aside. Everything you told me came true. I have to change my dealings with them, all of them, all the Tribes, especially the Dorians. I have to take my city in my hands at last and force it into the shape I need. But I don't know how to get from here to there. I need you to teach me how."

Unguarded, holding nothing back, he gazed into Akhaïdes' face. "You're behaving the way I expected you to: wary, resentful, discourteous. You're being as uncooperative as you can without being truly insulting. As if there were only ugliness between us. But I don't care how you behave, because I know where it comes from. Criticize me. Insult me. Refuse to look at me. Refuse even to touch me. *But I know you.*"

As always, when Temenus took up the truth, he did so fearlessly, with both hands.

"I need you. You need a place. Where can you go if not to me?"

Akhaïdes' right hand ached with the strain of holding it open.

Temenus turned his head and called quietly, "Deione."

From between two panels, limned for a moment by the sunlight behind her, came Deione. Wearing Makhawis's colors now, she walked to Temenus's shoulder with a lidded basket in her hands.

Temenus laid his palms on the table. Deione opened the basket and tilted it.

Out flooded ropes and ribbons and chains of gold, of silver, of gems and pearls. Bezels and filigrees, clips and rings. They rolled, poured, clattered, and finally settled and lay still, five times a double handful.

Akhaïdes saw their faces, and Kresphontes' most of all: flatly, dumbly, helplessly astonished.

Finally, Kresphontes said, "I know these things. That clip . . . the ring." He passed his open hands over the mound of treasure wonderingly, not touching it. He looked up at Temenus. "I know these things. These are Mother's wedding jewelry, her dowry."

Temenus didn't answer.

"But it all was stolen years ago, even before she died."

"No," Temenus said. "She hid it away and said it was stolen."

"Father killed three men as thieves!"

"Even he didn't know. Only she and I knew." Temenus said to Akhaïdes, "I always had enough to redeem you, but I wouldn't. I had only this and had to reserve it for myself."

More silence.

"My Return was more important than anything else—even you."

"You were right."

"At the moment the priest died, when I realized what you were, I went out to dig this up. Before I even could start, Aristodemus went to our dead. I finished digging, burned my brother, changed clothes, and brought this here for Hippotes' purification and your redemption. But I was too late." A hard, fearful light came into his eyes. He closed them. "I was too late."

Every man sat silent. Kresphontes still looked shocked and bewildered. At Temenus's shoulder, Deione watched Akhaïdes gently.

Temenus murmured, "I will pay for Hippotes because you told me that everything he did was my fault, and I finally believe you."

He opened his eyes again. The flame still smoldered in them. He used the edge of one hand to divide a small portion of the treasure from the rest and slide it to one side. He said, "This is for Hippotes. The rest was for you."

He asked, "Who are you? If you still are the Akhaïdes I know, I will say, 'I need you,' and you will come. Because what you need most is to be needed. You need responsibility, duty. Work of your own that no one else can perform. I can give you that. And I can give you more, besides."

He tightened his lips and touched them with his tongue—so familiar a sign. "If you will serve as my lawagetas in our Return, I will give you the land of Elis in freehold forever, and my sister Makhawis for your wife."

Akhaïdes stared at him.

"What are you? A derelict, unwanted bastard Pelopeid. You could walk out into the dawn tomorrow as the married king of Elis, and lawagetas to the rightful High King."

"Magic," Akhaïdes managed to say.

"If you like." Temenus sat back, his arms still open. "Your own needs: not gold, not power, not fame, but duty, loyalty, responsibility, authority. Love."

Akhaïdes said, almost inaudibly, "Hippotes claims Elis."

Temenus moved his head negative. "Hippotes is outlawed ten years for the priest's murder. I will pay his penalty so that he can fight at Rhion, but he can't have Elis. Even if his claim were valid, which I doubt, and even after his exile is over, like every Herakleid, he is subject to me. If I say Elis is yours, it is yours. If Hippotes disputes it, he will answer to me.

"And I doubt very much that he would challenge you again. Not you"—Temenus looked intently at him—"and not your sons after you. Come back to us. Come back to me."

He waited, palms up, guileless, patient. Akhaïdes knew those hands so well: their shape, their warmth, their strength. He looked at his own spread fingers: lean, crooked, callused, scarred, with Orestes' ring glowing coolly. He still didn't remember putting it on.

He looked at Kresphontes, who met his eye urgently, without malice. The young man with the ancient heart, holding the oldest beliefs. He, sooner than anyone, would accept this.

Akhaïdes said to him, "You didn't cut your hair. For your own brother, for Aristodemus, you didn't cut your hair."

Kresphontes ducked his head. "I cut a finger length. The rest has to wait for our Return. We swore long ago. I'll cut it all then."

Temenus said, "You see? You're already with us. What can any other place give you? Contempt? Treachery? Futility? Is that why you lived so long: to die unnoticed in some rock pile?"

"I won't die that way."

"A king, a married man, my lawagetas. Makhawis agreed. It was her idea."

Akhaïdes did not answer.

"Don't let resentment disserve you."

Akhaïdes looked at the hands, the mouth, the eyes he knew so well. He groped and found a cup of wine, raised it to the six corners, and drained it.

Temenus watched him do that, watched how he drank and how he set the cup down too hastily, unevenly, so its foot clattered on the boards. Temenus said, "You have never refused me. Don't do it now, when you could lose so much by it." He started to say something else, then stopped.

A slave came quietly to refill Akhaïdes' cup.

Temenus's gaze drifted away, and he just sat waiting. He knew all too well how to wait for Akhaïdes.

Around the edges of the space, murmured conversations began. Someone stepped closer to the table, ostensibly to take another share of bread, but also to get a closer look at the treasure. Kresphontes still sat unmoving, all expression washed away.

A slave came in with a tray of dried fruit, which she carried from man to man. She glanced twice at the treasure, then went on. Voices rose as Temenus sat looking at nothing and Akhaïdes sat watching him, and Deione began, piece by piece, tucking the jewels back into her basket.

Then a clerk came in cautiously and leaned over Temenus with a tablet. Temenus waved him off, but he came carefully back, showed the tablet again, and asked a question. Temenus glanced at it; then something caught his attention and he asked a question of his own. Another clerk came in, and they both launched an explanation. Temenus listened irritably at first, then finally began to agree. He snapped his fingers to emphasize something he said, and two dogs came to him. He cuffed them away. Yes, he had changed.

Akhaïdes stood. Kresphontes watched, but Temenus seemed not to notice. Akhaïdes lifted his cup from the table and moved quietly back toward the wall, into familiar shelter between Xanos's and Meydon's shoulders. He touched Xanos's arm.

Xanos placed a hairy paw over Akhaïdes' hand and said, "Every time we think we know what's going on, it all changes."

"Why are you all here—a delegation? A chorus?"

"Exactly," said Satnios, grinning wickedly. "All here to remind you how much Nafpaktos loves you and how you'd be so happy if you came back again."

"Not at all the way it used to be," Meydon added cheerfully. "Now it's all flowers and music and dancing children."

"Girls," Satnios corrected him.

"Dancing girls," Meydon agreed. "Lovely, nubile girls with big, soft breasts and no brothers at all."

"Drinkable wine."

Deione finished with the jewels and tapped the lid back onto her basket. There were many ways to leave this space, but she crossed toward Akhaïdes so closely that she had to step around him. At the last possible moment, she turned her eyes sharply to his, then went out between two cloth panels.

Akhaïdes said to Meydon, "Your mother is here."

"She is."

"This is what kind of trap, exactly?"

"The oldest kind," Meydon smiled. "Rarely fatal." He was suddenly serious. "And Temenus wants you alive in it."

Temenus was talking to the clerks, one hand moving in a gesture that Akhaïdes remembered. Kresphontes leaned in to join the discussion, and the clerks turned to him with relief.

Xanos murmured, "Temenus has changed even more than you see. Be careful."

Akhaïdes parted the panels, then glanced back. From across the complex, crowded space, Temenus looked up instantly.

You think you know me. What will I do now?

Temenus surely knew.

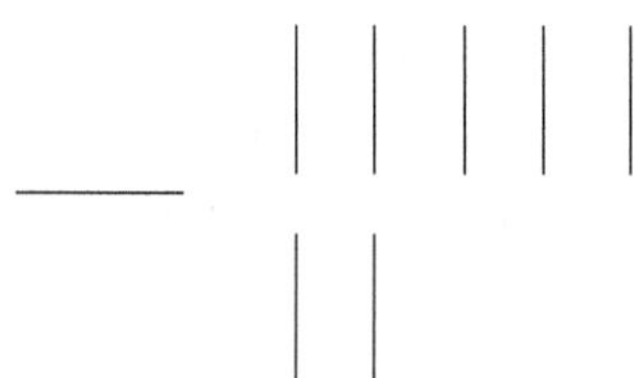

And when you can see your unborn children in her eyes,
You know you really love a woman.[xvi]

— *Adams, Kamen and Lange*

The sunset blinded him for a moment, but Deione was waiting. He followed the blur of her figure through a busy crowd of equally indistinguishable women and felt their surprise that a man would intrude in their work area, then surprise again as they recognized him.

Deione scratched at the front of the ivory-hued pavilion, then raised the flap. Akhaïdes half-turned to fling the contents of his cup in a shining arc over the grass. He looked up for a moment at the sky, colorless even though it was sunset. The full moon was modestly transparent now but would thicken as the sun left. He turned and bent to pass under Deione's protective arm, into the pavilion, to whatever waited there.

Makhawis was already crossing the rug-paved space, as if her walk to meet him had begun at the same moment as his to meet her. Her vast skirts dragged pillows along. They both stopped at the same moment and stood looking at each other. She held a wine ewer in both hands and smelled of olivewood and roses. Her hair was more richly spangled with silver than he remembered. She had circled her eyes with black.

He said, "An ordinary woman would say, 'I knew you'd come.'"

Her face lit up. "Then the ordinary man would say, 'How did you know?'"

She crossed the remaining space and lifted her ewer to fill his cup, then set it down on the ground. He raised the cup to all the parts of the earth and drank of her gift, raised it again, this time only to her, and drank again. She took it from him, turned it, and drank from the same place on the brim. When she handed it back, their fingers brushed and burned.

A slave moved to close the tent flap. Makhawis led Akhaïdes to a mountain of cushions, and he sat down obediently. He had forgotten the power of sexual compulsion, but her nearness woke it with a force that blasted away everything else: reason, restraint, even the most elementary caution. He wanted her, this clever, taxing woman he knew so well, as much as he had ever wanted anything.

What had the Serpent said? *Always believe Makhawis. She is the key.*

A slave brought a leather-topped stool, and Makhawis sat on it, very near but just beyond his reach. "My brother," she said. "He told you what he wants."

"He told me that the best parts are your ideas."

Another slave came to carry away the ewer and bring Makhawis's cup to her. She sipped wine, watching him over the rim. Deep, clear eyes and a mouth that could hide nothing ever—but still struggling, at this moment, to keep something from him.

He rested his wrist on his raised knee, suspending his cup by the rim. "How well I know so little about you," he said, quoting her.

She smiled, no doubt remembering. "Yes, Elis and marriage were my ideas."

Her slaves began moving around the space, lighting lamps. He said, "You are perceptive, Makhawis."

"And you fear that if I know you need this light, Temenus

must also know. But he does not know. Your habits are contagious: I never tell anyone the truth about you."

She took a deep breath and rearranged her skirt over her knees. Looking past him, she finally said, "Karnus's death is my fault."

He raised his head. "What? It can't be."

"I wasn't blamed and I won't be punished, but it's my fault."

He started to speak, and she raised a hand to stop him. "Let me do this. I'm practicing your habit of taking on all the blame in the world.

"If you had known, you would have stopped me. You would never have traded Karnus for yourself. It was my own choice to try to protect you, so it's my fault alone."

They paused, watching each other. He wondered whether he should tell her what the Serpent had said about her, and that the Serpent knew her name.

"Is Temenus being ever so nice with you today?"

"Sweet as honey," he answered.

"The conceit is breathtaking, isn't it?" she said, "that he could have for his lawagetas the High King's eldest son? A lawagetas that might even outrank *him* and would certainly unnerve the Mycenaeans when they saw him at the head of the Tribes." Her voice was a shade too harsh from her pleasure at Temenus's dilemma.

"Penthilus has a whole army of Oresteides that are of no consequence."

"Orestes never acknowledged them. He must feel differently about you."

He raised the cup, then lowered it again without drinking, cradling it in both palms. The right hand did not close as far as the left, and the cup tilted a little. He said, "I thought my life was done, but that judgment was . . ." He looked into the cup, then back at her. ". . . premature. Nothing is ever over."

"Arcadian, aren't you? Perhaps what you're meant to do next

is teach me to ride a horse." She smiled to disarm the suggestion, then lifted her cup and tapped it softly against her front teeth.

"I would do anything for you, to the end of my life. Anything that would do you good. I would like to say no harm will ever come to you, but I can't promise that."

She stopped all her frivolous motion. "And who are you to judge what's good for me and what isn't? What's harm and what's not? You are spectacularly incapable of making any move that would benefit yourself. Why should you be any better at helping someone else?"

The line of her jaw tightened. "I don't care about promises, and I don't want this . . . this delicacy about my feelings. I want a real home. I want to be a real wife. I'm sick of camp after camp, husband after husband, and only more children to show for it."

She looked away, then back again. "You are the only man in the world, and have been since I saw you the first time, sitting on the floor of my brother's megaron, in a cloud of Erinyes, and giving off such power that no one dared come near you, or even look at you, except to stare and see nothing. I didn't know it. Then I didn't believe it. But I remember the times you didn't touch me, better than I remember any of my wedding nights. Those memories are my fate. You and I, here alone—that is also my fate. It's all my own, and if it harms me, then so be it."

Akhaïdes did not answer, but he did what no man ever did: he touched his forehead to a woman.

She breathed in carefully. "And what about you? You offer nothing in one hand, everything in the other. But the first hand is all anyone ever sees. Is it really only Temenus and I who see the other?" She swallowed. "Is it only Temenus who will profit from what he sees, because he knows better than I how to misuse you?"

He sat still, giving her time.

Her eyes slipped away. "Can you touch someone like me now, or are you too . . . rare? Since I'm a woman, it doesn't matter if your position is higher than mine. It only matters that since I have no husband, I belong to my brother, so you're exactly where he wants you to be. You know the law. If you're still here at dawn, my brothers will come, and we'll be—"

He said softly, "Makhawis. Stop talking."

And for a moment, she did. Then she bent her head and said almost timidly, "I don't even know your true name."

A slave came to her. Makhawis gave the woman her cup and took back the ewer. Akhaïdes raised his cup. To pour his wine, she had to rise and come nearer, sloshing half of it over his hand.

She said, "I'm sorry," and sank down to her knees to take the cup and lick his wrist dry. Her hair swept over his forearm. He took her face in both hands and drew it to his. This close, he caught the quick flash of dread in her eyes.

And then it was too late. They were already kissing, hesitantly at first, just tasting each other's lips and faces, then deeper, then coupled at the mouth. She moaned aloud or he did, and she took him in her hands and led him through the maze of skirts to where he had to be.

They both whimpered. She coiled around him, and they were truly coupled—bound by hands and mouths and legs and hair and the sound of their own ragged breathing, driving and driving together. He rose to his knees, carrying her with him, his naked teeth against her throat, the skirt jammed between them.

She wormed under his shirt, and they felt the galvanic fusion of their skins. The shirt hung on one wrist, inside out. He shook it free. Makhawis pawed his face as if she were blind. He chewed her fingers. She ate at his lips through her own hands.

He drew her tongue into his mouth, embracing it with his. Tears sluiced down her face and neck. He licked her throat, sucked her breast—salt and sweet. She cried out, eyes wide but unseeing.

He laid her on her back and rose away from her, flung his head up as her nails raked his arms and her legs gripped his hips. She dragged him deeper with every stroke. There was fire inside her: scorching heat and a soft melting core—the heart of Makhawis.

He couldn't stop touching her. He whispered to her in Bajgana, the most vivid language for this, invading himself even more than her. Her hands clutched the dragon on his shoulders.

He closed his fists in her hair, forcing her head back. She clawed him closer, tighter, harder. A moan swelled from the center of her, and she arched against him, writhing and quaking as he emptied himself into her until nothing was left of him that was not hers, was not of her, in her—all Makhawis and nothing else at all.

* * *

She woke in deep night. No light shone in through the walls, and the lamps were trimmed so low that their illumination just trickled over the brims and faded at once in midair.

She had thought she wouldn't sleep, could never sleep again, but she had drifted off at last. Someone had spread a single cover over them both together, as if they were ordinary lovers.

He lay so near, facedown and turned away from her, his hair screening the pictures on his back, his beautiful hands open and guileless, his scarred wrists exposed. Just to see him there made her sex clench. She moved to stroke his extended arm. By the time she reached his hand, he was fully awake. His fingers locked with hers. He turned onto his back and drew her, hand over hand, to him. She pressed her face to his chest, his neck, his armpits, inhaling his smells and the smell of them together: sweat, blood, semen, horses, snakes, olivewood, roses.

She kissed him. Their mouths flexed and shifted. He moved

as he always moved, with that hitched fluidity that had always stopped her heart. He eased her over and onto him. She should sit astride, feel his whole reach inside, but she couldn't stand to be so far away. She clung to him.

"Open your eyes, Makhawis."

Even in this thin light, she saw the strong curve of every hair in his mustache: red, gold, white. She saw the narrow scars over his cheekbones, and the swollen gash on his lip where she had bitten him or he had bitten himself. She touched it with the tip of her forefinger. Now she was allowed to do that.

"Look at me," he told her softly.

She lifted away from him. Any other man by now would be hidden, impregnable, glaring vaguely past her, as if unwilling to admit that either of them was actually here, actually doing this. But Akhaïdes' eye, the very set of his bones, showed that nothing mattered but this mating, their claiming of each other. Nothing beyond the reach of their arms existed.

The fillet hid nothing. His face was built around it, the absence drawing more attention than anything present, like . . . Here her mind moved suddenly from familiar domestic notions to things alien and cool . . . The lost eye called attention to itself like a tent-size gap in a row of tents, like a riderless horse in a mounted troop, like a birdless sky.

The eye left to him, which had always concealed everything, now was bare as bone, lucent and undefended. And she could not bear this: he looked appallingly open and transparent, as if at any moment he might smile or weep or tell a secret.

She whispered, "Have you no pride at all?"

"None. I lost it recently, and I don't miss it. Don't close your eyes again."

There was no defense to that. She did not close her eyes. He sat erect, cradling her in his folded legs, his hands open against her back, her legs around him. They rocked together.

These arms, these hands, this mouth, this fierce body, had

savaged every man who ever crossed him. All this power and violence, all this intelligence and wariness, all this selfless, hopeless compassion, were hers to master, to take inside herself.

Literally wrapped in him, she could be no closer. She whispered against his ear, "I love you, Akhaïdes."

His head moved negative.

"I love you."

"Don't."

"I love you."

He began then to break apart, so carefully that she didn't notice at first. It was like the slow collapse of a complex structure—a statue, a palace—dismantling itself, piece after piece discreetly sliding away.

His breath hissed through his teeth, and then he groaned like someone dying and sank down in her arms. She held his head at her breast, her hands tangled in his hair.

She had held him this way before. She knew how. He was shivering, not resisting. In a moment, he would surrender.

She bent her head over his. "It's safe," she murmured. "It's safe to love me."

He gave a huge shudder, as if heaving off an enormous weight. Then he was still, no longer shaking, seeming not even to breathe.

She waited. His eye came open. He fumbled for her hand and sketched a line across the palm.

"This is where the rein lies." He touched the space between two fingers. "It comes through here, across the palm, and out here."

Her throat constricted.

"You control by just closing your hand. You needn't move your arm at all. To control without force is the hardest part to learn—that and balance."

She swallowed. "Balance."

"You don't stay on by strength, but by balance. To follow

wherever the horse moves, without effort, to know what it will do even before it knows. Strength is only for fighting, for getting on and off at speed. For tricks. Emergencies. War."

He closed her hand, then lifted it to his mouth and kissed it. "Women make excellent riders for that reason. They don't force. They persuade."

He looked directly at her, over their coupled hands. He would say something now; he would open another door between them that could never be closed again.

He said, "My wife was a superb rider. Much better than I. Even after six children."

She was going to weep. He wouldn't mind, but she would. "I don't have a pony," she whispered.

"You must ride a horse. Ponies are too quick, less predictable."

"Where would I get a horse? Temenus can't even get one for himself."

His voice was suddenly droll. "You're asking *me* that?"

She laughed aloud. "Oh, yes! Steal a horse for me! May I have a black one?"

"Black, red, solid gold. Woven all over with birds and fishes."

He eased them both down, her back to him, snugged against the warm curve of his body. His arms were half the thickness of Hippotes', but she knew their strength. They held her so safely that she could say anything—anything except the word "juchii."

She knew that he held her this way, not facing him, so it would be easier for them to speak together. Respecting that measure of separation, she dared to say, "There's no woman in Mycenae, Athens—anywhere—highbred enough for you, except me. But marry me for *my* reasons, not Temenus's. Marry me and instantly reconcile our brothers and our fathers and grandfathers, and stop this war before it starts. Save the lives of two thousand men, with two words. Take me to live with you—in Mycenae if you want, or in the land that is yours for those few words. Give me a home finally, where I can live the rest of my life with what's mine. Let me finally be a wife. Give me the right to make sons for you. Give me your brother so I can love him, too. Give me your household to rule, your clothes to sew, your wounds to mend. Give me the last of your terrible secrets. Give me your first unguarded smile. Give me your hand to hold as you leave the world; then take me with you because I could not stay here without you. Love me to the end of your life."

His hard fingertips closed her mouth so gently it was like a caress.

"My brother," he whispered, "is with the dead."

How like him to choose from a list of prizes the one that could hurt him.

"There is Tisamenus."

"But there was Elawon. I led him into danger he didn't understand, and it killed him." He breathed out softly. "I do that to people. I won't do it to you."

"But it was Elawon who made you go to Nafpaktos."

If not for Elawon, she would never have known him. The thought made her heart jump with alarm that something so precious might have depended on the whim of someone like Elawon.

If he felt that, he made no sign. "The idea of leaving his place, of going to Nafpaktos, wouldn't have come to him if not for me."

"I think that if it rains tomorrow, you'll find a way to blame yourself."

His breath was warm in her hair. "It was I who was outlaw. I was always at fault. Chance had already decided."

"Fate," she said softly, and he did not disagree.

There was, she realized quietly, a second reason that he held her this way, with her back to him, her hips nestled against his groin and his arms around her. This was what he was accustomed to. Somewhere, a place so alien it did not even have a name, men and women typically made love this way. Her heart twisted a little with the understanding that he had lain with another woman for so a long time, so easily and so regularly, that his body unconsciously retained the habit of her.

As if he felt her apprehension, Akhaïdes pressed his hand gently against her abdomen. Then his hand moved lower and caressed her, his fingers startlingly wise to the parts of a woman. She shivered and sighed, opening to him as the other woman must have done before, feeling, for a moment, an alien inhabit her own skin.

They had shared men before, she and Temenus, but they had never shared love. Left unharried, Akhaïdes would find his way between them with grace, with skill, with such honesty that neither would feel the lesser for it. Each could give him what the other could not, and his gifts to each would be equally singular. If he went to Temenus, later he would come to her. He would always come to her, and when he was with her he would be with her completely, just as he would be with Temenus completely— each of them, both of them, the true loves of his life.

Proud of herself and of him, Makhawis stretched herself against his hand and gave him her long, luxurious orgasm. When it was over, she brought his hand to her mouth and kissed his fingertips.

She lay against his warm skin. Nothing else existed.

"If you were born into responsibility for evil," she said, "then Elawon was, too."

"No."

"Why not? Because I'm wrong, or because you prefer that it be you? You *want* to be responsible. You volunteer for sacrifice."

"Responsibility is not sacrifice. Sacrifice isn't direct. It always is averted. It must never be confused with retribution. They are opposites."

She was quiet, absorbing this. The feel of his open fingers against her abdomen was heartbreaking.

She said, "You may never leave me."

His arms held her with so much love that in this moment, she could believe it.

She said, "So you were cast out and Elawon became chief of Ladon."

He drew breath, like a diver coming up from deep water. "Hyades accepted him. The . . . the sacrifice bound them to that and removed any suspicion of pollution from Elawon at the same time."

"When you killed your brothers, it wasn't madness, evil, or anything the story says. It was deliberate and logical in some way that no one else knows. And then, to seal it all, you sacrificed yourself."

"But it wasn't I who died."

She answered softly, "Yes, it was."

She turned and laid her head on his chest to hear the strong, patient cadence of his heart. The sound was so simple, so factual, it was as if she had spent her life listening to it. "All that was ugly, but it was over. There must be more—whatever you were so afraid of about Elawon that, so many years later, you would let him lead you around like a puppy on a rope. What is that secret?" She slid her hand over his mouth. "I'm not asking you, because you would lie."

He waited, barely breathing.

She murmured it as if posing a riddle: "Who was Elawon? Who was he? Why did you have to protect him, yet he must not know why? There must be more."

She lifted her hand from his mouth, and he lay waiting. She asked, "What could the last secret be? He was Hyades' son. Your sacrifice confirmed Elawon as his heir. What could be wrong with that?"

She waited. He waited. She lifted her head to look at his face. His eye was closed. He was waiting.

What had he said? *Suspicion of pollution.* Unexpected tears rose to her eyes and flooded down her face. She whispered, "Oh."

His eye opened. In a moment, he would look away and she would lose him. Once lost, he could never be reclaimed. She caught his head in her hands and held it.

"Don't turn away from me. You don't ever have to do that."

He stared at her for a moment, then wrapped his arms around her and held her so tightly, she could barely breathe.

As long as he held her, she knew he would recover. It was when he turned away that he did himself the most harm. She felt a rush of gratitude for Temenus, that he had been able to reach Akhaïdes when Akhaïdes could accept no one else. She would never forgive Temenus and never trust him, but perhaps she would love him again.

Now she felt, with glad relief, the power of Akhaïdes' will like a physical effort, dragging himself together again.

She waited until his grasp loosened, until he was again completely aware of her presence. She had to ask, "Are you sure? You were still very young. Maybe you're mistaken."

She felt his negative gesture. "I don't know. I absolutely do not know."

"He never suspected? No. He harassed you, to make you tell about his other brothers and why you killed them. He thought that was your only secret."

"If I told him the one part, I'd have to tell the other. How could I do that?"

"He despised you. Wrongly, but still. No, you couldn't tell him." She laid her hand against the side of his face. He turned into it a little, still wanting her touch. "Did you talk with the Serpent about this?"

"She knew. The Shaman guessed. No one else."

Your mother certainly knew, she might have said now. *His mother. And the man you thought was your father.*

She remembered suddenly her light and easy talk with Temenus. How long ago was that? What had she said? *"He can't*

*be a very competent murderer if he killed all his brothers but one.
Why leave one? And now, why leave him to trouble your life?"*

But she only said, "Like Oedipus, you punish yourself since
no one else will do it to suit you. And you punished your mother
by forcing her to live as an unwilling heroine with a husband she
hated and a child that would remind her every moment of you. I
don't understand everything you've told me, but I understand
how she felt when you left her."

She kissed his mouth then—he raised a hand to fend her off,
but she caught it gently and moved it aside—kissed the fillet
over his eye. She turned his right hand over, and he closed it
tightly. She set her mouth against the knuckles. Her cousins
had crushed this hand under their heels, at her brother's order.
It had broken again on her husband's face. Now it wore the High
King's ring.

She whispered against his fist, "I will say one thing, and you
tell me if I'm right or not. Just yes or no." She swallowed. "Juchii
was the name of your son."

She expected him to stiffen, to pull away, to rise and leave
her forever, to perform some unimaginable violence.

He said, "Yes,"

"Then it will be the name of ours, too."

Now he did stiffen, did stop moving. Stopped breathing.

She kissed his hand, purposely softly, casually, as if words
were only words, lingering until the hand relaxed completely and
she felt his breathing begin again, against her hair. Someday, in
some future year together, he would tell the story of the first
Juchii. She could wait, and so could. . .

His hand turned and began to stroke her as if she were a pet
or a treasure. As if his fingers would read her skin as a blind
man's would.

Under his touch, she was falling asleep. She yawned
enormously and snuggled her face into the side of his neck.
"You're in danger of becoming a wonderfully sweet man. I

thought I should warn you."

"And you are a prideful, fearless, self-satisfied, far too intelligent, spoiled woman."

"Spoil me more."

"All right."

They drifted into silence.

In the moment before sleep, she remembered to add, "There was nothing of you in Elawon," and felt the quiet breakdown of the last of his defenses. He buried his face in her hair.

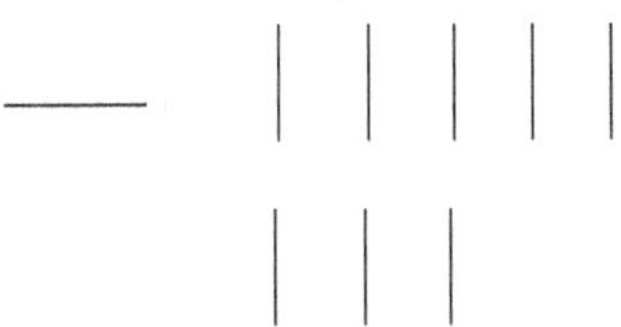

I may hold you close to me,
But these ties will never bind you.[xvii]
— Estefan and Santander

Akhaïdes woke to whispering voices. He lifted his head. Makhawis's eyes were a span from his own, screened by their entangled hair, and wide open. Too wide. He pulled himself the rest of the way awake and turned to see the contour of a crouching woman. Deione.

"Fire on the mountain. The High King Orestes is gone to his dead."

It was like counting to release an arrow: *one, two, three,* and then the surge hit like a kick under the heart.

"Have they seen it? Temenus's pickets?"

"I don't know."

Makhawis said, "Find out. If they haven't seen it yet, make sure they don't."

In the dark behind Deione, other heads were lifting, women rising.

Deione backed away, and another slave took her place. "What orders for me?"

Makhawis looked at Akhaïdes. "He'll do anything to keep you," she said.

He watched the thoughts race across her face. If she shouted, if she only called out, a score of men would be here in moments. He would not do something so grotesque as to fight his way, naked, out of her pavilion. He would simply let them take him. He saw how clearly she knew this.

She whispered, "Tell me about him. Your brother."

"Tisamenus is the only person ever to give me a gift and ask nothing in return. Expect nothing. I don't know why he thinks I deserve that. I don't know how he can be that way."

She watched him, perfectly still.

He added, "You might say he is younger than he should be."

"Like Satnios," she whispered.

"Like Satnios, and different. He has far less reason to trust, and yet he still can. And he's alone. If I can help him, I must."

He kissed her forehead and looked into her eyes. "How could I live as a ceremonial warlord for Temenus? I am not . . . decorative enough, or ambitious enough. You know that I have to act."

"A tool wants to be used even if it risks breaking. You said that."

"Temenus talks about finally listening to me, but he won't."

"You could be a king."

"A pet king. Trotted out in a bit and bridle for certain occasions."

"With a king's work to do the rest of the time."

"In a kingdom already well run, among strangers who don't want me. And even if that weren't true, how could I take a reward that I've done nothing to earn? You, him, everything you offer between you, the treasure he would have given—I couldn't take anything that way. None of it belongs to me."

"He loves you."

"And how does that make anything different? See it. See it as it is."

She did not answer.

"On the other hand, I've lived in chains. I can do it again."

"He would do more than bridle or chain you. To keep you,

he'd hamstring you and blind you. He'd cage you forever in bars of gold. But you'd die there."

"Maybe not. All you have to do is call out."

Women still knelt beside them, awaiting instructions. Makhawis said to them, in a perfectly even voice, "Find his clothes. Get food to carry with him." She turned to another woman. "Find his horse and its harness. Bring it as near as you can without anyone knowing." She raised her voice only a little. "Make no sound," she told them all. "No one can know."

Their hair was knotted together. A woman squatted behind them to untangle it. Slaves were running in all directions, but silently and without light. Makhawis said to him, "What else? If you think of anything, tell them."

"My belt and axe and wolfskin coat. The priests have them." A passing woman altered her course in mid step and slipped outside.

"My blanket in the slaves' house." Another woman darted away.

They were sitting up in a maze of pillows, the woman's hands working in their hair. Makhawis stroked his face with the tips of her fingers.

"And how will you live now? Don't be what you were before."

He touched his own forehead, mouth, and heart, then touched her lightly—forehead, lips, heart, as he had touched himself.

As cautiously as if she might release something perilous, she whispered, "What does that mean?"

"It is Arcadian. It means I claim you. You are my responsibility."

"I don't want to be! I don't want to be another burden. I want . . ." She saw his face and stopped. "The Warrior. He was Arcadian, wasn't he?"

"Yes."

"Don't be like that!" she commanded fiercely. "Don't end up

like that!"

Because she wanted it so much, he said, "I won't."

She sank back and brushed a finger over his bitten lip. "Say it," she whispered. "Say it just this one time."

It was here in this room, here all around him. He rubbed his face with his open hands. Makhawis sat still, eyes closed, hands upturned in her lap, doing nothing more. A woman bent over them to say that the horse had come.

* * *

Outside the pavilion, the night was bitingly damp. Slabs of moonlight lay as thick as snow on every surface. The king's tent, picked out in white and black, was unlit but alarmingly near. Temenus had gone serenely to sleep, confident of his sister and himself. Any outcry, any at all, would wake him.

Akhaïdes followed a woman to the road, where dust muffled the horse's restless steps. It settled when it saw him.

He looked up. High against a curtain of rock and scree, so high it might be one of the million ordered stars, even he could see it: a wavering reflection of flame against stone. Kepheus's fire burned at last. He imagined the stout old man, stamping and puffing, banging ancient logs into final position, tucking a mass of shirttails between hairy knees as he squatted by the firebox, coals casting red light upward as he lifted them out of their cage . . . Powerful envy squeezed Akhaïdes, and he stood suspended for a moment in its grip.

Above the road, silhouetted against moonlit walls, figures moved silently. On this night of nights, all the priests were waking. Even this soon, they had much to do, to safeguard Orestes' departure and protect his successor.

Tisamenus would not be sleeping. He would be performing some necessary ritual, as the priests did, to ease his father's going. Perhaps he was already cutting his hair.

And Temenus. *You think you know me. What will I do now?*

Something touched his elbow, stirring him out of himself. It was Deione, and he leaned to hear her whisper, "I didn't have to do anything. All the pickets are asleep. Temenus might be the only man in the world who doesn't know about this."

He smiled at the edge of contempt in her voice.

"But when the town learns, they'll all start to mourn. That will wake him. Be far away by then."

The belt clattered softly as he buckled it, and the axe tapped his thigh. The horse stretched, yawned, and shook itself. Akhaïdes shrugged the wolfskin coat on. He shouldered the bag another woman gave him, and mounted.

Deione whispered, "Travel well."

Down among the tents, in the portal of a dark pavilion, stood Makhawis, wrapped to the eyes in a blanket, only her hands touched by the bright, fecund moon.

Always believe Makhawis. She is the key.

The horse strode out willingly, knowing the ground and glad to be moving. Its hooves made almost no sound.

As the road curved toward the sanctuary, Akhaïdes saw, under the cypress trees, four, five, six figures, come to stand and watch him pass, their faces identical white ovals. One of them must be Menetor, another the purifying priest, another the black-haired boy. He could not tell who was who, and it didn't matter; he knew them all. And he would not see them again.

Glowing faintly in the roadside grass, the dry corpses regarded his passage without resentment. They had expected nothing, had never been fooled about his future, would not miss him among them.

He looked back, but Makhawis was lost in the dark already, and his chest constricted with a moment's grief that was so far beyond mere sorrow, there was no word for it in any language he knew. The horse snorted, objecting to his distraction as it carried him on the road to Mycenae.

* * *

She was afraid to wait for Temenus to come to her, so she went to him. She stepped into his tent before the town's wailing could wake him. His attendants scrambled up from the floor, and Temenus himself sat upright on his pallet when he saw her standing there wrapped in a blanket, her hair wildly disordered, the kohl smudged in dusky circles around her eyes, two of her women, as always, behind her.

He tossed off his blanket as someone stirred the lamps to light. In a white sleeveless vest and plain kilt, he crossed to her and took her hands.

He looked carefully into her face. She knew what he saw there—a woman fully loved and sated. Then his eyes tightened. He asked softly, "Why are you here?"

Fear closed her throat. She glanced past him. Kresphontes was also awake, sitting up on his pallet, his face showing the awareness that something was catastrophically wrong.

She had to answer. "It's not dawn yet. He's gone."

"*What?*"

In the distance, the outcry was beginning: voices in the town asking, demanding, answering, murmuring. Soon they would begin to wail.

"Fire on the mountain," she said. "The High King is gone to his dead."

Kresphontes groaned softly.

Temenus stared at her, as if still not comprehending. Then his eyes widened and dimmed. His hands crushed hers.

"He can't have left me. How could he do that? Where would he go?" But he already knew, already understood everything, and his hands shifted to grip her upper arms. His lips tightened, and he touched them with his tongue. Then he murmured, "You bitch. You stupid, stupid bitch. You let him get away."

All that she had planned to say died unspoken.

* * *

An easy, reaching walk was restful to both horse and man, and safe enough on the coarse, light-flattened road. Even at this pace, no man on foot could catch him, and Temenus had brought no chariots. Akhaïdes' blinded eye and his right hand ached with the cold. He wrapped the coat around himself, tucking it under his calves to keep his knees from stiffening.

As the gray horse skirted the tall mass of Hyampeia, an unseen spider's thread broke across Akhaïdes' face. Brushing it away, he breathed in the scent that clung to his hand: olivewood and roses, and the rich seashell aroma of the most private parts of her body. It whisked him away to a similar intimate, alien scent on a twist of foreign driftwood on a foreign beach, at the moment he realized he had reached beyond his right to know. And so he had now, as well. He saw again, agonizingly vivid, the damp, crisp hair between Makhawis's legs, just starting to gray. He had been moved beyond words by its poignant beauty. He exhaled against his fingers and drew in her scent and held it.

* * *

"You let him go!" Temenus gripped her arms, his eyes clouded with the rush of thought behind them.

She refused to wince. "It was you who gave him choices. How could I stop him?"

"How? *How?*" His fingers pinning her flesh. "The way you stop every man: by sticking him between your legs!"

She snatched one hand free and slapped him. Stunned for only a moment, he closed his fist and hit her jaw. She staggered, then braced her back and flung her head up. If he killed her, he would have to do it where she stood. And she was glad, viciously glad, that Akhaïdes would never know. This was between her and Temenus and no one else—not even its object, who would never live a peaceful hour with anyone he loved.

Temenus grasped her head, snatched it to him, kissed the place he had hit, scraping the ragged inside of her cheek against loosened teeth. Then, nose to nose, he whispered as if lovingly, "You let him go. You probably helped him." His voice rose, desperate. "He was my hope. My future and my fate, and you let him go!"

She could barely whisper, "You don't want him in chains. You don't want him that way."

"Blinded, castrated, in chains. How do you know what I want? Never, never, *never* tell me what I want!"

"He loves you so much."

"And shows it this way? That!" He slapped her face hard, then regained his grip on her head, "That for your love! That for all of it, both of you!"

Her eyes stinging from the blow, she whispered, "I've lost him, too."

"And what do you care? Screw one man, screw another. What's the difference to you? Go spread your legs again, Makhawis, while I . . . ."

He faltered at last, his eyes losing focus. "What is it like for you, to make love with Akhaïdes?" His hands tightened, his fingernails digging into her scalp until her eyes watered. "Never tell me. That, I will kill you for."

* * *

For one hallucinatory instant, Akhaïdes saw himself old, as old as Orestes, stooped and blind and limping but intensely alive, led by the hand through the deep shade of olive trees, past a solemn, earnest child carrying another, smaller child on his arm. The trees and the hills beyond them were all his own. The children's fluting voices and his low, patient replies attracted songbirds that circled fearlessly around them, and a few pet dogs that trailed after. The children's faces were familiar, though he did not yet know their names.

All she had had to do was call out.

* * *

A cousin cleared his throat cautiously. "We can go after him, Wanax."

Temenus turned on him. "On wings? You could never catch him. No one could. And if you caught him, what would happen then?"

The cousin said, "He'll betray you."

Kresphontes spoke at last. "No. He won't."

Temenus agreed. "He'll never betray me. But I promise you, he will kill me."

* * *

The horse stopped. It had been restless, eager to move, but now it stood still.

They were alone on a path thick with cold, white dust. Too late for wolves, too early for eagles, the only sounds the hiss and rattle of the wind, and the horse's patient breathing. Their moon-cast shadow splayed clumsily over dry bones of bushes, and angles and edges of rock.

He had never feared night, dark, solitude, thieves, the moon, monsters, death. He had not guessed that rebirth would make him so human as to be troubled by such ordinary threats. How human he might eventually become, he could not guess.

On this open edge of the mountain, anything could come at them. Through shadows, rising from clefts in the stones, something as mundane as Phocian robbers or as exotic as a pack of gryphons. Up there hung the vast and staring moon and the million eyes of the stars that Akhaïdes could not see but that were watching nonetheless. Up there, all the silent flying things of the night soared and plunged. Nothing could come at them here without their both knowing, but knowing would not protect them. The deer had known the lion and still had died. The lion had known Akhaïdes. Akhaïdes knew the perytons, the Erinyes, the Serpent, Temenus.

Temenus had held him in the most intimate of embraces and whispered, "We are lovers."

Temenus had told him, "I would give you to Arcadia. I would give you to Delphi. I will not give you to the side of some road to nowhere that matters."

Temenus had turned his hands up beside an inexplicable mound of riches and said, "I need you."

Temenus had closed his eyes over the grim fire of that need and whispered, "I was too late."

Temenus had sat quietly waiting. He knew so well how to wait for Akhaïdes.

Temenus had reasoned with him, argued with him, surrendered his dignity to plead with him before his own dependents. And in return, Akhaïdes had run away.

Temenus had made love with him when no one else would touch him.

Makhawis had said, "He would chain you. To keep you, he'd hamstring you and blind you if he had to. He'd cage you forever in bars of gold."

Yet there were as many ways to live as ways to die, each different, none really any worse than the others: outlaw, suppliant, lover, husband, prisoner, prey, trophy, slave. King. Monster food.

When would he regret that she had not called out? When would he begin to hunger for her, for Temenus, each in a unique and unbearable way? Once the hunger began, when would it stop?

If he went back, would he stand before them? Lie down at their feet? Take them in his arms? The right action would come to him. When he looked into the faces he loved, he would know what to do. His beautiful, willful, reckless Herakleids.

* * *

Temenus turned back to Makhawis, still holding her head in his hands, his eyes clear again, his fingers deep in her thick, sex-scented hair. "He's gone," he told her softly, lovingly. "The next time he and I meet will be on a killing field. Everyone you know will die, and it will be your doing."

* * *

They had closed no doors between them. As Akhaïdes rose to leave Temenus in his pavilion, he had said nothing, had not even touched his forehead in good-bye.

"*If you're still here at dawn,*" she had started to say. But he had stopped her before she could finish. Then, as he rose to leave her, she had said, "Say it. Say it just this one time." But he could not. Not because it wasn't true, but because it was.

If something came right now and killed him, ate him, shat him out on the mountainside, his body would be more useful in death than in the life they wanted for him.

* * *

The cousin murmured, "Wanax, you shouldn't talk that way."

"Why not? It's true." Temenus did not move. He was still watching Makhawis, so close. "The augury can't be satisfied. My three-eyed man is gone, my sister is not married, and we are ruined." He closed his eyes at last. "So tell them. Tell everyone. Send them home, wherever home may be. The Return is over."

* * *

The gray horse waited. The wind hissed and whispered; branches shifted; stones whined; hooves and claws moved quietly along the path, skin and dry feathers along the sky.

He had owned, for a time, a talking bird. Its wings had been trimmed for so many years that it never tried to fly. It paced along a wooden perch, reciting platitudes in four different languages. When Juchii took pity on it and tried to release it, it refused to go, clinging to his hands with all its claws, its hard black eyes terrified.

"The story of the birds," he had told Temenus, *"was for you."*

He laid the reins on the horse's neck, leaned forward, and lifted the wolfskin coat to cover his head. Huddled against the warm mane in that black, inhuman cocoon, he waited to be taken, to turn back, to go on.

"Never name a horse," he had told her son. *"You don't know when you'll have to eat it."*

i "Myxomatosis*"* Larkin, Philip, 1954

ii "The Stolen Child" Yeats, William Butler, from The Wanderings of Oisin and Other Poems, 1889

iii Heart of Darkness, Conrad, Joseph, 1899

iv "Measure for Measure," Shakespeare, William

v Twain, Mark, *Letter to Mrs Foote, Dec. 2, 1887*

vi "The Secret Sharer" Conrad, Joseph, *Harper's Magazine*, 1910

vii "Words From A Totem Animal" Merwin. W S,

viii Hold Still, La Cour, Nina, *Speak; Reprint edition* 2010

ix "Modern Man in Search of a Soul" Jung, Carl, Harcourt Harvest, 1955

x Dear Theo: the Autobiography of Vincent van Gogh, Stone, Irving, Plume, 1995

xi Johann Wolfgang von Goethe

xii Middlemarch, Eliot, George

xiii "Put Your Lights On" from *Supernatural*, Everlast, 1999

xiv "The Snake" Brown, Oscar, Jewel Music Ltd, 1963

xv "Stray Birds" Tagore, Rabindranath, The Macmillan Company, 1916

xvi "Have You Ever Really Loved a Woman?" by Bryan Adams, Michael Kamen and Robert John "Mutt" Lange, 1995

xvii "Steal Your Heart" from *Destiny*, Estefan, Gloria and Kike Santander, 1996